SURGEON'S SECOND CHANCE IN FLORENCE

KATE HARDY

THE VET'S UNEXPECTED HOUSEGUEST

JULIETTE HYLAND

MILLS & BOON

SURGEON'S SECOND CHANCE IN FLORENCE

KATE HARDY

MILLS & BOON

With love and thanks to the three editors
who worked with me on this book.

Julia, I'll miss you; Megan, thank you for caretaking;
Laurie, welcome back!

CHAPTER ONE

'SAMANTHA CLARKE! JUST the woman I wanted to see.'
Will Reynolds, the head of the department, smiled at
Sam. 'Can we have a quick word in my office?'

Sam, assuming that her boss wanted her to talk to
her about a new case, smiled back and followed him to
his office.

'Have a seat,' he said, perching on the edge of his desk.
'First of all, I have some good news—that research grant
we applied for has been confirmed, and we can start in
three months' time. I'm delighted to say it means we'll
be promoting you to consultant.'

Sam beamed at him. 'Thank you, Will! That's fantastic.'

'I knew you'd be pleased,' Will said. 'And, secondly, I
have an interesting case for you. Triplet pregnancy from
IVF—twins and a singleton.'

That was unusual enough in itself, but Sam guessed
there would also be a complication which might need surgery, or Will wouldn't be talking to her about it.

'And there's suspected twin-to-twin transfusion syndrome,' he said, confirming her thoughts.

'What stage?' she asked.

'They're doing another scan today at her hospital,'
he said. 'If it's still stage two—' which Sam knew was

when you couldn't see the smaller baby's bladder on the ultrasound, but it hadn't progressed to abnormal blood flow in the vessels around the heart '—then obviously amnioreduction is a possibility.'

When babies were still mildly affected by TTTS, doctors could try draining the excess fluid from one amniotic sac to resolve the problem. 'But you're thinking it's more likely to have progressed further and we'll need to do endoscopic laser ablation?' Sam had been working more intensively with foetal laser surgery over the last few months, so it sounded as if this was a mum and three babies who'd end up under her care.

'Got it in one,' he said.

'OK. When are they coming in?'

'That's the catch,' he said. 'They're not coming here.'

'So you're sending me to a different hospital in London?'

'Nope.' He wrinkled his nose. 'You know that the Muswell Hill Memorial Hospital is twinned with the Michelangelo Hospital in Florence?' At her nod, Will continued, 'Ricardo Fanelli, who's my equivalent in Florence, is setting up a new unit in foetal medicine. Professor Henri Lefevre from Paris is going to Florence for three months to oversee the unit and start training them, but Ric has asked for you to go over and treat this particular mum and her babies and work on secondment there until the research project starts.'

It was a fabulous opportunity, plus she'd always wanted to visit Florence.

Sam quickly suppressed the memory of the last time she'd visited Italy—and the last person she'd visited Italy with. That part of her life was over. Besides, as far as she knew, Angelo lived in Rome, so she was hardly likely to cross paths with him in Florence.

'Sam?'

She shook herself. Angelo had nothing to do with this. This was work. 'I'd love to do it, Will. When do they want me to start?'

'That's the other thing.' He wrinkled his nose. 'How's your Italian?'

'Conversational rather than medical,' she said. 'And it's horribly rusty.' She hadn't spoken Italian in two years, since Angelo had dumped her.

'They can probably help you with a translator, at least to start with,' Will said. 'But I'd advise you to get an app or something and start brushing it up again, and learning a few medical terms, because they want you to start on Thursday morning.'

'Thursday?' She felt her eyes widen. 'As in three days from now?'

'I know it's practically no notice, but that's when the mum's coming in again for another review,' he said.

'Well, that flat I was buying fell through, so I'm still staying with my parents. As long as you can cover me here, and I can get a flight, and someone in Florence doesn't mind helping me to find somewhere to stay, then...' She shrugged. 'I'm good to go.'

'That's great,' Will said. 'Though, as I said, I want you back for that research project. So no getting swept off your feet by a gorgeous Italian doctor, OK?'

Been there, done that, and won't make the same mistake again, Sam thought. 'No chance of that,' she said with a smile. 'If you don't mind me taking my break early, I need to tell my mum and sort out my flight.'

'Great. I'll ring Ric and tell him the good news,' Will said.

'Stop *worrying*. I'm perfectly fine,' Ruggiero Brunelli said.

Angelo wasn't entirely sure his dad was telling the

truth. A visit every other week and a video call every day didn't feel like enough support. He loved living in Florence, but maybe he should move back to Rome to be closer to his dad?

'Angelo. You're the best son anyone could ask for,' Ruggiero said gently. 'And I'm not going to have a relapse. I'm eating properly, I go swimming three times a week, I see friends regularly, and I have Baffi to keep me company.' He gestured to the black and white cat who was snoozing in a patch of sunlight.

'I know.' But Angelo still worried. His father's addiction to painkillers had turned Angelo's life upside down two years ago. Angelo had been in England at the time, and on the cusp of asking Sam to marry him. But when his Uncle Salvatore had called to put him in the picture, Angelo had known he needed to move back to Italy and concentrate on helping his dad. And there was no way he could've dragged Sam into it. Even if he'd ignored the potential scandal of a senior doctor self-prescribing narcotics—something that would've got Ruggiero struck off the register—there was the addiction side of things. Sam's younger brother had been an addict, and he'd died from an accidental overdose; she'd still been grieving when Angelo had first met her. How could he have asked her to support him through his dad's rehab, and bring all those painful memories back for her? Especially because he'd missed all the signs; how could he trust himself with her heart, when he'd let his dad down?

To protect her, he'd pushed her away—knowing that he was hurting her, but also knowing that if she stayed with him the situation would hurt her even more. And in a way, it had protected him as well; he'd felt helpless when he'd lost his mum, whereas ending it with Sam meant that at least he was in control. He'd done his best to minimise the potential hurt for both of them. Even though it had ripped his own heart out, lying to her and saying that he didn't love her any more.

He'd spent a year in Rome, supporting his father through the miserable months of rehab and then he'd been offered the job in Florence. He hadn't managed to persuade his dad to come with him and make a fresh start, but Ruggiero had encouraged him to take the job. And at least the hour and a half on the train between Florence and Rome was quicker and easier than doing the train-plane-train trek from London.

'I still wish you'd move to Florence,' he said. 'We could get a house in the hills so you have a garden. And it's probably the best place in Italy for art. You know how much you loved visiting the Uffizi with me.'

'I was born in Rome and I'll die in Rome,' Ruggiero said.

Angelo thought of the car crash that had left his father hooked on heavy-duty painkillers. How easy it could've been for his dad to forget how much he'd taken, accidentally overdose and die, the way Sam's brother had. Or was this his father's way of telling Angelo he'd had enough of living on his own and wanted to be with Angelo's mum? He winced. '*Dad.*'

'I didn't mean it like that.' Ruggiero returned the wince. 'Sorry. Let me make it clear. I'm absolutely not suicidal and I'm not going to take an overdose, accidental or otherwise. I simply meant I'm stubborn, I love my home city and I plan to stay right where I am. I'm *fine*, son. Really.'

Though Angelo couldn't help running through a mental checklist: sweating, dilated or pinpoint pupils, co-ordination problems, itching…

His father was scratching his arm.

Ruggiero rolled his eyes as if he'd guessed what was going through Angelo's head. 'Pruritis has quite a few probable causes. Mine happens to be from an insect bite. See?' He held his arm so Angelo could see the reddened lump. 'Yes, I know scratching a bite is the quickest way to get it infected. I'm going to put a cold compress on it to stop the itching, after you've gone. And, no, I'm not going to take ibuprofen to reduce the swelling. I've got some antihistamine cream somewhere.' He gave Angelo a gentle smile. 'I might be ancient and two years out of practising medicine, but I can still just about remember my training.'

'Sorry, Dad.' Shame mingled with relief. 'You've got thirty years more experience than I have in medicine.'

'I made very a stupid mistake. I should've asked for help instead of thinking I could sort things out myself. And I've learned from that mistake,' Ruggiero said. 'When you come to see me, I really would like to see my son the man, rather than my son the doctor. I'd like to go out with you for good food and a glass of wine and tell you terrible jokes, and not have to worry that you're worrying about me.' He paused. 'And I'd like you to come to spend time with your dad, not to visit a patient who might lapse back into his painkiller addiction and needs watching like a hawk.'

Guilt surged through Angelo. 'I know. I want that, too.'

'But you still worry about me, whatever I say.' Ruggiero gave him a hug. 'It's supposed to be the other way round, you know, with the parent never stopping worrying about their child. You had the worry of your mum's breast cancer through your student years, and now it's me. Though, actually, I worry about you. I think you need someone in your life, Angelo: a partner, not a difficult parent.'

'You're not difficult,' Angelo said.

'If you weren't worrying about me, you'd relax,' Ruggiero pointed out. 'You'd date someone for more than a couple of months before backing off. You'd let someone close.'

Except Angelo knew that whoever he dated would never measure up to Sam. And he'd left it way too late to fix things between them. He'd learned that the hard way when he'd gone back to London. 'I'm fine,' Angelo lied.

'Hmm.' Ruggiero looked at him. 'If you're worrying that I wouldn't accept a male partner, then let me reassure you that I don't care whether you're gay, straight or somewhere in between. That doesn't matter. I just want you to be happy—and to be *loved*.'

Angelo blinked back the tears that unexpectedly stung his eyes. 'For the record, Dad, I'm straight. But I'm glad you'd accept me if I wasn't. I've seen friends go through a rough time until their families accepted who they were—even now.'

'Love is love,' Ruggiero said. 'Being a recovering addict has taught me a lot about acceptance. About not judging. And I want you to have a *life*, Angelo.'

'I do have a life,' Angelo protested. 'I have a job I love, good friends, and a flat with an amazing view.' Which was all true. Provided you didn't look beyond the surface to see the empty spaces.

'But you spend your time worrying about me instead of embracing life. You keep yourself at a distance from people,' Ruggiero said. 'So let's do a deal. I promise that I'll keep going to the addiction support group every week, and they have my full permission to contact you if they're even the slightest bit worried about me. Your uncle keeps an eye on me, too. And you—you make sure you date someone before your next visit to Rome, and send me a selfie of you together. Agreed?'

Angelo was fairly sure he could talk one of his colleagues into posing for a photograph to make it look as if they were dating. If that would keep his dad happy, it'd be worth asking for a favour. 'Deal.'

'Good.' His father gave him a hug. 'Safe journey. Text me when you're home.'

'Of course I will. Have a good week, Dad.' Angelo hugged him back.

But on the way back to Florence he picked up a message from his boss, Ric Fanelli.

Muswell Hill Memorial Hospital is sending one of their team to us for a three-month secondment in the new unit. She starts Thursday. Can I ask you to help her settle in and translate?

As Angelo was half-English and had trained in London, he wasn't surprised by the request. But then he saw the name of their new doctor.

No.

It couldn't be her.

Surely.

He clicked on the link to her profile on the hospital website, and the photograph took his breath away.

Sam Clarke. Two years older and two years more beautiful.

He'd had no idea that she'd moved into foetal surgery. He hadn't seen her since he'd come back to Italy; their break-up had been by phone, because he hadn't trusted himself to go through with it if he'd looked her in the eye. Though, a year ago—when his dad was stable enough for Angelo to be sure he wasn't leaving Sam open to potential hurt—he'd gone back to London, ready to open his heart to her and apologise for the way he'd left. To tell her the truth about his dad's addiction and the way he was still coming to terms with losing his mum, and ask her to forgive him. He'd turned up at their old department at lunchtime, hoping he might be able to find out when she was off duty. The receptionist was someone he didn't know, so clearly she'd joined the department since he'd left.

'I used to work here,' he said, 'and I wanted to look up some old friends while I'm in London. Would you be able to tell me what shift Sam Clarke is on, please?'

'Oh, Sam's not in today,' the receptionist said. 'She's gone to Liverpool for the weekend with Greg.'

'Greg?' Who was Greg? Another new person in the department?

'Her boyfriend.' The receptionist smiled. 'He's so lovely. Swept her off her feet. I wouldn't be surprised if he pops the question, this weekend.'

What?

Sam was dating someone else, and it was getting serious?

For a moment, he couldn't quite piece it all together, and then the realisation slammed into him.

He'd left it too late.

But, if she was happy, it wouldn't be fair to turn her life upside down again. He'd been miserable for the last year, feeling guilty that he'd missed all the signs with his dad and wishing that his mum had still been around to share his worries and help him work out a plan. What could he really offer Sam, except more of the uncertainty that came with addiction? And what if it was too much for her and she left him anyway?

All the pain and longing would've been for nothing.

So maybe it would be better to do the right thing and go back to Italy without seeing her.

'Do you want to leave a message for her?' the receptionist asked.

'No, you're all right,' he said, forcing a smile he didn't feel. 'Thanks, anyway.' He'd managed to square his shoulders and saunter away as if his heart wasn't breaking into tiny pieces all over again.

And now it looked as if their paths were going to cross again for the next three months.

Had the woman been right and Greg had asked Sam to marry him, that weekend? Were they engaged, or even married?

Sam's profile on the hospital website was focused on professional matters, and they weren't friends on social media, so he had no idea. At least he had a couple of days to get used to the idea of seeing her again. But the prospect of having Sam back in his life, even temporarily, made him feel as if he was hurtling down from the top of a rollercoaster at full speed. Just how was he going to deal with this?

On Wednesday morning, Sam caught the plane to Pisa. When she'd collected her luggage, she checked the notes on her phone: next was the people-mover from the airport to the train station, and then the train to Florence.

She bought the tickets she needed, along with a sandwich and a bottle of water, took the people-mover to the train station, then found her seat on the train to Florence and enjoyed looking out at the scenery. Tuscany was such a pretty part of Italy, with its tall, narrow cypress trees and spreading vineyards; the river Arno ran alongside the train tracks, broadening into beautiful water meadows. Now, in the spring, everywhere was green, feeling fresh and new.

According to the map on her phone, her new flat was easily within walking distance from the station in Florence. And it turned out to be a gorgeous walk: narrow streets with flagstone paving, lined by four-storey buildings in tones of saffron and dark cream with shuttered windows. Everywhere she looked, there were ancient churches and towers; there were statues on corners and in niches, and stunning little details on every bit of ironwork she saw. No wonder Florence was a top destination for art-lovers.

Then she turned a corner and the famous cathedral was right in front of her, with the octagonal Duomo and its red-tiled roof. From photographs, she'd always thought the facade of the building was black and white, but up close she could see tones of dark green and cream and red. It was absolutely stunning. And to think she'd go past this every day on the way to work: how fantastic was that?

Smiling, she headed to the concierge's office to pick up her keys. Her flat was in a sixteenth-century stone building; there was a huge wooden doorway with a lion's head knocker. How many people had used that knocker and walked through that door, over the centuries?

Although there was no lift to the top floor, she didn't mind. Taking the stairs would keep her fit. At the same time, she was glad she'd travelled relatively light and only had the one suitcase to haul up three flights of stairs.

She unlocked the door and left her case by the doorway while she explored inside.

Most of the walls in the living room had been painted white, but Sam was thrilled to see that the top of one wall actually had the remains of an ancient fresco. Compared with her very modern flat in London, this was incredible: a building with art that someone had made five hundred years ago.

There was a comfortable-looking sofa in the living room, with a stripped wooden floor and a rug in rich tones of blue; a small bistro table and two ladderback chairs stood next to an archway that led to a compact kitchen. The kitchen area, too, was decorated in neutral tones, with pale counters and light wood cupboard doors; here, the flooring was terracotta flagstone.

The marble-tiled bathroom had a good-sized shower. The last room was a bedroom, again with stripped wooden flooring and a rug; there was a wrought-iron double bedstead, a gilt-framed mirror and a large wardrobe. The window had wooden shutters; Sam opened them to see the view, and then realised with delight that she could actually see the Duomo above the terracotta rooftops.

She took a snap to send to her mum and her best friend, captioning it.

A room with a view—it doesn't get more amazing than this!

It was still hard to believe that she was going to be living right in the historic centre of a city she'd always wanted to visit, doing a job that she loved.

And she couldn't wait for the next three months to start.

The concierge had given her an envelope along with her keys. She opened it to discover a note written in perfect English from one of her colleagues, welcoming her to Florence. Lidia had left her some milk and fresh coffee in the fridge, a loaf of bread and a bag of delicious-looking cookies in the cupboard, directions to the supermarket and a note of the best places to buy bread, cheese, fruit and vegetables locally, as well as advice about a couple of good places to eat nearby.

Sam made herself a quick coffee to go with the cookies—which tasted even better than they looked—to restore some of her energy from travelling, then headed out to buy food, plus some flowers to say thank you to Lidia. And she was pleased to discover that her language skills, helped by the app she'd been using for the last few days, were starting to come back; the shopkeepers were more than happy to help remind her of some of the words she'd forgotten.

Words that Angelo had taught her, patiently guiding her initial stumbling efforts and rewarding her with kisses…

She shook herself. That part of her life was over and done with. What was the point of wishing for what might have been? Angelo had made it clear enough that he didn't love her any more. He'd said he needed to go back to Italy to sort out some family stuff, and when she'd asked him what she could do to help he'd mumbled vague excuses. He'd barely answered the supportive texts she'd sent. And then he'd called her, out of the blue.

'Sam, there isn't a good way to say this, so I'm going to be honest with you. Things aren't working out between us.'

She'd been so shocked that she hadn't been able to say a word.

'I'm staying in Italy,' he'd continued.

'But—I thought—' She'd stumbled over the words. They'd been so good together.

'I'm sorry. I realised when I was here, I don't love you the way you deserve to be loved.'

'But—'

'Sorry. Be happy.' And he'd ended the call.

She'd been devastated. Angelo had met her a few months after her brother's death, when she'd been a walking shadow of guilt and misery, convinced that there must've been something she'd missed and she could've saved Dominic. They'd become friends and he'd made her realise that addiction was hard to help and nobody could've done more for her brother. And friendship had turned to love…or so she'd thought.

But Angelo hadn't loved her, after all.

And she didn't have a clue where it had gone wrong. It had taken her months to pick herself up and dust herself down again. Not that she'd made a huge success of it. Even though Greg from the Emergency Department was a lovely guy, she'd realised that she was dating him on the rebound and that wasn't fair, so she'd told him as gently as she could that they needed to go back to being just good friends. She hadn't dated since, burying herself in her work.

But maybe Florence would help her move away from the past. A summer in the Italian sunshine. And when she returned to London, after her secondment, she'd be ready to try again.

On the way back to her flat, Sam walked along the riverbank, enjoying the view of the bridges—and particularly the huge stone arch of the Ponte Vecchio, with its little shops and its perfect reflection in the River Arno. She took another snap to send home, then headed through a courtyard and found herself in front of a huge and very famous statue indeed: Michelangelo's *David*. She knew it was a copy, with the original housed safely in a nearby museum, but it was still a surprise—and a joy—to see famous sights almost everywhere she turned.

She took yet another snap to send home, and then she headed back to her flat. Florence, she thought, was going to be an incredible experience.

The next morning, Sam went for a run before her shift; the artists were just setting up their stalls by the Duomo and getting ready to paint more small watercolours for the tourists, and she could hear the bustle of market stalls being set up nearby. Cafés were starting to open, and she could smell the scents of coffee and freshly baked bread. Late spring flowers were everywhere: climbing up walls, spilling over window boxes and blooming in the large terracotta pots she always associated with Italy. The streets here were cobbled, and somehow the city managed to look completely ancient and thoroughly modern all at the same time.

Endorphins from the run and pleasure from the views set her up for the day, and Sam was still smiling when she walked into the Michelangelo Hospital. At the reception area, she picked up the lanyard with her ID card, and asked for directions to Ricardo Fanelli's office.

When she reached the maternity department and pressed her ID card to the reader, nothing happened; clearly her card hadn't been activated yet. Not wanting to be late on her first day, she pressed the buzzer.

There was an answering buzz, and a few seconds later the door opened.

And her knees buckled for a moment when she saw who'd opened the door to her. She almost dropped the flowers she'd bought to thank Lidia.

It couldn't be Angelo. How could he be working in Florence, when she knew he lived in Rome?

But the name on the lanyard round his neck was very clear: *Dottore Angelo Brunelli*.

The love of her life. The man who'd told her he didn't love her any more.

CHAPTER TWO

'HELLO, SAM,' ANGELO SAID. 'Welcome to the Michelangelo Hospital.' He held out his hand, offering her a formal handshake, as if to prove that they'd both got over the past.

The second her palm touched his, her skin felt as if it was fizzing. Memories bubbled over, of how she'd touched him in the past. Linked her hand with his as they'd walked along, talking. Wrapped her arms round him as they'd danced together. Slid her hands through his hair as he'd kissed her. Stroked his bare skin as they'd made love...

She hadn't been prepared for this. She'd thought she was working in a brand-new unit with Ric Fanelli and Henri Lefevre. She'd been so busy over the last three days, packing and sorting out her flight and accommodation and saying goodbye to everyone, that it hadn't even occurred to her to look up the rest of her new department.

But clearly Angelo had known she was coming here, because there wasn't the slightest trace of surprise in his expression.

'I didn't realise you worked here,' she said, forcing herself to sound calm and collected—even though seeing him again had sent her into a spin. 'I thought you were in Rome.'

He inclined his head. 'I moved here a year ago.'

And he looked just the same as she remembered. The same unruly hair that he tried to keep neat for work, but it insisted on curling and tended to stick out everywhere by the end of a shift. The same dark, soulful eyes with their incredibly long lashes. The same beautiful mouth that had made her heart feel as if it had done a triple somersault whenever he smiled at her.

She glanced at her watch, affecting a coolness she most definitely didn't feel. 'I'm meant to be meeting Professor Fanelli and Professor Lefevre,' she said. 'If you could perhaps point me in the right direction—and also tell me first where I can find Lidia—that would be appreciated.'

'Of course,' he said. 'Actually, Ric asked me to help you settle in and translate for you.'

She went cold. Oh, no. Please don't let everyone in Florence know that Angelo was her ex. This would be beyond awkward.

'On the grounds,' he continued, 'that I'm half-English and trained in London.'

She almost sagged in relief as she realised he was telling her that nobody knew about their shared past. That he was going to pretend they were strangers. 'That would be kind.' It wasn't how she felt about it at all, but she needed to keep things professional.

'I'll take you to Lidia,' he said, and ushered her down the corridor.

Lidia turned out to be one of the midwives, half-Italian and half-Jamaican, with a broad smile and kind eyes.

'I just wanted to say thank you,' Sam said when Angelo had introduced them, 'for settling me in to the flat. I really appreciated being able to make myself a coffee when I got in. Those cookies were utterly delicious.'

'No problem, *cara*,' Lidia said. 'And these flowers are gorgeous. Thank you.' She smiled. 'If you're free for lunch and I'm not with a mum, come and find me.'

'I'll do that,' Sam said.

Angelo made no comment, but took her down to Ricardo Fanelli's office, rapped on the door and opened it at the call of, '*Avanti!*'

'Dr Clarke's here,' he said, and gestured to her to go inside. 'Welcome again to the department, Dr Clarke. Enjoy your first morning.'

'Wait, Angelo—you might as well stay,' Ricardo said as Angelo turned away, 'because Dr Clarke will be working with you.'

Sam really hoped that the dismay didn't show on her face. She still hadn't come to terms with the idea of Angelo working in the same city as her, let alone working closely with him.

'Pia Bianchi—the mum with triplets and twin-to-twin transfusion syndrome,' Ricardo said, 'is on Angelo's list. But let me introduce everyone, first. Professor Henri Lefevre,' he gestured to the man seated beside him, 'meet Dr Samantha Clarke and Dr Angelo Brunelli.'

There were smiles and handshakes all round.

'I prefer to work on first name terms,' Ricardo said, 'so please call me Ric. May I ask, Samantha, how much Italian do you speak?'

'Please, do call me Sam. I've been trying to brush up my Italian since my boss asked me to join you, but it's still a bit rusty,' she said, not daring to look at Angelo, who'd taught her nearly all of the Italian she knew, 'and I'm afraid my vocabulary's much more social than medical.'

'You'll be surprised by how quickly you get a language back,' Ric said with a smile. 'And you'll soon pick up the medical side; in the meantime, Angelo can help translate for you. He's half English and trained in England.'

Yeah. She knew that already: his mum had been an English GP and fallen in love with his dad while on holiday in Rome. She'd met the English side of Angelo's family and liked them very much. Not that she could say so without things getting really awkward.

'Of course,' Angelo said, sounding very professional. No doubt this was going to be as difficult for him as it was for her. And, as the head of department had clearly decided that they were working together, Sam knew she and Angelo were going to need a chat to clear the air.

Thankfully the meeting itself was relatively brief, more of a welcome and an explanation of everyone's roles. Ric was working on strategy, Henri was overseeing the surgical team, and Sam was treating patients and training staff—starting with Angelo.

A quarter of an hour later, Angelo said, 'We need to get going, Ric. Pia Bianchi is having a scan right now. I want to review the scan before her appointment, and I also need to brief Dr Clarke on the situation.'

Ric said, 'If you and Angelo decide on surgery for the triplets, Sam, then it would be a good teaching case.'

'Agreed,' Sam said. 'Provided they give me permission, of course.'

'Of course. See the Bianchis, then Angelo can show you round the department and introduce you to everyone,' Ric said with a smile. 'I'll catch up with you later.'

So it was official that they'd be working together. At some point they were going to have to talk about the past. Quite how they were going to do that, she wasn't sure. For now, she'd stick to talking about work.

She followed Angelo to the consulting room in silence. He didn't speak as he logged into the computer and brought up the scan file, but she could see from his expression that it wasn't great news.

'Right. Pia and Tommaso Bianchi,' he said. 'Pia's thirty-six. It's her first pregnancy. She had problems conceiving and was diagnosed with PCOS. The third round of IVF was successful, and she's twenty-two weeks pregnant with twins and a singleton.'

The brief patient history hid what sounded like months and months of worry, and Sam's heart went out to Pia.

'Throughout the pregnancy, she's been well. Obviously, because triplet pregnancies are more complicated than singletons, we've been monitoring her fortnightly since sixteen weeks,' he said. 'Last week, I suspected the beginning of TTTS. I wasn't happy with Monday's scan because there was a noticeable difference between the twins—they were at stage two—and I'm even less happy with this morning's scan, because I think we're at borderline stage three.' He twisted the monitor round so she could see the two scans side by side. The second scan definitely showed a difference; they clearly needed to step in rather than watch and wait.

'Agreed,' Sam said. 'What's her delivery plan?'

'Originally it was for a managed delivery at thirty-five weeks—' which Sam knew was standard for an uncomplicated triplet pregnancy '—but, now TTTS is involved, I want to revise that to thirty-three weeks.' He grimaced. 'To be frank, I think anything after thirty weeks would be a bonus, and I'm planning to give her steroid injections at twenty-nine weeks.'

To mature the babies' lungs in case they needed an emergency delivery; it was a sensible plan, Sam thought.

'Would I be right in thinking that the twins are MCDA?' she asked. Monochorionic diamniotic twins—meaning they shared a single placenta with a single outer membrane, but two inner membranes—were the type at highest risk of developing TTTS.

'Yes.' He gestured to the screen. 'So what do you think?'

'My gut feel is we need to do laser surgery rather than amnioreduction—and I think my boss had the same view or he wouldn't have sent me out here,' she said. 'But we need to give the parents all the options and let them make an informed decision. We can give guidance, but at the end of the day it's their choice and our job is to support them.'

'Agreed,' he said.

She was relieved that Angelo's attitude towards parents was the same as it had been when they'd last worked together: that their views were important, and his job as a doctor was to give them all the information to help them make the right decision for their situation and then support them. At least she wouldn't have to fight him on that score.

'Is there anything else you need to know before I call the Bianchis in?' he asked.

'No, you've covered everything.'

After getting the parents settled, he introduced Sam as the new surgeon on their team.

'I trained in England,' she said, in careful Italian, 'and I'm here because I work with babies inside the womb.'

'We can speak in English, if you prefer,' Tommaso said.

'That's very kind, but it's not fair to you to have to think in a different language when you're already worried,' she said with a smile. 'I'll do my best to be clear in Italian.'

'And I'll help with any translation issues,' Angelo added.

She smiled her thanks at him.

'Signor and Signora Bianchi, I see that you've already had an ultrasound, a foetal MRI and an echocardiography of the babies' hearts today,' Sam said, glancing at Angelo to check she'd got the terms right and relieved to see his nod. 'I'm sure Dr Brunelli—Angelo—has already explained about twin-to-twin transfusion syndrome to you, but I'd like to be sure you have all the information you need to make a decision on how you want us to help you, so forgive me if any of this is repeating things for you. The condition is to do with the placenta rather than the baby, and it's absolutely not your fault. It happens in around one in seven twin pregnancies, and we don't actually know why it happens. What we do know is that the babies share some of the blood vessels in the placenta, so the blood flow between them isn't equal.'

She drew a quick diagram on the whiteboard. 'So we have your three babies: one with his own placenta, and the twins sharing another placenta. The one on his own isn't affected. But the connection between the blood vessels on the twins' placenta means that blood is transferred from the donor—let's call him twin one—to the recipient. Let's call him twin two.' She circled the first twin. 'Twin one doesn't have as much blood flow as he should, and the body prioritises blood flow to the brain so his kidneys aren't getting enough blood. He's dehydrated, he isn't growing as much as he should, he isn't producing as much urine as he should, and he doesn't have as much amniotic fluid around him as he should.'

She paused to check that the Bianchis were following. At their nod, she circled the second twin on the whiteboard and continued, 'Twin two is the other way round: he's getting too much blood and producing more urine than he should. His bladder will become enlarged, he's got too much amniotic fluid, and his heart has to pump harder so the condition will put a strain on his heart.'

'Are they going to die?'

Pia Bianchi was biting her lip, and Sam reached over to squeeze her hand. 'We're here to help, and we want your babies to arrive safely,' she said gently. 'Dr Brunelli and I have discussed your situation, and there are three choices. They're your babies, so how you both feel about the options is important. But we want you to know exactly what everything entails, so you can make an informed decision.'

The Bianchis both looked relieved.

'The first option is that we just wait and see,' Sam said.

'But we wouldn't really recommend that,' Angelo said. 'We've looked at the scans, and you can see the difference in size between twin one and twin two even since Monday.' He showed the screen to the Bianchis. 'And I can see your bump's a lot bigger than when I saw you on Monday, Pia.'

'It feels as if I'm nine months pregnant, not five and a half,' Pia admitted. 'It's not very comfortable. I did wonder if it was because I'm carrying triplets.'

'No. It's the twin-to-twin transfusion causing that. If we wait and do nothing,' Sam said gently, 'then I'm sorry to say I think it's very likely you'll lose both twins, and in turn that's likely to trigger the miscarriage of your third baby.'

'You're a surgeon, Dr Clarke—does that mean Pia needs to have surgery?' Tommaso asked.

'In my view, yes. And there are two things we can do to help the babies,' Sam said. 'The first one is that I can drain the excess amniotic fluid from twin two, which should help, and we'll do another scan in a couple of days to see how you're all doing. If draining the fluid has worked, then we can go back to weekly monitoring. Though I should warn you that draining the fluid doesn't correct the problem with the blood vessels that causes the excess fluid in the first place, so we might have to repeat the operation.'

'What if draining the fluid doesn't work?' Pia asked.

'Then we have a second option: laser surgery,' Sam explained. 'That's where I'd seal off the blood vessel connections that aren't working properly in the placenta, and then I'd drain the excess fluid. You'd need to stay in hospital for a day after the surgery, and we'd reassess the babies again before you go home.'

'Or you can go straight to laser surgery without trying to drain the excess amniotic fluid first,' Angelo added.

'Surgery.' Pia was white-faced. 'Will our babies survive?'

'We'll be honest with you,' Angelo said.

Strictly speaking, the Bianchis were on his list rather than hers, so Sam understood that Angelo wanted to be the one to answer the question—just as she would, in his shoes. At the same time, she appreciated the 'we', because he was including her and making it clear they were a team. They might be poles apart in their personal life but at least here they were on the same side.

'There's always a risk with surgery, and this is an invasive procedure so, yes, there is a risk of miscarriage,' Angelo said. 'At the moment, that'd be a ten per cent chance of miscarrying.'

'Ten per cent's an awful lot,' Pia said, looking horrified.

'If you look at it the other way round, there's also a ninety per cent chance that at least one of the twins will survive,' Sam said. 'The risk of miscarriage decreases after you reach twenty-four weeks, plus we'll keep a very close eye on you.'

'What are the chances that both of the twins will survive, if you do the surgery?' Tommaso asked.

'The chances for both of them are slightly lower than they are for just one of them,' Sam said. 'As Angelo said, with all surgery there's a risk. But the chances of them both being fine is much higher than the risk of losing both of them.'

'Could we wait to do the operation until I'm twenty-four weeks, when the risk of miscarriage is lower?' Pia asked.

'Given the changes in the scan since Monday, I really wouldn't want to risk waiting another two weeks,' Angelo said. 'But, whatever you choose to do, please be reassured that we'll keep a very close eye on you and we'll support you. If you're concerned at any point, then we want you to call us rather than staying at home and worrying.'

'There are three babies,' Tommaso said. 'If we have the surgery on the twins, will the other baby be safe even if—if one of the twins doesn't make it?'

'I've worked with triplet pregnancies involving twin-to-twin syndrome in London,' Sam reassured him, 'and I'm pleased to tell you I delivered all the babies safely in every case. As we've said, there's always a risk with surgery, but the odds are in your favour.'

'What would you do if they were your babies?' Tommaso asked. 'Take away the fluid or have the surgery?'

'If I'm honest, the option I'd prefer—both as a doctor, and if I was in your shoes—is laser surgery,' Sam said.

The Bianchis looked at Angelo.

'The same goes for me,' he said quietly. 'I believe it will give the babies the best chance.'

'How does the laser surgery work?' Pia asked.

'Your scan shows me the placenta is on the back wall of your uterus, so you'll have a local anaesthetic and sedation. That means you'll be awake for the procedure, but you won't feel any pain,' Sam explained. 'I'll make a small incision in your tummy and put a metal tube into your uterus.'

'A metal tube?' Tommaso's eyes widened.

'It's much thinner than you're probably thinking,' she reassured him. 'Thinner than a drinking straw. I promise you, it's not going to hurt Pia. Then I'll put a special kind of camera—called a fetoscope—through the tube to let me see all the blood vessel connections on the surface of the twins' placenta.'

'The camera's that small?' Tommaso asked, looking surprised.

'Yes. It's fibre optic,' Sam said. 'Through the camera lens, I'll be able to see which blood vessels aren't working properly, and I'll put a laser down the tube and use the laser to seal those blood vessels and disconnect them. That means the blood will be flowing normally again to both twins. Finally, I'll drain the excess amniotic fluid, which will make you feel a lot more comfortable, too.'

Pia looked thoughtful. 'If you have to operate on the placenta, does that mean I can't have a vaginal delivery?'

'That's entirely up to you,' Sam said. 'I'll sever all the blood vessels that shouldn't be joined, so it'll be safe to deliver vaginally. But if you decide you'd rather have a Caesarean section, that's also fine.'

'Because there's been a complication during your pregnancy, we'll want you to deliver the triplets a bit earlier than we originally planned,' Angelo said.

'How soon?' Tommaso asked.

'We'd aim for thirty-three weeks, but I'll be honest and tell you that anything after thirty weeks will be a bonus. They'll be tiny at thirty weeks, and they'll need special care, but they'll be old enough to cope with life outside the womb,' Sam said. 'We'll need to give you an injection of steroids at twenty-nine weeks to mature their lungs, Pia, just to be on the safe side. But it's very likely that the babies will need to be in the special care baby unit for a while after they're born.'

'We can't say how long they'll be in the special care unit—it depends on how the babies respond. But we can arrange for you to have a tour of the unit before the babies arrive,' Angelo added, 'so you'll know what to expect and it'll make the unit feel much less scary.'

'Don't panic, and don't think you have to make a decision this very second,' Sam said. 'You've got time to go away and talk it over with your family and friends. Right now the twin-to-twin syndrome is borderline stage two to three, so I don't have to whisk you straight into theatre. If you want to go ahead, we can do the fluid reduction or the laser surgery tomorrow.'

'What I would advise is don't look up complicated birth stories on the internet,' Angelo said. 'You'll find too many stories that will worry you.'

'I can print you a leaflet that explains the procedures, so you don't have to try to remember it,' Sam said. She glanced at Angelo, who nodded.

'I'll do that now,' he said, and tapped a couple of keys on his computer.

'It's a lot to take in. I'd advise you to go and sit somewhere pretty so you can think about it,' Sam said. 'Have a drink and something to eat. Talk to the people you love, write down all your questions, and come back and see us this afternoon so we can work through every single question and be sure you're happy to make a decision.' She shook their hands. 'The main thing is—and I know it's a lot easier to say than do—try not to worry. We're here. And we'll support you, whatever you decide to do.'

'If you'd like to come with me,' Angelo said, 'we can pick up that leaflet from the reception desk.'

'And we'll see you this afternoon,' Sam said.

Sam had always been kind, Angelo remembered. And the Bianchis had definitely reacted to her warmth.

She sat in with the rest of his clinic, that morning; most of his cases were straightforward, though there was another set of twins that they'd need to keep an eye on. At the end of the clinic, Angelo took her round the department to introduce her to as many of the other staff as he could find. Then he glanced at his watch. 'We've got half an hour for a lunch break.'

'I was going to lunch with Lidia, if she's not in with a mum,' she said.

'Let me check for you.' Angelo made a brief enquiry, then shook his head. 'She's in the delivery suite. Why don't I show you where the canteen is and buy you lunch?'

'Thank you,' she said politely. 'That's kind of you to show me round, but I'd prefer to buy my own lunch.'

Sam had always been independent, he remembered. Plus he couldn't ignore the way things had ended between them: he knew he'd hurt her badly. Of course a sandwich and coffee wasn't even going to begin to make up for that, and she wouldn't want to accept anything from him. In her shoes, he'd feel the same. Though he wasn't quite sure how to broach the subject. Or how to apologise in a way that she'd know he really meant it—other than by telling her the truth. And that would be tricky. He didn't want to hurt her even more.

'I know you'd probably rather not spend time with me,'

he said, 'but we need to clear the air a bit, since we'll be working together.'

'Agreed,' she said.

How did you apologise for breaking someone's heart?

He couldn't help glancing at her left hand. There was no ring, but that didn't mean anything. She was a surgeon, and hygiene regulations meant wearing no jewellery. Had she ended up marrying the guy she'd been dating a year ago? Her name was the same, though she might've decided not to change it after marriage. But how could he ask without it seeming crass? It was none of his business.

She still looked the same as she had two years ago, except she'd had her blonde hair cut short, in a choppy pixie cut that suited her. Still had the same cool grey eyes, the same beautiful rosebud mouth—a mouth he'd kissed until it made him dizzy. Seeing her made him feel dizzy now, and there was nothing he could do about it. Though at least she'd agreed to talk to him. That was a start.

In the canteen, he bought himself a sandwich and coffee, waited for her to do the same, and found a quiet table.

'It looks as if we're going to be working together for the next three months,' he said. 'And I know we're both professional enough to put our patients first. But I know that what I did…' God, this made him feel like a teenage boy, without the social skills to deal with an awkward situation. 'What I'm trying to say,' he said, 'is that I don't want things to be difficult between us at work. And I owe you an apology.' What he really owed her was an explanation, but it was a messy and complicated story—and the staff canteen most definitely wasn't the right place to tell it.

She shrugged. 'It was a long time ago. We're both older and wiser.'

'For the record, Sam, I'm truly sorry I hurt you,' he said quietly.

For a moment, he thought he saw the sheen of tears in her eyes. There was a time when he could've reached across the table and squeezed her hand. A time when he could've wrapped her in his arms and told her everything was going to work out just fine. But he'd forfeited that right when he'd walked out on her.

But then she blinked. 'I really wasn't expecting to see you here. I thought you lived in Rome.'

'I did.' Though she didn't need to know about the year he'd taken off work to look after his dad. 'I was offered a position here, a year ago. The Michelangelo is a good place to work, and Florence is a lovely place to live.' He paused. He already knew the answer to this, but he needed to find some way of making conversation before this got too awkward. 'So you're here for three months?'

She nodded. 'I'm helping to set up the new unit with Professor Lefevre, and doing some of the training. I gather from Ric that I'll be training you, so if the Bianchis opt for laser surgery and give their permission, maybe you can do some of the ablation.'

'Thank you. I'd like that,' Angelo said. 'What made you specialise in foetal medicine?'

'I went to a series of lectures at the London Victoria,' she said. 'And it just fascinated me: the fact that you could make such a difference to the outcome of a pregnancy and treat a baby inside the womb. I talked to my boss about it and asked if I could do some work in the area. He agreed, and I've gradually specialised. I moved to Muswell Hill a year ago, and I'm looking forward to working with the team here.' She looked at him. 'And you've stayed with general obstetrics rather than specialising?'

'Yes.' Just not in the hospital, the city or even the country where he'd originally planned to work. 'The team here's really nice.'

'Good to know.'

Reduced to small talk, after all they'd shared. This felt like nails raking down a blackboard. But Angelo knew it was his own fault. Two years ago, he'd believed he was protecting Sam by walking away instead of involving her and bringing back all the memories of her brother's struggle with addiction and eventual death. He'd thought he was protecting himself, too—that if he was the one to end it, he wouldn't be so badly hurt. What he'd actually done was to make the biggest mistake of his life. He should've been honest with her about his dad's situation and given her the choice, instead of making the decision for her. At the time, he'd thought he was being noble and doing the right thing. Now, he was beginning to think that maybe he'd just been arrogant. Either way, he'd been stupid. And he shouldn't have left it a whole year before going back for her.

Seeing her again had stirred up all the old feelings, and it had also made him understand exactly why all his relationships had fizzled out since he'd been back in Italy: because nobody had ever matched up to Sam.

Somehow he managed to keep talking to her about trivial things—good places to eat in the city, must-see attractions and the best times to avoid the crowds—and then it was time to go back for afternoon clinic.

They saw three more sets of parents before the Bianchis came back in.

'We've looked up the websites you recommended, made notes and talked it over with our families,' Pia said. 'And we've decided.' She and Tommaso shared a glance. 'We want to do the laser therapy because we think it'll give the twins their best chance.'

'Then I'll slot you in for first thing tomorrow morning,' Sam said. 'I know you've made your decision, but do you have any questions for us?'

Pia nodded. 'You did say to write them down.'

'Absolutely. That way, you can make sure you've asked everything, instead of getting nearly home and remembering something you forgot to ask,' Sam said with a smile.

Pia brought out her phone and opened a list.

Sam dealt with each question calmly and patiently, and Angelo was pleased to see that the Bianchis both looked a lot less tense by the end.

Sam gave them a quick reminder of what they needed to do before the operation, then smiled. 'So tomorrow afternoon you're going to feel a lot more comfortable, Pia— and you'll both be a lot less worried about the babies.'

'We've been a bit frantic, ever since the last couple of scans,' Tommaso admitted.

'We'll do our best to keep your babies safe,' Sam promised him. 'I do have a couple of questions for you, if that's all right?'

'Sure,' Tommaso said.

'Angelo and I will be in Theatre with you tomorrow, along with a couple of midwives, one of the neonatal team and the anaesthetist, which is pretty much standard. Would you mind if we had three or four other people in the team observing the procedure?' Sam asked. 'Obviously there's no pressure to say yes. I completely understand if you'd rather not.'

'But, if you don't mind Sam using the procedure to teach others,' Angelo said, 'it means you'd be under even closer supervision.'

'And, if you don't mind, I'd like Angelo to do some of the lasering—which will be under my close supervision and instruction,' Sam said. 'Again, please don't feel that you have to say yes. We'll completely understand if you'd rather not, and it won't make any difference to the way we treat you. Our main aim is to support you, and I want you to be comfortable.'

The Bianchis exchanged a glance. 'No, that's all fine,' Pia said. 'You've been very open with us. Kind. We trust you.'

Once they'd finished clinic, Sam turned to Angelo. 'I know you've got ward rounds now, but I'd like to catch Ric and Henri and tell them about tomorrow's op,' she said.

'Of course. Do you need me to show you again where Ric's room is?'

'It's fine. I'll find it,' she said. 'And thank you. I know this isn't easy for you.'

'It isn't easy for either of us,' he said.

'No.' She took a deep breath. 'I appreciate you being so accommodating.'

That was one way of putting it, Angelo thought. But what other choice did he have?

Three months, and she'd be out of his life again.

He could work with her for three months. Just keep it cool, calm and professional. And put a lid on the feelings that threatened to spill out.

CHAPTER THREE

'So HOW WAS your first day?' Nina, Sam's best friend, asked down the phone.

'Good,' Sam said with a smile, curling up on her sofa.

'Are your colleagues nice?'

'Yes. Ric Fanelli's a sweetie, and although Henri Lefevre's a tiny bit scary I think he'll be nice when I get to know him.' She took a deep breath. 'But, um, I did have a bit of a surprise today.' Which was the understatement of the year. 'Angelo works here.'

'What, *your* Angelo?' Nina sounded shocked.

'He hasn't been mine for two years,' Sam reminded her dryly. 'But, yes, Angelo Brunelli.'

'Ouch. That's going to be awkward. He's not on your team, is he?' Nina asked.

'You know that twin-to-twin transfusion syndrome case Will told me about, the one they brought me over to treat? The mum happens to be on Angelo's list—so, yes, I'm working with him. We're doing some laser ablation together tomorrow.'

Nina sucked in a breath. 'Oh, that's tough. Are you going to be OK?'

'I'll have to be, if I want to be part of this project,' Sam said. 'Which I do.'

'It's still awkward.' Nina paused. 'Has he changed?'

Sam had no idea. 'He looks exactly like he did in London,' she said carefully.

'Like a Raphael cherub, with that messy hair. He always was cute,' Nina said. 'And I really liked him—before he dumped you by phone.'

'It was all a long time ago,' Sam said. Though it still stung. Why hadn't he had the guts to call it off face to face, before he went to Italy?

'So is he married now? Does he have kids?'

'I don't know. We stuck to small talk and patients only,' Sam said. 'For what it's worth, he did apologise for hurting me.'

Nina coughed. 'That's a bit late. And he more than hurt you, Sam. He broke your heart.'

And Sam had never been quite able to move on, even though she'd dated. She'd liked Greg very much, but when he'd wanted to move their relationship to something more serious she'd realised that she wasn't ready. They'd stayed friends, but she'd concentrated on her career rather than her love life ever since. 'It is what it is,' Sam said. 'On the plus side, Florence is even more gorgeous than the photographs. I'm going to start exploring the city properly at the weekend. Everywhere you look is beautiful.'

'Sounds amazing. Send me lots of pics,' Nina said.

They chatted for a bit longer, and then Sam heard a wail. 'It sounds as if Lily's just woken up.'

'Yup. And that's definitely a "hungry" cry,' Nina said.

'I'll let you go. Give my goddaughter a cuddle for me,' Sam said. 'Talk to you soon.'

Part of her felt wistful as she ended the call. She'd hoped that she and Nina would end up having babies around the same time, and their children would grow up being close, though it hadn't worked out that way. But at least her best friend was happy, and Sam enjoyed being close to her goddaughter. To brush the gloominess away, she headed out for a walk along the river, enjoying the bustle of the early evening in the city.

But Nina's question had made her wonder. Had Angelo moved on? Was he with someone else, now? And, if so, was it serious?

She tried looking him up on a couple of social media sites, but his settings were locked so that only his friends could see whatever he posted and she was left none the wiser. She could hardly ask at work, without stirring up gossip.

Maybe she'd find a way of broaching the subject tactfully tomorrow.

On Friday morning, Sam went for a run to clear her head before breakfast, had a shower, grabbed a coffee and a warm pastry at the small café round the corner from her flat, and walked to the hospital.

Today would be a big day—both for the Bianchis and for the new unit. Along with the team who'd be there as part of the operation, two professors, the senior midwife, two junior doctors and another from the neonatal team would be watching the procedure, and Angelo would be there to assist her with the operation and translate any questions or answers where her language skills fell short.

She'd practised her new vocabulary all evening, wanting to show everyone in the department that she was trying to make an effort to be part of the team and work with them in their own language, rather than expecting everyone to accommodate her by speaking in English. But her own nervousness would be relatively minor compared to the way the Bianchis would be feeling, she knew. She went to see them before they were due to see the anaesthetist, just to reassure them and answer any last-minute questions.

Angelo was already there. He looked up and smiled as she walked in, and it made her heart feel as if it had done a backflip.

Not here, and not now, she reminded herself. She and Angelo had stopped being a couple two years ago. And, even if he turned out to be single, she wasn't giving him the chance to walk out on her again.

'Are you ready?' she asked Pia.

'I think so.' Pia swallowed hard. 'Actually, no. I'm scared.'

'Anyone would be, in your shoes. But, I promise you, I've done this before. You might feel a little bit of discomfort at times, but it won't be painful and it won't hurt the babies.' Sam squeezed her hand in reassurance. 'Try not to worry. The nice thing is that you'll actually get a proper look at your babies in the womb today. So you've got something to look forward to. Hold on to that instead of the worry.'

'Thank you,' Pia whispered.

The anaesthetist came in and Angelo introduced her to everyone.

'Time for Angelo and me to go and scrub up. We'll see you in Theatre,' Sam said with a smile.

Even though Sam's presence stirred up all kinds of feelings that Angelo would rather keep stuffed in their box, he was looking forward to the operation, intrigued to see how she'd handle it.

She chatted to him as they scrubbed up, treating him the same as she did all her other new colleagues, then talked him through exactly what was going to happen with the laser and what she'd need him to do. 'If you need me to go through any of that again,' she said, 'that's fine. I'm happy to repeat myself a dozen times, as long as you're comfortable with what you're going to do.'

'You made it very clear,' he said. 'Though if I can do the ablation for two of the blood vessels—one where you talk me through it step by step, and one where I talk you through what I'm going to do just before I do it and you stop me if I've got anything wrong—I think that would be useful.'

'That's fine,' she said. 'See how you go. It depends how many blood vessels there are; you might get the chance to do more than two.'

When they'd worked together before, they'd been equals. Now Sam was his senior; plus she was teaching him a new procedure. Though, in a way, it reminded Angelo of when he'd first started to teach her Italian, correcting her pronunciation and encouraging her to broaden her vocabulary. She'd been a good student, methodical and consistent, and he had a feeling that she would be just as good as a teacher.

Though she wouldn't be rewarding him the way he'd rewarded her, with kisses...

He shook himself. Letting the memories flood in really wasn't going to help. They were colleagues. End of.

When the rest of the team was assembled in Theatre, she introduced herself to them and ran through the operation; she was patient with questions, answering them as clearly as she could.

Then Pia was wheeled in, Tommaso by her side and holding her hand, and the anaesthetist on the other side.

Sam introduced them swiftly to everyone.

'Now, you can change your mind if you want to,' she said gently to Pia, 'and I'll ask everyone to go away. But if you're happy for them to stay it'll mean you'll get to meet more of the team, and also you'll have the chance to ask them any questions you like.'

'I just want it over with, so my babies are safe,' Pia said. 'I really don't mind your colleagues being here.'

'Great. Let's get started. Now, even with the anaesthetic, you'll feel a little bit of pushing, Pia. As I said to you earlier, it might feel a little bit uncomfortable, but it shouldn't hurt. If you're worried about anything, just say and we can stop. We've got all the time in the world,' Sam reassured her.

Angelo reached over to squeeze Pia's free hand. 'Sam's going to be concentrating on the surgery, so talk to me first and I'll do my best to answer any questions. I'll tell Sam if you need her to stop for any reason, OK?'

'Thank you,' Pia said.

'I'm going to talk through everything I do, as I do it,' Sam said, addressing Pia and the team. 'Pia's placenta is on the back wall of the uterus, so we're using a local anaesthetic and sedation. I'm going to make a small incision in her abdomen and then put a metal tube into her uterus to support the instruments I'm using.'

Angelo watched, fascinated by how deft Sam's movements were.

'And now I'm putting the fetoscope in—that's the telescopic camera, Pia.' She slid the instrument down the tube. 'And here we can see the babies.' She indicated the screen. 'Feet, legs—ah, this is what I wanted. Faces. Just as I promised. So now you get to see your babies properly, Pia and Tommaso.' She smiled. 'Meet your twins.'

'This is incredible,' Pia said, staring at the screen.

'Our babies.' Tommaso's voice was filled with awe. 'Twenty-two weeks old, and we can actually see their faces inside your womb, Pia.'

'I just wish it was for…' Pia bit back a sob.

'For a different reason. I know,' Angelo said, squeezing her hand. 'But we're doing the best we can for all of you.'

'Now, I'm going to take a closer look at the placenta,' Sam said. The screen was filled with shades of blue and red and purple; the veins were very evident. 'You can see the first connection that shouldn't be here,' she added to the team. 'I'm going to look all the way along, so we can see all the blood vessel connections before I seal them. We'll take our time and do this thoroughly.'

She was cool, calm and competent, and Angelo could feel Pia relaxing as Sam talked her way through the procedure.

'Next, it's the laser,' Sam said. 'I'm going to use it to seal the blood vessels and disconnect them, so their circulations are separate and blood flows normally again to both twins. You won't feel anything happening, Pia. I'm shining the laser through the tube, and in a second you'll hear a pop as we break the connection and seal the blood vessel. But don't worry about anything happening to the babies, because the blood will clot immediately. All we're doing is separating their blood circulation so they'll each have the right amount of blood. This won't hurt them.'

The pop when she fired the laser was louder than Angelo had expected, sounding like a light switch turning on.

She did two more blood vessels, then turned to him. 'Angelo?'

She talked him through the first one; her instructions were clear and easy to follow.

And then it was his turn to talk through what he planned to do, doing each step once she'd given the go-ahead.

Part of him was terrified; one wrong move, and it

could be catastrophic. On the other hand, part of him was thrilled to bits. He was helping to perform an operation that would give the twins the best chance of life—an operation that wouldn't even have been possible when he'd first started training. This was the cutting edge of medicine, and he could really understand why Sam loved it. It felt like having his own personal magic wand.

Sam encouraged him to do two more blood vessels, then took over again to finish sealing the last few connections.

'And now I'm going to drain the excess amniotic fluid, Pia, which will make you feel a lot more comfortable,' she said.

Once Sam had finished the procedure, Pia was wheeled out to the recovery area to rest, they scrubbed out, and Sam debriefed the team and answered questions.

Angelo was there to support with the translation, but she'd clearly remembered more than she realised because she didn't need to turn to him for help. He still couldn't help remembering when he'd taught her how to speak his language: the smile in her eyes when she'd said, '*Te amo*, Angelo.'

He'd loved her, too.

So very much.

He'd planned to take her to Rome, that summer, to meet the Italian side of his family—she'd already met his mum's side, in England, and they'd all adored her. And, more importantly, he'd planned to take her to the garden of oranges at the top of the Aventine Hill and ask her to marry him…

Then he realised that Sam was looking at him—and so was everyone else. Clearly she was stuck on the vocabulary she needed to answer a question; lost in his memories, he hadn't been paying attention. 'Sorry,' he said, thinking on his feet. 'I'm still a bit stunned about what we just did. If someone had told me when I was a student that one day I'd get to do *in utero* surgery with a laser, I would never have believed them. And, best of all, it means these babies have a much better chance in a complicated pregnancy.' He smiled. 'Sorry. Can we have the question again?'

Thankfully, he was able to help Sam with the answer. But he really needed to stop dreaming. He had no idea if she was in a relationship, and he probably didn't have the right to know. They had a job to do, and then she was going to leave. Maybe he and Sam could become friends again, but it was clear that would be the limit. He'd hurt her so badly.

And he needed to focus on his job.

All the same, he couldn't help suggesting that they grab a coffee in the staff kitchen, when everyone else had gone back to their own clinics and offices.

'That was amazing,' he said. 'I totally get why you fell in love—' Oh, no. Seriously bad choice of phrase. 'With that kind of surgery,' he added swiftly.

There was a faint stain of colour in her cheeks. 'I like the precision. The fact you can make such a huge difference with such tiny, tiny instruments.'

'And it was good working with you again,' he said, before he could stop himself.

The colour in her cheeks deepened. 'We always did work well together.'

Personally as well as professionally. Yeah. They'd *fitted*.

And he could still remember how it felt to hold her close. Her warmth. Her shape. Her scent. All he'd have to do would be to take one step forward and slide his arms round her...

...and she'd run a mile.

Though something about the way she wouldn't quite meet his eyes made him curious: did she, too, wonder how it would feel to hold him again, feel his arms wrapped round her?

'I, um, need to get on with the paperwork,' she said, sounding a little flustered—unless it was his imagination working overtime and he was hearing what he wanted to hear. 'See you with the Bianchis in a couple of hours,' she added, and left the kitchen.

Had his thoughts shown on his face, and that was what had made her practically bolt from the room? Or had it been her own wayward thoughts driving her?

Angelo shook himself. He needed to get a grip. Keep things professional. And stop dreaming about the might-have-beens.

'How are you doing, Pia?' Sam asked.

'OK. I think.' Pia's face was lined with anxiety. 'I was hoping I'd feel the twins move a bit more by now. I mean, there are three babies, and I'm twenty-two weeks...'

'Even though there's less space in your womb, with triplets,' Sam said, 'you still won't feel them move any earlier than if you were carrying just one baby—and in a first pregnancy that's usually around twenty weeks. It's still really early days. Try not to worry.'

Pia's face said it all for her.

'It's a lot easier said than done,' Sam said ruefully. 'Let's go for a scan and see how the babies are doing. I think you could both do with the reassurance.'

'It's hard,' Tommaso said, 'not being able to do anything to help.'

'I'd say you're doing the best thing possible to help,'

Angelo reassured him, 'because you're here and Pia knows she isn't on her own.'

In the ultrasound suite, Angelo rubbed the gel over Pia's stomach, and Sam stroked the head of the transceiver across Pia's bump.

Had the surgery worked? he wondered. Or were the Bianchis going to have their hearts broken today?

Sam looked at the screen—which she'd turned away from the parents, in case she needed to prepare them for bad news, and Angelo noticed that the sound was off, too. For Pia and Tommaso's sake, he really hoped that this would be good news. The longer Sam looked at the screen, the more the muscles in his back tightened with worry. Had the babies survived the operation? Was Sam going to confirm Pia's worst fears?

But then she smiled and flicked a switch. 'Listen to this. This is twin one's heartbeat.' The sound was steady and regular. 'Twin two.' Again, the heartbeat was steady. 'And baby three.'

A single tear leaked down Pia's face. 'They're still alive. All of them. They're still *alive*.'

Sam turned the screen so they could see it.

'I know you're not feeling the movements very much,' Angelo said, 'but you can see on the screen they're definitely kicking and moving around. The heartbeats are all nice and strong.'

'You've saved my babies,' Pia said. 'I can't even begin to thank you both.'

'It's still early days,' Sam warned quietly, 'and I want you staying in the ward overnight to rest. But the signs are all looking excellent, so far.' She smiled. 'I hope you're feeling a bit less worried, now. I'm afraid I do have another patient to see, but I promise I'll call in and see you before I go home.'

'My next ward round isn't for another half an hour, so I can stay with you for a bit longer,' Angelo said. 'I'll clean up the gel, Pia, and I'll see you both back to the ward.'

Sam called in to see Pia and Tommaso after her shift, and spent a while just chatting to them; thankfully, Pia was starting to feel more foetal movements. Then she walked back to her flat and cooked herself a quick supper before calling her mum to let her know that the operation had gone well. She also emailed Will to give him a rundown of how things were going in the new department.

But, once she'd done the washing up and put everything away, she felt oddly flat.

Friday night in Florence, with nowhere to go. All the museums and tourist attractions were closed in the evenings; though, even if they had been open, Sam didn't have anybody to go with. She really didn't feel like going out and having a drink in a bar on her own. She wished she'd thought of asking some of her new colleagues if they were free that evening, before she'd left work. Yesterday evening, she'd been too busy learning Italian to think about anything else; tonight, she felt lonely.

'Enough of the pity party, Samantha Clarke,' she told herself crossly. 'It's been a long day, with a stressful operation, and you've spent most of the day practically thinking in another language. That's why you're out of sorts. What you need is a shower and an early night with a good book or a comedy.'

The shower helped, and the comedy made her laugh; though neither of them distracted her quite enough to stop her thinking about Angelo and how he'd worked seamlessly with her in Theatre. In some ways, it felt as if those two years they'd spent apart had never happened. And when they'd talked in the kitchen, there had been a moment when their eyes had met. When he'd said it was good working with her again and she'd stupidly burbled about them working well together. She'd meant professionally: of *course* she'd meant professionally. But for a second she'd seen a glint in his eye that told her he'd remembered the personal side, too. All the old feelings. The feelings for him she'd thought she'd buried had flooded back as if they'd never gone away, and she'd had to look away, not wanting him to see.

And maybe that was the real reason she felt so out of sorts. Because seeing Angelo again had brought home how much she'd loved him—and how much she'd missed him.

She spent a restless night, and was awake a good hour before her alarm. Maybe a run would sort her out; the endorphins might boost her mood. She brushed her teeth, changed into her running gear and headed out along the banks of the Arno. She'd been running for about ten minutes when she heard her name being called.

Stopping, she looked round, and saw Angelo.

Her heart skipped a beat. Even in ancient, slightly scruffy jogging bottoms and a faded T-shirt, he looked gorgeous. She'd always loved the way his hair was so easily mussed: as her best friend had once pointed out, he looked like a Raphael cherub.

'I would ask if you were out for a run, like me, but it's pretty obvious what you're doing,' he said with a smile. 'I assume your flat must be nearby?'

She nodded. 'And you obviously live near here, or you wouldn't be out for a run here.'

'Yes. The river walk is good for running, as long as you go early—that way you can avoid the crowds,' he said. 'If you head west, Cascine Park is pretty, or if you want a challenge you can cross the river and run up the

Viale Michelangelo to the Piazzale, and you'll get stunning views of the city as a reward for running up a hill.'

'Thanks for the tips,' she said. 'I'll try to remember that for the future.'

'Are you due at the hospital, this morning?' he asked.

'Yes. Are you?'

He nodded, and glanced at his watch. 'Do you have plans, or would you like to join me for breakfast?'

She could make an excuse and say that she needed to finish her run. But her path would still cross with his at the hospital, and he'd realise she'd been trying to avoid him outside work, which would make it feel even more awkward.

Perhaps having breakfast with him would be a good idea. If they were in a neutral space, she could make it clear that she saw him only as a colleague. Even though, if she was honest with herself, that wasn't quite the truth. Seeing him again had made her feel so mixed-up.

She took a deep breath. Might as well face the other bit head-on. 'Would your partner mind me joining you for breakfast?'

'There isn't anyone to mind who I have breakfast with,' he said.

Angelo was single?

That was a shock. She'd assumed that he'd started dating someone else at some point in the last two years. Then again, she knew from experience that he didn't commit, or maybe it was just that she'd been the one he hadn't wanted to commit to.

'Just to be clear, I'm asking you to breakfast as a new colleague who's just moved to the area and my boss has asked me to help you settle in,' he added.

Was that his way of telling her she didn't have to worry that he was trying to reignite their old relationship? And maybe this would give them a chance to work out how they were going to handle things.

'In that case,' she said, 'breakfast would be lovely. And I'll do the rest of my run later today.'

He took her to a café not far from the Duomo.

'This is my bill,' she said as they reached the doorway. 'And that's not negotiable. It's a condition.'

'You always were independent.' He shrugged. 'OK. Thank you. I'll have pancakes with sliced bananas, walnuts and caramel sauce, please, and a skinny cappuccino.'

She blinked. 'You haven't even looked at the menu.'

'Everyone orders pancakes, here,' he said. 'It's the house speciality. The coffee's good here, too.'

She ordered pancakes and coffee for both of them, while he found a quiet table in the corner.

'How are you settling in to Florence?' he asked when she joined him.

'Fine, thanks,' she said. 'My flat's lovely, and the hospital seems a good place to work—it's a nice team.'

'It is,' he said. 'I've been here a year, now, and I'm really enjoying it.'

The waitress brought their coffee, and Sam took a sip to bolster her courage, enjoying the slight bitterness of the brew. 'When I agreed to come here, I wasn't expecting you to be part of the team,' she said.

'When Ric told me your name, I was sure it was just a coincidence,' he said. 'Until I looked you up on the hospital website.'

So he'd had time to prepare himself for seeing her again.

Would she even have come here, if she'd known it would mean working with him for three months? Her first reaction would probably have been to refuse, but then again this might give her the chance for closure.

'So are you still with Greg?' he asked.

She stared at him, slightly taken aback. How had he known about Greg? Had he stayed in touch with some of his old friends in London and they'd told him she was dating someone else? Not that it mattered. 'No,' she said. 'He was a really lovely guy, but it just didn't work out.' Mainly because she'd dated him on the rebound, trying to get over the man who sat opposite her right now.

It hadn't worked.

'Nowadays, I'm completely focused on my career,' she said, wanting to make the point.

'Me, too.'

So they were on the same page. 'Did you get everything sorted out in Rome?' she asked.

His eyes widened. 'Rome?'

'The family stuff you went to sort out.'

'Yes,' he said, his voice suddenly clipped.

But he didn't elaborate, and it felt too intrusive to ask anything more, when he was sending out such obvious 'keep off' signals.

The silence was excruciating. Which was sad, because in their two years together, they'd never stopped talking. They'd been so in tune: which made that phone call all the harder to understand. It had come out of nowhere and Sam still didn't understand why.

Had he met someone else? She didn't think so, because Angelo wasn't the type to lie or cheat. But she really couldn't work out what had gone wrong.

Fortunately the pancakes arrived, to distract them from the awkward silence.

'You're right. They're excellent,' she said after her first taste.

'Good.' He tackled his own pancakes.

Maybe it was the carbs doing the hard work for them,

but the silence between them gradually became easier. She sneaked tiny glances at him, wondering what was going on in his head. He was still the most gorgeous man she'd ever met, from the curve of his mouth to those ridiculously long eyelashes. But it wasn't just his looks; the Angelo she'd fallen in love with had been bright and passionate, and his enthusiasm for the Romans and his heritage had ignited her own interest. She'd found history a bit dull, at school, but Angelo had made it come alive for her. He'd made a list of every single bit of Roman London that could be visited: not just the pieces of Roman wall that still stood around the city and in basements, but also the amphitheatre under the Guildhall, as well as the villa with its hypocaust in Billingsgate. He'd done the same in Paris, insisting on going to Cluny to see the Roman baths as well as walking hand in hand round the art galleries with her so they could enjoy the Monets.

Maybe that was a way back to some kind of friendship. 'So you've been here a year?' she asked.

'Yes.' He looked slightly wary.

'I assume you've found every single bit of Roman remains in the city?'

The wariness dissolved. 'Most of them,' he said with a grin. 'There's a Roman temple beneath the Duomo—hence the mosaics. The main Roman forum was at the Piazza della Repubblica, there was an amphitheatre near Piazza Santa Croce, and there are the ruins of a theatre under the Palazzo Vecchio.'

'And you've got a list?'

He smiled. 'You remember my lists?'

She nodded. 'You taught me a lot I didn't know about London.'

He looked thoughtful. 'Is this your first visit to Florence?'

'Yes.' She hadn't been back to Italy since she'd gone to Venice with him.

'Maybe I can show you around when we're off duty,' he said.

Was this another example of him being a kind colleague, or was there more to it than that? Was he, too, reflecting on the fact that they were both single, and maybe wondering if they could repair the damage between them? Her skin tingled at the idea.

'Exploring a new city with someone who knows it, rather than a guidebook, means you get to find the interesting bits more quickly,' he said.

The anticipation flattened before it had a chance to rise much further. The way he was talking, it didn't sound as if he was asking her out on a date.

'And we're colleagues.'

Definitely not a date, then. Which the sensible side of her knew was a good thing, because dating him last time round had left her with a broken heart, but part of her felt disappointed.

'I know I hurt you, Sam,' he said, 'and I'm so very sorry for that, but maybe we can find our way back to some kind of friendship. It'll make things easier for both of us at the hospital.'

And maybe it would give her some closure, too. Maybe, if they became friends again, she could finally let herself move on from him instead of wondering where it all went wrong and coming up with a blank. 'All right,' she said. 'Offer accepted.'

'Are you busy after work today?' he asked.

'I was going to finish my run,' she said, not wanting to seem too eager.

'If you wouldn't mind going for a walk instead,' he

said, 'there's a public garden I'd like to take you to see. It's pretty special at this time of year.'

'All right,' she said.

'Then I'll meet you outside the hospital after our shift.' He glanced at his watch. 'Thank you for breakfast, Sam. I need to shower and change before work, so I'll catch up with you at the hospital.'

'Starting with the Bianchis,' she said. 'I want to do another scan this morning and check the babies' hearts.'

'OK.' He smiled at her. 'It's good to be working with you again.'

'And you,' she said politely, even though right now she felt too confused to know whether seeing him again would be a good thing or a bad.

CHAPTER FOUR

ANGELO TURNED THE temperature down on the shower, hoping the coolness of the water would do something to restore his common sense.

It didn't help.

All he could think about was what Sam had told him: she was single.

And she'd agreed to spend time with him today, after work.

OK, so he'd suggested it in terms of a colleague showing her round the city. And he'd told her that he was focused on his career.

It was all true. Up to a point.

But he'd never forgotten the woman he'd fallen in love with. The slightly shy doctor he'd met when he'd moved from Hampstead to the London Victoria. He'd been attracted to her right from the very first moment, and not just because she was pretty; there was a warmth and sweetness about her that had drawn him. He'd asked her to join him for a drink after work. She'd refused, and the hospital grapevine had told him that her younger brother had recently died. Knowing it was the wrong time to be pushy, he'd made friends with her instead. Over the next few months she'd gradually opened up to him; then, the night of the hospital's Valentine ball, he'd kissed her for the first time.

They'd quickly become inseparable, until the day his uncle had phoned him about his dad's addiction problem. Ironically, Sam was the one person who would've understood and given him sound advice about helping an addict; but how could he have opened up her wounds, knowing that her brother had accidentally overdosed on cocaine? He'd given her a vague story about needing to sort out some family stuff in Rome; when it was clear that his dad needed him to stay, Angelo had made the phone call to break up with Sam. He'd lost his mum, he'd lost his dad, and if Sam walked away from him it would be too much. Better to end it now than risk losing his heart completely.

Every word, every lie he'd told, had shredded his heart a little more: but wasn't it better that she should believe him shallow and callous than for her to get dragged into his family's problems and relive the misery of her own past? When he'd told her he didn't love her, he'd almost stumbled over the words, but it was the only way to keep her away. To keep them both safe.

But now she was back.

And he was still lying to her, claiming that he saw her as just a colleague.

If they were to have any chance of getting true closure on the past and moving forwards—maybe together—then he needed to tell her the truth. But he needed to find the right words, so he didn't hurt her even more.

He towelled himself dry, dressed and headed for the hospital. Before his ward rounds, he dropped in to see the Bianchis.

'Good morning. How are you feeling, Pia?' he asked.

'Much more comfortable, thank you,' Pia said. She

bit her lip. 'But the babies still aren't moving as much as I expected.'

'I know you're booked in for another foetal echocardiogram this morning before you see us,' he said, 'but for now let's have a listen.' He checked with the Pinard stethoscope—to his relief, everything sounded normal, but he knew that Pia was worried. 'It all sounds fine, but I'm going to get another scanner rather than making you try and be a contortionist,' he said, and fetched the portable Doppler scanner, knowing that Pia and Tommaso both needed the reassurance of hearing their babies' heartbeats. 'Here we go. One heartbeat, nice and steady.' He moved the head of the Doppler. 'Twin two.' He smiled. 'And, finally, baby three.'

The Bianchis both looked relieved. 'They're holding on,' Tommaso said.

'They're doing fine,' Angelo reassured them. 'So now you can try to relax during the scans this morning, and I'll see you with Sam a bit later, OK?'

When he'd finished doing the ward rounds, he caught up with Sam in her office.

'Just the man I wanted to see,' she said.

For a moment, it felt as if they were back in London. That she too had lived for the moments when they were together.

But of course it wasn't. She'd simply been expecting him to join her for the Bianchis' appointment this morning. When she added, 'I've just had the Bianchi triplets' scans through,' it confirmed why she'd wanted to see him. Obviously. And he needed to stop being ridiculous.

'I saw Pia and Tommaso first thing,' he said. 'Pia was worrying earlier that she couldn't feel the babies moving very much, so I checked their heartbeats. I used the portable Doppler so the Bianchis could hear the heart-beats for themselves.'

'Good call,' she said. 'Have a look at the echo results and see what you think.' She brought them up on screen.

Angelo studied them. 'That's wonderful,' he said. 'I can't believe how much difference there is since yesterday.'

'It's pretty dramatic,' she agreed.

'You know, doing the laser ablation felt almost as if I was waving a magic wand,' he said.

She nodded. 'That's what I love about this field of medicine. We're making such a huge difference to the parents of babies who weren't very likely to make it without our intervention. We're giving the parents hope and the babies a real chance.'

He knew she meant a general 'we' but, again, this felt personal. As if she were talking about just the two of them, and it made him feel warm from his very core. 'Yes,' he agreed.

'Ready for to see the Bianchis?' she asked.

He nodded. 'I'll call them in.'

Pia and Tommaso still looked slightly anxious when they walked into the consulting room.

'So how are you feeling, Pia?' Sam asked.

'OK. Well, scared,' Pia admitted. 'Even though we heard their hearts beating, I guess I worry that...' She stopped, clearly not wanting to voice her fears in case talking about them made the worst happen.

'Angelo and I have reviewed your echo results, and we're really pleased,' Sam said gently. 'Let's do the ultrasound so we can see what's happening.'

Angelo assisted, squeezing Pia's hand and Tommaso's shoulder in reassurance as Sam stroked the transceiver over Pia's abdomen. He was pretty sure this would all be fine, but there was always that tiny, tiny margin of doubt.

But then Sam angled the screen towards the Bianchis. 'Twin one. Twin two. And baby three.'

Pia burst into tears—happy tears and Tommaso hugged her. Angelo couldn't help wrapping his own arms round Sam, overcome with relief and joy that the procedure had worked so well, and for a moment Sam hugged him back.

Something shifted in the region of his heart, and he pulled back. Her gorgeous grey eyes were wide with an emotion he couldn't quite name. Had she, too, felt more than the joy of the moment? Her lips parted, and for a crazy moment the whole world disappeared and it was just the two of them in the room.

But then Pia asked, 'So it's all as it should be?'

Sam shifted back into professional mode. 'Yes. They've all got good movements, and more importantly the scans earlier showed me the blood flow and I'm very happy with it. So your job now is to relax, rest, and do something that will help distract you from worrying.'

'And we'll see you for a regular check-up on Friday,' Angelo said, battening down his feelings and going into professional mode, too. 'Obviously, if you have any concerns before then, call us.'

'I'm pleased to say we're happy to send you home,' Sam said with a smile, 'provided you rest.'

'I'll make sure she rests,' Tommaso said.

After clinic, Sam was called in to help with an emergency delivery of a baby in distress, and Angelo didn't see her again before the end of his shift.

He waited for her outside the hospital, as they'd arranged.

She'd agreed to go out with him this evening—strictly

as friends—but she'd had a day to think about it, between seeing patients. Would she have changed her mind? He knew she'd turn up; she'd always been meticulous about keeping her word and he didn't think that would've changed. But she might have had second thoughts about spending the evening with him. Especially after that hug. He could probably explain it away as relief, but they'd both know it wasn't.

Would it make Sam back away?

Adrenalin shimmered through him, making him feel as nervous as if this was a first date. Which was ridiculous. This was merely a situation where one colleague was showing another around a new city, that was all, he told himself.

And then he rolled his eyes. Who was he trying to kid? He hadn't been able to stop thinking about Sam since he'd seen her again on Thursday morning. Though, until he'd been honest with her about why he'd walked away from her in the first place, he couldn't really ask for her forgiveness. And that was a conversation where he didn't have a clue how to start.

Angelo looked in a world of his own, leaning against the wall near the hospital entrance and gazing into the distance. Was he regretting his offer to take her to show her the gardens and wishing he hadn't burdened himself with her company? Sam wondered. Or was he, too, thinking about their situation and wondering quite where they went from here? Was he, too, thinking about the moment they'd hugged each other and the way their closeness had triggered all the memories of their past?

She walked up to him. 'Penny for them?'

He jumped slightly, then looked at her and smiled. 'I'd

be overcharging you,' he said. 'Sorry. Miles away. Are you still OK to go and see the gardens?'

His expression was completely inscrutable, and she had no idea whether this was his way of giving them both a let-out, or whether he was simply trying not to put any pressure on her.

Maybe he, too, needed closure. Maybe this would give them the opportunity they needed to really talk, and finally put the past behind them. 'I'm fine to go, if you are,' she said.

He smiled, then. She'd forgotten how his smile could make her feel as if the world was all lit up.

'Let's head into town,' he said.

He pointed out some of the buildings to her as they headed into the historic centre. 'We're going to take the quicker route up to the Piazzale Michelangelo today,' he said, 'but I can show you where the running route comes out.'

'Thanks. That'd be good.'

Once they'd crossed over the Ponte Vecchio, they walked alongside the river for a while. 'The Bardini Gardens are also worth a look, when you've got a free afternoon,' he said, pointing out the entrance to the gardens as they passed. 'They've got a tunnel of those purple flowers you like. The ones you once dragged me to see in Notting Hill.'

'Wisteria,' she said with a smile. 'And you have to admit it was gorgeous.' She still had pictures somewhere of them together next to the wisteria, with the white-painted walls of the house a perfect backdrop to the flowers. 'So where are we going?'

'The Giardino dell'Iris—the Iris Gardens,' he said. 'The gardens are only open while the irises are blooming, so you're in Florence at the perfect time.'

They walked up to a honey-coloured stone archway. 'This is Porta San Miniato, one of the gates in the old city wall,' he said. 'And we're going to walk up the steps along the outside of the rose garden.'

The steps looked wide and shallow, but she soon discovered that the hill was steeper than it looked—and a lot longer.

'Don't turn round to look until you get to the top,' he said. 'I promise the view's worth it.'

Sam had always enjoyed walking through a city with Angelo. Whenever they'd taken a mini break together, he'd researched the city thoroughly beforehand and made a list of places he wanted to visit, so they could make the most of their time and see as much as possible.

He'd done the same in London, making a list of the places he wanted to visit, and splitting them between rainy and sunny days. At the London Victoria, they'd sorted out the rosters so they were off duty at the same time, and they'd gradually worked their way through Angelo's list, seeing everything from the weird jars of specimens at the Hunterian Museum and the butterflies at the Horniman, through to the bluebells in Highgate Wood and the summer roses in Regent's Park.

She'd just bet he had an amazing list for Florence.

Maybe he'd share the list with her, if she asked—even if he didn't want to go to the different places with her.

At the top of the steps, he gestured to the bronze replica of Michelangelo's David. 'Keep walking over to the statue—don't look anywhere else—and *then* you can turn round.'

She did, and gave a sharp intake of breath as she saw the view of the city, with the mountains behind it as a backdrop. 'That's so pretty, with all the old buildings running along the side of the river. I know that's the Duomo and the bell tower—but what's the other tall tower?'

'The Palazzo Vecchio, which is definitely worth a visit,' he said. 'There are some great sculptures, and there's a good view from the top of the tower.'

'I'll add it to my list of things to see,' she said.

From his expression, she guessed that he, too, was remembering his old London list and how they'd worked their way through it. Would he offer to join her with her list in Florence, or would he keep his distance?

'Good idea,' he said, and she felt the lurch of disappointment in her stomach. He'd clearly chosen distance.

'Let's go and look at the irises,' she said. 'I assume from the name that it's mainly irises in the garden?'

'And olive trees,' he said. 'But it's dedicated to irises, so it's only open when the flowers are blooming.'

'So why specialise in just one flower with a short blooming season? Why not plant the kind of garden that has something different every month?'

'It started out as a competition garden. Apparently there's been a competition every year for decades to produce an iris the exact shade of the red one on the Florentine coat of arms,' he explained. 'There are a couple of thousand varieties of iris, but it seems it's really hard to breed a red one.'

She frowned. 'I thought it was a lily on the Florentine coat of arms. A fleur-de-lys.'

'They look similar, but the symbol is actually inspired by an iris,' he said.

She believed him. Angelo always had done his research. Besides, the garden was pretty and she enjoyed walking round the narrow, winding stone pathways with him, shaded by olive trees. There were birds singing and flowers everywhere; as well as the shades of blue, purple, white and yellow she was used to, there were irises in shades of apricot, peach and pink, and even black. They ranged in size from the tiny ones she'd grown on a windowsill to truly gigantic, and everywhere she looked she could see frilly petals, with the grey-green leaves of the olive trees as the perfect background to the riot of colour. Behind the trees, the hills loomed, and above them fluffy white clouds scudded along a blue, blue sky.

It was idyllic. If she and Angelo had come here together when they were still a couple, she would've loved every second; it was so romantic. By the pond in the lower garden, she almost forgot herself and reached for his hand. At the last moment, she realised what she was about to do and touched his arm instead. 'Look. Dragonflies.' She indicated the blue and orange dragonflies hovering over the water.

'And the frogs are definitely trying to compete with the birds,' he said with a grin. 'I don't think I've ever heard such loud croaking.'

'Thank you for bringing me here. This is lovely.'

'I hoped you'd like it.' He smiled at her. 'There are great views from the rose garden we walked beside, too. And the Piazzale itself is a good place to sit and watch the sunset.' He wrinkled his nose. 'I should've thought to pick up some things at lunchtime for a picnic.'

A picnic at sunset. It was the sort of thing she'd once loved doing with him, but she wasn't sure she could handle it now. There would be too many memories. Too much sadness about what they'd lost. 'Maybe some other time,' she said.

'I was wondering,' he said. 'Given that you bought me breakfast, would you like to join me for dinner tonight?'

'Dinner?'

'Nothing fancy,' he said. 'I thought we could walk

back down the hill. There are some good places to eat on this side of the river. And the Ponte Vecchio looks at its best around sunset.'

This wasn't a date, she reminded herself. She needed to think of him purely as a colleague she'd once known, who felt he owed her dinner in return for the breakfast she'd bought him. Besides, if she said no it meant she'd be spending another evening alone in Florence, because she hadn't arranged anything with anyone else. 'OK. That'd be nice,' she said.

Tell her now. Now, when the world was full of flowers and butterflies and sunshine. When there was enough space round them that it wouldn't become painfully intense...

But Angelo couldn't find the words. Knowing that he was being a coward and avoiding the conversation they really needed to have, he talked about the city instead. Was it his guilty conscience, or did Sam's expression say that she knew why he was keeping her at arm's length? Then again, she wasn't raising the subject, either. Maybe they'd needed time to get used to each other again before they could talk about their unfinished business.

When they'd finished looking at the irises, they walked through the rose garden, and Sam enjoyed hearing the hum of bees and watching butterflies flit between the flowers. The scent was incredible, as were the views, and Sam took snaps to send later to her mum and Nina. Then they took a winding path back down the hill, ending up at another of the old medieval gates. Angelo led her through a maze of narrow cobbled streets, with tall buildings either side painted in tones of ochre and saffron and cream, their narrow windows flanked by shutters.

He took her to a tiny restaurant whose tables had red

checked tablecloths, and there were candles stuck in raffia-covered bottles.

'The decor's a bit retro,' he said, 'but the food's fantastic.'

The waiter brought them breadsticks and explained that the day's menu was on the chalkboard; when he asked what they'd like to drink, Angelo looked at Sam. 'Chianti OK with you?' he asked.

'Lovely,' she said. 'And maybe a jug of water?'

'What do you recommend to eat tonight?' Angelo asked.

'The meatballs are good,' the waiter said. 'And for sides, the potatoes and spinach.'

'Sounds good to me,' Sam said, and Angelo ordered for both of them.

When the waiter had brought the wine, Angelo lifted his glass in a toast. '*Saluti.* Welcome to Florence, Sam.'

'*Saluti,*' she said, clinking her glass against his. 'Mmm, this is good.' She paused. 'So, as you've been here a year, I assume you've already worked your way through the places you want to see in the city?'

He grinned. 'Most of the things on my list, yes.'

'What do you recommend?'

'All the churches,' he said. 'Every one has something different, whether it's amazing sculpture or ancient frescos that look as if they were painted yesterday instead of hundreds of years ago. And it's definitely worth going up inside the Duomo, because it's fascinating to see how it was all put together, though you'll need to book a few days in advance.'

'I'll book a ticket for next week, on my day off,' she said.

'And there are Roman mosaics in the basement. Keep an eye out for the peacock.'

Sam grinned. 'Of course. Roman stuff.'

'But Florence,' he said, 'is more about the Renaissance. The Medici.'

'And the art,' she said.

'It's definitely worth buying timed tickets for the galleries,' he said. 'My favourite's the Uffizi, for the Botticellis. And, believe me, even though you might think you know what *The Birth of Venus* is like from all the reproductions, it's really something else in real life. All the little details. It's stunning.'

'I'll add that to my list.' She wondered if he was going to suggest going with her, and her stomach swooped in disappointment when he didn't. Which was crazy. They weren't even considering getting back together. He'd dumped her two years ago without any real explanation. Why would he change his mind now? And she wasn't sure she was ready to handle a conversation about what had happened. Not yet. So she deliberately kept the conversation light during dinner; the chicken and ricotta meatballs in tomato sauce were excellent, along with the side dishes of tiny roasted potatoes with rosemary and garlicky, buttery spinach.

She didn't have room for pudding, but the coffee was fantastic.

They left the restaurant just in time to see the sun setting across the river. The amazing colours in the sky were reflected on the river, and the Ponte Vecchio had turned golden in the sunlight. 'I need to take a snap of this for Mum and Nina,' she said. 'I can see why so many people take photographs of the bridge. It's so pretty.'

'The ground floor is shops and the middle floor is housing, but the top level's the Vasari Corridor,' he said. 'It was built for one of the Medici dukes to connect the Palazzo Pitti with the Palazzo Vecchio. They made all the owners of the towers on the bridge agree to let them build the corridor through their property—except for the Mannelli family, who refused, so the corridor had to go round their tower.'

'Someone actually stood up to the Medici and survived?' She raised her eyebrows.

'Surprisingly, yes,' he said.

When they sun had finally set, he turned to her. 'I know you can look after yourself and Florence is a safe city, but I'd still rather walk you home.'

'I won't argue,' she said, 'because you're saving me having to get my phone out to check that I'm remembering the right way to get home.'

At the door to her building, she said, 'Thank you for this evening. It's been really nice.'

'I enjoyed it, too,' he said.

Should she ask him in for coffee?

If they'd been new colleagues, new friends, she probably would have asked him in. But this was Angelo. They had history. And they couldn't turn back the clock—even though it would be oh, so easy to lean towards him and kiss him on the cheek, to let one thing lead to another…

And then things would get really complicated.

Better to let things be. She was only here for eleven more weeks, and they were colleagues. She couldn't afford to let her feelings get in the way.

'I'll see you at work on Monday,' she said.

'Enjoy your day off,' he said politely. 'See you Monday.'

Angelo waited until Sam had closed the door behind her before he headed back to his own flat. Spending the evening with her had been bittersweet; the teasing light in her eyes when she'd asked him about the Roman bits of

Florence had brought back so many memories of trips he'd taken with her to see Roman ruins. London, Paris, Bath, the Roman villa at Fishbourne…

And he'd been so close to kissing her goodnight on her doorstep. If he'd just leaned forward—would she have met his lips? Would she have kissed him back? Would she have asked him in, to spend more time together?

But there was a huge, huge boulder in their path: the way he'd dumped her, two years ago. He really needed to apologise properly and tell her why he'd really left London. He knew he should've done it this evening; except he'd been enjoying spending time with her and he hadn't wanted to spoil it by bringing up past hurts.

'You're such a coward, Angelo Brunelli,' he told himself. 'You can't turn back time. But you can't go forward until you've sorted it out.'

He just had to find the right words. Somehow.

Sunday was another gorgeously sunny day, and Sam spent the day exploring Florence. She'd bought a timed ticket for the Uffizi, on Angelo's recommendation, and enjoyed the gallery hugely. The exhibits were stunning and, as he'd told her the previous day, the Botticelli paintings were amazing in real life, full of tiny details. The gallery itself was a work of art, too, with its painted ceilings and marble floors, and Sam loved the dome with its ceiling covered in shells. She lingered by the windows, enjoying the views over the city, then sat on the café's balcony in the sunshine, next to the terracotta pots filled with herbs and shrubs, sipping coffee while she looked across the rooftops to the Duomo and the bell tower.

Yet, although she was enjoying herself, she was aware there was something missing.

Angelo.

Which was ridiculous. They hadn't been together for two years. She'd moved on and, was focussing on her career.

Though last night had reminded her of so many days out she'd spent with Angelo, discovering nerdy things together and delighting in obscure facts. If he'd been with her today, she knew he would've told her something about every single room or exhibit in the Uffizi.

But, if he'd wanted to spend time with her, surely he would've said so? The fact that he hadn't made it clear he didn't want to resurrect the past.

They'd established a good working relationship, now they'd moved beyond the initial awkwardness.

Wanting more than that—well, she would just be setting herself up for disappointment.

She was going to enjoy her temporary secondment, make friends with her new colleagues and explore her temporary home.

And then she'd go back to London and forget about Angelo Brunelli.

CHAPTER FIVE

FOR THE NEXT WEEK, Sam was busy at the hospital; when she wasn't seeing new cases in the foetal medicine unit, she worked with some of the more complex cases in the main maternity department. Over the next few days, she got to know her new colleagues a lot better and even spent a couple of evenings out with some of them, enjoying drinks and a meal and learning more about Florence. She noticed that Angelo didn't join them; was he trying to avoid her outside work? So much for thinking that they'd be able to get some kind of closure and find their way to a friendship. Perhaps he hadn't meant it after all?

Ten more weeks.

She could keep a professional attitude towards him for ten more weeks.

On the Friday morning, the Bianchis came in for a check-up and scan, so Sam had to work with Angelo.

'I'm really pleased with the way things are going,' she said when she'd finished doing the scan. 'One of the twins is still smaller, but he's starting to catch up.'

'I still worry,' Pia admitted.

'Of course you do. That's completely normal,' Angelo reassured her with a smile.

'Will you be here when the babies arrive?' Pia asked Sam.

'You're twenty-three weeks pregnant, and I'm here

for another ten weeks,' Sam said. 'Given our plan to get you to thirty-three weeks if we can, I'm pretty sure I'll be here. And if I'm not on duty when you deliver, I'll come in anyway. I'll make sure there's a note on the file to call me.' She smiled. 'Apart from anything else, I can never resist a cuddle with a newborn. And in your case that's three cuddles, so that's a real bonus.'

Pia looked pleased. 'It wouldn't be the same without you there.'

'That's kind.' Sam smiled. 'Is there anything either of you want to ask me?'

Pia and Tommaso looked at each other, and then shook their heads. 'I think you covered everything.'

'Then we'll see you next week,' Sam said. 'Take things easy.'

'I'll make sure she does,' Tommaso promised.

Angelo was busy catching up with paperwork in the early afternoon when Lidia put her head round the door. 'I need you to do a scan, and possibly a section.'

'What's up?'

'Raffaella Costa's just come into the labour ward. She's thirty-nine weeks, but the baby's breech.'

Angelo thought back. 'Am I right in remembering that her baby seemed to have a plexus cyst earlier on, but it sorted itself out?'

Lidia nodded. 'But the baby's head feels a bit large. I'm not happy.'

If there was fluid on the baby's brain, it could cause the baby to have breathing problems after birth. 'Can you get the portable scanner?' he asked. 'I'll check the notes, then grab Sam and brief her.'

She was in clinic, and he felt guilty about interrupting,

but at the same time he knew that this was going to be a complex case—one where he really needed her expertise.

'I'm so sorry to interrupt,' he said to the parents in her consulting room, 'but I need a very quick word with Dr Clarke.'

'Problem?' Sam asked when they were in the corridor.

'Potentially, yes. Lidia has a mum who's just come in—Raffaella Costa. She's thirty-nine weeks pregnant. At twenty weeks, the scan showed the baby had a plexus cyst on her head, but it resolved naturally and her last scan, at thirty weeks, was fine.' He grimaced. 'But Lidia's not happy. She feels the baby's head is too large.'

'Potentially fluid on the brain?' Sam asked.

He nodded, knowing that Sam would be aware of what complications might follow on from that. 'And the baby's breech. I'm going to do a scan, but I think it's quite likely that Rafaella will need an emergency section. Given your experience with more complex births, we could do with your input.'

'OK. I assume the neonatal team are on standby?' Sam asked.

'Already sorted.'

'Right. I'll finish up with my parents here. Then I'll prime Carla on reception that I might need to either get the parents to wait a bit for the rest of my afternoon's clinic, reschedule their appointments or maybe see someone else if Carla can get cover. Once that's sorted, I'll come in to check the scan results with you. Which room will you be in?'

'Room four,' he said.

'OK. Give me a few minutes.'

Angelo had just done the scan, confirming that there was indeed fluid on the baby's brain, and was telling the Costas that he wanted to do a Caesarean section when Sam came in. He introduced her quickly to Raffaella and her husband Mauro. 'This is Dr Samantha Clarke, a specialist from England who's with us for the next three months,' he said. 'Sam, this is Raffaella and Mauro Costa.'

'Hello,' Sam said with a smile. 'I'm here to support you along with Angelo and Lidia. Angelo's told me the history of your pregnancy, and I'm sorry you've had so much worry.'

'I so wanted a normal birth,' Raffaella said. 'But Lidia and Angelo say I need a section because the baby's breech.'

'Babies never do anything according to plan,' Sam said. 'I don't think I've met anyone whose birth went as they'd planned it, and plenty of my mums have made their birth plan into a paper plane, over the years. From what I've just seen on the scan, I agree with Lidia and Angelo that a section would be safest for you and for the baby.'

Raffaella bit her lip. 'Is she going to make it? When she had that cyst, the information leaflet said she might have fluid on her brain, and that might mean she can't breathe when she's born. And if she can't breathe… If she…' Her voice choked off.

'That's why we'll have the neonatal team in with us, to make sure your baby has the right support. Plenty of babies need a little bit of help after the birth,' Sam reassured her. 'Don't try to think of what *might* happen—that's way too scary. Focus on the fact that Lidia's a great midwife; she's kept a careful eye on you and she isn't going to let you take unnecessary risks.'

'But I can have a Caesarean section and still be awake, can't I?' Raffaella asked.

'Given that this is an emergency section, we'd rather

do it under a general anaesthetic,' Angelo said. 'It's safer for both you and the baby.'

Raffaella's eyes widened. 'Will Mauro still be there for the birth?'

'No, but he'll be able to see the baby very soon afterwards,' Sam reassured her.

Raffaella clutched Mauro's hand. 'Promise me you'll take a picture of her, Mauro. In case—' her voice cracked '—in case our little girl doesn't make it before I wake up.'

'She'll make it,' Mauro said. But his tone was hollow.

'Promise me,' Raffaella insisted.

'I promise,' he said, his face looking haunted.

'Try not to worry,' Sam said. 'You'll be cuddling your daughter very soon. I'm just going to sort out my appointments for the afternoon while you see the anaesthetist, and I'll be there in Theatre, OK?'

Though Angelo recognised that tiny pleat between Sam's eyes. Something was definitely worrying her. But, despite the complication of a breech birth and the size of the baby's head, the Caesarean section itself should be relatively straightforward.

'What's wrong?' he asked when she was back from sorting out her appointments and they were scrubbing in.

'I…' She shook her head. 'It's fine.'

Her smile was a bit too brittle for his liking, but now wasn't the time to push her to talk. They had a baby to deliver safely.

The anaesthetist had already done her work and Raffaella was on the operating table. Sam did the 'knife check'—making sure the consent form had been signed, confirming Raffaella's identity and running through the risk of a bleed; then Raffaella was prepped and draped for the operation. Sam checked with the anaesthetist that they were ready to go; when the anaesthetist nodded, Sam made the incision and between them she and Angelo performed the Caesarean section.

When Sam lifted the baby out, the baby's head was definitely bigger than average; she was covered in vernix, and, more worryingly, she was silent. Angelo couldn't see any sign of her breathing. Her skin was blue, and he wasn't happy with the look of her muscle tone. It was normal for a baby born after a Caesarean section to have a slightly lower Apgar score—the first assessment of the baby's health scored on the appearance, pulse, grimace response, activity and respiration—but this baby needed resuscitating.

Sam removed the placenta, leaving the cord attached to the baby without clamping it; Angelo knew in a minute or so it would be time to clamp and cut the cord, making sure the baby had the optimum blood from the placenta.

Lidia took the baby from them and began rubbing her vigorously with a towel. 'One-minute Apgar score of three,' she said.

Breathe, baby, Angelo thought. *Please breathe. Breathe and pink up. Cry. Move your arms. Grimace.*

Sam's face had lost all colour, beneath her surgical mask; he was pretty sure she was as worried about the baby as he was. She did the routine check of Raffaella's reproductive organs, then started to sew up the incision she'd made in the uterus. Angelo admired her quick, deft, work, but he was aware that both of them were waiting anxiously to hear the baby's first cry.

The longer it took, the more help the baby was likely to need.

He remembered the desperation in Raffaella's eyes when she'd asked Mauro to take a photo of the baby. Her conviction that their daughter wouldn't make it. Had it been maternal instinct?

Please, baby, just breathe, he begged silently.

'Cord, please, Angelo,' Lidia said.

He clamped the cord and cut it. One of the neonatal team had put an oxygen mask over the baby's face.

Still there was no sound other than the low, worried murmuring of Lidia and the neonatal team. There was no sign of the first, stuttering cry that they were all desperate to hear.

Sam met his gaze for a moment, and her eyes were suspiciously shiny; then she blinked and continued stitching.

Please let the baby make it. Please.

Angelo continued to worked alongside Sam, handing her the things he knew she'd need the moment before she needed to ask him for them.

And then finally, just as he thought the neonatal team would have to intubate the baby to support her breathing, there was a faint cry.

'Good girl,' Lidia crooned. 'That's what we all wanted to hear. Five-minute Apgar score of five.'

Sam said nothing, but she stopped stitching and closed her eyes for a moment in apparent relief. Five out of ten still wasn't as high as they would've liked, but it was a move in the right direction, and Angelo knew Lidia and the neonatal team would do another score in three minutes' time to keep a check on the baby's condition.

'We're going to take her to Neonatal Intensive Care to warm up a bit and help her breathe,' the neonatal specialist said. 'And then we'll sort out a head scan. I'm not happy with the size of the baby's head, either—I think you might be right about fluid on the brain.'

'OK. I'll get a message to her dad—he's in the waiting room,' Angelo said. 'Can he come and see her?'

'Of course,' the neonatal specialist said.

'Well done, everyone,' Sam said, her voice heartfelt. She looked at Angelo. 'I'm OK to finish here. Go and see Mauro and tell him the good news—that he has a little girl.'

Mauro was pacing up and down the waiting room.

'Is—?' He stopped, clearly terrified of the answer. Had the baby made it?

'Your daughter's on her way to the neonatal unit to warm up a bit and to have a little bit of help breathing,' Angelo reassured him. 'Right now, she's holding her own.'

Mauro sagged in relief. 'I was trying to be strong for Raffaella's sake, but deep down I thought the same as her, that the baby wouldn't make it.' A tear slid down his cheek. 'Is my wife all right?'

'Sam's finishing sewing her up, and then we're going to wake her up and take her through to the recovery room. You can go and see the baby now, if you like. Take that photograph for Raffaella; by the time you come back, she'll be awake and desperate to see the baby.'

'Thank you,' Mauro said hoarsely. 'If the baby hadn't made it, I don't know what...'

'I know,' Angelo said, patting his arm. 'The team's going to organise a scan of the baby's head, later today. But whatever happens we're here to support you, OK?'

When he got back to Theatre, Raffaella was in the recovery room, coming round from the anaesthetic. He went to find Sam, to debrief her; she was scrubbing out, and he noticed that her eyes were wet.

'What's wrong?' he asked.

'Nothing. I'm fine.'

He knew she wasn't telling the truth. 'Sam,' he said

gently, 'you looked worried sick in Theatre and you're crying now.'

'Relief,' she said. 'Because for a while there I didn't think the baby was going to make it.'

He'd felt that same fear, but he wasn't in tears. There was more to this than met the eye. 'What happened?' he asked softly.

'If you must know, I had a case, a couple of years back,' she said, 'where the baby was a breech birth with an emergency section. The baby didn't make it. And this time we had the extra complication, with the extra fluid on the baby's head. I don't often lose a baby, so doing the section brought back some tough memories.'

Acting entirely on impulse, Angelo slid his arms round her and held her close for a moment.

Sam relaxed against him, and he couldn't stop himself resting his cheek against her hair, stroking her back.

To have her in his arms again, after all these years... It felt like paradise.

Did it feel like that for her, too? Had she missed him as much as he'd missed her?

Then Sam's muscles tensed, and it brought Angelo sharply back to the present. This was incredibly inappropriate. Unprofessional. No matter how upset she was, he shouldn't be hugging her in the scrub room. He released her and took a step back. 'Sorry. I just thought you could do with a hug from a colleague,' he said, feeling the blood rush to his face.

'Thank you,' she mumbled, not looking at him.

'I, um…' Since when had he been this incoherent? 'I'd better let you get back to your clinic.'

'Uh-huh,' she said.

Keep it professional. Focus on the patients, he reminded himself. 'Mauro's with the baby. He's going to come back to the recovery room when he's taken a picture for Raffaella.'

'That's good,' she said. 'Catch you later.'

That hug had really thrown Sam. A moment of comfort when she'd needed it—just as Angelo had comforted her on rough days years ago, days when she'd missed Dominic and struggled to come to terms with his overdose. Angelo had made her see that her best *had* been good enough, that nobody else could've done more to stop Dominic on his tragic path.

That brief physical contact in the scrub room had brought back so many memories, so many times when Angelo had held her. And she missed it. Missed it so much, it was a physical ache.

Right now, they were trying to work their way back to some sort of friendship. But could it be more than that? Could they find their way back to the closeness they'd once had? Or would she be setting herself up for more heartache? She was only here temporarily and her career—her life—was back in London.

It was hard to think straight. She needed to focus and get on with her job. Work, at least, was safe.

She apologised to the parents who'd had to wait while she'd been in Theatre, and stayed well after the end of her shift to make sure she caught up with everyone. Then she headed through to the neonatal intensive care unit to see how the Costas were doing.

Raffaella and Mauro were sitting either side of a tiny cot, each with a finger held by the baby.

'Sorry I couldn't get here earlier,' she said. 'I was in clinic.'

'Don't apologise. We know you put all your other mums on hold so you could deliver Paola,' Raffaella said. 'And I'm so, so grateful. Lidia told me, she wasn't doing so well at first.' A tear trickled down her cheek. 'If we'd lost her...'

'I know,' Sam said gently. 'You said her name's Paola?'

'After my grandmother,' Mauro said.

'That's lovely.' Sam smiled. 'So how's she doing? How was the scan?'

Raffaella swallowed hard. 'They said there are cavities in the brain, and the fluid acts as a shock absorber, but Paola's got a lot more fluid there than she should have.'

'That sometimes happens when a baby's had a plexus cyst,' Sam said.

'They said she's at risk of having seizures and learning difficulties,' Mauro said, his voice cracking slightly. 'Our little girl.'

'That's an awful lot to take in,' Sam said. 'I'm sure the team here has already told you that "learning difficulties" is a very broad spectrum. Try not to think the worst. It might simply be that Paola doesn't crawl or sit up as early as other babies do, or she might be a bit slower to start talking.' Or it could be a lot more serious; right now it was too early to tell. 'But it's early days and there's a lot of support you can access.'

'We're just grateful she's here,' Raffaella said. 'I was so scared we were going to lose her.'

Sam peered into the cot. 'She's beautiful. I can see both of you in her.'

'Thank you for all you did,' Mauro said.

'I'm so sorry you couldn't be awake for the birth, and that Mauro couldn't cut the cord,' Sam said. 'I know that's really disappointing for both of you.'

'But Paola's here now. She's safe, and so's Raffaella. That's the main thing,' Mauro said.

'I'll leave you to get to know your little one,' Sam said. 'But I'll pop in to see you when I'm next in the hospital.'

When she went into the staff room, she was surprised to see Angelo there. 'I thought your shift finished ages ago.'

'It did. I was waiting for you,' he said.

She frowned. 'Why?'

'Because you've had a tough day, and in your shoes I know I could do with some company and some carbs,' he said gently. 'Do you have anything planned for this evening?'

She could fib and say that she was meeting up with some of the maternity team, but the lie would be too easily unravelled. 'No,' she admitted.

'Then how about I cook you dinner?' he asked. 'Nothing super-fancy and no strings: it'll be whatever I've got in the fridge and the freezer. Just dinner with...' He paused. 'With an old friend.'

He'd been a lot more than just an old friend, and they both knew it, but she let it slide. Even though there had been a happy ending today, the case had brought back memories of the baby who hadn't made it. It had been the first complicated operation she'd done after Dominic's death, and she'd always wondered if there was something she'd done wrong: if she'd let herself get distracted by her personal life and missed something crucial that could've made a difference. She'd been over it again and again, and eventually her boss had sat her down and told her that it wasn't her fault; whoever had performed the operation, that particular baby still wouldn't have made it because the odds had been just too high.

But Sam had never quite stopped feeling bad about it. Right now, she didn't want to be on her own and she needed something or someone to distract her.

'OK,' she said. 'Dinner would be nice. Thank you.'

Angelo waited for Sam to get her things from her locker; then they walked back to the city together.

'I'd like to contribute something to the meal,' she said.

Angelo shook his head. 'It's really nothing fancy: just gnocchi with tomato and mascarpone sauce. I made the gnocchi last week and it's in the freezer. It'll take all of five minutes from start to finish, and it's as quick to cook for two as for one.'

'Can I at least buy the wine?' she asked.

'I think I can just about afford to give you some wine,' he said drily. 'No. You're fine.'

His flat was in a quiet street, on the fourth floor of a cream-coloured building with olive-green shutters. 'I'll give you the thirty-second tour,' he said with a smile as he opened his front door. 'Bathroom.' He indicated the first door, then led her past a second door—which she assumed was his bedroom—through to the living room. 'Living room.' It had wooden parquet flooring, a comfortable sofa, a bookshelf and a coffee table; there were photographs on the mantelpiece—one of his parents that she remembered him having in London—and a couple of prints of Rome on the walls. At one end of the room there was a small table and chairs; in the middle of the room there were large glass doors. 'That's the balcony. It's just about wide enough for a table and two chairs. I thought we could eat there tonight.' He gestured through the glass doors. 'And the kitchen.' It was a narrow galley kitchen with terracotta flooring and a view of a church and the hills outside the city. She noted the fresh herbs on the windowsill. The entire flat was immaculately tidy, but it definitely felt like a home rather than a show flat.

'I'll start cooking dinner,' he said. He set water to

boil in the kettle, took two portions of gnocchi from the freezer, and put two saucepans on the hob.

'Can I do anything to help?' she asked.

'You can slice some bread and take it through to the balcony,' he said. 'And maybe lay the table. The key to the door is in the dish on the table, and everything in the kitchen is in an obvious place.'

The crockery was on open shelving, the bread bin was on top of the microwave—and the top was clearly the cutting board—and she found the cutlery and a bread knife in the drawer next to the sink.

She sliced the bread and put it on a plate, then took it and the cutlery out to the balcony. The balcony ran the whole length of the living room; it had a terracotta tiled floor and wrought-iron railing. There were pots of geraniums clustered by the railing, and a bistro table with two chairs was set in the middle. The view was beautiful: the narrow street and a garden opposite that was stuffed to bursting with flowering shrubs.

When she went back to the kitchen, the gnocchi was cooking in boiling water and the tomato sauce was bubbling; Angelo was scooping out the gnocchi as they floated to the surface of the water.

'Anything else?' she asked.

'Wine. Red's in the rack, and there's a bottle of white in the fridge, so pick whichever you'd prefer and open it,' he said.

Sam had missed this kind of domesticity. Greg hadn't been interested in cooking, leaving it to her and sorting out the clearing up instead. But she'd always enjoyed working with Angelo in the kitchen; they'd been a team.

She found glasses and uncorked a bottle of red; by the time she'd done that, Angelo had added the mascarpone to the tomato sauce, added the gnocchi and filled two bowls.

'Let's go and eat,' he said, and ushered her out to the balcony.

'You've got a fabulous view,' she said.

He smiled. 'I think that goes for just about anywhere in Florence, particularly if you're on a higher floor. You get the iconic view of the rooftops, the hills and the sky— and maybe a tower or two.'

'It's a beautiful city,' she said.

'Agreed.'

'This is very good,' she said after her first taste of the gnocchi. 'You always were an excellent cook.' And the carbs were just what she needed.

He inclined his head. 'Thank you.'

To Sam's relief, Angelo kept the conversation light during dinner. She didn't have room for pudding or cheese, but she accepted the offer of coffee.

He took a deep breath, as if nerving himself to say something, and then he looked her in the eye. 'Sam. There's something I need to tell you.' He paused. 'When I left London... I lied to you.'

CHAPTER SIX

SAM STARED AT ANGELO, not quite making sense of his words. He'd lied to her? About what? And why? 'I don't understand.' She found it hard to believe that Angelo would've cheated on her; she'd been absolutely sure he was the faithful type. But what other explanation could there be? 'Are you telling me you left me for someone else—someone in Rome?'

'No. Of course there wasn't anyone else.' He frowned. 'I mean I lied about not loving you any more.'

That still didn't shed any light on it for her. Why would he lie about that? 'Why?'

'Because I was trying to do the right thing.'

She shook her head, trying to clear it. 'Right thing? For whom?' She still didn't get it. How had breaking her heart been 'the right thing' to do?

He sighed. 'I don't know how to tell you. I didn't want to hurt you.'

'But you *did* hurt me.'

'And I'm sorry. But I didn't know what to do, Sam. Whatever I did, I knew it was going to cause you pain. If I'd told you the truth, it would've…' He shook his head. 'I went for the option with the least collateral damage. I thought if I pushed you away, made you think I didn't love you any more, it would protect you.'

'Angelo, you're not making any sense at all.'

His face was filled with anguish. 'OK. I need to tell you what really happened. And I'm sorry, Sam. I'm sorry I hurt you, and I'm sorry because I know I'm about to hurt you all over again.'

Worry made her sharp. 'Just tell me.'

'The ripping-off-the-plaster quickly version? All right.' He took a deep breath. 'My dad was an addict.'

An addict.

Like her little brother had been.

And Sam could still remember the day she'd had to identify him in the mortuary. Dominic, who'd struggled so hard to stop taking the stuff, but the cocaine had finally beaten him. The boy she could remember as a newborn, when she'd taken him a teddy to welcome him to the world. All that life, all that hope, had turned into a cold body on a cold slab.

'He was taking coke?' she whispered.

'No. Codeine.'

She knew the opiate painkiller that could start to become addictive if it was used for more than a week, which was why doctors were super-careful about prescribing it. 'What happened?'

'Dad was in a car accident,' he said. 'It wasn't his fault; he'd stopped in a queue of traffic, but the guy behind him was texting instead of paying attention to the road and didn't brake in time. Dad ended up with what he told me was a minor case of whiplash.'

'Except it wasn't,' Sam guessed, knowing that codeine wasn't the kind of painkiller prescribed for minor pain.

'No. He had horrendous backache, and the only thing that stopped the pain was codeine. The hospital prescribed them for two weeks, and assumed that Dad— being a doctor himself—would know how to taper them off properly.' Angelo grimaced. 'Of course he knew what he was supposed to do. Except he was still in pain, and nothing else he tried came close to helping. Hot and cold compresses, physio, a TENS machine—' a transcutaneous electrical nerve stimulation machine that sent little electric impulses to the affected area, to help block the pain signals going to the brain, and which several of their mums used during labour '—and he even went to a psychologist for cognitive behavioural therapy, to try and help himself think differently about the pain and try to manage it better. But the only thing that took the edge off and helped him to function normally was codeine. So he kept taking it. Without it, the pain stopped him sleeping, and he was worried that he'd make a mistake at work and end up prescribing the wrong drug or the wrong dosage for a patient.'

Broken sleep was incredibly debilitating; the worse you slept, the harder it was to manage a difficult medical condition. Angelo's dad had clearly been trapped in a vicious circle.

'Your poor dad,' she said. 'He must've been desperate.' Just as Dominic had been. His friends at work had all taken cocaine at the weekends; the drug had given him an edge he'd felt he'd needed to keep up on the trading floor at work, so he'd started taking it during the week as well. When it affected his judgement at work and he was sacked for gross misconduct, the truth about Dominic's addiction had come to light; Sam had taken her little brother to rehab and helped him try to put his life back together. Except he'd relapsed again and again and again. Told lie after lie after lie, broken promise after promise after promise.

'Addiction's hard—for the addict and for their families,' she said. 'You know what happened with my brother. You know I wouldn't have judged your dad. Why didn't you let me help?'

'Precisely because I knew what happened with your brother,' he said. 'How you took him to rehab. How you let him stay with you so you could support him. How he lied to you and stole from you and went back on the coke. You spent two years trying to get him clean, never giving up on him even when he relapsed. And then…'

He didn't say it, clearly trying to spare her feelings, but they both knew. Dominic had accidentally overdosed. And Sam had found him too late, lying on her bathroom floor. She hadn't been able to bear living in her flat, after that.

'It broke you, Sam,' he said softly. 'I met you six months later. I knew how badly it had hurt you. How could I drag you back into that kind of situation and bring all those memories back?' He swallowed hard. 'And it wasn't just the addiction.'

'How do you mean?'

'Dad started prescribing codeine for himself.'

Oh, no. Self-prescribing was seriously against the rules, and doing it could get a doctor struck off the medical register.

'He knew you're not supposed to do it unless there's nobody else who can assess you and prescribe something for you, and either it's an emergency or it's to avoid serious deterioration in health. And you're supposed to keep a clear record stating exactly what you prescribed and why,' Angelo said.

It sounded as if his dad hadn't done any of that.

'One night, the pain was so bad, he prescribed codeine for himself. And he didn't make the proper notes. He knew what he'd done was wrong, so he covered it up.' Angelo dragged in a breath. 'He only meant to do it once.

But the pain just wouldn't go away. And he knew if he asked he wouldn't get the prescriptions. So he kept going.'

'How long did he take codeine?'

'Two and a half years,' Angelo said dryly.

'What?' Sam's face was filled with shock. 'But codeine's prescription only. Surely someone must've noticed at the practice, or at the pharmacy where he got the prescriptions filled. They would've kept records and seen that the prescriptions were going on for much longer than doctors usually prescribe codeine.'

'He used online pharmacies at first,' Angelo said. 'There was a loophole in the law, so he could refuse permission for them to access his medical records, and also make the pharmacy withhold the information from his doctor about his online purchases.'

Sam frowned. 'But pharmacists know you're not supposed to take opiates for more than a week, and then it needs tapering off. And if someone's had a lot of prescriptions filled for codeine, it's pretty obvious they have a problem. How did he get away with it?'

'He only asked for a week's supply at a time, to avoid arousing suspicions. There are a lot of online pharmacies that he could cycle round, and they don't share data,' Angelo said grimly.

'Why didn't he go back to his doctor and ask for a referral to a pain clinic?'

'He did. There was a waiting list,' Angelo said. 'A really, really long one. Obviously Dad was prepared to pay for a private appointment, but the clinic he went to wasn't that helpful. He asked about an epidural steroid injection for the nerves around the painful area, but they said it wouldn't work for him.'

'That's rough,' Sam said.

'He tried to find another way. But, the longer he was

on codeine, the more his tolerance grew, and the more he needed to take to deal with the pain. He never put any of his patients at risk, but he needed to find a way of managing the pain so he could function.' Angelo spread his hands. 'And he chose the wrong way. I feel horrible that I didn't have a clue about it. I mean, I rang him every week. He always seemed fine on video calls. When he wouldn't come to London, I assumed it was something to do with London having too many memories of Mum and he couldn't handle it.'

Angelo's mum had been an English doctor who'd trained in London; Angelo had followed in her footsteps and trained at her old medical school. Sam knew that his mother had died from breast cancer in his Finals year, and he'd almost chosen oncology as his specialism in his mum's memory, but during his rotations he'd fallen in love with working on the maternity unit and seeing the wonder of new lives.

'I couldn't pin my dad down to a time when I could take you to meet him in Rome. I assumed he was being cagey because he'd finally started dating someone and didn't want to say anything in case it didn't work out.' He shook his head. 'I just wish I'd realised he was hiding something a lot more serious.'

'How did you find out what was happening?'

'One of his self-prescriptions came to light during an audit,' Angelo said. 'The senior partner at his surgery investigated the issue, and made him retire on grounds of ill health. They weren't trying to dump him; they were trying to avoid him being struck off for self-prescribing, because they knew then he'd feel even worse about the situation. Though retiring really didn't help; without working as a doctor, Dad felt he didn't have anything left in his life. His colleagues tried to help him with the back pain, but nothing worked. He refused to go to rehab, and his mood got lower and lower.' He sighed. 'Dad never dated again after Mum died, so he didn't have a partner to step in and hold his hand through it, either. His brother—my Uncle Salvatore—knew something was wrong. Eventually he persuaded Dad to tell him what was going on; he didn't know how to deal with it, so he talked to me. Obviously in London I was too far away to be of much help.'

Now Sam understood why Angelo had gone straight back to Rome. 'So that was the family business you mentioned.'

He nodded. 'I wanted to get Dad into rehab so they could wean him off the codeine. Once he was out again, I wanted to be there to support him, and help him get that back pain sorted out properly. I needed to put him first.'

'I understand that, I truly do,' Sam said, 'but why didn't you just tell me the truth?'

'I was worried sick, I wasn't thinking straight, and I felt so guilty for not realising it.'

She understood that, too; she'd felt guilty for not being able to help her brother.

'All I could focus on was the fact my dad was in a lot of pain, he'd kept everything to himself instead of letting me or my uncle help him, and he'd resorted to self-prescribing codeine,' Angelo continued. 'As a doctor, he knew the risks of addiction, and he knew that taking codeine long-term could cause problems—everything from mild confusion through to severe respiratory depression. But he still did it, because for him putting up with the pain was harder than dealing with the possible risks. And all I could think of was, what if he just stopped breathing in the night because he was taking such high doses of codeine?'

'I would've been there for you, if I'd known about it, just as you were there for me,' she said quietly. 'I would've supported you. *Both* of you.'

Angelo nodded. 'I'm sorry. I know you wouldn't have judged my dad. But losing Dominic almost broke you. I didn't want to bring back all the bad memories. The only way I could think of to protect you was to push you away. That's why I said what I did. I'm sorry I hurt you, and I'm sorry I lied.' He bit his lip. 'I did the wrong thing. I know that.'

She thought about it.

Angelo had wanted to protect her, and he'd wanted to help his dad. She could understand that. But the way he'd gone about it… 'I loved you so much, Angelo. I was devastated when you dumped me. I thought we had a future together. When we went to Venice, I almost asked you to marry me.'

'I thought about proposing to you in Venice, too,' Angelo said. 'But I was planning to take you to Rome in the summer, to meet Dad and the rest of my Italian family. And then I was going to whisk you off to this amazing garden of orange trees and ask you to marry me.' He shook his head. 'But how could I drag you into what was happening in Rome? You deserved better than that.'

'I deserved better than you saying it wasn't working out and you didn't love me.'

He winced. 'I know. And I'm sorry. It wasn't true. I really, really loved you,' he said quietly. 'When things with Dad had finally settled down, I came to London to see you. To apologise, to tell you the truth about why I went away, and to ask you to give me another chance.'

'When?' She frowned. 'Until I came to Florence, I hadn't seen you for two years.'

'Because I didn't go through with it,' he said. 'The day

I came back to London, there was a new receptionist on our ward, someone I didn't know. I asked her if you were on duty, and she said you'd gone away with your boyfriend Greg for the weekend and it was getting serious.'

So *that* was how he'd known.

'I wanted you to be happy,' he said, 'so I didn't want to get in your way. I came back to Rome without seeing you.

'Ironically, that was the weekend I broke up with Greg,' she said. 'He wanted to get serious—and I didn't. I knew I wasn't being fair to him. So we agreed to be friends. He's dating someone seriously now, and I really hope she gives him everything I couldn't.'

'That was how I thought, when I heard you were dating someone,' Angelo said. 'And I've barely dated, too. That first year in Rome, I was focused on Dad. I took a year out to support him, and then I went back to my training. I was too busy for relationships, between work and keeping an eye on Dad. Though he got a bit fed up with me being under his feet all the time, and he was the one who persuaded me to take the post here.' He shrugged. 'I wasn't sure at first, even though I wanted the job; I didn't want to leave him. But he pointed out that he was a lot better, he needed to stand on his own two feet, and it's quicker to get to Rome from Florence than it is from London.' He smiled wryly. 'And he said I needed to get a life. So I gave in and took the job.'

'How often do you see him now?'

'Every fortnight,' Angelo said. 'And I call him every other day in between.' He sighed. 'I'm in Rome tomorrow. I'm supposed to send him a selfie to prove that I'm dating someone.'

Sam raised her eyebrows. 'Why?'

'Because he worries about me as much as I worry about him. Because he wants a visit from his son, not a

doctor who's checking him all the time for signs of a relapse. When I saw him a fortnight ago, he kept scratching his arm.' He winced. 'And, yeah, my first thought
was itching and codeine. I didn't say it, but it must've
shown on my face and he called me on it. It was an insect
bite, not a skin reaction to codeine. I felt so ashamed; I
should've trusted him instead of jumping to conclusions.'

'I was the same with Dommy,' Sam said. 'And your
dad's right. You do need to see him as your dad, not as a
patient. Otherwise it's going to drive you apart.'

Angelo grimaced. 'I know. But how do I stop worrying about him?'

'It's hard,' she said. 'I sometimes think if I'd made
Dommy feel that I really trusted him, it might've taken
off some of the pressure and helped him stay away from
the coke. I think you just have take a leap of faith. Has
your dad taken codeine—or anything similar—since he
came out of rehab?'

'No,' Angelo said.

'You know how much hard work it is, recovering from
an addiction. Why would he throw it all away, knowing
he'd have to go through it all over again?'

'I guess,' Angelo said.

'Plus you supported him through it last time. So if he
gets to the point where he's not managing as well as before, he'll talk to you about it instead of trying to hide it,
because he knows you understand the situation and he
trusts you to help him,' Sam pointed out.

Angelo thought about it. 'You're right. The irony is, he
doesn't even take paracetamol, let alone anything stron-
ger.'

'So how has he managed his back pain?'

'It turned out that the clinic he went to got it wrong.
He saw another specialist, who recommended radiofre-

quency ablation—and that worked,' Angelo said. 'He still misses being at the surgery, but by now he would've retired anyway, so I think he's coming to terms with it. He keeps himself busy pottering about in his garden, and he's taken up watercolour painting and baking. As he pointed out to me a fortnight ago, he lives a good life. He sees his friends, he eats well, he goes swimming three times a week, he goes to his addiction support group every week, and he has Baffi for company.'

'Baffi?'

'His cat.' Angelo wrinkled his nose. 'Though the one thing I think that's missing in his life is a relationship. Mum definitely wouldn't have wanted him to spend the rest of his life on his own. But if I nag him to start dating someone, then he'll nag me even more to do the same thing.'

'So why don't you date someone?' she asked.

'I have, from time to time.' He shrugged. 'But nobody's ever matched up to you. It's never felt the same. It's always fizzled out.'

Which was exactly the way she'd felt. 'I've changed since you knew me, Angelo,' she warned. 'Just as I'm sure you've changed.'

'I've grown up, and I think we're both older and wiser. For what it's worth, Sam, I've always regretted what I did. And I'm sorry it didn't work out with Greg. I really wanted you to be happy.' He held her gaze. 'Though there's a selfish bit of me that's glad you're single.'

Her breath caught. Was he going to suggest that they tried again?

And, if he did, should they?

It had gone so badly wrong, last time. He'd left her flat, lonely and miserable. But it sounded as if he'd been just as lonely and miserable, too.

'I know it's a big ask,' he said, 'and I won't sulk or harass you if you say no. But I've missed you, Sam. I miss *us*.'

Her heart skipped a beat. She'd missed him, too. But she needed to be sensible. 'Angelo, I'm only here on secondment for three months,' she said. 'And then I have to go back to London. I've been trying to set up a research project; the funding comes through when I get back, and I'm being promoted to consultant.' She grimaced. 'That sounds a bit boastful. What I meant is, I've worked hard and it's all finally coming together.'

'You deserve it,' he said. 'But would you consider giving me a second chance while you're here? We could see how things go. If it doesn't work, then we'll part—this time, as friends. And, if it does work, then maybe before you go back to London we can talk about it, decide together where we go from there.'

The man who'd broken her heart wanted her to give him a second chance.

If she did, would she be setting herself up for yet more heartbreak? Or could they both learn from the past and make it work, this time around?

And if it did work out…would she have to be the one to make all the sacrifices? Or would they be able to work out something that was fair for all of them?

'Let me go and make that coffee I promised you,' Angelo said. 'Then you can have a few minutes to think about it without any pressure from me.'

He disappeared into the kitchen, and Sam stared out into the distance, thinking about what he'd said.

She'd never been able to forget Angelo. The attraction was definitely still there between them. He'd explained why he broke her heart the way he did, and she understood his reasons—even if she didn't entirely agree with them.

Going back to him would be a risk.

She could say no and keep their relationship strictly professional.

Or she could say yes, and see where things took them.

She looked up as Angelo walked onto the balcony, put two mugs of coffee on the table and sat opposite her.

'Right now, I feel like a teenager who's just asked the girl of his dreams if she'll go out with him and is terrified she's going to turn him down,' he said.

'That makes two of us,' she admitted. 'Part of me's scared. If I say yes, how do I know it won't go wrong again?'

'If you'll give me another chance,' he said, 'then I'll do my very best not to make the same mistakes. I'll talk to you about things instead of being arrogant and thinking I know how to deal with everything, when I clearly don't. And I know you're strong enough to understand my situation and support me.'

'That's fair,' she said. 'And you're going to Rome to see your dad tomorrow, right?'

He nodded. 'Though, even if you do decide to give me another chance, I wouldn't expect you to come with me tomorrow. I think we need time to get used to each other again before I introduce you to Dad or the rest of my Italian family.'

'That's a good point. I'm not sure I'm ready to meet your dad yet, either,' she admitted. 'But there is one thing.'

'What?'

'You promised him a selfie of you and a date. Do you have one?'

'No.' Angelo's cheeks tinged with colour. 'I did think

about asking someone at work to pose with me, just to keep him happy, but there isn't any point in lying. So I'm just going to have to be honest with him and say I didn't manage to keep my end of our bargain.'

'Bargain?' Sam asked.

'He'll keep going to his addiction support meeting every week, as long as I start dating someone.'

She stood up and took her phone out of her pocket. 'Better keep your end of the bargain, then. Come and stand with me.'

His eyes widened. 'You're going to take a selfie of us to keep my dad happy?'

'I'm going to take a selfie of you and your new—well, sort of new—girlfriend,' she said.

He actually blushed as he came to stand beside her, and she smiled. 'You always were cute,' she said softly. 'Like those Raphael cherubs.'

'You mean the ones lurking at the bottom of the painting, looking a bit bored?'

'Looking wistful,' she corrected. 'You always stuck your hand in your hair when you were studying, and your hair's always messy by the end of the day. It's one of the things that made me fall for you.'

He smiled. 'Apparently the cherubs were based on the children of Raphael's model for the Madonna. He painted them exactly as he saw them.'

She rolled her eyes. 'Trust you to know that.'

He spread his hands. 'What can I say? I've always had nerd tendencies.'

That was something else she'd liked about him.

The only answer she had was to reach up and touch her mouth to his.

He wrapped his arms round her and kissed her all the way back.

She'd forgotten how it felt to kiss Angelo: the warmth, the sweetness, the coil of desire in her stomach that tightened and grew hotter.

When he finally broke the kiss, Sam's head was spinning and Angelo looked dazed.

'Sam.'

'I know.' She traced his lower lip with the tip of her finger. 'Me, too.'

He laid his palm against her cheek. 'I can't think straight. Right now, I want to pick you up and carry you to my bed. At the same time, I don't want to rush you. We've both changed over the years, and I want to give us time to get to know each other again. And in any case,' he admitted, 'I don't actually have any condoms.'

'Me neither.'

He gave her a wry smile. 'So now you know I wasn't planning anything. I really, honestly, just meant to cook you dinner and be there as a friend. Except I don't…' He brushed his mouth lightly against hers.

He didn't need to finish the sentence. She felt exactly the same way: that they weren't friends. They'd been lovers, knew each other intimately. And it would be oh, so easy to fall for each other again.

'Sit with me for a while?' he asked.

'It'd be a shame to waste that coffee,' she said lightly.

He smiled, moved one of the chairs away from the table, then sat down, scooping her onto his lap and wrapping his arms round her waist.

She rested her head against his shoulder. 'It's years since I sat like this with anyone.'

'Me, too,' he said.

'That photo for your dad—we still haven't taken it.' She cuddled into him and tilted her phone screen. 'Smile.' She took the snap. 'I'll message this to you later.'

'Thank you.' He twisted so he could kiss the tip of her nose. 'So we're giving it another go?'

Right now they couldn't promise each other an easy, simple future. She had a job she loved in London, and Angelo was tied to Italy because of his dad. If they were going to be together, one of them would have to make a huge sacrifice. And there were no guarantees everything would work out. 'Let's just take it one day at a time,' she said, wanting to take it cautiously.

'OK.' he said.

They sat there together until they'd finished their coffee. Then, half reluctantly, she slid off his lap. 'You've got a long journey tomorrow. I'd better go.'

'I'll walk you home,' he said.

And how different it felt, walking through Florence hand in hand with Angelo. All the colours seemed brighter, even though the sun had set. Everything seemed in sharper focus. And all around she could hear snatches of love songs.

When they reached the door to Sam's entrance hall, Angelo kissed her. 'Tomorrow evening,' he said, 'if you're not busy, maybe I can see you when I get back from Rome?'

'I'd like that,' she said.

He smiled. 'Until tomorrow evening, then.' He stole a last kiss. 'Sweet dreams.'

CHAPTER SEVEN

'GOOD TO SEE YOU, Dad.' Angelo hugged his father.

'And you.' Ruggiero returned the hug. 'Now, this time, I have my son visiting, not a doctor, right?'

'Right,' Angelo confirmed.

'Good. I thought we'd have lunch in the garden,' Ruggiero said. 'I bought cheese and tomatoes at the market yesterday, and I made bread this morning. The way your *nonna* taught me.'

'Sounds great,' Angelo said. 'I brought *cantucci*. Though they're not home-made.'

'I'm not judging. You don't have time to bake,' Ruggiero said. His eyes narrowed slightly. 'Though you look different.'

'Different how?'

'I don't know. More relaxed, perhaps. Work's going well?

'Yes.' And talking about work was a good way of introducing the subject of Sam, Angelo thought. 'You know I told you my boss is setting up a foetal medicine unit?'

'Yes—and it sounds fascinating. It's amazing to think you can do surgery in the womb,' Ruggiero said.

'We have a professor from Paris and a specialist from London,' Angelo said. 'I have a mum on my list with triplets—a singleton, plus twins with twin-to-twin syndrome. The London specialist did laser ablation on the placenta, and I got to laser a couple of the blood vessels.'

'When I was your age, I would never have believed it possible that one day we could do *in utero* surgery,' Ruggiero marvelled.

'It felt like waving a magic wand,' Angelo said. 'We've given those babies a real chance. And it's more effective than simply draining the amniotic fluid from the recipient twin, because we've corrected the problems that caused the fluid imbalance in the first place.' He paused. 'But it's more than that. It turned out I already knew the specialist from London.'

'Someone you used to work with?'

'A bit more than that.' He smiled. 'It's Samantha.'

'What, *your* Samantha?' Ruggiero asked. At Angelo's nod, he winced. 'That must be a bit awkward.'

'Surprisingly not, once we'd got over the shock of seeing each other again. We're both older and wiser,' Angelo said. He'd never actually told his father why he'd split up with Sam, not wanting his dad to feel he was to blame for the break-up; instead, Angelo had fudged the issue, saying instead that he and Sam had grown apart.

'So you're managing to work together without a problem?'

Angelo nodded. 'Actually, it turns out that she's still single, too.' He paused. 'We've talked about how things were in London, and while she's in Florence we're…well, seeing how things go.' He took his phone from his pocket. 'I promised you a selfie of me with my date. Here you go.'

Ruggiero studied the photograph. 'There's something about her smile that reminds me of your mum.' He looked at Angelo. 'I'm sorry I didn't meet her when you were in London. At the time, I didn't want to travel—I couldn't face having to use uncomfortable seating that would make my back worse. And I didn't want you to come to Rome, either, in case you guessed that things weren't really all right with me.'

'I assumed you were secretly dating someone and didn't want me to know, in case I thought it was too soon,' Angelo said. 'Which, by the way, I didn't. You've been on your own for nearly a decade, Dad. Maybe it's time to meet someone.'

Ruggiero made a dismissive gesture. 'I'm not interested in dating. I could never replace your mum.'

'You wouldn't be replacing her, or dismissing her memory,' Angelo said gently. 'You'd simply be opening your heart to someone new. And I can say this because I loved her, too: Mum definitely wouldn't have wanted you to be on your own. She would've wanted you to have company. Someone who loved you.'

'I'm fine as I am,' Ruggiero said. 'Now, I thought we could go for a walk before lunch.'

In other words, he didn't want to discuss it. But hopefully, Angelo thought, he'd planted a tiny seed in his dad's head. 'A walk sounds great,' he said with a smile.

It was the most relaxed day he'd spent with his father since he'd come home to Italy two years ago. They talked easily, and Angelo didn't find himself checking surreptitiously for signs that his father might have relapsed. Maybe he had Sam to thank for that; she'd made him think differently, and make the effort to trust his dad.

On his way back from Rome, he texted her from the train.

How do you fancy cocktails this evening and maybe a bit of dancing?

Her reply came back.

Sounds good. What time?

Meet you at your place, about eight?

I'll be ready. How was your dad?

Fine. And thank you for making me see him differently. Today's been a lot better. x.

There was a pause, and then YVW followed by a heart.

He couldn't help smiling.

If anything, Sam had become sweeter with age. He liked the woman she'd become. And he really, really hoped that they'd find a way for this thing between them to work.

Sam had brought only one suitcase with her to Florence: work outfits, jeans, and casual tops. She didn't have a dress, or anything remotely suitable for going out dancing and for cocktails. And now she had roughly an hour until the shops closed. Would that be long enough to find a dress and shoes she could dance in but that looked stylish as well?

She checked the internet to find out where the clothes shops were, and called Nina on her way out. 'Are you around, for the next hour?'

'While your goddaughter's napping, yes,' Nina said. 'Why?'

'Because I need your fabulous fashion sense.'

Nina laughed. 'What, matching spots of baby dribble on each shoulder?'

Sam laughed back. 'Not quite. I didn't pack a dress, and I'm going dancing tonight, so I need shoes and a dress, and the shops close in an hour, and...'

'Stop panicking and breathe,' Nina cut in. 'I take it you're going on a work night out, and you forgot about it until the last minute?'

'Not exactly,' Sam hedged.

'Don't tell me you're going on an actual *date*?'

'Um, yes. Cocktails and dancing.'

'That sounds fun,' Nina said. 'So tell me about your date. I'm assuming he's someone you work with? What's his name? What's he like?'

Sam squirmed. 'You already know him. It's Angelo.'

'Angelo?' Nina sounded shocked. 'Are you sure dating him is a good idea, Sam?'

'We're just seeing how things go,' Sam said. 'Keeping everything low-key.'

'He broke your heart, last time.'

'I know, but we talked last night. I mean *really* talked. I understand why he walked away, now.'

'So he had a good reason?'

'It's complicated,' Sam hedged. 'And it's not really my place to talk about it. Let's just say it was a family thing, and I understand now.'

'Right.' Nina didn't sound in the slightest bit convinced.

'He came back for me, Nina. I had no idea. The receptionist in our old department told him I was away for the weekend with Greg. Angelo wanted me to be happy, so he walked away.' She sighed. 'How ironic is it that *that* was the weekend we broke up?'

'I just don't want you to get hurt again,' Nina said.

'I won't get hurt. Angelo's changed, and so have I.'

'Hmm. I'm reserving judgement,' Nina said. 'But, in the meantime, you need a dress and shoes. Something you can dance in. Is Florence really fashionable?'

'It's Italy,' Sam said dryly. 'Everyone looks like a model.'

'OK. Play it safe. Go for a little classic black dress, and black court shoes that are high enough to make your legs long but won't give you blisters for work. Did you take any jewellery with you?'

'Uh,' Sam said. 'Do I need jewellery?'

'Yes. Get the dress and shoes, then head for an accessory shop. You'll need a bag as well,' Nina said. 'Honestly. The first time my best friend buys a dress in *years*, and she has to do it hundreds of miles away instead of letting me have the fun of bossing her about on a shopping trip.'

'I was planning on taking photographs in the mirror and sending them to you,' Sam said. 'It's the next best thing.'

'I'll hold you to that,' Nina said.

Fifty-six minutes later—having tried on eight little black dresses and ended up going back to the very first one she'd seen—Sam was in possession of a dress, a wrap, shoes, a bag and a chunky necklace.

'Video call me when you've done your hair and makeup,' Nina said. 'And eat carbs, if you're drinking cocktails.'

'To line my stomach. I know,' Sam said. 'Call you in a bit.'

She texted Angelo just to double-check that they weren't eating, then went to the little pizzeria round the corner to grab something to take away. Once she'd showered, done her hair and make-up and finished dressing, she video called Nina, balanced her phone on the windowsill and did a twirl so Nina could see her outfit.

'Gorgeous,' was her best friend's verdict.

'I feel ridiculously nervous,' Sam said. 'It's like being seventeen again.'

'Have fun—but maybe don't let your heart get involved, this time,' Nina advised.

'Got it,' Sam said. But the butterflies in her stomach had turned into a stampede of ostriches by the time her doorbell rang.

'Coming down,' she called into the intercom, hoping her nervousness didn't show in her voice. This was crazy. She *knew* Angelo. They'd dated for two years. They'd been at the point of settling down together. OK, so it had gone wrong, but now she understood that it hadn't been because of anything lacking in her. It had been circumstances outside both their control.

She draped the light wrap round her shoulders, locked the door and went down to meet him.

Angelo was waiting for her in the street; he looked incredibly stylish in dark formal trousers and a jacket, a pale formal shirt and highly polished shoes.

'Hi.' He looked at her and smiled, and her heart skipped a beat. 'You look lovely.'

'So do you,' she said, feeling ridiculously shy. 'How was your dad?'

'Good.' He smiled. 'I did what you said and tried to make him feel I trust him. And we had a really nice day together.'

'I'm glad,' she said, meaning it,

'Ready for cocktails?' he asked.

'Yes,' she fibbed.

He took her hand and they strolled through the cobbled streets, heading towards the river. For a moment, she wondered whether he was planning to take her to watch the sun setting from one of the bridges; the sky was washed with peach and pink as the sun neared setting point, and the reflections in the river would look amazing. But then he ushered her through an unobtrusive doorway into a reception area.

He glanced at her shoes. 'Lift, I think. Save your feet for dancing.'

The lift was small, only big enough for two people. Standing this close to him, she could smell the woody scent of his aftershave, and it sent a shiver of desire down her spine.

'Samantha.' He rested his hands lightly on her waist and looked her in the eye.

Two years ago, he would've kissed her. Would he kiss her now?

He leaned forward, and every nerve-end tingled.

His lips brushed just below her ear. 'Whatever just put that look in your eyes, hold on to that thought.'

'I was thinking about kissing,' she said, her voice husky with need. Right now, she really, really wanted him to kiss her.

'That's what I'm thinking, too,' he said, drawing her a tiny bit closer. His mouth skimmed the curve of her neck, and she closed her eyes, but then a ping signalled that the lift doors were about to open. 'Hold that thought for later, *carissima.*'

She was glad that Angelo was holding her hand as they left the lift, because her knees felt decidedly wobbly. It was nothing to do with the height of her heels, and everything to do with the fact that he was going to kiss her later.

He led her round the corner and through another doorway, and to her delight she realised they were on a rooftop garden with a panoramic view of the city. Although they didn't have a view of the river, they could still see the sunset and the iconic buildings of Florence rising above the terracotta rooftops.

'This is gorgeous,' she said.

'I thought we'd start with drinks here, while the sun's setting,' he said, 'then move on to the dancing.'

'Sounds perfect,' she said with a smile.

'What can I get you to drink?' he asked as they reached the bar.

'I don't know.' She smiled at the barman. 'What would you recommend as the most typical drink in Florence?'

'If you'd like a cocktail, then it has to be a Negroni,' the barman said. 'It was invented in Florence a hundred years ago.'

'What's in it?' Sam asked.

'Bitters, red vermouth and gin,' the barman said. 'Or, if you'd like something a little lighter, you could try a negroni *sbagliato*, where you swap the gin for Prosecco.'

'I think I'd like the lighter version, please,' she said with a smile.

'And I'll have a traditional negroni, please,' Angelo said.

The barman mixed their drinks expertly, adding ice and a slice of blood orange to each glass. 'Enjoy,' he said.

'Thank you,' Angelo said, and walked back out to the terrace, still holding Sam's hand. 'Where would you like to sit?'

'Where we can see the Duomo, please,' she said. 'I love that building.'

'Maybe I can get tickets for us to go up inside it one day after work,' he said.

'But haven't you already done that?'

'It's worth repeating.' He found them a table, then lifted his glass in a toast. *'Salute.'*

'Cheers,' she said, lifting her own glass.

He took a sip of his drink and grimaced.

'Not great?' she asked.

'I think it's more that I'm not really much of a cock-tail person. I'll order a glass of red wine, next time,' he said. 'How's yours?'

'Lovely,' she said. 'Try a sip. Bubbles make every-thing better.'

'Even if they're terrifyingly sweet Bellinis.' He rolled his eyes. 'Do you remember that evening we drank Bell-inis in Venice?'

'In St Mark's Square, sitting outdoors by the heater because it was February, but it wasn't raining and we wanted to look up at the stars. And then dancing in the square.'

'We were the only ones dancing,' he said softly.

And it hadn't mattered. It had felt like the most roman-tic place in the world: just them and the music and the stars and the wide, wide square, back in the days when they'd definitely been in love with each other.

Yet, two months later, it had all fallen apart.

This time round, would it work out? Or would some-thing else get in the way of their happiness? She shivered.

'Cold?' he asked, moving to shrug off his jacket.

'No, I'm fine.' She looked at him. 'Venice was a long time ago.'

'When we were different people,' he said. 'So let's focus on the here and now.'

'Agreed,' she said.

When they'd finished their drinks, Sam insisted on buying the next round: chianti for Angelo, and another negroni *sbagliato* for her. Then they headed for the other side of the river.

'I haven't actually been here before,' Angelo said as they reached another unobtrusive doorway, 'but it's got good reviews. We're going retro.'

Once they'd checked in his jacket and her wrap, Sam

was delighted to discover that the club was playing music that reminded her of her student years—including the kind of line-dance songs that had everyone joining in. 'I'd forgotten how much I enjoyed this sort of thing,' she said, when they'd taken a break to get some water.

'I've forgotten most of the moves,' Angelo said ruefully. 'But I agree; it's fun.'

They danced for the next hour, but then the DJ slowed everything down and Angelo drew her closer.

Sam closed her eyes, enjoying the feel of their arms wrapped round each other as they swayed to the music. Everything and everyone else in the room melted away; all she was aware of was the beat of Angelo's heart, the way the blood pulsed through her veins in exactly the same rhythm as his.

His cheek was against hers; she couldn't resist turning her head slightly and pressing a kiss to the corner of his mouth. His arms tightened round her, and he twisted so he could brush his mouth against hers.

The next thing she knew, he was really kissing her, and the long years of loneliness melted away. This was Angelo's touch, Angelo's kiss, Angelo's body heat. The man she'd loved and lost, and had somehow found again…

When someone accidentally bumped into them, apologising, he broke the kiss. Sam was hideously embarrassed to realise that the music had changed tempo, and they'd both been so lost in kissing each other that they hadn't noticed everyone else was jumping around the dance floor.

Angelo took her hand and drew her off the dance floor.

'I can't believe we just did that,' Sam said, her face heating. 'As if we're seventeen.'

'Blame it on the music,' he said, his eyes glittering with amusement. 'I don't know about you, but everything they played reminded me of our student days.' He laughed. 'No wonder we've both dropped a decade and a half off our age.'

She smiled back at him. It wasn't the music at all, she knew; it was his nearness. But she appreciated the way he'd managed to keep things light. 'Shall we find somewhere a bit quieter?'

'Sounds good to me,' he said.

When they'd collected their things, they walked back through the narrow cobbled streets to the bridge, crossed back into the old town, and strolled through the centre of Florence with their arms wrapped round each other.

Eventually, they ended up outside the entrance to Sam's building.

'Would you like to come up for coffee?' she asked.

'Yes—but I'm not going to,' he said.

She frowned. 'Why?'

'Given that we kissed each other stupid in a crowded nightclub, not noticing that the music had changed,' he said softly, 'it's obvious what will happen if we're somewhere more private. And I don't want to rush you or take you for granted. I want us both to be sure about where this is heading, first.' He stole a kiss. 'I'd like to date you again, Sam. Do things properly. Are you busy tomorrow?'

'I'd planned a hot date with a washing machine and a vacuum cleaner,' she said.

He smiled. 'Maybe you could take a rain check? The weather's meant to be nice tomorrow. I thought it might be nice to go for a drive, so I can show you some of the countryside around Florence.'

'You mean, the Roman half of you has found a ruined temple or something you want to explore,' she said drily.

'Now you mention it, there's this amphitheatre…' He

laughed. 'Though we can go and see something else, if you'd rather.'

'Actually, I used to enjoy going to see your Roman ruins,' she said. 'Though even *you* couldn't find Roman ruins in Venice.'

He rubbed his cheek. 'Ah. I hate to tell you this, Sam...'

'No *way*,' she scoffed. 'The earliest bit of Venice is that church we saw at Torcello.'

'Back then, yes. But I read an article, a couple of months ago,' he said. 'Apparently, the sea level was a couple of metres lower in Roman times, so bits that are submerged now were accessible by land back then. Archaeologists have found evidence of a Roman road in the lagoon, along with remains of a possible dock. Obviously they're not accessible to the public, but the point is there really are Roman remains in Venice.'

She smiled. 'It always surprised me that you never became an archaeologist.'

'I did think about it, when I was about twelve,' he admitted. 'But, with both my parents being doctors, medicine was the obvious career choice.' He stole a kiss. 'I promise you lunch to make up for dragging you round the Roman stuff. And in the afternoon we can have a stroll round a garden. One with wisteria.'

'I'd really like that,' she said. 'I'll walk over to you. What time?'

'Nine?' he suggested.

'I'll be there,' she promised.

'Good.' He kissed her. 'See you tomorrow. Remember a hat—and not one that can blow away easily.'

The next morning, Sam woke with a smile on her face. A whole day with Angelo, exploring the hills around Florence. Remembering days they'd spent like this in the past, she dressed for walking, grabbed a quick coffee and some toast, filled a water bottle and put it in her bag, then headed over to his flat and rang his intercom.

'Dr Clarke, reporting for duty to explore ancient ruins,' she teased.

He laughed. 'I'll be right down.'

His car turned out to be low-slung and sleek and red, with a soft top; now she realised why he'd been so specific about the hat not blowing away easily. She felt like a million dollars as he drove them through Florence and out to the hills. Italy in the summer, in a soft-top car and with the sun shining: it didn't get any better than this.

'So where are we going?' she asked.

'Fiesole—though I'm taking the long way round, as it's a pretty drive and I think you'll enjoy it,' he said.

The countryside was gorgeous, all rolling hills and patchwork fields and cypress trees. Sam couldn't resist taking snaps as they drove along. Fiesole turned out to be a very pretty town, its main square lined with little cafés as well as being a backdrop for the cathedral and its bell tower.

They explored the ruined Roman baths with their stone arcades and the amphitheatre, marvelling over how much had been preserved.

'Stand here by the arcade,' Angelo said. 'You've got the bell tower in the background, too—that'll make a nice photo for your mum. I'll take it on my phone and send it over to you.'

When they'd had their fill of the ruins, they walked up the steep, narrow street to the priory. At the top, they could see the hillside sloping down to olive groves and a line of cypresses, and then Florence rising up in the distance with the Duomo clearly visible in the centre.

'That's just stunning,' Sam said. 'Thank you for bringing me here.'

'My pleasure.' He stole a kiss. 'I hoped you'd like it here. And it's good just to spend time with you.'

After lunch in the town square, Angelo drove them to a villa with formal gardens; to Sam's delight, there was a wisteria in full bloom, and she insisted on taking photographs of them together next to it. The gardens were beautiful, full of box hedges and fountains and geraniums spilling out of terracotta pots; the formal terracing led to a perfectly turquoise lake. Even in the heat of the afternoon sun, the gardens felt deliciously cool, and Sam enjoyed the fact that Angelo kissed her in every single secluded corner.

She enjoyed a drive through the hills; the scenery was spectacular, and made her fall in love with Italy all over again.

She gave Angelo a sidelong glance. It would be easy to fall in love with him all over again, too. The day they'd spent together reminded her of so many days out they'd had before. They liked the same things, saw the world the same way.

But, even though she understood now why he'd walked away from her, she couldn't quite let herself relax fully with him. How could she be sure that he wouldn't shut her out again, the next time life threw him a curveball? If she trusted him with her heart, would he break it all over again?

Spending today with Sam made Angelo realise how much he'd missed her. How much he'd missed *them*.

But he knew he needed to give her time. If he rushed her now, she'd back away. They needed to get to know each other again, and she needed to learn to trust him.

Would the few weeks she had in Italy be enough for them to sort things out between them? Maybe he needed to take the leap of faith with that, too.

He parked the car, and smiled at Sam. 'I guess I'd better walk you back to your hot date with the laundry.'

She wrinkled her nose. 'The laundry won't mind waiting, and I don't want today to end just yet. Can I take you to dinner?'

He didn't want today to end, either. 'Thank you. I'd love that.'

So he found himself walking hand in hand with her across the Ponte Vecchio to Oltrarno. Past the padlocks inscribed with lovers' initials attached to the railing, past the jewellery shops, through the narrow streets lined with workshops making everything from violins to mosaics to shoes, and finally they found a tiny restaurant with a barrel-vaulted brick roof, red-and-white-checked cloths on the tables, and a chalk board stating the day's menu.

Sam gazed through the window. 'I've seen plenty of restaurants with wine bottles used as a candle-holder, but never as lampshades for the overhead lights. This is so pretty. Can we eat here?'

'Sure,' he said.

They ordered tortellini, followed by chicken stuffed with Gorgonzola and wrapped in Parma ham, and the waiter brought them a jug of Chianti.

'I need to find one of these for Nina,' Sam said, admiring the deep blue pottery jug with its white daisies. 'This'd be perfect on her kitchen windowsill, full of flowers.'

'How is Nina?' Angelo asked. He'd always liked Sam's best friend.

'Fine. Since you last saw her, she got married and had

a baby. Lily, my goddaughter, is the most amazing baby
in the world,' Sam said with a smile.

Was that a hint of wistfulness in her eyes? Angelo
wondered. Did Sam want children? They'd never really
had a serious discussion about children, but he'd assumed
that eventually they'd have a family together.

'Hang on—you can see for yourself,' she said, and
fished her phone from her bag. She flicked into the photo
app and brought up an album entitled 'Lily', then passed
the phone to him.

It started with pictures of Sam sitting on Nina's hospital bed, cuddling a tiny baby. As he scrolled through the
photos, he could see Sam as a proud godmother holding
the baby in a christening gown, and he could see Lily
growing and changing before his eyes, rolling over, sitting up, crawling, and finally pulling herself up onto the
furniture with a look of mingled glee and satisfaction.

'That one was a couple of days before I came to Florence,' Sam said. 'She's cruising, now. And I have to admit
that's the thing I'm missing most, over here: the fact I
won't be there for when Lily starts walking all on her
own,' she said ruefully. 'Though Nina's promised to send
me a video. She sent me that one yesterday of Lily waving to me.'

Angelo watched it, then handed the phone back. 'She
looks adorable.'

'She is.' The wistfulness was back in Sam's expression, but vanished as the waiter came over with their
tortellini.

He kept the conversation light during dinner, then held
her hand all the way back to her flat. He'd intended to
just kiss her goodnight on the doorstep, but then she said,
'Come up for coffee.'

How could he resist?

'That's an amazing fresco,' he said when she showed him into the living room.

'Isn't it just? I can't get over how there's so much gorgeous art everywhere you look in Florence.'

'It's pretty spectacular,' he agreed.

'Better than Rome?' she teased as she started making coffee.

'Rome has more fountains than Florence,' he said. 'Not to mention the Pantheon.'

'Didn't I read somewhere that it's slightly smaller than the Duomo?'

'Very slightly,' he admitted. 'But Rome has the Colosseum.'

'Yeah, but Florence is all Michelangelo.'

He coughed. 'Sistine Chapel, anyone?'

She laughed. 'I love it when you go all pompous about Rome. And you just annexed the Vatican as Roman.'

Angelo laughed back. 'That's Dad's influence. Everywhere leads back to Rome. But, growing up in Rome, with all the ruins mixed in with new buildings, it's as if you can blink and go back two thousand years. It's always fascinated me.'

'Dad's the same. I think if you ever went to Pompeii together, Mum and I would have to leave you both there for a week.'

'That might *just* be long enough,' he teased back.

He honestly meant to just have coffee and leave. But the only place to sit was next to Sam, on the sofa. He ended up with his arm round her, and that led to kissing—until he was almost dizzy with need.

This had to stop.

While he still could.

He broke the kiss and stroked her face. 'I'm trying really hard not to rush you. So I'm going now. But thank you for spending today with me. It's been perfect.'

She brushed her mouth lightly against his, and every nerve-end she'd touched tingled.

'I enjoyed it, too,' she said. 'Tuscany's gorgeous.' She held his gaze. 'So are you.'

It felt as if all the air had just emptied out of his lungs, and he couldn't speak.

Crazy. They'd been apart for longer than they'd been together. But he'd never been able to forget her. Never stopped missing her.

But if he rushed her now, he was scared she'd end up regretting it. Regretting him. Regretting their second chance.

'Sam. I'd better go,' he said softly. 'I'll see you at work tomorrow.' Reluctantly, missing her warmth the moment he moved away from her, he got to his feet.

She, too, stood up. And her kiss goodbye at her front door made his blood feel as if it were fizzing all the way back to his own flat.

Taking it slowly was going to drive him insane. But if it meant he'd get her back for good, he'd do it.

CHAPTER EIGHT

BACK ON THE WARD, Sam and Angelo treated each other strictly as colleagues, and if they had lunch together it was always as part of a group. They worked together on the more complicated cases on Angelo's list, and Sam was busy teaching new procedures to a group of medics that didn't always include Angelo.

As part of taking their new relationship slowly, they'd agreed not to see each other every evening. On Tuesday, Sam went to an aerobics class with some of the midwives and out for a healthy dinner with them afterwards. On Thursday, she and Angelo were both on an early shift; after work, he took her to the Bardini Gardens. She was utterly charmed by the long flight of baroque steps in the centre of the garden, which led to a terrace with stunning views over the city. But her absolute favourite part of the garden was the bit Angelo told her he'd saved until last: the wisteria tunnel. The sweet, musky scent, the gorgeous purple of the flowers cascading down like a waterfall, the butterflies alighting to drink their fill of nectar…

'This is perfect,' she said.

'I knew you'd like it,' he said, looking pleased.

The week zoomed by; the following Thursday, Angelo came into the Foetal Medicine Unit to find Sam, who was in Henri's office.

'I've got a possible new case for the unit,' he said. 'And I think you're the parents' last hope, as well as mine.'

'OK. Talk us through it,' Henri said.

'Rosa Pozzoli is twenty-five weeks pregnant,' Angelo said. 'The baby has a growth in the lung. It's a non-cancerous tumour, but it's grown since the last scan, three weeks ago, and it looks as if it's starting to squash the baby's heart. I'm worried that the baby's starting to go into heart failure.'

'Can we see the scans?' Sam asked.

'Of course. May I?' Angelo gestured to Henri's computer.

Henri vacated his seat. 'Go ahead, Angelo.'

Angelo logged in to the system, brought up two scan pictures on the screen, and huddled round the desk with Sam and Henri. 'This one's the last scan—and this is today's.'

'Your diagnosis is spot on,' Henri said. 'If we leave operating until after the birth, the baby won't make it.'

'So we need to operate now.' Sam zoomed in on the area round the tumour. 'It looks as if there's just one blood vessel feeding the tumour—or have I missed something?'

'No, I agree,' Henri said.

'If we use an interstitial laser to seal off the vessel,' Sam said, 'it should stop the tumour growing.'

'How strong is the baby?' Henri asked. 'Because we need to tell the parents there's a possibility the baby's heart might stop under the strain of the procedure.'

'The baby's weaker than I'd like. But, as you said,' Angelo reminded him, 'if we leave it, the baby will die. Cutting off the blood supply to the tumour will at least give the baby a chance.'

Henri inclined his head. 'All right. Do you want to take this one, Sam?'

'I've done something similar to this,' Sam said, 'but

not a case that involves a heart. If the parents are happy for us to go ahead, then yes, I'd like the chance to do the operation—but I'd like you to be there, Henri, in case I need you to step in.'

'That's fine,' Henri said.

'Are the parents with you now, Angelo?' Sam asked.

'No. I sent them off to go and have a walk round the hospital gardens while I talked to you, to see if anything can be done. There's nothing worse than being stuck in a room, waiting and worrying about what the doctors are going to say,' he said.

'OK. Bleep me when you're ready,' she said, 'and meanwhile I'll take a closer look at these scans.'

Angelo went back to his consulting room, saw his next set of parents, and then bleeped Sam when the Pozzolis came back.

He introduced her swiftly to the Pozzolis. 'Sam, this is Rosa and Cosimo Pozzoli. Rosa and Cosimo, this is Dr Sam Clarke, a specialist in foetal medicine from London who's here with us in Florence on secondment,' he said. 'She's been looking at your scan.'

The Pozzolis both looked worried sick. 'Can you do anything to help our baby, Dr Clarke?'

'There's a blood vessel feeding the tumour. I can use a laser to seal off that blood vessel, which should mean that the tumour will stop growing,' Sam said. 'But I do need to warn you that it's an invasive procedure, which always carries a risk of miscarriage, and there's also a possibility that your baby's heart might stop during the operation.'

'But if you don't do the operation, the tumour will keep growing and the baby will die anyway,' Cosimo said. 'This is the best chance we have of her surviving.'

'We understand that there are risks,' Rosa said, 'but

the operation will also give us all hope. If you can save our baby, then please—whatever it takes, do it.'

'Let me talk you through the operation before you make a decision,' Sam said. 'The thing is, when we operate on babies outside the womb, they're still. Inside the womb, they're moving in amniotic fluid. I need the baby to be as still as possible, because I have to be very exact with the laser. This means I'll need to give the baby an anaesthetic during the operation.'

Cosimo looked amazed. 'You can give an unborn baby an anaesthetic?'

Sam nodded. 'I've done it before. What we do is put the needle in the baby's bottom.'

Rosa bit her lip. 'That sounds very risky.'

Cosimo said again, 'But if we don't do anything, Rosa, the baby will die.'

'Have you done an operation like this before?' Rosa asked.

'I've done something similar,' Sam said, 'and if you choose to go ahead, I'll have Professor Henri Lefevre from Paris with me when I operate. If I have even the slightest doubt about anything, I'll refer to him.'

The Pozzolis asked a few more questions, some of which Angelo could answer, and then Rosa took Cosimo's hand. 'This is our baby's best chance. So yes, please, we'd like to go ahead.'

'I promise to take the very best care of both of you,' Sam said. 'I'll schedule you in for tomorrow morning. You'll be awake for the operation, Rosa, so you'll know exactly what's happening, though you won't feel any pain. And we should be able to give you a bonus view of your baby's face, so you have something to look forward to. I know it's hard, but try to concentrate on that rather than worrying.' She smiled. 'If you think of anything else you want to ask, write it down and we'll talk about it tomorrow. I'll leave you with Angelo for now. See you in the morning.'

After work, Angelo had booked them tickets to go inside the Duomo. He'd been before, but he enjoyed the experience—and even more than that he enjoyed seeing the amazement on Sam's face as they climbed the narrow, winding staircase inside the narrow, low-ceilinged passageway and saw the dips in the centre of the steps made by hundreds of feet before them.

'This last bit's almost vertical!' Sam whispered in horror. 'I can't believe how far apart the steps are.'

'Use the handrail to pull yourself up,' Angelo whispered back. 'I'll be behind you. I won't let you fall.'

They climbed the last few steps and then they were back in daylight, the deep blue Florentine sky above them with puffy white clouds, and could walk round the base of the lantern at the top of the dome to see the whole of the city spread out before them. From this high up, even the bell tower next to the cathedral looked small. Angelo pointed out the different churches and buildings that rose above the terracotta rooftops.

'And all those villages dotted about the hills—it's so pretty,' Sam said.

She took a selfie of them at the top, with the glorious views around them.

'Are you glad you did it—even though it's four hundred and thirty-six steps?' he asked.

'For views like this, definitely,' she said with a smile. 'And it was incredible to see the frescoes on the inside of the dome close up, too.'

Once back at the bottom of the stairs, they looked around the cathedral, and then Angelo enjoyed showing her the peacock mosaic in the crypt. 'There's a list of names in the mosaic, showing the people who paid for the floor,' he said. 'It even says how many feet of floor space they paid for. It says the peacock was paid for by someone called Obsequentius.'

'Incredible—and it's still here, all these hundreds of years later, the colours still bright,' she marvelled.

Back outside, they bought ice creams from one of the gelateria near the cathedral, then strolled through the city centre, hand in hand.

'Thank you for distracting me,' Sam said. 'I really needed that.'

'Are you nervous about tomorrow?' he asked.

'A bit,' she admitted. 'I'm usually nervous, the night before an operation, because I'm so aware of just how tiny my patients are. There's no room for error. Even a millimetre can make the difference between success and heartbreak.' She grimaced. 'This evening feels worse than usual, though I guess it's because it's the first time I've done this particular procedure.'

'I've watched you operate,' he said, 'and you're good at what you do. Plus you said you've done something similar before. This won't be very different.'

'No.' She wrinkled her nose. 'I guess now's the right time for me to worry and fret and feel nervous, because there's no room for nerves in my operating theatre.'

'Look at the flip side,' he said. 'You're giving hope to parents who would definitely have lost their unborn children without intervention.'

She nodded, and glanced at him. 'Are you busy this evening?'

'I'm not doing anything in particular,' he said.

'I could do with a little bit more distraction,' she said. 'Tell me your worst jokes.'

'If you want terrible jokes, you really need someone

from Paediatrics,' he said with a smile. 'But I can offer you an alternative. How about streaming a comedy show on the TV and a glass of wine?'

'That sounds wonderful,' she said.

Angelo took her back to his flat and set her in front of the TV with the remote control and a glass of wine. 'I'll make us something to eat,' he said.

'Anything I can do to help?' she asked.

'It's fine. Just sit and chill,' he said with a smile.

He made chicken risotto with lemony steamed green beans, which they ate on his balcony; then they curled up together on the sofa. Angelo glanced down a few minutes later and could see that Sam was almost asleep. He was tempted to ask her to stay the night, but then she'd be in a rush in the morning. It wouldn't be fair to add to the stress of the delicate operation she'd be performing.

'Hey, sleepyhead. I'll walk you home,' he said gently.

She stretched, yawned and got to her feet. 'Thank you,' she said. 'For putting up with me having a fit of doubts. I really appreciate it.'

'Any time.'

He walked her home, and kissed her goodnight on her doorstep. 'Call me if you can't sleep,' he said. 'Even if it's stupid o'clock. I'll be there.'

She kissed him back. 'Thank you. See you tomorrow.'

The next morning, Sam went for a run to shake off the last of her nerves. She showered and washed her hair, and by the time she'd walked to work she felt every inch the professional she normally was.

She had her weekly appointment to see the Bianchis with Angelo, first thing, and she was really happy with the scans; the triplets were all doing well, and the smaller twin was starting to catch up to his sibling.

She caught up with the Costas, too, in the special care unit. 'I'm due in Theatre, but I wanted to see how you were getting one,' she said.

'We're allowed to take Paola home today,' Raffaella told her, beaming.

'That's fantastic news,' Sam said, taking the opportunity for a cuddle with the baby. 'She's looking well. Did you get the scan results back?'

'Yes. She's been diagnosed with Weaver Syndrome,' Mauro said.

It was a rare genetic condition associated with rapid growth, Sam knew, and it explained why Paola's head had been so large.

'Apparently she might have very mild learning difficulties and, because her bones will develop faster than average, she might have problems with balance and co-ordination,' Raffaella said. 'But the main thing is she's with us and she's healthy, and we'll do our best to give her all the support she needs.'

'We just can't wait to get her home,' Mauro said. 'And we can't thank you enough for what you did.'

'It wasn't just me. It was the whole team,' Sam said. 'And I'd better give this little one back, even though I could sit here and cuddle her all morning.'

When she'd taken her leave of the Costas, she checked in with Rosa and Cosimo—who were with Angelo—then went to scrub in.

'How are you doing?' Angelo asked as they headed for the scrub room.

'A lot better than yesterday,' she said. 'Thanks again for putting up with that wobble, last night.'

'You're welcome,' he said. 'And you would've done the same for me.'

She finished scrubbing in, then went into the operating

theatre and talked the team through what was going to happen. Everything was ready before Rosa was wheeled in: the needle, the laser fibre, the setting of the machine.

'You're going to feel some cold antiseptic on your tummy, Rosa, and then a sharp scratch with the local anaesthetic,' she said. 'You won't feel any pain, but you might feel a little bit of pressure from time to time. Anything you're worried about, tell Angelo—and if you need me to stop, that's fine.'

'I'm OK,' Rosa said, though her eyes were wide with worry.

Once the anaesthetist had checked that Rosa was numb, and she could see that Angelo was focused on getting Rosa to breathe slowly and calmly, Sam got to work. Guided by the scanner, she put the anaesthetic into the baby's bottom, then slid the laser fibre through the narrow metal tube.

One tiny blood vessel.

If she got this right, she'd be saving a life.

If she got it wrong…

She closed her eyes for a moment and took a deep breath, then guided the laser fibre so it was next to the blood vessel feeding the tumour.

'OK. Fire,' she said coolly.

She checked on the screen, and relief flooded through her: the blood vessel was blocked. She watched the area for a few more moments, checking that there wasn't even the tiniest leak, and was satisfied that all was well.

'All done,' she said quietly, and removed the laser.

She checked the baby's heartbeat. 'Nice and steady,' she said. 'The blood vessel that fed the tumour is blocked, so the tumour should stop growing, and the baby's heart and lungs will have space to grow and mature,' she said. 'And I promised you that you could see the baby's face,

Rosa and Cosimo.' She moved the scanner head and the baby's head came into view. 'Here we go. Meet your little one.'

Cosimo's eyes were wet. 'Thank you. I can't begin…' His voice broke.

'It's all good. This is my job, and being able to make a difference is what gets me up in the mornings,' she said softly. 'Rosa, you're in for observation for the rest of today, but if all's well you can go home tomorrow. Take it easy. And I'll call in to see how you're doing, OK?'

Once she'd debriefed the team, the day sped by; she saw the rest of the patients on her list, checked in again with the Pozzolis, and went out for an aerobics class and dinner with her friends on the midwifery team.

She hadn't had a chance to see Angelo since the operation, but they'd texted to arrange going out together the next day; he'd promised to take her exploring another part of Tuscany. Sam was growing to love the area, and she could completely understand why painters were drawn to it.

But she was beginning to think that it wasn't just the beautiful countryside and architecture that made Florence feel so special. It was because Angelo was here. The more she got to know him again, the more she thought she was falling back in love with him.

On the one hand, she didn't want to rush into things, only to find she'd made a mistake. On the other, she only had a few weeks left in Italy. At the end of her secondment, would Angelo want her to stay?

That would mean giving up the research project she'd worked so hard to set up—and her promotion. Yet if Angelo came to London with her he'd be too far from his dad.

She couldn't see a solution that would work for them

both, without either of them having to give up something important. They really needed to talk about it, but for now she wanted to enjoy their summer together.

Even if it had been pouring with rain, Angelo thought, it would've felt as if the sun was shining brightly—because he was spending the whole day with Sam.

When his doorbell rang, he practically skipped down the stairs to meet her.

'Good morning.' He couldn't resist stealing a kiss.

'So where are we off to, today? Finding more Roman stuff?' she asked.

'There's a bit, yes, but it's a place that's meant to be really pretty. And it's somewhere I haven't visited yet.'

'Mystery tour, hmm?' She grinned, and stole a kiss. 'Bring it on.'

He drove them to the medieval city of Lucca; once they'd parked, he took her hand and they walked through one of the gates in the enormous brick wall surrounding the city. 'There's a walk along the top of the walls,' he said. 'I thought it might be nice to do that first, then find somewhere for coffee and pastries.'

'Sounds good to me,' she said.

A narrow passageway and some steps led them up through the defensive wall. At the top, there was a wide path, lined with trees on both sides.

'I really wasn't expecting this,' she said. 'When you said a walk along the walls, I assumed it'd be like the city walls at York, where it's quite narrow and you have to squeeze past people, but this is almost like a boulevard in Paris. I bet it's really lovely here in autumn.'

'And what a view,' he said. 'The city to one side, and the mountains to the other. I can see why Lucca is called the city of a hundred churches.'

Once they'd strolled around the walls, their arms wrapped round each other, they headed back down the steps and went into the centre of the city. They went through an archway and found themselves in an enormous oval piazza. The tall cream, white and yellow buildings followed the line of the square, and many of the doorways on the ground floor seemed to be arches, garlanded with climbing plants.

'This square used to be the site of the Roman amphitheatre,' Angelo said. 'I love how the buildings have kept the shape of it.'

There were plenty of cafés to choose from; they found a table under a parasol with a view of the square and ordered coffee and delicious-looking cinnamon pastries.

'I hope you don't mind, but I booked tickets for one place that intrigued me,' Angelo said. He glanced at his watch. 'Though we've plenty of time for coffee and looking round other bits of the city, first.'

When they'd finished their coffee, they went in search of the remains of the amphitheatre in the outer perimeter of the walls, and found thin Roman bricks in the shape of archways set into saffron-coloured stucco.

'Another one to tick off your list,' Sam teased.

They made their way through a narrow street, and then Angelo said, 'Look up.' A fourteenth-century brick tower loomed on the skyline.

'Hang on—are those *trees* on the top of that tower?' Sam asked, sounding surprised.

'Seven oak trees,' he confirmed.

'I've heard of rooftop gardens, but oak trees?'

'I looked it up. Apparently, when the Guinigi family built the tower, there were seven brothers, so it's thought that one tree was planted for each brother,' he said. 'We're right on time for our tickets, so let's go and work off those pastries.'

In the centre of the tower, they looked up to see the metal openwork stairs hugging the walls all the way to the top. 'Ready?' Angelo asked.

The climb was relentless, but finally they reached the top. The oak trees gave some shade against the heat of the sun; the terracotta rooftops of the city were spread out before them, dotted with bell towers or churches and greenery showing the gardens. In the distance, Mount Pisano loomed, and behind them they could see the huge ellipsis of the piazza where they'd had coffee.

Not far from the tower was the Roman house that had been found in the basement of a restaurant, during renovations.

'I knew there'd be something Roman,' Sam said with a grin when they stopped outside.

When they'd had their fill of the museum, they visited the cathedral to see the tomb of Ilaria del Carretto.

'Those ringlets—I've never seen such realistic carving,' Sam said. 'And that headdress with the flowers is so pretty. I can see why they call her the "sleeping beauty".'

'And the little dog at her feet,' Angelo said. 'Apparently she died in childbirth.'

'Six centuries ago.' Sam sighed. 'Nowadays, we could've saved her.'

'And you're saving babies,' Angelo said softly, 'who couldn't have been saved even ten years ago, let alone six centuries back.'

'It's a privilege,' Sam said. 'And I love what we do. I love cuddling a baby we've helped through a tough time.' She smiled. 'Even if I'm off duty, I want to be there when the Bianchi babies arrive. Three cuddles.'

'My favourite bit's the first cry,' he said. 'And when

you look into a newborn's eyes and see all the wonder of the universe.'

'All the promise of the future,' she agreed.

The promise of the future.

Angelo was really starting to hope that it might happen for them. That he and Sam could finally put his stupid mistakes behind them, and get back together for good.

Though at the same time he was aware that there were issues. He was trying hard to trust his dad not to relapse, but London was too far away for him to keep a proper eye on his dad and it wasn't fair to ask his uncle to take on the burden. And Ruggiero was adamant that he wouldn't leave Rome. Yes, he could ask Sam to stay, but that would mean she had to give up the research project she was looking forward to starting, plus she'd be turning down a promotion. It wasn't fair to ask her to make all the compromises.

He racked his brain, but for the life of him he couldn't find a fair solution.

CHAPTER NINE

OVER THE NEXT few weeks, Sam fell into a routine with Angelo; one night a week, they did something in Florence followed by having dinner together, and on one of their days off they explored Tuscany. Together, they'd made a list of places they wanted to see—everything from the famous leaning tower at Pisa, where they took pictures of each other 'holding' the tower up before climbing up the worn steps to the top, to Siena with its stunning cathedral. They drove through Chianti country and stopped to tour one of the vineyards and taste the wine, and they explored the rocky coastline, discovering a quiet beach with golden sand and clear turquoise water that was more than worth the steep climb down the steps to get to it.

With every day they spent together, Sam was finding herself falling more in love with Angelo again. Yet, at the same time, she was aware of the ticking clock. She was due back in England at the end of July. Could they make their relationship work long-distance? Or would one of them have to compromise and move to the other's country?

Or maybe she was getting ahead of herself, because he'd still kept her at the holding hands and kissing stage.

Maybe, she thought, she needed to let him know that she was ready to move their relationship forward. Not quite back to how they'd once been, because they'd both changed: but back to that old closeness.

On Wednesday evening, Angelo had done the handover and was ten minutes away from finishing organising some follow-up appointments when one Emilia, one of the junior midwives, rushed in to his office. 'Angelo, I've got a mum in birthing room three. I think the baby has shoulder dystocia. I called Lydia for help, and she's with the mum now, but she asked me to come and get you.'

Shoulder dystocia, where a baby's shoulders got stuck in the mum's pelvis during birth, was a condition that could cause serious problems for both the baby and the mum. For the baby, there was the risk of a brachial nerve injury—the nerves between the neck and shoulders—that could cause weakness or even paralysis in the upper arm; for the mum, there was the risk of a serious tear or heavy blood loss after the birth. There was a range of manoeuvres that could help free the baby, but if they didn't work the mum would need an emergency section.

'I'm on my way now,' he said. 'Give me thirty seconds to send a text, and then fill me in on the way.' He'd had plans with Sam for a late dinner, that evening, but he wasn't going to walk out on a mum and a team who needed his help, so it was fairer to cancel now than to leave it to the last minute.

Sorry, have to cancel dinner. Baby with suspected shoulder dystocia. Call you soon as I can. xx.

As soon as the text had gone, he focused on Emilia. 'Tell me the mum's history.'

'Nicoletta's twenty-eight, forty-one weeks pregnant, and this is her second baby. Her daughter was born two years ago, and everything was normal, though the baby was quite big.'

First babies tended to be smaller than subsequent babies; she'd gone just over term with this baby, so the chances were that this baby would be bigger.

'This time round, the pregnancy's been uncomplicated—she's not diabetic and her BMI's under thirty—and all her scans have been normal. She came in very early this morning, three centimetres dilated, so the team on the shift before me encouraged her to continue walking about. Four hours later, her membranes ruptured, but she was still three centimetres dilated.'

A longer second stage, then. 'Did you give her anything to help with labour?' Angelo asked.

'The night team gave her a syntocinon infusion and we were monitoring the baby with CTG. Everything was fine when I took over as her midwife,' Emilia said. 'Four hours after the infusion, she was at seven centimetres, and four hours later, she was at ten centimetres and started pushing. When the baby's head crowned, her chin seemed to be wedged against Nicoletta's perineum. I tried delivering the baby's shoulders during the next two contractions, but it didn't happen—that's when I asked Nicoletta to stop pushing and called Lidia. She asked me to come and get you.'

'Have you come across many cases of shoulder dystocia before?' Angelo asked.

'The is the first one I've actually come across—I'd only ever seen a "turtle head" presentation on a training video before today. I know the theory,' Emilia said. 'We go through the "helperr" mnemonic.'

'Starting with calling for help, and then E for "end pushing", which you've already done,' Angelo said. 'Hopefully between us we can help Nicoletta change position and it will get the baby unstuck. In about ninety per cent of cases, the McRoberts manoeuvre does the trick.'

In the delivery suite, Lidia introduced him to Nicoletta and her partner.

'I'm sure Lidia and Emilia have explained what's happening,' he said gently, 'so what we're going to do now is try changing your position to give the baby a bit more room inside you, and that will hopefully help the baby move enough so her shoulders come unstuck and we can help you deliver her safely. We'll try each manoeuvre for thirty seconds or so, and if it doesn't release the baby's shoulders we'll move onto the next one.'

'I just want my baby to be safe,' Nicoletta said. 'Do whatever you have to.'

'Thank you,' he said.

'I've assessed Nicoletta for an episiotomy,' Lidia said, 'and I don't think it will help.'

Angelo knew how experienced the senior midwife was, and he trusted her judgement completely. 'OK,' he said, and turned to Emilia. 'First manoeuvre?'

'L,' she said. 'Legs. The McRoberts manoeuvre.'

In nearly every case Angelo had seen, it had done the trick and the baby's shoulders had come unstuck, though he had a funny feeling about this one. He couldn't put his finger on why, but every instinct told him this was going to be tricky.

'We're going to help you press your legs up with your thighs against your belly, Nicoletta,' Angelo said; together he and Lidia helped Nicoletta to flex her hips.

The baby was still stuck. He glanced at Emilia.

'P—suprapubic pressure,' the junior midwife said, and pressed on Nicoletta's lower belly just above her pubic bone; when the baby didn't move, she tried a rocking motion. She glanced at Angelo and shook her head.

Still stuck.

'Next?' Lidia asked.

'E—enter manoeuvres,' Emilia said.

'I'm going to try to rotate the baby's shoulder and help the baby's arm out of the birth canal,' Angelo told Nicoletta.

But although he'd done the procedures before, in this case they didn't work.

'R—roll onto hands and knees,' Emilia said.

But helping Nicoletta roll over onto all fours didn't release the baby's shoulder, either.

'R—refer,' Lidia finished wryly.

Which meant they needed to act fast. The big risk now was of the baby suffering from hypoxia; she needed to be delivered in the next five minutes.

'Nicoletta, the baby's really wedged,' Angelo said. 'We're going to need to give you a Caesarean section—and I'll need to push the baby's head back into your pelvis.'

He sent Emilia to get the anaesthetist and the neonatal team, gave Nicoletta medication to reduce her contractions, then rotated the baby's head and pushed it back.

Within a couple of minutes Nicoletta had been whisked into Theatre, with Lidia holding the baby's head in place while Angelo scrubbed in.

A minute later, he'd delivered the baby. As always, he was on tenterhooks until the first cry came; then he relaxed and finished sewing up Nicoletta while Lidia, Emilia and the neonatal team concentrated on the baby.

He examined Nicoletta; thankfully there was no sign of a severe tear, but he'd talk to the next shift and ask them to keep an eye on her drain and the blood loss.

'How's the baby doing?' he asked the neonatal specialist.

'She's doing fine. Five-minute Apgar score of nine.

There's some brachial nerve damage on the arm that was stuck, but that should resolve itself, and there's no sign of hypoxia.'

'That's good to know,' he said.

Once he'd debriefed the team, and Nicoletta had come round from the anaesthetic enough to cuddle her baby and for him and the neonatal specialist to talk to her and her husband about what had happened and what it meant for the baby and any future pregnancies, he wrote up his notes and texted Sam.

Ended up in Theatre. Mum and baby both doing well. x.

The reply came back almost immediately.

Good to hear. Have leftovers here if you want dinner? x.

He wasn't that hungry, and he was tired; it had been a long day.

Tired and a bit out of sorts. Not fair to make you put up with that. x.

I don't mind out of sorts. Maybe you'll feel better if someone makes a fuss of you. x.

He couldn't help smiling. Seeing her would definitely make him feel lighter.

On my way now. x.

It didn't take long to walk to her flat and press the Entryphone buzzer. She let him up, and as she opened her front door to him he could smell something delicious.

Suddenly he realised he actually *was* that hungry, and wolfed down the chicken wrapped in Parma ham that she'd served with a simple salad.

And then then were strawberries with the most perfect vanilla ice cream.

'I bought a take-out carton from the gelateria round the corner,' she said.

'Excellent idea,' he said. 'Thank you for feeding me. I feel human again, now.'

'Shoulder dystocia where McRoberts doesn't work is scary stuff,' she said. 'I'm glad to hear the mum and baby are fine.'

'The baby has Erb's palsy,' he said. 'Edoardo thinks it will resolve in a few days, but it's still not great for those poor parents. And there were no real red flags to make any of the team think the baby would get stuck. Yes, the baby was big, but half the babies with shoulder dystocia weigh less than four kilos. It was her second pregnancy, there weren't any complications and her last birth was uncomplicated.'

'Sometimes it just happens.'

'That what I told Emilia. She's been fretting that she missed something.'

'The main thing is you delivered the baby safely,' she said.

'Yeah.' He rubbed a hand across his eyes. 'How was your day?'

'Mostly follow-ups,' she said. 'But I do have an operation tomorrow you might like to sit in on; the baby has a hydrothorax which is compressing the lungs. We did all the work-ups today as well as a high-resolution ultrasound and echo, to see exactly what's going on.'

'So what's making the fluid form in the baby's chest?' he asked, intrigued.

'In this case, we're not sure,' she said. 'I've ruled out anaemia or a cardiac problem.'

'What are you going to do—a thoracentesis?'

She shook her head. 'In nine out of ten cases, after you've drained the fluid, you get a recurrent build-up. A thoracoamniotic shunt—a catheter in the baby's chest which drains fluid into the amniotic sac—will stop the hydrothorax and decompress the chest so the lungs can develop properly.' She spread her hands. 'Obviously there's the usual risk with foetal surgery, that the mum will go into labour: but the baby's twenty-nine weeks. I'm giving the mum steroids to mature the baby's lungs, and we'll do it under sedation tomorrow.'

'What happens to the shunt at the birth?' he asked.

'We take it out, though the baby might need intubation and respiratory support, and possibly a chest tube for a few days to keep draining fluid. But once the shunt's in place we'll check it every fortnight to make sure it's working properly. If it gets blocked, we just redo the shunt.'

'It sounds fascinating,' he said. 'What time are you in Theatre?'

'Nine,' she said.

'I'm on a late shift, but I'll come in to watch,' he said. He glanced at his watch and kissed her. 'I know I'm being horribly rude, but I'm tired.'

'You're not being rude. You stayed late at the hospital,' she reminded him. She stroked his face. 'Or you could stay.'

Part of him desperately wanted to agree.

But he wanted their first time back together to be special. And when he wasn't half asleep. And when he didn't have to get up early for work, the next day; he wanted to savour waking up with her in his arms. 'Hold that thought,' he said. 'Because I'd love to wake up with you. But on a day when we can take our time about it.' He held her gaze. 'We're going exploring on Saturday. And we're both off on Sunday. Maybe,' he said, 'we can go out to dinner when we've finished exploring, then go back and sit on my balcony with a glass of wine. And I'll make you breakfast in the morning.'

'Saturday night,' she said, and kissed him. 'It's a date.'

Angelo was still thinking about Saturday night when he walked to the hospital, the next morning.

'Someone definitely got out of the right side of bed today,' Lidia said with a grin. 'And you're three hours early.'

'I'm going to watch Sam's operation,' he said.

'Hmm,' Lidia said, but her eyes crinkled at the corners.

Watching Sam work was fascinating; she had the ultrasound on to guide the movements of her surgical instruments, and deftly fitted the tiny shunt to the baby's chest. She talked the team through every move she made, and the reasoning behind it, and at the debrief afterwards she barely needed support from him on translating the medical terms.

Once Giannina Gallo was fully awake after sedation, Sam sat down with her and her husband Enzo.

'I'm pleased to say the operation worked very well,' she said. 'I'd like to keep you in for the rest of the day, but if all's well you can go home this evening. I'd like to see you every two weeks for the rest of your pregnancy for a scan, to check the shunt is still working as it should be. There is a possibility it might get blocked, but if that happens I'll redo the shunt.'

'But it worked,' Enzo checked.

She nodded. 'I could see from the scan that the fluid's already started to drain from the baby's chest.'

'Thank you.' Giannina took Sam's hands. 'If you hadn't done the operation, our baby wouldn't have made it.'

'It's what I'm here for,' Sam said with a smile.

'If we have more babies in the future,' Enzo said, 'will they have the same condition?'

'It's very unlikely,' Sam reassured him. 'Now, is there anything else you'd like to ask? The last thing I want is for either of you to worry.'

'No. Last night and this morning were awful. I kept thinking the worst. But now…' Giannina smiled. 'Now, I feel as if the sun's shining again.'

'Good.' Sam patted her hand. 'I'll take you through to the ward, and get you settled in. But if there's anything at all worrying you, talk to one of the midwives—and ask them to call me if they need to, OK?'

'So how are you doing, Chiara?' Angelo asked his next patient when she came in and sat down.

'I've had a bit of a headache all morning, and I feel a bit sick,' she said. 'I took some paracetamol, but it hasn't worked. And everything's a bit blurry.'

A red flag went up at the back of Angelo's head. 'Let's take your blood pressure,' he said, 'and I'll see if I can find something to help with that headache. Whereabouts is the pain?'

'Here.' She rubbed the front of her head.

'OK. Have you been sick at all?' he asked.

'No.'

Her blood pressure was up on the previous reading,

and although her temperature was fine her heart rate was a little fast for Angelo's liking.

'And you're feeling the baby kick as normal?' he checked.

'Not as much as normal,' she said.

Another red flag.

'Are you OK for me to examine you?' he asked. At her nod, he checked her over; her uterus was soft, but she winced when he touched the area beneath her ribs on her right side. And he noticed that her legs and fingers had some mild swelling.

'I'm a little bit concerned,' he said. 'I'd like to do some blood tests, and admit you to the ward.'

'Is something wrong with the baby?' Chiara asked. 'Is that why I'm not feeling him move so much?'

'I think you might have pre-eclampsia,' he said.

'But—isn't that something you only get if you're really fat or over thirty-five?' Chiara asked, sounding shocked.

'It happens in young mums, too,' Angelo said. Chiara was twenty-two, and because her periods had been irregular she hadn't realised she was pregnant until she was twenty weeks. 'We don't know exactly what causes it, but it's to do with the blood vessels in your placenta.'

'Can you give me something to make it stop?'

'The only cure is delivering the baby,' he said.

'It's too early—he's meant to be thirty-six weeks, but because I didn't know my dates we're not really sure,' Chiara said, looking distraught.

'He's got a good chance of doing well, even at thirty-six weeks. When babies are born early, sometimes they struggle a little bit with breathing, but we can give you some steroids to help mature the baby's lungs.' Angelo reassured her. 'Once I've got your blood results back, we'll know exactly what we're doing, but you're very likely to have the baby either today or tomorrow. Can we call anyone to come and be with you?'

Chiara shook her head. 'My mum's a panicker and she'll just make things worse. The baby's dad isn't around any more.'

'A friend? A sister?' he suggested.

'My best friend's at work. She won't be able to get the time off. There's nobody,' she said.

It was tough enough to have complications during pregnancy, he thought, but to be on your own as well…

He took the bloods and sent them off. On the ward, he settled Chiara in and introduced her to Emilia. 'Emilia will look after you today,' he said. 'And I'll be back to see you after clinic.' He gave her an antihypertensive to reduce her blood pressure, administered steroids and set up a magnesium sulphate infusion to reduce the risk of Chiara having an eclamptic fit.

'Emilia, can you catheterise her and keep an eye on her urine output, please?' he asked.

'And if it's low, call you,' Emilia said.

He nodded. 'And if you can put the baby on CTG—Chiara says the baby hasn't moved as much today.'

'Any signs of foetal distress, I'll let you know,' Emilia said.

'I've sent her bloods off. When the coagulation screen's back so I know what's going on, and her blood pressure's under control, it's very probable that I'll take her to Theatre.' He grimaced. 'She's on her own, poor kid.'

'I'll spend as much time with her as I can,' Emilia promised.

Angelo had just made himself a mug of instant coffee in the staff kitchen, filling half the mug with cold water so he could drink it straight down, when Sam walked in.

'Are you OK?' she asked. 'You're looking a bit out of sorts.

'I've just admitted a young mum with pre-eclampsia,' he said. 'She's on her own and hasn't got anyone who can be with her. I'd keep her company myself, but I have clinic.' He shook his head crossly. 'I've given her steroids, antihypertensives and mag sulph, and I'm waiting for bloods to come back.'

'I've only got paperwork for the rest of the day,' she said. 'I can take a break now and finish it later. Come and introduce me to her, and I can sit with her until you're ready to take her into Theatre.'

'Are you sure?' Angelo asked. 'This is above and beyond.'

She shrugged. 'It's fine. If she's sitting on her own, worrying, it's not going to help with her blood pressure, is it?'

'I really appreciate this,' he said.

He introduced Sam to Chiara, and after his clinic had finished he checked Chiara's blood results. As he'd expected, there were raised levels of liver transaminases, urate and creatinine, and her platelets were at the lower end of normal.

The CTG results showed that the baby was starting to be in distress, but thankfully Chiara's blood pressure had stabilised and he was able to take her straight to Theatre to deliver the baby. The little boy was absolutely fine, and when he accompanied Chiara back to the ward her best friend was waiting for her.

Relieved that she wasn't alone, he went down to Sam's office, where she'd said she'd be catching up with her paperwork.

'Baby boy, good weight for thirty-six weeks, and he didn't need any help breathing,' he said.

'That's great.' She smiled at him.

'Thank you for what you did. That was kind.'

'She's a nice kid. I hate it when our mums don't have any support,' she said. 'And my paperwork could wait.'

'Her best friend was there when I took her back from Theatre,' he said. 'How did she know Chiara was here?'

'Between us, Emilia and I persuaded Chiara to send her best friend a text, and her friend came straight after she finished work,' Sam said. 'So at least Chiara will have some support now.'

'Thank you,' he said.

'No problem.' She smiled. 'You supported me this morning. I'm just returning the favour.'

He risked stealing a kiss. 'I'd better get back to the ward. See you tomorrow morning.

On Saturday morning, Sam walked over to Angelo's flat. He greeted her with a kiss. 'Ready to do some exploring? I've got a bag with towels.'

'Are we going to the coast?'

'Not quite,' he said. 'But I think you might enjoy what I have in mind.'

He drove them through the Val d'Orcia; the roads were lined with cypress trees, and everywhere she could see vineyards, olive groves and cornfields.

'I know this is being greedy, considering how gorgeous the views are here, but I always thought there were huge fields of sunflowers in Tuscany,' she said.

'There are. But the best time to see them is the end of June. I'll definitely add them to our list.'

They stopped in a little village overlooking the valley, and walked through to the main square. Sam stared in surprise: the whole of the central square was taken up by a large pool. The water was a clear green, and there was steam rising very gently from it. 'That's not just a pond, is it? It looks like the Roman baths in Bath,' she said.

'That's exactly it,' he said. 'The piazza was built over the source of the hot springs here, and apparently it was on the pilgrim route. Although you're not allowed to bathe here in the town square, you can follow the springs down the cliff and sit in them.'

'Now I know why you brought towels,' she said, smiling. 'Great idea.'

They walked down the path by the cliff; the water beside them was turquoise and sparkled in the light. Sam bent down and dabbled her fingers in the water. 'It's gorgeously warm.'

At the bottom of the cliffs, they sat on the edge of the pool and dipped their feet in the water, enjoying the sunshine.

'It's amazing to think people have been doing exactly this for hundreds of years, here,' she said. 'The more time I spend in Tuscany, the more I'm falling in love with the place.' And back in love with Angelo, though she wasn't quite ready to say it.

When they'd had their fill of the pool, Angelo drove them to a vineyard, where they had a tour of the vines and then tasted some of the different produce; and they took the long, scenic route back to Florence.

Angelo dropped her back at her flat. 'I'll shower and change,' he said, 'and then I'll come and collect you for dinner.'

He'd made a reservation on a rooftop restaurant where they had a view of the sun setting over the river; then they walked hand in hand back along the river.

'Come and have a glass of wine on my balcony?' he asked.

She nodded, butterflies swirling in her stomach. This

wasn't just wine. This was moving their relationship on to the next stage—and putting the past behind them.

They didn't even make it to opening the bottle; as soon as he closed the front door, they were kissing, and he was scooping her up in his arms and carrying her to his bed.

CHAPTER TEN

AFTER THAT NIGHT, 'taking it slowly' was out of the question. Sam and Angelo spent alternate nights at each other's flats, went for a run together before work, and spent as much time as they could together outside the hospital.

Towards the end of June, Angelo drove Sam into the countryside. 'Right. From here, close your eyes and no peeking—even when I stop,' he said.

'Got it.' Obviously he wanted to surprise her with a gorgeous view, she thought, but she did what he asked and kept her eyes closed.

He parked the car in what she assumed was a lay-by. 'Keep your eyes closed,' he reminded her.

She heard his door close and hers open; he unclipped her seatbelt, stole a kiss, and led her out of the car.

'OK. You can look, now,' he said.

And the view completely took her breath away.

There was a massive field of sunflowers in front of her, all their faces turned towards her. Behind the sunflowers, the hills rose up, crowned by a walled town and its castle.

'This is stunning,' she said. 'I've never seen so many sunflowers in one place.'

Angelo looked pleased. 'You did say you wanted to see sunflowers, and this spot's famous for it.' He kissed her lightly. 'Turn round so the sunflowers are behind you, and I'll take a picture for your mum.' He took a snap on his phone.

'And now one for your dad.' She beckoned to him to stand beside her; once his arm was round her, she took a selfie of them smiling.

'This is perfect,' she said. 'It doesn't get better than this.'

Halfway through the next month, Angelo was catching up with paperwork when one of the ultrasound team knocked on his door.

'I'm doing the twenty-week scan for one of your mums, and there's a problem. I'm not happy with the way the baby's left hand looks—I think some of the fingertips are missing—and the left foot looks swollen.'

Angelo frowned. 'Do you think it's amniotic band syndrome?'

'I'm not sure. The senior radiographer's on a break. Would you mind taking a look?'

'Of course,' Angelo said. 'But I'd like to bring Sam Clarke in as well—if it is amniotic band syndrome, she'll know and she'll also be able to do something about it.'

'Sam from the Foetal Medicine Unit?' the radiographer asked. 'I haven't met her, but I've heard she's very good.'

'She is,' Angelo said. 'Give me a couple of minutes, and I'll come down.'

He went to see Sam. 'Got a minute?'

'I've got clinic starting in ten minutes,' she said. 'So, if you're quick, yes.'

'One of my mums is having her twenty-week scan,' he said, 'and the ultrasound team isn't happy. The baby might have some fingertips missing on the left hand, and the left foot looks swollen. It could be amniotic band syndrome. They've asked me to come and have a look—and I think this might be one where you could help.'

'OK. I'll come down as soon as I've asked Carla to apologise to my first parents and let them know I'll be a bit late,' Sam promised.

In the ultrasound department, Angelo greeted Amara and Tino Albano, then introduced them to Sam when she came down.

Sam looked at the screen, asked the radiographer to check a couple of things, and then turned to the Albanos. 'I think Gianni's right, and you have amniotic band syndrome.'

'What's that? I've never heard of it,' Amara said. 'Did I do something wrong when I was first pregnant?'

'No. It's absolutely not your fault,' Sam reassured her. 'We don't know why it happens, but the inner layer of the amniotic sac has been damaged at some point.' She grabbed a piece of paper and drew a diagram. 'There are two linings in the amniotic sac; it's like a balloon being blown up inside another full balloon, and between them is a sticky substance that fuses the linings together by the time you're sixteen weeks pregnant. Sometimes they don't fuse together properly, and bands form on the inside lining. They're really thin strands of tissue.' She indicated the screen. 'Can you see those tiny, tiny white threads?'

Tino nodded. 'What does it mean for the baby?'

'Because the baby's moving around in fluid, the amniotic bands can sometimes tangle round the baby and restrict the blood flow. Gianni picked up that the baby's left foot looks a bit swollen and some of the fingertips on the left hand are missing,' Sam said. 'From the look of the scan, there's still blood flow to the foot—the nerves are the last things to be damaged, and if there's blood flow it shows the nerves aren't irreversibly damaged and we can do our best to save the baby's foot.'

The Albanos looked utterly shocked.

'So our baby might lose his foot?' Tino asked. 'But you said you could save it. How?'

'I'm a surgeon in the new foetal medicine unit,' Sam said, 'and I operate on babies inside the womb. Obviously, with any surgery in the womb, there's a risk that your waters could break, Amara, and at twenty weeks your baby's too little to make it.'

'But if you don't operate, our baby will lose his foot,' Amara said slowly. 'And could the bands tangle round his neck?'

'It's very rare,' Sam said, 'but yes.'

'How does the operation work?' Tino asked.

'I'd do it under a general anaesthetic and make an incision in Amara's abdomen, and then two tiny incisions in her uterus so I can put a camera in one and a cutting instrument in the other. And then I'd cut the band to release the baby's foot,' she said.

'If you do it, we might lose him. If you don't do it, he'll lose his foot,' Amara said. 'I...whatever we do, it's bad.'

'I'm sorry. It's a horrible situation,' Sam said. 'But please let me reassure you that it's nothing that you've done wrong. It's not genetic, and it's very rare—it's highly unlikely to happen in a future pregnancy.'

Amara put her face in her hands. 'I don't know what to say. I can't think.'

'Don't make a decision now,' Sam said. 'Talk it over. Take your time. And, although I'm in clinic this afternoon, you can get a message to me via Angelo and I'll come down as soon as I'm not with a mum-to-be and I'll answer any questions you might have.'

* * *

In the end, after another meeting with Angelo and Sam, the Albanos decided to go ahead with surgery, and to allow some of the team to view the operation. The next day, Sam reassured the Albanos before Amara was anaesthetised, then went to scrub in and brief the team.

'I'm using tiny instruments, to reduce the risk of breaking Amara's waters because I don't want her going into labour,' she said. 'Obviously operating in a womb means we're operating in water, so there's movement and we need to take extra care. What we're doing is cutting the band round the baby's foot. I'm putting two incisions in the womb—one for the camera, and one for the cutting instruments. Angelo's going to sort out the camera while I do the operation itself.'

She made the incisions, and Angelo inserted the tube with the camera.

'Now we can see the baby. And you can see the amniotic bands inside the womb—those white strings,' she said. 'Can you show me the baby's left hand, Angelo?'

He manipulated the camera so she could see the baby's left hand. 'The thumb's fine,' she said, 'but three of the fingertips are missing. It's not the whole of the fingers, so the baby should be able to manage just fine with a little support as he grows up.' She turned to Angelo. 'We need the left foot, now, please.'

The white band around the baby's foot was much more visible.

'If we leave the bands as they are, they'll tighten and amputate the baby's foot,' she said. 'So my job here is to release the foot, and with luck the swelling will go down and the foot won't be badly affected.'

She pulled the band away from the baby's foot; then, careful not to nick the baby's skin and cause a bleed, snipped through the band with the tiny scissors. 'Done,' she said.

She closed up, checked the baby's heartbeat, then debriefed the team while Amara was in the recovery room. Once Amara was awake, Tino by her side, Sam went in with Angelo to talk to them. 'I'm pleased to say the operation was a success,' she said. 'You lost some amniotic fluid during the surgery, Amara, but the baby's heartbeat is nice and strong.'

'I'd like you on bed rest here for the next five days, so we can keep an eye on you. If you're worried about anything, call the midwife and they'll get hold of me or Sam,' Angelo said. 'We'll do another scan tomorrow, to see how his foot's looking, but in the meantime try to relax.'

Thankfully, the next day, the scan showed that the swelling in the baby's foot had gone down considerably, and his heartbeat was still strong; Amara was able to go home four days later.

In the middle of July, Ric asked Sam to come in for a quick chat.

'Sam, thanks for making the time to see me,' he said. 'There are a couple of things I'd like to talk to you about. Firstly, we'd like you to give a presentation to senior management next week, about the work you've been doing here.'

'Of course,' she said.

'Secondly, your secondment's due to end next week. We're delighted with the way you've settled in to the team, and we'd like to offer you a permanent position here.'

Which meant she could stay here, doing the job she loved, with Angelo.

They'd said they would see how things went, put the past behind them... But neither of them had had the courage to bring the subject up.

If she went back to London, she'd be going home to a job she loved just as much, with the added bonus of a promotion and starting the research project she'd been looking forward to. She didn't want to turn that down.

How could she choose between them?

'Ric, I really wasn't expecting this,' she said. 'I'm flattered. Really flattered. But please can I have a bit of time to think about it?' She needed to discuss it with Angelo, and find out what he wanted for the future. If she turned down everything she'd been offered in London and then discovered that Angelo wasn't sure she was what he wanted, she'd be left high and dry.

'Sure,' Ric said. 'No pressure. Maybe you can give us your answer after the presentation. But we like your work and we definitely want you.'

She thought about it all day. Angelo was working late, so she went back to her flat and called her mum. 'I need your advice, Mum,' she said. 'Ric has just offered me a job here.'

'I'm not surprised they want you to stay in Florence,' her mum said. 'But I thought you were only there for three months, until the funding came through for your research project? Or has that fallen through?'

'It's still going ahead,' Sam said. 'But I don't know what to do, Mum. I mean, I really want to work on that research project. And it means I'll be a consultant. But I'm happy here in Florence, too.'

'Would you be staying for the job, or for Angelo?' her mum asked.

'That's the big question,' Sam admitted. 'Angelo and I… We haven't really worked out where things are going with us. And I know I'm being a coward, not pushing him to talk about it.'

'Not talking is why you split up in the first place,' her

mum said. 'I think we all learned from Dominic that we need to be open and honest about things. You need to talk to Angelo—*really* talk to him—and work out what you both want.' She paused. 'What do you want, Sam?'

'Everything,' Sam said wryly. 'I want Angelo and I want to work on the research project in London.'

'Can he move back to London with you?'

'Not with his dad's situation.' She filled her mum in swiftly. 'He can't really move, can he? So I can't have everything. It's Angelo or London.'

Her mother sighed. 'You need to talk it over together. Make a list of pros and cons. Think about what you're prepared to compromise on and what you're not.'

'Do I go with my heart or my head, Mum?' Sam asked. 'On paper, I know London is the sensible choice.'

'There's a huge "but" in your voice. I think you've just answered your own question,' her mum said.

'Actually, I haven't,' Sam said. 'My head says come back to London; my heart says stay in Italy. Either way, I lose something I really want. But, if I stay in Florence, I'm scared it's all going to go wrong again.'

'Talk to Angelo,' her mum said again. 'Find out how he feels. Once you've got all the facts, it will help you decide. But you've got time to make a decision. Don't rush into it.'

'Thanks, Mum.'

But, the more Sam thought about it, the more confused she got. Did she follow her head or heart? Or was there a middle way where she could follow both?

Later that evening, Angelo called round to Sam's flat. 'Everything OK?' he asked, noting that she looked un-usually frazzled.

'Yes—and no,' she said. 'Ric's asked me to do a presentation to senior management next week, before I go back to London.'

'That's a good thing, isn't it?' He looked at her. 'Wait. He wants you to do the presentation in Italian?'

She nodded.

'I'm pretty sure your language skills are good enough to cope, but if you need a hand with any of the vocab while you're prepping, give me a yell.'

'Thank you,' she said. 'I was hoping you might be at the presentation, too, in case I get stuck on any questions.

'Of course I'll be there,' he said. 'Though you won't need me.' But he could tell there was something she wasn't saying. 'What's the not OK bit?' he asked gently.

'It's not a bad thing. Just… I need to make a decision. Ric's offered me a job in the new unit,' she explained.

So there was a reason for her to stay in Florence, besides him.

Which brought them to the thing they still hadn't talked about; they'd both ignored the ticking clock, wanting to see how things went between them before they had the really important conversation.

It looked as if their hands had just been forced.

Though he absolutely couldn't put any pressure on her. If she stayed, it had to be because she wanted to be there, not because she was trying to please him. 'Are you going to accept?' he asked, trying to keep his voice as neutral as he could.

'I don't know,' she said. 'I've been thinking about it all day, and I talked to my mum.'

'What did she say?'

'Make a list of pros and cons, talk to you and be honest,' she said.

He smiled. 'That's one of the many things I've always liked about your mum: her common sense.'

'She likes you, too. Well.' She wrinkled her nose. 'If I'm being honest, she *used* to like you.'

'Until I made a massive mistake and hurt you,' he said. 'In her shoes, I'd be the same. And I hope I can make things right with her as well as you.' He paused. 'So I assume you've made a list?'

She nodded. 'Where my career's concerned: if I go back to London, it's to a promotion and to a research project I'm dying to work on. If I stay here, it's swapping my current job for the same one, just in a different hospital.'

'That makes London the logical choice,' he said.

'So you're saying I should go back to London?' Her eyes widened.

He knew what she was really asking: did he want her to stay here for his sake? 'Sam, I don't want to get in your way. You have your career to think of. You've worked hard, and I'm not going to be selfish and ask you to turn down something I know you really want to do.'

'So you don't want me to stay.'

'That isn't what I said,' he pointed out. 'I just don't want to complicate your decision. You need to do the right thing for you. If you were going back to exactly the same job as you're doing here, then I'd say stay. But staying here would mean a sideways move and turning down something you've worked hard for.' He looked at her. 'This is the conversation we've been avoiding.'

She nodded. 'This decision doesn't just affect me. So I'll be brave and ask you for an honest answer: what do *you* want?'

'I want you,' he said. 'But I want you to be happy. I don't want you to stay here for my sake, then end up resenting me in the future because of everything you've had to turn down to be with me.'

'But if I go back to London, what does that mean for

us?' she asked. 'You've got your dad to think of. You wouldn't have a problem finding a job in London, but you can't leave your dad.'

And his dad wasn't going to leave Italy.

He wanted to run with his heart, but for her sake he needed to work with his head. 'I think,' he said, 'we need some time to work out what all the options are and which one is the best for us. When do you need to give Ric an answer?'

'Next week. And I need to talk things over with my boss, too, to see what the options might be in London.' She looked at him. 'But the bottom line is, you can't leave your dad—and I wouldn't ask you to do that. If anyone had asked me to leave Dominic to cope on his own while I went hundreds of miles away with them, I would've said no. It's too much to ask.' She paused. 'So that gives us two choices: either I stay here with you, or I go back to London without you.'

'It's my turn to be brave and ask for an honest answer. What do *you* want?' he asked.

'I want you—*and* my research project,' she said. 'But that's greedy. I can't have both.'

'Are you sure about that?' he asked. 'Not about what you want, I mean, but whether you have to choose? There might be some room for negotiation.' He looked at her. 'We're juggling Rome, Florence and London. Maybe we'll have to spend some of the week apart, but our hospitals are twinned. Does your research project all have to take place in London?'

'That's where the funding is,' she said. But her face brightened. 'Though you have a point. I'll talk to Will and see if at least some of it can be done here.' She looked at him. 'But I want to be with you, and I want to work on that research project.'

He wrapped his arms round her. 'If your boss says no, find out what the barriers are, and we'll find a way round them. Because I want you, and I want you to do the job you love.' He kissed her. 'I love you, Sam.' He'd never stopped loving her. 'I want a future, with you.'

'That's what I want, too.' She smiled. 'I love you, Angelo.'

'Then we'll find a way to make it work.' He kissed her again. 'Together.'

This was their second chance. And they weren't going to let it pass them by. They could make it work, couldn't they...?

CHAPTER ELEVEN

SAM SPENT THE week negotiating with Will and Ric, working at the hospital and practising her presentation in front of Angelo. Early on the afternoon of the presentation, Pia Bianchi came in for her elective Caesarean.

'You made it to thirty-three weeks. That's fantastic,' Sam said, giving her a hug.

It was probably the most crowded delivery room Sam had ever been in: three midwives, three neonatal specialists, the anaesthetist, Angelo and herself, as well as Tommaso being there to hold Pia's hand and cut the cord.

The babies were all good weights: two point one-five kilograms for the recipient twin, two point zero nine for the singleton, and even the donor twin was one point nine-eight. And, considering they were premature, they all had good Apgar scores.

Pia and Tommaso were smiling through tears of joy as they cuddled their babies.

'That's brilliant,' Sam said. 'Well done. And can I be really cheeky and ask a favour?'

'Of course,' Pia said.

'I'm doing a presentation to the senior management today. You were my first patients, and it would be so lovely to show everyone a picture of you with the babies so they could see what a difference the unit made to you.'

'Use my phone,' Tommaso said, 'and I'll send you the picture. And good luck with your presentation. Tell them from us, we think you're brilliant.'

Sam laughed. 'Thank you. I will.'

'And we were thinking,' Pia said. 'We'd like to name the twins after you—Angelo and Samuele.'

'That's so lovely,' Sam said, a lump in her throat.

When Pia and Tommaso had gone with their babies to the special care unit, she looked at Angelo. 'All those weeks ago, the odds were really against the babies. And now they're here, all safe. Days like this don't get any more perfect.'

'We'll definitely celebrate tonight, after your presentation,' he said. 'I have a bottle of something nice chilling in the fridge.'

'I'll hold you to that,' she said. 'In the meantime, I have notes to write up, then I need to go home and change.'

'Me, too,' he said. 'See you at the presentation.'

Angelo was halfway home when his phone shrilled.

He glanced at the screen and his heart missed a beat. Why would his uncle be calling him at this time of day?

'Tio Sal, is everything all right?' he asked.

'Angelo, your dad's in hospital. He collapsed in the street,' Salvatore said.

It took a few seconds for the words to penetrate. *His dad had collapsed.* 'I'm on my way,' he said.

But, when he checked the train times to buy a ticket online, he discovered there was a problem with the line and the trains to Rome had been cancelled for the rest of the day.

Which left him with no choice: he'd have to drive.

And it meant he'd have to let Sam down.

He swiftly typed a text while he hurried back to his flat.

Dad collapsed and is in hospital. Trains all cancelled so have to drive. Sorry can't make presentation. Will ring when I get to Rome. Sorry to let you down, but you'll be fabulous. xx.

He slid the phone into his pocket, ran the rest of the way to his flat, grabbed his car keys and headed for Rome.

When Sam got out of the shower, she saw the notification on her phone screen. She flicked into the message and scanned it. Oh, no. Angelo must be frantic. She typed back.

Take care. Hope your dad is holding his own. Let me know if I can do anything. Don't worry about anything here. xx.

She finished getting ready, then went to see Ric in his office. 'Angelo can't be here for the presentation,' she said, 'so can you help with any questions if I get stuck, please?'

'Of course,' Ric said. 'You look worried, Sam. What's happened?'

'Angelo's dad has been taken to hospital, so Angelo's had to go to Rome,' she said. 'I'm assuming he'll call you as soon as he knows what the situation is.'

'I'll arrange cover for him in the meantime, so at least he doesn't have to worry about making it back to the ward by tomorrow,' Ric said. 'I'll message him now, while you're checking through your slides. If there's anything you need, come and get me.'

'Thank you.'

Sam uploaded her files and ran through the presentation swiftly, double-checking that everything worked; then she slipped out into the corridor to check her phone. There were no updates from Angelo, so she sent him a text.

Phone on silent. Thinking of you. Doing presentation now. xx.

When she went back into the lecture hall, it had filled up. Ric came on stage to introduce her; she took a deep breath, reminded herself that she knew her stuff and she had support if her language skills let her down, smiled, and went through the presentation.

At the end, she brought up the photograph she'd taken of the Bianchis and the triplets. 'The very first case I told you about—the mum with triplets and twin-to-twin transfusion syndrome—made it to thirty-three weeks, and she came in today for an elective section. I'm pleased to say that all the babies are doing well in neonatal special care, and I'd like to introduce you to Tommaso, Angelo and Samuele Bianchi.'

Everyone applauded, and then it was time for the questions and answers.

As soon as she could excuse herself from the drinks reception, she checked her phone. There was still nothing from Angelo. Maybe he'd been stuck in traffic—or maybe things were really serious with his dad. She didn't want to call him, in case he was still driving or talking to a medic about his dad's condition, but at the same time she didn't want him to feel abandoned. She texted him.

Presentation went well. Hope your dad's doing OK. Call me if you need anything, even if it's stupid o'clock. Love you. xx.

Ruggiero was sitting up in bed when Angelo walked in.

'Dad!' Angelo hugged him. 'I'm so glad to see you like this. I drove here, expecting you to be flat on your back, on oxygen or worse.'

'Sorry for worrying you.' Ruggiero looked sheepish. 'Sal should've called you back and told you I was fine and not to come.'

'You're *not* fine, Dad. Sal said you'd collapsed and you'd been taken to hospital. Even if he'd called me again, of course I'd be here to see you for myself.' Angelo hugged him again. 'What happened?'

'I slipped on the stairs, and it set my back off. I was going to take ibuprofen to try and calm it down enough so I could get to see my doctor. Except there was a bottle of codeine at the back of the drawer and...' Ruggiero shook his head. 'I'm sorry. I only took one. I was on my way to see my doctor. Obviously my blood pressure must've dropped a bit, thanks to the codeine, because the next thing I knew I was in an ambulance and the paramedics had called Sal.'

'Oh, Dad.' Angelo wasn't sure whether to be more worried or angry.

'I made a mistake. I won't make another,' Ruggiero said firmly. 'I'm going to take the rest of the codeine to the pharmacy to get it disposed of safely—or I'll give it to you, if you feel you can't trust me.'

'We'll sort it out,' Angelo said. 'Now I know you're OK, I'm going to talk to your doctor.'

The doctor confirmed that they'd run tests to check there wasn't something more sinister causing Ruggiero's collapse; his blood pressure was back to normal, and they were happy to send him home.

Relieved, Angelo went into the corridor so he could call Sam. He saw her messages and his heart squeezed;

typical Sam to be warm and concerned, even though he'd let her down. And that 'love you' made him stop feeling so miserable and hollow.

And it was good to know that the presentation had gone exactly as he'd expected. Hopefully the board liked Sam enough to agree to the proposals the two of them had put together over the last week, in consultation with Sam's boss and his own.

He called her. 'Hey. So you were a superstar, then?'

'I was just myself,' she said, 'but it seemed to go down well with the board. More importantly, how's your dad?'

He filled her in on what had happened. 'He's well enough now to be discharged, but I want to stay in Rome for a few days, just to keep an eye on him.'

'Absolutely.' She paused. 'Angelo, I probably shouldn't have this conversation with you by phone, but I've been thinking about it all evening. I know we had plans, but right now they're not going to work. We can't spend half our time in Italy and half our time in England, because you'll be too far from your dad if anything happens. He needs you and you can't leave him.'

Angelo went cold. Please don't let her be breaking up with him, in a horrible echo of what had happened last time; then, he'd been the one to walk away, but now it seemed that she was the one walking away. He leaned against the wall, not quite trusting his legs to hold him up. 'What are you saying?'

'I'm saying,' she said gently, 'that we need to put *us* on hold. Not for always, but for now. Right at the moment, your dad needs you and I'm only going to distract you. So I'm going back to London.'

No. *No.* This wasn't what he wanted. At all. He dragged in a breath. 'You're walking out on me?'

'No. I'm giving you space to help your dad sort things

out,' she said. 'Remember, I've been there with Dommy. Several times. It's hard when you're helping someone through a relapse. You don't need someone else demanding your attention when you have to concentrate.'

Angelo disagreed. He needed *her*. But she sounded implacable. How was he going to get her to change her mind, if they weren't even going to be in the same country?

'Sam, please don't go back to London before I'm back in Florence. At least let me see you before you go,' he said.

'There's no time. My flight's tomorrow,' she said. 'You know I was always going back to London tomorrow. Just... I'll be staying there for a bit longer than we'd planned.'

How much longer? For good? He couldn't bring himself to ask that.

'We'll find our way back to each other, if it's meant to be.'

This definitely sounded as if she was bailing out on him. Trying to let him down gently.

He needed to be with his dad, but he also needed to be with Sam. And he couldn't split himself into two. There had to be a way round this. There just had to be.

'Sam. I love you,' he said, desperately wanting her to know that he didn't want to break up with her. 'I want to be with you.'

'I love you, too,' she said. 'That's not in doubt, Angelo. I promise.'

'Then don't give up on us,' he begged. 'Please.'

'I'm not giving up on us. I'm giving you *space*,' she said.

He didn't want space. Not when he'd found her again. But arguing with her on the phone wasn't going to solve this; all it would do was make both of them miserable. 'I'll find a way round all this,' he said. 'Just don't give up on me. I'll find a way.'

When he ended the call, it felt as if all the weight of the world sat on his shoulders.

He went back to the ward, where his dad sat waiting on the bed, fully dressed and ready to go.

'You look as if the bottom's just fallen out of your world,' Ruggiero said.

He could be brave about it, or he could tell the truth. 'It has.'

Ruggiero frowned. 'What's happened?'

'Sam's going back to London. Without me.'

Ruggiero looked shocked. 'Without you? Why?'

Because you need me and I can't split myself in two.

But Angelo couldn't bring himself to hurt his father by saying it so bluntly.

Or maybe it showed on his face, because his father winced. 'Is this because of me ending up in hospital today?'

'No,' he fibbed.

'Angelo.' Ruggiero frowned. 'Be honest with me.'

Angelo raked a hand through his hair. 'All right, then. Yes. Sam and I thought we'd worked out a compromise— that we'd spend half our time in Italy and half our time in England. Our hospitals are twinned, so we could've worked together. We'd got agreement in principle from our bosses, and she was going back to London to work out the details. But what happened today made her realise I can't live in London even part-time, Dad.' Sam had been right about that much. 'It's just too far away from you.'

'I can *manage*,' Ruggiero said. 'This was a minor hiccup.'

'I know you can manage, Dad. I'm not saying you're

too weak to fight the addiction. But there are a whole host of other things that could happen,' Angelo pointed out. 'You might slip on some ice and break your hip. Or you might get pneumonia during the winter. Something that means I'd want to be there to look after you. I need to be near you. Which means I need to be in Italy, not London.'

'I can manage,' Ruggiero repeated stubbornly. 'Don't sacrifice your life for me.'

'You might be able to manage with me being hundreds of miles away,' Angelo said, 'but I can't. You're my dad. My closest family. If I go back to London, I'll worry myself sick about you every single day. Which is nothing to do with the codeine,' he added swiftly, before his father raised that particular objection, 'and everything to do with the fact you're getting older. And if Sam and I are lucky enough to have children, I want them growing up seeing a lot of their *nonno*. I can't do that if you're in another country. The alternative is that Sam has to give up everything she worked for in London—her promotion and the research project she really wanted to do— and stay apart from her family. It's not fair to ask her to do that. I mean, I know she'd do it, if I asked her, but I'm scared that years down the line she'll regret it and she'll regret me.'

'She might not,' Ruggiero said. 'If she loves you and wants to be with you, that's the most important thing.'

'Mum moved to Italy for you,' Angelo said. 'Tell me honestly—did she ever wish she hadn't?'

'No. Even when she was ill. She wanted to be here, with me,' Ruggiero said.

'Would you have moved to London for her?'

'She never asked me,' Ruggiero said.

'That isn't what I asked you, Dad.' Angelo regarded his

father. 'Hypothetically and honestly. If Mum had asked you to move to London for her, would you have done it?'

Ruggiero was silent, clearly considering it. In the end, he sighed. 'Yes. I love Rome—but I loved her more.'

'Then I'm going to ask something of you, something that's difficult because I know how you feel about Rome,' Angelo said quietly. 'I want to be with Sam. Her life's in London. But I don't want to leave you. London's too far—even Florence is too far, if we're being honest about it. I need to find a compromise, something that will work for everyone.' He paused. 'So would you consider moving to Florence?'

'Moving from Rome.' Ruggiero looked thunderstruck.

'Living near us,' Angelo qualified. 'I don't want to take away any of your independence, so I'm not insisting that you live with us. But if you had your own place near us, so if you needed us we could be there in ten minutes—would that work for you?'

Ruggiero blew out a breath. 'Your mum's in Rome.'

'Mum,' Angelo corrected, 'is in your heart, and mine. She'll be with you whether you're in Rome or Florence.' He took a chance. 'Or London.'

'London,' Ruggiero repeated.

'The way I see it,' Angelo continued, happy to leave the seed of the idea of moving to London in his father's head, 'her grave's a place to take flowers, but Mum's with me every day, because I'm part of her—just as I'm part of you.' He took his father's hand. 'I know I'm asking you to uproot your life for me, and it's a huge thing to ask you. But the only way this is going to work for all of us is if we're a family. Together.'

'Have you discussed this with Sam?'

'No,' Angelo admitted. 'But I know Sam. If it works for me, it'll work for her.'

'We might not even like each other, when we finally meet,' Ruggiero warned.

Angelo grinned. 'More like the pair of you will gang up on me. Just think about it, Dad. Or help me find a solution that works for everyone.'

Ruggiero hugged him. 'You're the best son I could wish for. And I know you're trying to balance this so everyone wins. Let me sleep on it. I need to come to terms with things, my way.'

'I'll wait until you're ready,' Angelo said. 'For now, let's go home.'

The next morning, Ruggiero was already making coffee when Angelo came downstairs.

'I was born in Rome, and I planned to spend my life in Rome and be buried in Rome,' he said, and put a mug of coffee in front of his son. 'But if moving to Florence—or London—means that you have the kind of love with Sam that I had with your mother, then I'll move.' He patted Angelo's shoulder. 'As you said last night, you're part of me and you're part of your mother. And I like the idea of seeing my grandchildren grow up instead of relying on video calls.' He paused. 'I've been thinking about it. It's not fair to make Sam's parents be the ones who have to travel to Italy every time they want to see the grandchildren. And I have your mother's family in England, as well as you.'

This was more than he could've hoped for. 'You'd move to England?'

'If your mother had asked me,' Ruggiero said, 'I would have moved for her. And you, as you so eloquently told me last night, are half your mother. If London works for you, then I'll live in London.'

Angelo could hardly breathe. 'You'll live in London.'

'You asked me to help you find a solution that works for everyone. This is it. In London, Sam gets her promotion and her research project. You have the love of your life and a job that makes you happy. And I…maybe for me it's a clean slate. A place to make new memories,' Ruggiero said.

'Oh, Dad.' Angelo hugged him. 'I can't believe you'd do this for me.'

'For all of us,' Ruggiero said. 'As long as Baffi comes, too.'

'I'll take you to visit him every day in quarantine,' Angelo promised.

'He won't need to be quarantined. He's microchipped and vaccinated,' Ruggiero said. 'I just need to sort out a pet passport. When does Sam's plane leave?'

'Lunchtime.'

'Better hope you don't get stuck in a traffic jam. I added cold water to your coffee, so drink it down and go get your girl.' Ruggiero handed Angelo a couple of cereal bars. 'Normally I would say you should have a proper breakfast, but you can eat this on the way. Now *go*.'

'I love you, Dad,' Angelo said. 'Thank you.'

He called Sam from the car, but her phone went through to voicemail. Maybe she was in the shower, or she was on the train in an area where the signal was spotty. 'I love you,' he said. 'I've talked to Dad, and I'm pretty sure we have a workable Plan B.' A perfect Plan B. 'I'm on my way to Pisa airport. Meet me by the baggage check-in.'

The journey seemed to take for ever. And when he ended up stuck in a traffic jam, he felt as if he was going to explode. Of all the days to be stuck in traffic, this was the worst. Sam still wasn't answering her phone. 'I'm definitely on my way,' he said. 'Don't set foot on that plane until you see me. Please.'

Finally he managed to park, and he ran all the way to the check-in desk.

Sam was there, glancing at her watch as if worried that she'd either miss him or miss her plane.

And suddenly the world felt back in balance: because she was here, right by his side.

He picked her up, swung her round and kissed her.

'That's not goodbye,' he said. 'It's *arrivederci*. And there's a difference.'

'I know. And I'm not bailing out on you,' she said. 'I'm just giving you space, until you've sorted things out with your dad. How is he?'

'A lot better than yesterday. Well enough to talk about Plan B,' he said. 'Plan A was juggling Florence, Rome and London. It didn't work. But Plan B does.'

'And Plan B is…?'

He grinned. 'London.'

'But how? You can't leave your dad.'

'I'm not leaving him. He's coming with us,' Angelo said. 'He'll live far enough away from us to have his independence, but near enough so I'm not worried about him all the time.'

She frowned. 'I thought you said your dad would never leave Rome?'

'We talked last night, more honestly than we ever have,' Angelo said. 'I asked him to help me find a solution that works for everyone.' He paused and wrinkled his nose. 'I might have promised him grandchildren. Which I know I should've talked to you about first, so I apologise.'

'You're safe. We're still on the same page,' she said. 'But are you sure about this?'

'Always,' he said. 'Where you are—that's where I

want to be. London works for all of us. I can get a job, you get your research project and your promotion, and we'll need to juggle a few lists while we work out where we're going to live and where we're going to get married.'

She coughed. 'Did I just hear the M word?'

He looked at her. 'Ah. I missed a step. Rewind.' He dropped to one knee, took her left hand and drew it to his lips. 'Ignore the fact we're in an airport. We're in some gorgeous gard—'

'It doesn't matter where we are,' she cut in. 'Just as long as we're together.'

He grinned. 'Samantha Clarke. You're the love of my life, and we've already wasted two years. So let's cut to the chase. Will you marry me, have babies with me and grow old with me?'

Sam smiled. 'Yes.'

EPILOGUE

Two years later.

ANGELO STOOD WITH his arms round Sam's waist, looking through the kitchen window to their garden in Muswell Hill. 'It doesn't get better that this,' he said. 'The perfect summer Sunday afternoon. My dad and yours manning the barbecue, your mum and Louisa making a fuss of the baby, Nina with Lily resting against Bump and Joe reading her a story—just like I hope we'll do, in a couple more years—and...' He spun her round and kissed her. 'And my chance to have five minutes on my own with you.'

She kissed him back. 'We're supposed to be getting the salads and another bottle of wine, Dr Brunelli.'

'It's not as if salad's going to burn,' he pointed out with a grin. 'Are you sure you're ready to go back to work tomorrow?'

'Yes. It's the best of both worlds: three days a week, so I'll still get to see plenty of Dommy.' They'd named Dominic Michael Ruggiero after both their fathers and her brother, reducing all their parents to happy tears. 'Though, after six months of maternity leave, I'm really missing the cutting edge of foetal surgery.'

'That pun is laser-like in its intensity,' Angelo deadpanned.

She leaned her forehead against hers. 'Poor Dommy. He's going to grow up hearing terrible puns from both parents, his godmother and all three grandparents.'

'All four,' he corrected. 'You didn't hear this from me, but Dad's planning to propose to Louisa tonight, and I'm pretty sure she's going to say yes.'

Ruggiero had met Louisa when he'd joined a group of volunteers to help set up a sensory garden, shortly after he'd moved to Muswell Hill, and their friendship had turned to dating, the previous summer.

'Oh, that's wonderful. She's lovely,' Sam said. 'And I think they'll be really happy together.'

'He's been worried about it,' Angelo said. 'That I'd think he was replacing Mum. Of course he isn't. He's just opening his heart a bit more. And I want him to be happy, not lonely.'

'I'm glad,' she said. 'And you don't regret leaving Italy?'

'Nope. Home's where you are,' he said. 'But I'm glad you came to Florence. That we got our second chance.'

She kissed him again. 'Me, too. I love you, Cherub.'

He groaned. 'You do know, since you let that slip, everyone seems to have made it a mission to buy me everything cherub-related?'

'Even down to the wrapping paper.' She laughed. 'At least you'll always know which mug is yours in the staff room at work.'

'And which desk,' he said wryly. 'The one with the paperweight, the drinks coaster, the card, the calendar and—' he rolled his eyes '—the bunting.'

'I dare not tell you what your dad's found for your birthday,' she said, her eyes glinting with mischief.

He groaned. 'I dread to think.'

'You'll love it,' she said with a grin.

'I love you. And Dommy. And our family. And our life,' Angelo said, and kissed her again.

* * * * *

THE VET'S
UNEXPECTED
HOUSEGUEST

JULIETTE HYLAND

MILLS & BOON

For Betsy.

I have written multiple draft dedications
looking for a way to say thanks
for the years of mentorship and friendship.

A few lines aren't enough, but thank you.

CHAPTER ONE

THE RHODES ANIMAL SERVICES sign swung in the wind as Dr. August Rhodes stepped from his beat-up truck. Either the paint he'd used as a teenager had remarkable staying power, or someone had made sure that the navy blue color his father enjoyed never faded. Probably the latter.

Dr. Jeffrey Rhodes set high standards for his clinic, and for his son. And when those standards weren't met, well, the wall of silence the man could build was impenetrable. The half a dozen sentences his dad had uttered today were the most he'd said since the day of August's high school graduation.

That explosion had been epic.

He still wasn't sure how his father could've been surprised by the fact that he wasn't one of the top students. But he'd graduated, a feat that even August hadn't been certain he could pull off when he saw his English score at the midterm.

Dr. Jeff's only concern was his vet clinic and his reputation as the best vet in town. And August had not been the best at anything. Hadn't even tried to meet the standards his father set. An unforgivable sin.

Still, he'd excelled at the local community college before transferring to the state school. To his surprise, he'd loved biology and animal husbandry. So, he'd applied to veterinarian school and been stunned when the acceptance letter arrived. The four years had flown, and he'd loved every minute.

August had hoped his new devotion to the career his father loved would change their relationship. He'd sent his dad an invitation to his vet school graduation. The olive branch had gone unanswered.

He'd sworn that day that he'd never try to prove anything to his father or anyone else. You could take him or leave him, but he was enough, just as he was.

So what am I doing here now?

The question had rattled around his brain as he'd hit the Tennessee state line. He'd almost turned the truck around several times, but he'd already finished his relief contract with the Stonybrook Veterinary Clinic. The small Arizona clinic had been a nice change after the cold of Alaska. When they'd begged him to stay on, to consider joining the practice as a partner, he'd considered it.

Then the wandering nature he'd inherited from his mother kicked in. His need to be somewhere else, anywhere else called to him. So, he'd said no, made his goodbyes and hit the road.

Maybe he wasn't meant to find roots. But he had a career he loved. As a relief vet, he made his own schedule, worked where he wanted, when he wanted.

And most importantly, August Rhodes was not his father. Clinics and the clients they served made him smile and brought him joy. But he refused to let his life revolve around one. Refused to push away the ones he loved for a practice. He was already more like the man who'd barely raised him than he was comfortable with.

Yet, here I am. If Dad got a call about me being in the hospital at three in the morning, would he have come to my aid?

August didn't want to consider that question too closely. He'd answered the call. That was what was important. The nurse had said his father had been injured in a car accident, that he'd be spending weeks in the hospital followed by at least a few weeks in a rehab facility. Then she'd asked him when he could be in Foxfield.

Bitterness had reared its ugly head as he almost told her never, but since he suspected that was the answer his father would give in this situation, August found himself saying two days.

Once he'd uttered the words, he'd felt honor bound to see them through. Just to prove that he wasn't like the man who'd sired him. The man who pushed away everyone he loved with impossible standards.

He'd stopped at the hospital first, another chore he probably should have left to later. But the small boy in him that cried out for his father's affection had never completely gone away. Though August swore that today was the last time that piece of his soul got a say in his decisions.

His father had looked tired, and so much older than he'd imagined. His tongue had been just as direct though. No words of affection after their long estrangement. No sorrys or regrets.

Nope, just orders about the clinic. His father claimed that the vet he'd hired a few years ago wasn't able to handle the load on their own. That he was worried about the vet.

Worried. That word hung in August's mind. His father didn't worry about people, only animals. Before he could ask more, his father had said he didn't want the animals to suffer. And he was concerned if the vet couldn't handle it, that it would hurt the clinic's reputation. And just like that the man he knew was back.

More concerned about the clinic than people. Still, with a list of faults that could stretch a mile, his father truly cared about animals.

It was the one quality August was proud to share with the crotchety doctor he was forced to admit he was related to. That was why he was standing in front of the place he'd sworn he'd never set foot in again.

Animals couldn't complain about what was bothering them, and for most owners they were part of the family. They deserved the best care, and if his father wasn't here to handle it, helping out for a few days, a week at the most, at least until he had a better plan was good start.

But all those thoughts didn't keep the keys his father pressed into his palm, after August had said he needed to find a hotel room, from burning. Nor did they stop the urge to simply walk away.

He didn't owe the man anything.

Flipping the keys over, he took a deep breath. He was already here. He looked at the keys, the first was to the clinic, and the second was to the small house his father maintained behind it. A rental that his father was constantly looking for new tenants for. Ones that would live up to the high standards he expected…demanded.

He tried not to let it hurt that his father had offered him a room there rather than his old bed at home. Not that he wanted to return home. And the rental was a huge improvement over a hotel… Still, being asked if he wanted to stay at home would have been nice.

He threw that thought away as he tried to push the emotions he'd kept behind walls in his heart back in their place. He was here for the animals, nothing more.

Focus, August.

The clinic had closed hours ago. He yawned. He should just head to the rental, crawl into bed and check the place out tomorrow. But August wanted to get a look at the clinic, reorient himself to it. Even though the clinic probably looked the same as it had when he left.

Dr. Jeff was set in his ways. Stubborn, unchanging…

When August had mentioned painting the waiting area to something besides the sallow yellow his mother had thrown on the walls when she was still speaking to his father, his dad had said that there was no need to change anything. That his clients came to him because he was the best vet for fifty miles. At that time he'd also been the only vet, but August had known well enough to keep that thought to himself.

"Standing in the parking lot, looking at the front door isn't going to get you a hot shower and a soft bed, August." When chiding himself didn't make his feet start moving, he pulled a hand across his face.

It was less than five hundred steps from the parking lot to the front of the clinic. It should not be this hard to cross the threshold.

Rolling his head, he stretched. Then August grabbed his beaten-up duffel bag from the truck cab and forced himself to step away from the truck.

Here goes nothing.

The door to the clinic swung open, and August reached for the light switch, prepared to step back into his past.

Except…

The front looked completely different. The waiting room was painted a light blue, there were pictures of animals doing silly poses and a wall listing valuable information for pet parents.

Pet parents…

August could not imagine his father using that phrase. The room was welcoming, inviting, almost soothing. And he was stunned by how much it sucked that it wasn't the same. That his father had waited until he left to finally make some changes to the old place.

Without him.

Maybe the vet hospital on the edge of town was costing his father business? It had certainly looked impressive when he drove past it. August had worked in a few fancy locations. In his experience, the corporate vet sites cared more about the bottom line and getting the most money for each procedure than about their patients. But that didn't stop a lot of people from taking their pets to the seemingly upscale locations.

The exam rooms here were clean and brightly colored with more happy pictures plastered on the wall. Either his father had hired a designer, or the man had had a distinct personality shift in the last fifteen years. Likely the former, since he'd shown no hint of any change in the short time he'd spent barking orders at August from his hospital bed.

Overall, there was no hint of the disorder his father had told him to expect. No indication that the other veterinarian was having issues. But looks could be deceiving.

His eyes wandered the walls again and stopped on the award shelf. That hadn't changed. His stomach flipped as he saw the framed certificates and handful of plaques. A reminder that his father excelled at things…and August didn't.

At least not in ways that put your name on fancy plaques and trophies. He swallowed the feelings building in him. He was not traveling that well-worn path tonight.

Flipping the keys in his fingers, August walked to the back door of the clinic and looked at the small house where his father had said he could stay. The front bushes were overgrown, and the flower gardens looked like they'd been haphazardly weeded. But it was a place to stay for the short time he was here.

His father had said that the house was stocked, and at least he knew August would be close by in case the clinic needed anything. He'd not asked after August's desires, or if he wanted to stay at home, just handed him the key for the house and returned his worries to the clinic.

That shouldn't have been surprising. And it shouldn't have hurt. But that didn't stop the ache in his chest as he looked over his shoulder at the clinic. If it magically evaporated, August wouldn't mourn its disappearance.

Rhodes Animal Services was Dr. Jeff's obsession. A truth his mother learned when she packed her bags and told him he had a choice, he could hire more vets to help him out and cut back on his hours or he could lose her.

He hadn't even paused when he'd said he wasn't hiring anyone to help at his clinic, and if she wanted to go, then she was free to leave.

To this day, August wasn't sure if he'd been calling her bluff. They'd never divorced, and his mother loved his father to the day she died, but they never slept under the same roof again.

August swallowed as he tried to pull the vision of his mother's face forward. It had faded over the years, but the memories of their trips together were still crisp. His mother had wanted adventure and she'd gotten tired of waiting for her husband to join her.

So she'd taken August with her. To Boston, England, South Africa, Alaska. Sometimes she'd throw a dart and just visit the city. It had been heaven.

Until an ice storm stole her away. And overnight he was left with the man who always saw him as an under-achieving burden.

He let out a sigh and started up the steps to the house.

This was why he'd never returned to Foxfield. He'd always feared it would bring back too many memories, and he hadn't been wrong.

He'd stay a few days. A week at the most. He mentally circled the date in his mind. A target he could focus on.

He had a few connections with relief vets who might want to do a short rotation in Tennessee. And he'd gently bring up the game plan in case his father wasn't able to return to full-time work.

Whoever the other vet was they were either a saint or another type A jerk who meshed well with his father to have stayed on for several years. The longest he'd seen another partner hang on was eight months.

But that was tomorrow's problem. Tonight he wanted a hot shower, a soft bed and at least eight hours of uninterrupted worries behind shut eyelids.

The front foyer was inviting as he stepped inside. Another shock to add to the growing list. An empty shoe rack sat by the door and more of the blue paint he'd seen in the waiting room covered the walls. The living room was stocked with comfy looking but well-used furniture and more than a few knickknacks littered the mantel. The look was cute, almost like the cottages and apartments he saw listed for weekend rentals online.

He stepped into the kitchen and smiled. The little table and the flower wallpaper just felt like a home. A ridiculous feeling given that he was staying in his father's rental house instead of his actual childhood home, but the feeling persisted.

The kettle on the stove let out a hiss, and August jumped. A kettle in an empty rental shouldn't have hot water.

"What the hell are you doing in my house?"

August turned as the words hit his back, dropped his

duffel bag and raised his arms as he stared at the beautiful brunette, with fire dancing in her eyes, who seemed more than willing to use the baseball bat held high over her head.

Dr. Kit Bedrick held the baseball bat above her head and prayed that despite being barely over five feet tall, she looked frightening to the far too handsome giant standing in front of her hot kettle. If she'd remembered to plug her cell in during her day at the clinic, she could have called for help. But no, she'd been too busy to pay attention to the draining battery. And Dr. Jeff had pulled the landline out of this rental a year before she signed the lease.

She'd considered running out the front door, but Bucky's leash was in the kitchen. There was no way she was leaving her one-year-old pit bull cross in the house with a stranger. And she'd been too busy at the clinic to train him to stay by her side outside without a leash.

The first thing he tried to do when he got outside was chase a squirrel. And she was far too exhausted to run after him tonight.

Another mark to add to the ever-growing list of to-do items that never quite got done.

"I said—" she waved the bat, mostly to hide the fact that her arms were starting to shake "—what are you doing in my house!"

As if this episode couldn't get more ridiculous, Bucky bounded to her side, finally awake from his nap. He waited a moment for Kit to pat his head, but when she didn't lower the bat, he moseyed over to the intruder's side.

Then the dog rolled over at his feet and smiled. She loved watching Bucky smile, it always warmed her heart, except he was at the feet of a stranger—granted one who looked as stunned to be found in her kitchen as she was at finding him.

"Some guard dog you are." She glared at the intruder, hoping that the raised hands meant that he wasn't intending harm to her or her dog.

"Kit—"

Her name coming from the hunk's mouth almost made her lower the bat. Foxfield had grown sizably in the last two decades, but there were plenty of ways for the Adonis standing in her kitchen to know her name.

But that did not mean he should be in her kitchen!

"Answer the question! What are you doing here?" She heard the terror rising in her throat. The kettle continued to squeal, and her heart jumped. "Bucky, come here!"

The dog wagged his tail and looked at her but didn't move from the intruder's feet. *Seriously!* She needed to find more hours in the day to focus on his training. He was a perfect angel in the clinic, but at home, he reverted to a mischievous devil.

"My dad gave me the key, and I suppose he forgot to mention he had rented the place out to you. Oh, God, did he sell it to you and…?" Crimson climbed his neck as he looked at her.

"August?" Kit blinked as the words he said rattled around her brain. *No.* There was no way that the man standing in her kitchen was the rebel who'd left Foxfield, determined never to return. Though whom else would Dr. Jeff have given his key to? "August Rhodes?"

"Yep. I swear, I didn't know the house was rented. My father…" He pulled his hand across his neck, then looked at the ceiling. "You'd think he'd have at least mentioned it."

Except it didn't surprise her that Dr. Jeff hadn't mentioned it. If it didn't revolve around the clinic, it barely registered on the man's radar. Though even if he had tried to call, her phone was dead.

But the fact that the rebel son of the local vet had finally found his way home stole all the words from her brain. They'd graduated high school in the same year, though they'd not shared a friendship group. Kit had hung with the kids mostly labeled nerds and overachievers. August… Well August's friends had been the exact opposite.

Had Dr. Jeff finally called him?

He'd never said it out loud, but Kit knew he missed his son. There was a picture of him in the desk draw, the edges of it worn.

"Any chance I can lower my arms and pet the handsome Bucky at my feet?" August's lips tipped up and the deep dimples that had made more than a few of the girls in their high school go weak appeared. God, the man really had gotten better with age.

But that did not excuse him barging into her house.

Unintentionally, Kit.

She could get mad at Dr. Jeff. But what good would that do now? Besides, if she were honest, she wasn't surprised that Dr. Jeff would give him the key to his rental rather than his home.

The man was a grump, but she knew it was loneliness speaking. A loneliness he did not seem interested in addressing. The few women who'd worked up the courage to ask him out were turned down quickly. He gave everything to his clinic. And despite lamenting the changes she'd made to it and complaining that none of it was necessary, he'd let her update things.

The more welcoming environment had not changed the acerbic vet's nature, with anyone, but he listened when she offered suggestions. And he'd started talking about retiring. *Finally.*

If she could just hold on for another year or so, Kit was certain she could convince him to sell the place to her. Then she had a real shot at taking on the Love Pets Vet across town.

Love Pets Vet had been *her* dream, once. She and her husband, Leo, had cut the ribbon with giant scissors provided by the local Chamber of Commerce. It was their place, their dream.

But sometimes life forced your dreams to change.

Now she was determined to make Rhodes Animal Services the best in town. If she could just win the Foxfield Finest Award, she'd be able to say it was the top clinic.

It was a silly local award with multiple categories with everything from Best Bakery to Best Mechanic. Local shops put the sticker on their door and merchandise. And Rhodes Animal Services hadn't won since she started working there. A fact that Dr. Jeff bemoaned when the awards were announced. Her mother's boutique won it each year too…something the woman never let Kit forget.

Love Pets Vet always came out on top. A fact her ex-mother-in-law called to gloat about every year. Never mind that they sent out email reminders and offered free cookies in office if their clients voted with their mobile phones right at the counter. Maybe the game was rigged, but Kit knew if she worked hard enough, it could be hers.

And then, perhaps, her former in-laws would know they'd made a mistake forcing her out after Leo died. At the very least she'd earn the award her mother coveted. Finally a first place for the perpetually second-place Kit.

But she needed to stay on Dr. Jeff's good side to do that.

She looked at August, her mouth watering as she looked from his chiseled jawline to the jeans hugging his body just right. He didn't seem like much of a threat to her.

"Fine. But don't move other than to pet Bucky." She lowered the bat as August lowered his hands. Her arms shook as she leaned the bat against the wall. Maybe in the imaginary hours she was compiling on her to-do list she should add strength training?

"Who's a good boy?" August's baby voice echoed in the kitchen as he bent and rubbed Bucky's belly.

Despite the trauma of finding him in her kitchen, her frustration at Dr. Jeff for causing the situation and the exhaustion pulling at her, Kit's heart melted a little. Tough-looking men with hearts for animals were her weak spot. And with a tattoo sleeve on his left arm, scruffy beard and loose T-shirt, August looked like the exact opposite of a man who would make the baby noises as he rubbed her dog's belly.

Bucky was a lost cause. He'd follow August anywhere now. But Kit wasn't that easy to sway. Her heart had stopped racing when her husband passed almost ten years ago. Now her focus was the clinic and the dog currently showing a preference for an intruder over her. Though that didn't mean she couldn't admire the man's beauty.

"Why did your father give you a key to my place?"

August shrugged as he continued to pet Bucky's belly. "If I had an answer to that question, I wouldn't have caused this scene. Want me to get the kettle off the stove before it runs dry?"

"Yes." Kit sighed as she looked at August. Maybe it was a mistake, but he didn't look like the rebel that had done the exact opposite of everything his father had demanded. The fight they'd had in the high school parking lot one morning because August had walked out of the house in torn jeans had been the talk of the school for days. Particularly when August had shown up with torn pants for the rest of the week.

He'd been the bane of many of the teachers' existence. August might have skipped more classes than he attended in high school, but their twenty-year reunion was next year. She wasn't the same person she'd been at eighteen, and she doubted August was either.

August lifted the kettle and pointed to the mug she'd set out. When she nodded, he poured water over the tea bag. "I am sorry, Kit. My dad said I could crash here in the spare room. Now that I think about it, him saying spare room should have sent warning signals dancing across my brain. But it's taken me two days of driving to get here from Arizona."

The spare room? She'd forgotten that clause in the rental agreement, one she wasn't sure was completely legal, but since Dr. Jeff had never exercised the option, she'd assumed he wouldn't. Which was her mistake.

She took the mug he offered and moved to the table. "There is a spare room that the lease says I have to let your father rent out, if necessary, but I figured he'd at least talk to me about it."

An uncomfortable laugh escaped her lips as the words left her mouth, "But it's not surprising he didn't give me a warning."

"I'm not staying long," August said as he slid into the chair across from her. "If you don't mind me staying tonight, I'll find a motel or something tomorrow."

"No, you can stay. The room is at the end of the upstairs hall and has its own bathroom. The sheets and everything are in the closet in there. It just caught me off guard."

The last thing she wanted to do was upset Dr. Jeff. She'd worked for too many years to get on the man's...

Well, he didn't necessarily have a good side, but he was cordial to her. Which was more than he managed with most of his staff.

They had an open account with the temp agency in town to supply a new receptionist when Dr. Jeff's crabbiness inevitably ran theirs off. But the man was going to retire at some point, and the clinic was going to be hers.

Then the few changes she'd managed to accomplish could become major initiatives. That day was close too, she could feel it. If that meant she had to host his son for a few days...

Well, August wasn't hard to look at.

She tilted her eyes to the tea mug in her hands, hating the heat creeping up her neck. It didn't matter that he was attractive. If she'd seen him on a street corner, or anywhere other than standing uninvited in her kitchen, she might have ogled him for just a minute.

But none of that was relevant. She'd been alone forever. He was hot, and these were just random intrusive thoughts as her body dealt with the adrenaline draining from her.

She finally looked up and shrugged. "Seriously, August, it's fine. I don't mind if you stay. Like I said, I technically agreed to it in the lease."

August raised an eyebrow and looked at his duffel bag. "Why don't we play it by ear for a day or so. I'm really not staying long. Just going to check in on the other vet. I guess Dad doesn't think they're able to handle the patient load without him."

That statement didn't surprise her. Dr. Jeff had an inflated sense of self, and he pushed his staff harder than he should. But she'd grown up with a mother who'd demanded perfection too. And her in-laws had taken those demands to the extreme.

Only Leo had loved her for her. Only he had cared about her dreams and the joy they brought rather than the money or prestige they could gather. But he'd been gone for almost ten years. Nine years longer than they'd been married.

Unfortunately August's father's assessment wasn't completely incorrect either. His patient load was less than hers these days but covering both sets of patients wasn't possible long-term.

And the car accident had crushed Dr. Jeff's left leg. Even if he fully recovered, it would be months before he could return to the patient load he'd managed before his accident. Assuming he even wanted to.

And she was struggling to manage her own load, even if she had no plans to admit it. She could do this. She just had to work a little harder. Be a little better tomorrow than she'd been today.

But why would he ask August to check on her?

The man had spent two years at the local community college, then disappeared. To the best of her knowledge, he hadn't returned home since then. Dr. Jeff never talked about him. A vet clinic, even a well-run one, could look chaotic. If he didn't have any experience in the field, he could mistake a normal day for an out-of-control nightmare.

"I'm managing fine, but I appreciate your father's concern." She laid her hand on Bucky's head. Hoping petting her sweet boy would calm the feelings of inadequacies pulsing around her.

She was fine. Fine. She was.

If she repeated the words to herself, could she make them true? It was the mantra she'd used through high school, college and veterinarian school. The trick had worked then, at least mostly. It had worked less often since Leo's death.

But she wasn't going to let her worries overwhelm her. Not tonight, and not in front of August Rhodes.

If he was surprised to realize that she was the vet, August didn't show it. Instead he looked from the dog at her feet to the mug of tea and then to her face. The look he gave her sent heat down her spine. How long had it been since someone looked at her with concern?

She wasn't going to spend time delving into the answer to that sad question.

"Are you okay?" He crossed his arms and leaned back in the chair. "Because even with another clinic in town, I can't imagine Rhodes Animal Services is an easy task for one vet. The place has grown by leaps and bounds since the last time I was here. I swear I barely recognize the city."

"New is relative, if you haven't been in town. Love Pets has been there over a decade." Her hand brushed her neck where the wedding band she'd worn for less than a year hung. Eleven years... The clinic had been there eleven years. Swallowing the emotions clogging her throat, she added, "There is even a new high school across town—it's only four years old."

"Changing subjects?" He raised an eyebrow and leaned closer to her.

Her cheeks heated as she took a sip of tea.

Why is his presence unnerving me?

"Not really. But it's easier to talk about the size of the town than to talk about the odds that your father will look into hiring a temporary replacement. So, I'm all the clinic's got." She raised her chin, daring him to contradict her.

He rubbed his face as he looked at her. "I suspect he

will rebel against that thought, at least until he has a good idea of whether or not he can come back at all."

"And if he doesn't come back—"

"I suspect he'll shut it down, sell the land and move. I can't imagine him being willing to sell it to anyone else. The place is his life. Not sure if he's capable of letting someone else step in," August stated, then he cringed as he looked at her.

Her face must have looked as low as that thought made her feel. "He's talked about letting me buy it." That was mostly true. He'd listened when she'd talked about the option, though he hadn't responded to her query about becoming a partial owner through a partnership.

"My dad really said he'd let you buy it?" His eyes held hers and he cocked his head. It was a motion similar to his dad's, but with more caring in his face. "Kit?"

"He didn't immediately say no." She blew across her tea, even though it didn't need cooling.

August made a noncommittal noise, then sighed as he looked at her with what she feared was pity. "The clinic across town looks like it can take care of the patient load. It certainly looks big enough to handle more than his office."

"Big does not equal qualified." Kit felt her brows furrow at the idea that Rhodes Animal Services would close without Dr. Jeff. She was more than capable of taking it over. Of hiring another vet to help her with the load. Of making sure the town knew that when it came to animals, Dr. Kit Bedrick was the best choice.

This was her home, her brothers and nephews were here. And she couldn't leave Leo. His spirit was gone, but leaving the town where she'd laid him to rest was a step she wasn't willing to take. Kit was staying in

Foxfield. Which meant she needed Dr. Jeff to sell to her...eventually.

August gave her a look that Kit didn't understand. "I bet they'd hire you. It looks to be more state of the art. My father's clinic—"

"Serves the animals just fine. And we have a full surgical suite, multiple specialists on call, an in-house lab and a mobile X-ray machine." She crossed her arms as she moved to stand. There were things she wanted to add, like oncology consults and a part-time radiology tech, when she finally bought the clinic. But even without those things, Rhodes Animal Services was still very capable. "The last thing I need is the prodigal son returning to Foxfield determined to cash in on his father's injury."

That was unfair, she knew it. But if August encouraged his father to sell to someone else, what would she do?

"I don't want a thing from my father."

"If that were true, then you wouldn't be here." August's eyes flashed as the words flew from her lips, but she didn't pull them back. Maybe he didn't want to admit he wanted something from his father, but actions spoke louder than any words.

But then who was she to judge? Her mother lived less than four miles from here, and she saw her on holidays and whenever she felt the need to drop by and lecture Kit on some failure—real or imagined.

Both her brothers were at the top of their career fields, Stephen the chief financial officer of a startup technology company. He had two of the cutest little boys and a lovely wife. And David was the founder of an engineering firm that built artificial intelligence machines.

Even as a successful vet, she was the black sheep of her family. She didn't own her own clinic and rented a house. All the things her mother expected her to have achieved by her mid-thirties were still just out of reach. Heck, she'd even come in last in height. In a family of six-foot giants, she could barely claim five-one.

"How many patients did you see today?" August's question hovered between them as she tried to figure out the shift in his tone. And tried to force the feeling of failure that always seemed to hover at her heels away.

"What?" She hadn't meant to let that question out, but life didn't have a rewind button. Rather than wait for him to ask the same thing again or to figure out that her mind wasn't focused on their conversation, Kit answered, "Almost forty…or maybe a few more. I haven't been able to reschedule all of your father's clients."

"Forty?" August shook his head as he patted Bucky. *Weren't dogs supposed to be loyal?*

She snapped her fingers, trying to get the dog to return to her side, but his ears appeared to be turned off. *Spoiled brat.*

"That isn't sustainable, Kit." He rubbed the bridge of his nose. "I can help for a few days and put out some feelers for relief vets to see if anyone wants to take a short rotation in Foxfield."

"You're a vet?" It was the wrong question. She knew it as soon as the words hit August's ears.

He shifted in his seat, the confident persona slipping for just a minute. "Yep. Guess Dad forgot to mention that when he brought me up."

Dr. Jeff never brought August up. But she wasn't sure hearing that would be helpful in the moment. So instead she pivoted the conversation again. "Do you have any specializations?"

"I have worked all over the place with all sorts of species, but no official specializations outside of dogs, felines and horses. Though in Idaho I helped birth more than a few cows. And of course saw all sorts of lizards and snakes when I lived in Florida." The tips of his lips tilted up.

That was nice. Most vets loved all animals, but reptiles were few vet's favorites. Occasionally one wandered into their clinic but not often. If any needed to be seen while August was in town, she'd happily let him.

"I've worked as a relief vet since I graduated veterinary school. I am certified in a few different states that have reciprocal licensing agreements with Tennessee."

The idea of having a helping hand, at least for a few days, was such a relief she hadn't even considered his license. She needed more rest than she wanted to admit. But there wasn't time. Since it opened, Love Pets Vet had taken nearly an eighth of the patient load from Dr. Jeff, and this was the first year that they were on track to have a net gain of clients. There wasn't time for resting.

"I appreciate you staying a few days, August. And I'll be at the clinic early. Feel free to stop by if you want to settle in."

"Tomorrow morning? It's Saturday. Is the clinic open for a half day?"

"Nope! It's open all day on Saturday. Nine to five. But I work seven days a week. Sundays I don't usually see patients, but paperwork and such…" Kit smiled. She was proud that she managed to keep such a schedule. The clinic and the animals she saw were her life. Though the look passing across August's face did not seem like he thought her schedule was something to be proud of.

Her chest squeezed but she ignored the feeling. It happened anytime she felt like she was disappointing someone. But it didn't matter if August Rhodes was disappointed in her.

He was a temporary vet, the prodigal son of her boss and already plotting his escape from Foxfield. They'd wanted different things in high school, and it was clear that while so much had changed, that hadn't.

Scooting back in his chair, he stood and grabbed his duffel bag. "I see why my father and you have managed to work together for more than a few months. I'll see my father's patients tomorrow. But Sundays are rest days. You can't help your clients if you're burned out."

She barely managed to hold her tongue as she sipped her sleepy-time tea. She wasn't going to argue the merits of her schedule, and she was certain he wouldn't agree.

"I'm going to grab a shower and crash. Been a long day."

"Spare room is at the top of the stairs, last room on the right. The bathroom for that room is attached to it."

August nodded, then took his leave.

She raised the now-cool tea to her lips. The certainty that August's comment regarding the length of the professional relationship she'd maintained with his father was not a compliment rattled around her brain. Her chest clenched again. It shouldn't bother her that the hunky intruder didn't approve. But the tinge of uncertainty pulsing at the back of her brain sent a bead of worry down her spine.

No. What August Rhodes thought of her did not matter! She stood and looked at the small blackboard by the cabinet. *Be the best* was written in pink chalk.

She knew what she wanted in life. What August Rhodes thought was not important.

Period.

CHAPTER TWO

AUGUST SQUEEZED HIS eyes closed, wishing there were a way to fall back to sleep. Not that he'd managed a particularly restful night. He'd spent more than a few restless hours tossing and turning reliving his interactions with Kit.

And the look on her face when she'd said she'd be at the clinic all day today. Most clinics saw a handful of clients on Saturday and were closed on Sunday.

He'd never brag about working seven days a week. Sure, he'd done it on a handful of occasions. But each incident had been in his work as a relief vet when a clinic had been overwhelmed by a natural disaster. It was an emergency situation, not an every-week opportunity. But it shouldn't matter to him that Kit was proud of it.

The overachieving salutatorian of their class had become an overachieving adult. It was textbook. And not his concern.

But there was the hint of something in her eyes. He didn't know her well enough to call it sadness, but she wasn't completely fulfilled. The ways she'd bitten her lip and rocked back in her chair when she was justifying herself. He wasn't even sure she realized it. But she was tired, exhausted and trying to prove herself. To whom he wasn't sure. But that called to him.

I see it in the mirror. Saw it in the mirror.

He mentally corrected himself. He wasn't trying to prove anything now.

His concern was for Kit. He was fine these days. And he'd be even better when he got back on the road. Maybe he'd look for a rotation in Washington. He hadn't been on the west coast in forever.

Life was short. You were only guaranteed one trip on earth. And he planned to spend his time enjoying it, not just working.

Besides his father, he doubted there were many people who would hope they'd spent more time at work when they reached the end of their days.

But maybe if he asked her if she wanted a day off…? Sometimes people just needed to be asked. *No.* He was not going to travel any mental paths related to the cute workaholic he'd be sharing a house with for a few days.

He rolled over and looked at the clock. Seven in the morning. He threw an arm over his eyes before blowing out a breath. Lying in bed wasn't going to accomplish anything.

Not that he needed to accomplish anything in this moment.

Not every second or even every day had to have a to-do list. That was something he'd learned in his father's house. In spite of his father. Today he was helping out at the clinic, that was enough.

Tomorrow maybe he could spend the day exploring the state park. See how many of the hiking trails he remembered from his youth.

Rolling off the bed, he grabbed a T-shirt and pair of cargo pants. His mind would function better after coffee. He tiptoed passed Kit's closed door. Oddly happy to see that it looked like the woman trying to hide her stress last night was sleeping in a little. If he needed to rummage through the cupboards for coffee, he'd make sure he was quiet.

Stepping into the kitchen he saw a mug, French press, coffee grounds and sweetener sitting in the middle of the table. He blinked as he stared at the layout. It was sweet, but a niggle of something he couldn't quite place settled in his stomach.

Had Kit done this last night? She'd looked as tired as he'd felt. But maybe she hadn't wanted to risk him waking her?

He stared at the offering before walking over to the sink. The mug she'd used for tea last night was sitting next to one with a little coffee in the bottom.

How early had she gotten up?

He shook his head as he filled the kettle with water and set it on the stove. Maybe she was just a morning person?

As he waited for the water to heat, he looked around the room. His eyes landed on a chalkboard by the pantry. The words *be the best* were written in bold script.

The kettle squealed, and he grabbed the French press. But his eyes kept wandering back to the chalkboard. *Best.*

It was a word that had haunted his teenage years. A word he now knew was a fiction. Best was a moving target. What was best to one was worst to others. An impossible target. But somehow it didn't surprise him that those words were in Kit's house.

Written as a mantra in the room where she was supposed to find sustenance. His room was sparsely decorated but in the morning light he stepped into the living room. Many of the knickknacks he'd paid little attention to last night now caught his eye.

A group of blocks said *seize the day*. A piece of reclaimed wood hung over the fireplace reminding the room's occupants to *ask if what you are doing today is setting you up for tomorrow's success...*

Sipping the coffee, he stepped onto the front porch looking forward to the morning air. Instead he felt his blood pressure rise further. The lights in the clinic were on. At seven thirty on a Saturday morning?

That was too much. It was one thing to work every day. Another to be at work before the sun had fully risen every day!

Their profession, like many of the healing professions, suffered from higher rates of depression and anxiety than the general population. A healthy balance between work and the clinic was necessary. Without thinking, August started toward the clinic.

He might never be able to convince his father to enjoy a break, but maybe he could talk Kit into enjoying a cup of coffee with him. Anything that made it so she wasn't living at the clinic.

Bucky barked as soon as he opened the door, his tail wagging as he sat on a plush bed with his name inscribed on it. The dog smiled at him but didn't get off the bed.

"Where's your mom, Bucky?" The tail rapped against the bed as he scooted to the edge, careful not to actually leave it. "Good boy." August patted his head, rewarding the dog. Kit must have trained him to stay on the bed when she was here, and he wanted to reinforce that behavior.

"I know, Mrs. Clingman. Bentley is an important part of the family. I understand." Kit's words floated over the desk.

Seriously? There was a client here? Did the woman set no boundaries?

He stood slowly, not wanting to scare Kit or the woman with her.

"Dr. Rhodes, so glad you're here." Kit nodded to him and then to Mrs. Clingman. "Bentley was hit by a car this morning. Can you help me with X-rays, and treatment?"

The woman with her sniffled, her eyes watering as she looked at August.

It was early, on a weekend. Rhodes Animal Services was not an emergency facility and he'd not even managed breakfast, but an animal needed help. "Of course." The words slid from his lips. There was no other choice, but how often did Kit do this?

"Bentley is part of the family." Mrs. Clingman reiterated as August started to follow Kit. "The kids will be devastated… I'll be devastated."

"We'll do everything we can." August tipped his head toward the middle-aged woman. He hadn't seen the dog, had no idea what the prognosis might be.

Dogs hit by cars had a variety of injuries ranging from broken bones to internal bleeding. And there were so many factors that could impact the outcome. What he told her was the only truth he could offer. He and Kit would do their best.

Following Kit into the treatment area, August was stunned to find a giant Saint Bernard panting on the floor. Somehow, he'd pictured finding a small breed or poodle with the name Bentley.

The Saint Bernard lifted his head as they walked in then laid it back down. At least he could still move it.

"How did you get him in here?" The dog had to be at least a hundred and fifty pounds.

"Special hoist your father bought a few years ago. With age, he's not as spry as he once was, though he does his best not to use it."

As if using a tool was somehow bad. He was young and in excellent shape, but he would never attempt to lift an injured Saint Bernard on his own. But there wasn't time for August to dwell on any of the issues his father had.

"What was Mrs. Clingman able to tell you about the crash?" August bent to look at the Saint Bernard's eyes. The dog blinked and his tail lifted a bit. "Don't try to wag your tail, big guy. Not until Dr. Bedrick is sure it's safe."

"Bentley was playing with Piper, their eight-year-old. Her ball rolled into the street, she went after it and Bentley ran after her when the car rounded the corner. Piper is fine. Bentley is here."

"Man, we don't deserve dogs." August rubbed the dog's ears. "You're a legitimate hero, big guy."

Kit handed him a muzzle and he gently placed it over the Saint Bernard's face. Even the gentlest dog could bite or snap when they were injured. And the safety of vets had to be protected too.

"I'm going to grab the X-ray machine. We'll also need to do an ultrasound to see if we can find any internal bleeding. The back leg is definitely broken but if we're lucky, it will be a clean break."

"Let's hope that is the worst of it." August rubbed the dog's ears one more time, then stood and went to the sink. He didn't know his way around the clinic. He'd do more good by staying here and keeping Bentley as calm as possible than he would wandering after Kit or getting in the way.

She was back quickly with the X-ray machine.

"I'll get started on this if you want to grab the ultrasound machine." He saw her hesitate. He'd told her he was a vet. And if he were honest, he was likely more skilled than his father given the wide range of hospitals he'd served in. But she didn't know him, or his skill. Still, even a vet fresh out of school could take X-rays. "So we don't waste any time."

"I want the legs and spine," Kit stated before she headed back out.

"Of course." He'd been a practicing vet for over ten years. But they didn't know each other... Still, he felt the need to prove himself to her.

A need that made him instantly uncomfortable. He'd sworn to himself that he would not seek anyone's approval. He did the work because he wanted to, not to prove anything.

Stuffing the unwelcome emotions down, he focused on the issue at hand. August draped the lead apron over himself, then positioned the X-ray over Bentley. "This will only take a second, buddy." He shot three images of the spine, then repositioned over the back legs. The left one hung to the side. If it wasn't a clean break, he worried they might have to amputate.

But dogs were resilient. They could get by with only three legs easily.

A light knock on the door echoed in the quiet room. "Can I come in?"

"Yes, the machine is off." August waited for her to enter and move behind the machine before he snapped the images of Bentley's legs.

As soon as he finished, Kit stepped up with the ultrasound. Her teeth pulled at her bottom lip as she moved it toward Bentley's middle. And raised a razor to shave the fur so they could get the best reading possible.

An ultrasound was the true test. Bentley could lift his head and wag his tail, so his spine was likely fine. Broken legs and ribs healed. But internal injuries...

It was too early in the morning to be facing this. But life often threw you curves.

"Bentley, you are an important part of your family. Did you know your mom told us that?" August knew the dog didn't know what he was saying, but he needed to keep the dog calm while Kit got the skin ready for the ultrasound. Even with all the pain medicine coursing through him, the Saint Bernard wasn't unconscious.

"Not gonna lie. I'm a bit jealous, big guy. Can you or Dr. Bedrick let me know what it's like for your family to call you important?" He looked up to wink at Kit and saw the color had drained from her face.

"Not something I can give you, August. Though maybe Bentley can give us both the inside scoop to that."

August blinked, his tongue frozen to the roof of his mouth. Kit had graduated second in their class, with more honor cords draped over her gown than almost anyone else. She was a veterinarian. How could she not be considered an important part of her family?

"Kit—"

He heard her breath blow out as she put a little a gel on the dog's belly. "Keep your fingers crossed for Bentley."

He nodded, uncomfortable with the shift in the room. But it was the furry guy on the table who was most important now. He held up his hand and offered a smile he didn't quite feel. "Fingers crossed."

She moved the wand slowly over the dog's belly. He wasn't in a position to be able to see the images Kit was seeing on the screen. So he watched the woman instead.

Despite her small size, Kit was a large presence. Her dark hair was trimmed short, and a little tussled. She'd probably run from the house to the clinic when she'd found out about Bentley's injury. But it was her shoulders he watched now.

The subtle breaths she was taking and the tightness

easing from her. So she must not be seeing anything too terrible on the ultrasound.

She was beautiful. But the exhaustion she'd had last night was still curled around her. The shadows under her eyes pulled at him.

How hard had his father been pushing her?

A woman who kept a be-the-best mantra on the wall in her kitchen was his father's dream partner. But who looked out for Kit?

Not her family apparently. Anger flared in his belly. He hated that his father hadn't cared for him, but at least he'd been a rebellious pain in the rear teen. That didn't make it fair or okay, but he could acknowledge that he'd not been an easy kid.

After his mom died, he'd lost his compass. The person who loved him for him. And he'd hated that his father had kept his cool following her loss, diving even further into his work. August had rebelled just to make his father react…or at least that was what his therapist believed.

But Kit was a dream child. Successful, hardworking, a natural leader. Heck, she'd been the vice president of their school class. The fact that she wasn't made to feel important sent fury ricocheting through him.

"Looks clear." Kit relaxed. "So, on to the X-rays."

August pulled up the digital file on the tablet. At least this office used a digital tablet system he'd used before. Today's learning curve was suddenly a lot shorter. The images popped on the screen, and he pushed them to the large television screen on the wall. As they flipped through them, August wanted to shout with joy.

"Only the broken back leg and cracked ribs. Lucky guy." Kit let out a small laugh and covered her mouth. "Sorry, nervous reaction I've never managed to get rid of." Her cheeks colored as she patted Bentley's head.

"Do I make you nervous?" He grinned, glad that the dog was going to be okay.

"I…" Kit looked at him, her dark eyes widening.

He held up his hands. "Sorry, bad joke. I know you're nervous about this big guy's injuries. When I'm coming off an adrenaline rush, I make bad jokes."

It wasn't exactly a lie. Jokes, particularly bad ones, were his coping mechanism. One clinic had given him a book called *The Best Worst Jokes Ever* as a parting gift.

But if he made Kit nervous, it might even the playing field. Because the woman next to him made him nervous. He didn't know her, but he worried about her.

That emotion didn't make sense. It was probably just because he knew what a demanding presence his dad was. That had to be the reason.

"Oh." She nodded. "Well, the good news is that we only need to cast the back leg. I want to keep him for observation tonight and then I can arrange for him to go home tomorrow morning if he's doing okay."

She looked at him and smiled. "Thank you for coming down so early. This would have been a lot on my own."

But she'd have figured out a way to make it work. If he hadn't wandered down here, Kit would have done this all by herself.

"I'm here to help, Kit. At least for a little while." The last words were an afterthought, and they tasted bad as they exited his lips. Still, it was the truth.

But she needed help. His father wasn't wrong in that assessment. The clinic needed a relief vet to handle his father's absence.

I could stay…

He pushed the thought away. He was more than qualified, and Kit needed help, but staying in such close proximity to his father was not an option. The old need to prove himself had already broken through its cage. It would be better to find someone else.

And probably a part-time relief worker for the weekend. Most clinics employed at least one relief vet. It wasn't a sign of laziness, but he was already mentally building the arguments to make his father understand.

But that was tomorrow's battle.

Kit's stomach growled as she leaned her head against the wall across from Bentley's kennel. Her stomach craved sustenance but she didn't want to leave Bentley alone quite yet. Unfortunately the granola bar stash she kept in her desk was exhausted.

She needed to go to the grocery store or at least schedule a food delivery. Another thing to add to her ever-growing mental to-do list.

At least August had been here today. She smiled. Her Saturday shift had been easier with August than it was with his father.

She was more relaxed with August's easy conversations and silly jokes. The clinic felt happy. Busy, exhausting, but happy.

For a day the clinic had felt like the kind of place she was hoping it would be when she finally took it over. The transformations she'd convinced Dr. Jeff to make were all surface level. The real work came with how you treated the staff and clients, and his crabbiness always cast a bit of an unwelcome glow. Today everything truly seemed in reach.

All of that should have equaled a relaxed Kit. Or at least a Kit that didn't have to mentally remind herself to relax her shoulders. Some relief from the tenseness that she wore.

But her body was wound tighter than ever. August's

easygoing presence made the clinic lighter. His laughter brought joy. But it also disrupted her carefully controlled life.

And not in friendly professional ways. No, today she'd found herself looking for him. She'd enjoyed them each trying to hide their smirks as they tried to coax Mr. Dolhen's cranky parrot from the top cabinet after he'd called in a panic, fearing it had hurt its wing. The only thing wrong with the parrot was a stubborn attitude as it made siren noises when asked to come down. August had laughed as its ambulance siren echoed in the room, asking the bird if it was really necessary to be such a drama king as dogs started barking all over the clinic.

She'd looked forward to the small head nods and smiles when they passed each other in the back after checking on Bentley. All professional reactions, but the way her body heated when his green eyes locked onto hers was decidedly unprofessional.

In some ways he reminded her of Leo. His love for animals, caring attitude and determination to have some fun. Her heart sighed as the memory of her lost love pulled around her. She could think of him now without getting teary. The good memories were much easier to pull forward than the last terrible day.

Today the clinic had been nearly blissful. The skeletal weekend staff relaxed as they dealt with a jovial colleague. She hadn't had to worry about outbursts from Dr. Jeff. No unhappy clients complaining because he just barked orders rather than discussed options with them for their pet.

She and August had been a near-seamless team. It had been like working with Leo again.

Is that why my heart picks up when he's around?

That was the easy answer. She and Leo had basically

lived at the clinic during their short marriage. All the dreams they'd started building…only to be yanked away by a drunk driver.

She blew out a breath. Two weeks before their first anniversary, she'd joined the uncomfortable kinship of widowhood. And before she'd had time to process her loss, to gather the pieces of their life together and try to find her place in the rubble, her in-laws had hired a lawyer. The summons had arrived less than a month after the funeral, claiming that they'd given the loan for the clinic to her husband, not her and demanding repayment.

The worst part of that day was that she hadn't been surprised.

Her in-laws, Karen and Robert had made no secret of that fact that they'd hoped their son would marry one of the socialites they'd preselected for him. They'd not hidden their dismay when he'd chosen veterinarian school with her over going to medical school. Blamed her for him not going into surgery like his father.

But she thought when they married that eventually they'd see her as family. A futile hope. When the lawyer successfully sued her for the loan money, she'd told them the truth. All the money had gone to the clinic. She and Leo had rented a small apartment while they set up their clinic and paid off her student loans.

She promised to pay them back as soon as she was able, but that hadn't been soon enough.

So the clinic had become theirs. A clinic they didn't want, staffed by vets they didn't know, but whose qualifications were impeccable. Top-tier schools, multiple certifications and the tendency to move on in the first two years.

And she'd landed here. Playing second to the cranky local doctor who drove most of his staff away. But who'd survived off the elderly clients who'd been bringing their pets to the doctor for the last several decades.

Today was the first day that the clinic had been fun. The first day she'd felt like herself in so long.

But August wasn't Leo. It was a memory she was craving, not the handsome tattooed vet who'd appeared in her house last night.

And he'd made no secret of the fact that he planned to get out of Foxfield as soon as possible. Several of the ladies had not tried to hide their frowns when August said he'd be moving on too quickly to meet their daughters…or granddaughters.

Kit had hidden more than one frown too.

The man was stunning. He was muscular without looking like he dropped barbells every evening in the gym. And when he bent over and went all googly-eyed with an animal, it was hard not to swoon. He was like the hero that wanders in at the beginning of a seasonal Christmas movie and sweeps the heroine off her feet.

But this wasn't a movie. He was a vet, not the hero in a sappy movie. And she wasn't the heroine either. She knocked her head against the wall, reminding herself that fiction was fiction for a reason. The real world rarely delivered happily-ever-afters.

And even when it did, it ripped them away.

Mentally she formed a list of the ways August differed from Leo. Maybe that would help her stop the racing tingles across her skin when he was near.

For starters he'd looked horrified when she said she'd be at the clinic for most of tomorrow doing paperwork. Like the mountain of paperwork would somehow do itself? This was a small business after all. Leo had understood that.

Instead of working tomorrow, August was planning

to go hiking. In fact he'd told her he was heading to bed early tonight so he could be out on the hiking trails at sunrise. And part of her had wished he'd invite her along. Not that she'd have accepted. But it would have been nice to be asked.

Ugh…she was supposed to be making a list of ways he wasn't like Leo. Not feeling sorry for herself that he hadn't invited her on a hike that she would have politely declined.

She was just lonely. She'd gone on dates with four different men following Leo's death. She hadn't made it past the third date with any of them.

The final guy had told her she was intimidating. That her goals were so lofty she'd be lucky to find any man who wanted to deal with her. It was cruel, and she'd told him so before blocking him. Then she'd sworn off dating.

She'd gotten lucky enough to find a partner that had loved her for her. His family hadn't, but he had. No one had loved her like Leo. Not even her mother. That was enough love to last her for a lifetime. It had to be.

"Kit?"

She blinked and looked at her watch. It was only seven o'clock, but she hadn't expected August to return. He walked through the door to the back of the clinic and held up a bag.

"Thought you might be hungry."

Her eyes stung as she looked at the brown bag in his hand. How long had it been since anyone worried over her? Considered if she'd eaten or was tired?

"You brought me food?" Her throat felt tight as she took the brown bag from his hands.

"I mean, I made a sandwich from the ingredients in your fridge, pulled a few carrots and cucumbers from your garden and sliced them. And…" he pulled two water bottles from his backpack "…brought water. It's nothing fancy."

But it is. She kept those words to herself as she pulled the sliced carrots out of the bag. "I'd like to offer you a few carrots, but I am so hungry I think I might devour all of them."

"No problem." August winked as he pulled another bag from his backpack. "I brought my dinner too."

It smelled delicious. She leaned over to look. Chicken smothered in some kind of tomato sauce with sautéed zucchini. "I ran to the grocery store. Didn't want to poach from your limited stash."

She nodded. She appreciated the thought, but her sandwich looked a lot less appetizing than his meal. "I keep meaning to go, but it's been…" She let her hand wander, gesturing to the clinic. "I'll try to remember to put in a delivery order tonight."

August tapped her shoulder with his, a friendly gesture but her heart skittered. How lonely was she that just a simple dinner could make her swoon?

"Or if you're not too picky, you can just use what I stocked the fridge with. I fear I may have gone a little overboard." He looked from his meal to her sandwich. "Do you want to switch? I only made you a sandwich because I didn't know if you had any special dietary restrictions. One of my good friends gets terrible stomach cramps if he breaks his strict diet and well, I figured you had enough going on."

She laughed, those dang nerves again. This wasn't funny. It was sweet. So terribly sweet. "I don't have restrictions, but I'd feel terrible stealing your dinner."

He reached for her brown bag. The tips of his fingers brushing against hers sent heat sprinting across her body. She swallowed as he laid the chicken in her lap.

"I insist." Then he took a giant bite from the sandwich, sealing the deal.

"Thank you." The whispered words hung between them as he looked at her. His green eyes were the same jade tone of his father's, yet they looked nothing like the man he'd inherited them from. They were kind, and sweet, and her body started to lean into him before she instinctively pulled back.

Lifting the fork to her lips, her mouth felt like singing as the flavors dashed across her tongue. It was a simple dish, but so flavorful. And completely different than the sad sandwiches and veggies she managed to grow when she remembered to water the bed.

"So how is our big boy doing?" August nodded to the giant kennel where Bentley was snoring. He took a carrot slice from the bag and then offered it to her.

She grabbed a carrot and looked at the kennel. "So far so good. He'll be on pain meds for several weeks, but soon he'll be back to playing with the whole family. I've had three conversations with them today. He is their baby."

"A giant baby." August laughed and then took a sip of his water. "I'm sure he'll be glad to get back home too. Being a very important member of his family and all."

"Yeah. Must be nice." She hadn't meant for those words to escape but she couldn't reel them back in now.

She could feel his stare, but she didn't look up from the chicken in her lap. Greeting his emerald gaze wouldn't make the truth hurt less, and it might make it worse.

"I find it so hard to believe that you aren't considered important to your family. Me, I understand. I was the screwup. But you were perfect."

"Ha." She kept her gaze locked on Bentley, the sleepy puppy a haven in a room suddenly full of potential mental landmines. "Perfection equals the best. I was the only Bedrick kid not to be valedictorian."

"Salutatorian—"

"Second is just the first loser." She mimicked her mother's voice, the one she still heard in her dreams. Even her subconscious didn't let her escape the standards set for her. "At least according to my mother. She constantly compares her children and I come up last every time. My brothers each own their own business. Their own homes. They've won awards for their work. Then there's me. Can't even win the Foxfield Finest Award when competing with the only other vet clinic." She sighed.

It shouldn't bother her. Practically she knew she was doing well. And somedays she even managed to convince herself that she didn't care. But tonight she didn't feel like lying to herself.

"Then she's an idiot," August stated firmly as he leaned his head against the wall. "You're amazing and anyone that has trouble seeing that needs their vision and their senses checked."

She knocked her shoulder against his. It was less than she wanted and still too much. But she couldn't help herself. "Well, the same could be said for your father."

"I appreciate the sentiment. But my father and I had a falling out over much more serious transgressions than my failure to graduate first in my class. I spent more time out of school than in it those last few years and made it a point to go against nearly every rule the man laid down."

August took another bite of his sandwich as he looked around the back room of the clinic. "He did a lot of things wrong."

She thought she heard a catch in his voice but August kept going before she could be certain.

"But if I am honest, I was not an overly loveable teen."

She laid her hand on his knee. She wanted to tell him he shouldn't have had to earn his father's love. Wanted to say that a parent should give that basic need freely, but she'd been what most of society deemed a good, loveable kid and it hadn't been enough. Saying the words aloud didn't change the circumstances you'd grown up in. Didn't relieve the pain that never quite vanished from your heart.

So instead she squeezed his knee. The connection was brief, but it was all she felt she could offer. August laid his hand over hers and their gazes locked.

The mood in the room shifted as his eyes held hers. Her breath caught as the moment stretched on. Heat pooled in her belly as fire danced across his eyes. Desire, or what she wanted to believe was desire called to her.

What if I lean in?

The thought shot across her brain, and Kit instinctively pulled back. They were at the clinic, watching over an injured dog, colleagues that barely knew each other. She was just lonely.

And he was gorgeous. Of course her brain would leap to the idea of scratching an itch. That was the reason her belly was tumbling, and heat was pooling in places that it hadn't for so many years. Nothing more.

Clearing her throat, she held up her empty dinner dish. "I really appreciate you bringing me dinner. I can't remember the last time anyone thought to take care of me."

Why had she said that last sentence?

There was no reason to open herself up like this. A simple thank-you was more than enough. August Rhodes didn't need pieces of her life story.

"You don't have to stay." The words rushed from her lips, words she wished she could call unintentional but ones she truly meant. "I mean, I plan to stay with Bentley tonight. But I know you want to go hiking early."

She was rambling. Rambling! Kit never rambled. What had the handsome rebel vet unleashed in her? Whatever it was, she needed to rein it back in.

"Actually, that was one of the other reasons I came down here."

"I hope you aren't going to ask me about the trails. I haven't been on them in ages."

"No."

Hurt ran across her chest at his quick and easy word. Seriously, she needed to get it together. She couldn't go, even if he wanted her to. Which he clearly didn't.

But she wanted to go. Her heart ached at the idea of being left behind, a stupid overreaction. Still, until her heart or libido or whatever was currently messing with her carefully constructed life was under control, she was going to limit her interactions with August.

"But I thought this might be helpful." He pulled out a fancy baby monitor and smiled. "This is the best on the market."

She felt her eyes widen as she shook her head. "I'll admit you could have pulled almost anything else out of that sack and I would have expected it more than a baby monitor."

"It has video and will wake you up if Bentley starts crying. Which, given the amount of pain medication in his system, is doubtful. I know there is a cot here. My father slept on it more than he slept in his own bed, but we'll be close enough that we can be here in less than five minutes if he gets whiny."

We.

Such a simple but powerful word. One she doubted August had meant to say. It had been so long since she'd been part of a *we*. She felt water invade her eyes and she blinked quickly to force the sensation away.

"Sleep is important. Work-life balance *is* important."

"Thank you, August." She grabbed the device and moved to set it across from Bentley. It was kind of him, but she didn't need better balance. She was fine. Though sleeping in her own bed tonight would be nice.

She slid back down beside him. "And thank you for dinner."

"Speaking of dinner—" he gestured to her lip "—you have a bit of sauce, just…"

Kit brushed her hand along her mouth, embarrassment crawling through her.

"It's still there. Hold on."

His thumb brushed her jaw and her insides melted. She didn't know how she'd managed to get sauce on her jaw, but the embarrassment she felt evaporated with his touch.

"I got it." He smiled and her heart melted.

Yep, she was attracted to August. But attraction was fleeting, and he was leaving in a few days. She could put a bit of distance between them, wrangle the desires creeping out of dormant places back in their holes and focus on what mattered—the clinic.

CHAPTER THREE

The Foxfield Finest Award is out. Love Pets Vet is first in the Best Vet category again. Just thought you might like to know in case you talk to Mom today.

KIT READ THE text from her brother David and sent back a quick thank-you. She didn't point out that she already knew. Didn't tell him that she'd set an alert on her phone to remind her to check the Chamber of Commerce's website this morning.

Like she needed a reminder. Like today wasn't seared into her brain. Although instead of staying up late worried about the clinic's placement, she'd spent the night thinking of August.

She bit her lip. Now was not the time to get distracted by the hot man upstairs.

Particularly because she'd failed to unseat her ex-in-laws' clinic—again.

Failed to be the best. To prove to her mother that she deserved a place in her high-achieving family too.

She could already hear the not-so-subtle disappointment her mother would level at her. *Trying isn't worth much if you don't accomplish it. Have you tried visual-*

izing your success? Focusing on only that? That's how I ensure my boutique's success.

And of course her mother's boutique was the winner in Best Boutique and Stephen and David's firms had taken first in their categories too.

Kit swallowed as the wave of words that hadn't even been spoken yet rolled through her. This had been the constant repetition since she was a child. Each second-place trophy tossed aside as her brothers' first-place achievements got displayed on the fireplace mantel.

She'd never earned a spot there. She shook her head, trying to force the pity and disappointment out of her brain. A trick she'd never accomplished. And today wasn't going to be when she mastered it.

Her eyes wandered to her phone and her fingers itched to check the website again. Like this time it would say something different.

But it wouldn't. No amount of wishful thinking was going to change the outcome. Rhodes Animal Services was listed as the runner-up.

Runner-up. Which was not much of a consolation when there were only two competitors in a competition that technically recognized three businesses in each category.

Second is only the first loser. Her mother's words echoed in her brain as she poured the coffee into her to-go mug, trying to convince herself that it didn't matter.

It was a silly local competition the Chamber of Commerce ran every year. Except Rhodes Animal Clinic hadn't won since she'd come on board. A fact Dr. Jeff lamented each year.

At least this year he isn't here to complain in person.

Kit bit her cheek as the unkind thought echoed in her brain. She should not be glad that an accident had sidelined Dr. Jeff for weeks. Or that it had delivered August Rhodes to her door.

But it was hard not to be grateful that she wouldn't have to listen to his complaints. She doubted August Rhodes would care about the clinic's rankings. He'd probably just shrug it off. Call it a marketing ploy and ask why it mattered?

That's what he'd done through high school. Thrown off everyone's expectations. Not cared what anyone thought.

They'd had exactly one class together. Junior year English Literature. She'd sat in the front row of Ms. Fornby's class. Trying her best to soak up as much information as possible. August had taken a different approach.

It was the back row for him. His head leaning against the wall most days, with his eyes closed. But he wasn't asleep. Whenever Ms. Fornby had asked him a direct question, he'd answered, usually with surprising insights into the reading.

The looks of appreciation or disappointment from their teacher never phased him. What was it like to have that much confidence? To truly not care what people thought of you? To not care what your family thought?

She looked at the clock—she needed to go check on Bentley. August was hiking today, and she couldn't pretend she wasn't lollygagging on the hopes that she might see him before he left for the day. August Rhodes wasn't whom she needed to be focusing on.

Today started the race over for best vet clinic in Foxfield—next year…

As if she was able to read her thoughts, Kit's phone dinged. Her mother's name popped on the screen with a text.

There's always next year. Maybe David can give you some pointers. He's successful.

The words hurt, even though they were expected. Second place wasn't recognized in the Bedrick family. If you weren't first, you may as well be last. She looked at the text. Leaving it on read without returning a response would upset her mother and result in a phone call. If Kit left that unanswered, it would ensure a visit. And she certainly didn't want that.

I'll see what tips David can offer me.

It hurt to see the words on the screen. David was a fantastic coder. And his tech company was doing great things. But there were few overlaps with the world of veterinarian medicine.

Still, she knew it was pointless to point that out to her mother.

Today was a new day. A new start. She looked at the sign by the pantry.

Be the best.

She could do this. She paused at the foot of the stairs. Still no sounds of August moving around. But that was a distraction she shouldn't be looking for.

She bit her lip and looked at the myriad of motivational statements on her fireplace mantel.

Is second really so bad?

Kit shook her head, forcing the wayward thought from her brain. She was not traveling that path. Maybe if they finally came in first, Dr. Jeff would go out on top and sell to her. Slacking was not an option.

It wasn't.

* * *

August's phone echoed in the quiet stillness of the trail, and he saw a few hikers turn to look at him. No one tried to hide the disappointment radiating off their faces. Not that he could blame them. Normally he'd have been furious at the interruption in the quiet hills too.

But today wasn't normal. Today, instead of leaving his phone in the car or turning it off on the trail, he'd kept it on. Worried that Kit might need him. And August wasn't sure how to deal with that.

It was his day off. He was substituting for his father but that didn't mean that he was tied to the clinic. There had to be boundaries. He did not work every day. Today was his time to recharge.

He'd stayed to help get Bentley loaded up into his family's minivan this morning. That was more than enough.

His head should be clear. Focused on the majesty of the hills around him. Free from thoughts about the clinic.

And they were...mostly. It wasn't the Rhodes Animal Services clinic rotating through his mind, but the woman so tied to it.

Kit.

He was drawn to her. Despite the be-the-best mentality she maintained, talking to her was easy. Working with her yesterday had been fun. She laughed and joked, and when she'd laid her hand on his knee last night, his soul had rejoiced at the simple connection.

Last night... A simple packed meal shouldn't have made for so much emotion. But for a moment he thought she might lean in to kiss him. And he'd wanted that. *Badly.*

He'd almost asked her to come with him today. She'd looked off this morning in the clinic. She claimed it was because she hadn't slept well, but he thought there was more to it. Something she wasn't telling him.

And why should she? You barely know each other.

Still, you didn't have to know someone well to know when they were exhausted. And Kit needed a day off. The hills could be so rejuvenating, and August had spent far too long thinking of excuses he might use to convince her to play hooky on whatever paperwork she claimed needed to be done.

Except he'd seen the determination in her this morning. Determination to spend the day at the clinic. To ensure she didn't break her seven-day workaholic streak.

It had torn at his heart to see the walls that had fallen when he'd given her his meal fly back up. So he'd bottled up the question, not wanting to get shot down.

It was a weird sensation. He'd never worried about getting turned down before. If a woman wasn't interested in his company, he accepted it. But with Kit...

There was something between them. He couldn't identify why he felt protective of her. Why he wanted to see her smile. Why he wanted to be near her.

But she was only focused on the clinic. She'd made that clear today when she'd said she had work to do, wished him well on his hike and marched into her office.

Which was why he should have turned his phone off. If she wanted to live at the clinic, it wasn't his concern. But that thought didn't stop him from reaching into his back pocket. He frowned at the unknown number on his phone.

Of course it wasn't Kit.

His finger hovered over the ignore button for a moment before he pushed answer. "Dr. August Rhodes."

"Is it really necessary to answer like that? I know who I called." His father's gruff voice shot across the phone.

Somehow August doubted his father would have appreciated a *Hello, Dad* either. Even if he'd known he was calling from the hospital number. Why wasn't he using his cell? There really was no winning with the man.

Refusing to return the gruff tone with his own annoyance, August stepped just off the trail to make sure he didn't disrupt any other hikers but kept the trail firmly in his sights. Hikers went missing with far too much regularity in the woods.

And Kit needed him right now.

That was an unwelcome thought. He swallowed as he tried to focus on the man on the other end of the phone. "I'm out on the Highland Trail, what can I do for you?"

"Is the clinic a mess?"

"No." He gave the honest answer, taking a bit too much pride knowing that knowledge probably made his father frown. Kit was overwhelmed and needed help, but she was handling the clinic on her own better than most. His father prided himself on his indispensability. But no one was indispensable.

"We do need to get at least one relief vet in to help Kit—Dr. Bedrick. Ideally, two, one for the week and one for the weekend, so she can get a break."

"I never used relief vets." The unwavering tone that had carried through his childhood echoed through August.

And that choice cost you your family.

Instead of stating the obvious, he made a noncommittal noise.

"And the clinic isn't going to start now."

Stubbornness was a trait his father valued. Though he'd call it determination. August called it foolishness.

There was nothing wrong with seeking help when you needed it. And Kit needed it.

"Kit needs support. You've run it with two vets for the last several years. Your client list is for at least two vets. You could easily support a third." He pinched the bridge of his nose as he tried to make his father understand. This wasn't the clinic he'd run when August was growing up. And he'd needed additional support then too, even if he'd been too stubborn to keep partners on for longer than a few months at a time.

"Your clinic is bigger than you seem to think it is," August ground out, then took a deep breath. He was not going to let his father's annoyance drive away his day. He was not the annoyed teenager trying to best his father in a game of words. He was a colleague, one with a significant résumé in a multitude of clinic types.

"Yet our clients never seem to think we're the best." His father's harrumph on the other end of the phone made August blink.

What was that supposed to mean? The clients brought their pets, their precious family members to the clinic. The level of trust that showed was immeasurable.

"Excuse me?" The conversation shifted, and August wasn't sure where his father was taking him.

"We came in second again on the Foxfield's Finest poll." His father's tone was not hard to read over the phone. The man had always put too much faith in awards. Particularly that one.

It was a local poll that the community prided itself on, but it wasn't a good measurement. Many of the larger businesses gave out coupons, cookies, and big discounts if customers could prove they voted for them. A practice his father refused to participate in. Smaller businesses might not win, but that didn't mean they weren't the community's true favorite.

"Haven't won a single time since Kit joined me."

Blood pounded in August's ears as his father's words echoed in his mind. "Are you insinuating that she isn't good enough, because…"

Before August could defend Kit's honor, his father interrupted.

"No. She's more than qualified. Hard worker too. But maybe it's time to sell." The words were low in the phone, and August wasn't sure if his father had meant to say them, or they'd slipped out.

Then his father continued, his voice wavering just slightly…or maybe it was the connection. "The Love Pets Vet owners have reached out a few times. They'd offer a good price. More than anyone else. Maybe…" His father's words died away.

August wasn't sure what the right answer was. The only thing he knew for certain was that Kit loved Rhodes Animal Services, and she deserved to get to stay if his father was really ready to retire.

"And Kit could stay on if they purchased it?" He'd known the woman less than forty-eight hours, but it mattered to him that she got to keep her place. He saw too much of himself in her.

"I doubt it." His father let out a sigh. "Her ex-in-laws run the place. Not a lot of affection there."

His mind raced with that information. She'd been married and divorced. Was it because of how much time she spent at the clinic?

He pushed the wayward thoughts away. It didn't matter. But Kit losing her place at Rhodes bothered him. Deeply. She'd worked hard, by his father's own admission. She deserved more than to be shunted off when he retired.

August wasn't sure if it was exhaustion or annoyance. "Then what about her?" He felt his stomach flame. This was the outcome he'd told Kit he'd champion if his father brought it up less than two days ago.

And he'd meant it then. He didn't want the clinic, didn't want anything from it. But to see it stripped from her seemed so unfair.

Before he could broach the topic again, his father continued, "There is another option."

The pause hung in the air as he waited for his father to say something. Anything. When the line remained silent, August finally prompted him. "What is it?"

"You take my place."

"Your place?" The words tumbled through him. Part of him wanted to scream no. Hang up the phone and leave Foxfield. He'd stayed away from this place to ensure he didn't become his father.

And because I hated seeing the disappointment on his face.

August kept his mouth shut as emotions rumbled through him. There'd been a day, not as long ago as August would have liked, when he'd have been excited to hear those words. When he'd craved them. But now...

He had a life. A good one. One he didn't plan to give up for a man who'd written him off when he was a child because he hadn't performed the way he wanted him to.

"Yes." Emotion clung to the word, but it disappeared almost immediately, "At least until I'm done with rehab. Six weeks or maybe eight. Then you can go back to your rambling ways."

Rambling. August felt the negative reply build in his throat, but he forced it down. That solved the short-term issue but wasn't a true solution. "What happens when you finally decide to retire? Kit will be back in the same position then. She is expecting you to at least offer her the option to buy the clinic."

If she owned the clinic, her family might see her for the caring, skilled veterinarian that she was. Though following in his father's footsteps hadn't earned August any additional love. But maybe Kit could finally see the pride radiate from her parents' faces that had alluded him.

"Stay until my rehab is complete and I will bring her on as a full partner, an *owning* partner. Then she gets a say no matter what when I finally decide to put myself out to pasture."

She should already be that. Another retort he bit down.

"I will hold you to that promise." He wasn't sure how. But somehow he'd find a way.

"I'm tired." And with a click, his father was gone.

Six weeks, eight at the most, in Foxfield. He'd dreaded getting stuck in Foxfield as he drove across country. Considered plans, developed excuses to use if his father tried to guilt-trip him. He should feel upset, angry that his father had forced this position.

So why was it happiness pooling in his soul as he stepped back onto the trailhead?

Kit signed her name across the bottom of an invoice for what felt like the hundredth time, then sat back in the chair. Leaning back, she looked at the ceiling and took a deep breath. As the smell of the clinic ran through her nostrils, she wished she were outside in her garden.

Or on the hiking trail.

The image of August, dressed in cargo pants and a fitted T-shirt, ran across her memory. The heavens must have paused to admire their work when designing August Rhodes. Dark hair, chiseled cheekbones, muscular frame. He was nearly perfection.

Heat wrapped around her, and she sat up.

No. She did not wish she were on a hiking trail with August.

She was doing what she loved, taking care of the clinic. This was her place.

Except it's not. Not really.

That truth struck her heart, but she wasn't giving in to dismay. There was work to be done.

Pursing her lips, she signed her name again and grabbed the stack of envelopes she'd printed out labels for this morning. All of this would be easier if Dr. Jeff would've let their former office manager sign up for on-line payments. And if he hadn't run off the office manager right before his accident.

At least the staffing agency was sending over a new hire this week. Then she could go back to just doing the vet work. This was a set of obligations she wouldn't mind leaving behind.

The phone rang, and she felt her eyes narrow as they locked on it. It was Sunday, and they were not an emergency clinic. But the clinic had lost more than one client to Love Pets Vet since it started offering emergency services on the weekend.

Just one of the reasons they were Foxfield's Finest. She bit her lip as her hand hovered over the receiver. Being the best came with sacrifices. Ones she was willing to make.

She forced her eyes not to stray to the clock as she picked up the phone. "Rhodes Animal Services. How can we help you?"

"So you're answering the phone on the weekend? How very adorable."

Her former mother-in-law's chuckle sent ice shards

to her heart. How she'd managed to raise such a caring and wonderful son was something Kit would never understand. Some families believed a daughter-in-law remained in the family if the unthinkable occurred. But not Karen and Robert. Kit had been a pebble in their shoe during her marriage. Now she was less than that.

It wouldn't do any good to tell Karen she'd been handling a few things and decided to answer in case a patient needed her. So instead she kept her voice level as she asked, "What can I do for you, Karen?"

Hopefully nothing.

"I was calling to find out Dr. Jeff's number. We made an offer on his clinic a few months ago. He said he'd consider it but never got back to us. Given his accident, and the ranking that came out this morning, we've decided since to increase our already very generous offer."

He said he'd consider it...

That line pounded in Kit's head.

It felt as though all the air had evaporated from the office. *No.* This was just a cruel trick. Just like when her former mother-in-law blamed her for encouraging Leo's running habit by getting him new running shoes and a GPS watch for Christmas.

Never mind that his parents still had all his cross-country medals in their home. Or that their son loved to run. Her gifting him things for Christmas was the reason he'd been on the road to be hit by a drunk driver.

It was beyond the point of cruelty. She'd initially thought it was just a part of the fog of grief, but all these years later, Karen still hated her. Still said that if she hadn't come into Leo's life, he'd have gone to med school, taken a job in his father's practice, and married one of the women they'd hoped for. In short, if he'd followed their path, he'd be alive.

And the worst part was they weren't wrong. They'd moved to Foxfield because of Kit. Because her brothers were here, and she'd wanted to come home. If they'd been anywhere else... But that wasn't something she could change.

"You offered to buy this clinic?" The words were choked, and she looked up to see August standing in the doorway. She blinked twice just to make sure her mind hadn't materialized him.

"Who is that?"

Kit didn't bother to cover the phone's receiver as she answered, "Karen Lloyd. The owner of Love Pets Vet. She wants your father's number so she can discuss purchasing Rhodes Animal Services."

"Who are you talking to?"

Kit ignored Karen's question as she looked at August. He'd said he'd encourage his father to sell. Now the option was here. Did she have enough money to buy the clinic?

Yes. But only if Dr. Jeff took a fair offer for the clinic. If Karen and Robert wanted to outbid her, they could. *Easily.*

August motioned for the phone, and she passed it over.

"This is Dr. August Rhodes. I spoke with my father this afternoon regarding your previous offer on the clinic."

Her ears were ringing, and Kit crossed her arms as she looked at August, hoping desperation wasn't dripping across her features.

She couldn't lose her place here. This was her home. God, what would her mother say if she lost this clinic? If she had to start over, again?

Black spots floated in front of her eyes. This couldn't be happening. It couldn't be.

Gripping the desk, she looked at August. His features were soft, but unreadable.

"My father isn't in any condition to take demanding calls." He smiled at her and then continued, "We've agreed that I will stay on in his place until he's completed his physical therapy."

Now her body was heating for a different reason. August was supposed to be leaving. Her plan to keep her distance was designed for a week in his presence. Several weeks, even months...

Her tongue was stuck to the roof of her mouth. She'd fail at that mission if she didn't keep her focus at all times.

Would that really be so bad?

She refused to acknowledge that wayward thought. August was staying—that was good for the clinic—and his father wasn't talking about selling to her ex-in-laws. At least not yet.

He handed the phone back to her. "So your ex-in-laws sound lovely. Is their son as vindictive as they are?"

Of course Karen would say something cruel before August hung up the phone. Personal growth was a foreign concept to her.

"No." She shook her head, and the memory of Leo saying it would just take time for them to love her floated across her brain.

What would he think now?

She pulled the ring from its hiding place behind her shirt and pursed her lips before she looked at him. "Leo was killed by a drunk driver while out for a run just before our first anniversary. Karen and Robert blame me for reasons that aren't rational.

"Love Pets was Leo's and mine. We opened it just after we got married. Didn't even honeymoon. His parents loaned us the money, or him the money, according to their lawyer." She shrugged. "He's been gone ten years, but their desire for revenge has never cooled."

Time had taken the fire from her anger, but she was still determined to make this the better clinic. To show her in-laws, her mother and herself that she didn't need them. To be the best...finally.

Next year. When the results of the local poll came out... Her brain faltered as so many thoughts rammed through it. So many ideas for bettering Rhodes Animal Services...ideas she doubted Dr. Jeff would be keen on.

"Wow. I am so sorry, Kit. When my father said they were your ex-in-laws, I figured it was a bad divorce. But that is so much worse. It's beyond cruel." August's arms wrapped around her, and he squeezed.

She sighed into his heat as comfort wrapped around her. This wasn't the desire that had ricocheted between them last night. It was soft, and comfortable, and just what she needed in this moment.

"It is." She didn't have the heart to lie. Her mother was disappointed that she didn't meet her definition of success, but Karen and Robert... Well their actions bordered on evil.

But she didn't want to discuss her ex-in-laws right now. Today was a new day and Dr. Jeff wasn't selling to Karen and Robert. Yet.

August squeezed her tightly, and she leaned her head against his shoulder for just a second. Enjoying the simple connection with another.

Then she met his gaze and her mouth watered. Suddenly the hug and the link between them felt decidedly different than the comfort he'd been providing a few seconds ago.

She forced herself to step away. "So you're staying?"

Kit's heart raced as she looked at August. This wasn't what he'd claimed to want, but he didn't look terribly put off by it.

Or maybe I just want to believe he's fine with the decision. That he wants to stay...with me.

"That is the deal I've struck with my father." August looked over the small office, then his gaze rested on her. "And I'm looking forward to working with you, Kit."

Tingles ran across her skin as her name slipped between his lips.

Then the other words registered. *Deal.* He'd struck a deal with his father...for her? But that meant Dr. Jeff had considered selling to Karen and Robert. That shouldn't have surprised her, but it hurt.

And August had stopped it. *For now.*

"What happens when your father is through with rehab?" She needed to know. Needed to know what the future held for her. If her plans for making this the best clinic, for being the best, for finally making her family proud were worth anything.

His hand moved and for just a moment she thought he was reaching for her. But he pulled back and ran his hand over his chin. "He told me that he plans to make you a full partner at that point. That was part of the deal. But..."

August offered her a small smile that didn't touch his eyes.

"But there is no way for you to guarantee that he will keep his word. Am I right?" Kit preferred the truth, and she was glad that August wasn't trying to sugarcoat it. She got on better with Dr. Jeff than anyone else, but he was consumed with the clinic.

She'd broached the subject of a partnership, just after her fourth year here. Cool didn't begin to describe his reaction. He'd said no, directly. Then told her that he wouldn't have a full partner. Another vet would have left, but leaving Foxfield meant leaving Leo's resting place, and her brothers and nephews.

This was her home. She was not leaving.

Dr. Jeff had mentioned selling when he retired, and she'd clung to that nugget. Desperate to make it real.

Would he hold to his promise to make her a partner if August stayed? Uncertainty stole through her. Dr. Jeff cared about this clinic. That she knew with all certainty. "So I have a few weeks to prove myself indispensable."

The tips of August's lips dipped, and she hated putting a frown on his beautiful face.

"No one is indispensable, Kit."

"I don't believe that." She crossed her arms and wished she could step back into his hold. Desperate to feel comforted again. However she stayed in place. "But the last thing I want to do right now is debate." Her stomach growled.

"Well—" she laid a hand over her stomach "—that was loud." Without thinking, she reached for August's hand. It was strong and warm in her hand. The connection sent a wave of emotions rolling through her.

Hope, worry, excitement...desire.

She squeezed his and dropped it. She should probably keep her distance from the man she was so attracted to. But tonight all she wanted was a bit of company.

"So instead of debating, how about dinner? You hungry?"

"I am."

He opened and closed his palm twice before stuffing it in his pocket.

Had he reacted to her the same way she reacted to him?

"Where do you want to go?" August's smile lit up the

room and the drama of the day seemed to float away as he gestured toward the door.

"Anywhere." Kit grabbed her phone and keys. As she followed him out of the clinic, she looked at his hand. How easy it would be to reach for it…

She blinked and put her hands in her pockets, mimicking him. This was a friendly night. Dinner after a long day of hiking and fighting with ex-in-laws.

So why did it feel like she was stepping onto a new path? Excitement coursed past the walls Leo's passing had placed around her heart. Tomorrow she'd find a way to put them back in place.

Tomorrow.

The crickets sang and gravel crunched under his feet as August walked behind Kit toward the small cottage that would be home for at least a few weeks. The day had been full of heavy decisions and topics. But somehow he wasn't worried about spending an extended period of time in Foxfield.

That should have been surprising but being here felt right.

At least for now.

Kit turned and the glow of the porch light highlighted her face. She looked relaxed. And he couldn't keep from smiling. Their dinner conversation had been light, no worries from the day allowed to creep in. He'd enjoyed every minute.

"Thank you." Kit crossed her arms as she stood at the door.

"For what?" August raised a brow. They'd split the dinner check, and she'd let him choose the tiny diner. It was a place where he'd gotten fried chicken, green beans and ice cream with his mom so many times.

Kit's teeth bit into her bottom lip as she looked over at her garden. "For cutting a deal with your dad. For going to dinner with me. For noticing me. It's been a long time since I had someone look out for me." She pushed a hand through her hair. "Not that I need it. But it's nice. So, thank you."

August nodded. "Well, a greasy diner meal isn't as relaxing as a hike on the trails, but it's comforting in its own way. And maybe I'll get you to play hooky with me one day while I'm here. You might like it."

"I have no doubt that I would." Kit's hand brushed his arm before she turned and put the key in the door. "But the clinic is busy."

"Mmm." He didn't argue. Not tonight. But August was going to get her to take a day off before he left. It didn't have to be with him…though he'd do anything she wanted if she asked him to tag along. "Good night, Kit."

He stared at her for a moment, his eyes memorizing the small freckles dotting her nose. She was so lovely, and part of him ached to drop his lips to hers. Tonight was not the right time; perhaps that time would never come. But if it did, August swore he'd remember every precious second of it.

CHAPTER FOUR

THE SCREECHES FROM the husky were still escalating as Kit stepped from the exam room into the back of the clinic. "Jenkins needs his nails trimmed." She handed the chart to Missy, one of the vet techs. "And as you can tell, the dramatics are already in full swing from his checkup."

"It's always the huskies." August grinned as he put the tablet chart in the charger. "I've never met a more dramatic dog breed."

"There is a reason I like to schedule them for the last appointments of the day. Their whines tend to disrupt the entire clinic. Beautiful dogs, but the label of drama queens does not even begin to describe the breed!"

"True." August looked at his watch and then her. "It's almost quitting time. Big plans for the night?"

He'd asked her the same question each night for the last week. And each time it got harder to find a way to avoid inviting herself to whatever activity the man had outlined for the night. So far he'd gone fishing, night hiking and watched a comedy marathon with the biggest bowl of popcorn she'd ever seen. He was always doing something, and she was fascinated by him.

But the heat between them had leveled off. They were simply solid work colleagues. No desire humming between them.

Or maybe she'd imagined the desire in his eyes after they'd shared dinner. Heaven knew she didn't have much experience with desire. She'd dated Leo through most of college and married right after they'd graduated vet school. She'd had a few dates since he'd passed, but sparks hadn't flown.

Until she met August.

But it was good that they were just colleagues. That was what she wanted. If her heart picked up when he was near or she hung out in the kitchen sipping coffee and enjoying a few minutes with him in the morning, that didn't have to mean anything.

She was just enjoying the company of someone who made her feel accepted. Who didn't bark orders or offer compliments designed to make her question herself. Her mother's specialties.

It's nice that you have Bucky. Dogs are good for protection... Of course a man is better. But dogs are okay.

Have you considered joining another clinic? One that wants you as a partner—assuming you could make partner there?

And her mother wondered why Kit didn't visit more often.

"No big plans." She barely resisted putting her fingers in her ears as Jenkins the husky started howling. Like getting his nails trimmed was traumatic...except everything was traumatic to a husky.

"That is one loud husky. But my last client of the day was a macaw who was less than thrilled with my service." He gestured to the large spot of bird poop on his shoulder before walking to the cabinet where they kept changes of clothes. "The bird told me to go to hell more than once."

"Frank is ornery. And since his parents divorced, he's

picked up a whole new suite of language. Their lawyers actually got involved on what they can train him to say."

Kit's breath caught as August stripped off the dirty shirt and grabbed another from the pile of clean scrubs. It was a normal action—most of the office just quickly redressed back here if necessary. Modesty was something that didn't survive long when animal waste was just part of the job.

Still, seeing August's chiseled back, a tattoo on each shoulder, stole her breath. Turning, she put a hand to her cheek, hating the heat radiating from it. What was with her?

"Kit?"

August's voice tore through her, and she plastered a smile on her face as she turned, hoping the desire pulsing through her couldn't be seen. "Yes?"

"I asked if you wanted to come with me to Shady Springs Ranch. I'm doing a night ride." August bent to pet Bucky's head as the dog leaned against him. Her dog had taken a strong liking to August.

She was more than a little jealous, but also it was so darn sweet to see the tattooed giant cuddling with her pittie-mix. Her heart pounded in her ears each time she saw it.

"Oh." The *no, thank you* was on the tip of her lips. But instead of saying those words, she heard, "I think I'd like that," slip through.

She could tell by August's expression that he'd expected her to say no. But the grin that followed lit up her heart.

"Do I need recent experience with horses to do this?" She'd agreed so fast. And she was already second-guessing herself. There was gardening to look after, and laundry and paperwork here she could do. "If there is—"

"Nope. You aren't backing out that easy." August raised an eyebrow as he looked at her. "I can already see the wheels spinning with other things you think you have to do."

"I mean I *do* have to do laundry, and paperwork doesn't do itself." Kit crossed her arms, unnerved that he'd read her so easily.

August stepped to her side. Her heart raced, her mouth watered and her eyes involuntarily traveled to his lips. Why was her body so receptive to his?

"This is the first time that you haven't immediately come up with an excuse when I asked you about your plans. You said no big plans. Every other time you've listed out a ton of chores that have to be done. So no, you do not need much horseback riding experience to do this. Evie and Anya Mitchell do this ride once a week on a giant trail with a small group of riders."

"Will they be able to add a plus-one then?"

"Yep. Because I told them I was going to bring someone." August winked. "I was hoping I might be able to convince you to take a night off. You've more than earned it."

"I…" Her throat tightened.

"You're not used to having anyone look out for you. I know. But as long as I'm here, I'd like the job."

The look in his eyes sent a wave of fire across her body and she felt her cheeks heat. But she didn't step back. He was right. No one had looked out for her since Leo passed. And she was so focused on being the best that relaxation was usually her last priority.

A sacrifice she was generally content to make. But for one night she wanted to let go. To just be Kit, not Dr. Bedrick, future clinic owner, future top vet, future… To live in the moment. Enjoy the present.

"So, we have to be at the ranch by seven. Want to grab dinner first?" His eyes sparkled as he grinned.

Is this a date?

Of course it wasn't. He was being friendly, like when he'd brought her dinner. Just because her mind jumped to other thoughts, thoughts she was not going to act on, didn't mean his did.

"Dinner sounds nice." Did her voice sound as hesitant as her mind felt? "Maybe the quick-serve taco joint?" Quick-serve tacos were delicious but not a date location. Not really.

"Tacos. Sounds perfect." He looked at his watch, then back at her. "Guess we should wrap things up here. Don't want to be late for our..." He cleared his throat.

Was he about to say date?

"For the ride." August crossed his arms. "So glad you agreed to come, Kit."

"Me too." It was the truth. Night trail riding was a lot more fun than laundry and paperwork. And those things would be there tomorrow. But August... Well August had an expiration date.

She could let loose for one night.

August's horse neighed as the owls hooted above them. He patted the majestic creature's neck as they ambled down the trail. Kit's back swayed with her horse's motions, and August felt the smile tug on his lips. She was really here.

Part of him still couldn't believe it.

Despite what he'd told her about planning for a plus one, August had fully expected her to say no when he asked if she wanted to come tonight. No matter what he'd proposed over the last week, she'd demurred. But he was determined to keep trying.

So, he'd asked the owner of the ranch, Anya, while planning his trail ride when the last possible moment was that he could add someone. When Anya had asked him why, he'd explained how Kit was working herself to the bone, and if he could get her to take a night off, he'd try his best.

Her sister, Evie, had overheard the conversation and said they'd keep one slot open on the off chance he could convince Dr. Bedrick. Apparently Kit was the ranch's vet, but she rarely took them up on their offers to go out on the trails. Despite being an avid horse rider in her youth.

He'd clung to that bit of knowledge. He liked getting to know Kit, the little she'd let go. The woman was fascinating, and the fact that her in-laws seemed intent to ruin the life of the woman their son had loved made him want to offer any protection he could.

It was a ridiculous feeling. Kit was more than capable of dealing with her own problems. But August always handled his own problems too. And it was lonely.

He was drawn to her. The dark eyes, fierce but gentle. A determined woman who needed a hug. When he'd held her the other night, his heart had soared. He'd offered the hug for comfort, one human to another, reminding them they weren't alone. The most important reminder one could give another.

Except when her eyes had met his, it had taken all August's control not to ask to kiss her. All his reserves to let his arms drop to his sides when she'd stepped away. So many times over the last week he'd nearly asked again. When he caught her looking at him, or after sharing a quiet moment over coffee. He ached for her.

But the desire pooling through him wasn't why he'd asked her out tonight.

Or at least not the main reason.

Kit needed a night off, and if all his short residency at his father's clinic accomplished was showing Kit that taking time off was okay, he'd count this stay as a success.

When Kit had shown up tonight, Anya and Evie had let out shouts of delight. Telling her how glad they were she was taking a night off and then leading her into the horse barn so she could pick her horse. He'd been practically forgotten, and enjoyed every moment.

She needed this. Even if she didn't want to admit it.

"This night is nearly perfect, August." Kit looked over her shoulder.

He couldn't quite make out her features in the dark, but he could hear the smile. It was precious. "Glad you came with me. It's been fun revisiting some of my old haunts. But I've enjoyed finding new places too. Like this. I would never have gotten on a horse in my teen years. Funny how life changes us."

"Mmm…" Kit sighed as the horse barn came into view. She pulled her horse to a stop and waited for August to pull up beside her. "I rode out here for years. Competition riding, of course."

"Of course." August hoped his voice sounded teasing. He didn't need the caveat. Life was too short for everything to be about accomplishments and wins. One could do something just for the pleasure of it. What did Kit do just for fun?

She let out a light chuckle. "My mother was determined that I would find a sport to excel at. My dad was a swimmer, though he dropped out of our lives before I could walk. I tried that but never got very fast. I'm built like a gymnast, but far too clumsy. I'm a horrid soccer player and basketball…" She gestured to her body. "Not a lot of need for a basketball player that is barely over five foot."

"I suppose not." If they weren't on horses now, he'd pull her into his arms. Funny, he remembered seeing Kit in school, watching her jump into her mother's car after school. His father never left the clinic to pick him up. They'd lived just close enough to the school that he hadn't been eligible to ride the bus, so after his mother passed, he'd been responsible for getting himself home.

He'd been jealous of people like Kit. People whose parents seemed to enjoy picking them up. Enjoyed being part of their kids' lives. But you never really knew what happened in other people's homes.

"I was actually pretty good at stadium jumping. My horse, Willow, and I were like one. I spent hours taking care of her. Decided to be a vet in this very horse barn. She's been gone almost six years now. Such a good girl." Kit stroked her horse's neck as she looked toward the barn.

He knew many vets who had similar stories. Animals they'd loved growing up, making them realize this was the profession they wanted. Not him. He'd been fascinated by the science. He loved animals, but it was the science that had gotten him to vet school.

"Stadium jumping." August held the reins loosely in his hands. "You were a great stadium jumper and yet asked me if you needed much horse experience for tonight?" August chuckled. "So you really were just trying to find a way out, after saying yes to accompanying me."

"Technically, I asked if you needed recent horse experience." Kit laughed.

It was a gorgeous sound. The melodic noise made his heart leap.

"Besides, I wasn't great." Kit stuck her tongue out at him. "My childhood closet is stuffed with second-place trophies. Never managed to capture first for my mom to put on the mantel."

He noticed that it was the trophies she focused on rather than his statement of the fact that she'd been trying to get out of spending tonight with him.

"So many second-place trophies."

He saw the frown form on her lips and wished there were a way to wipe it away. Tonight was about fun and relaxing. Besides, there was nothing wrong with second-place trophies.

His father likely would have screamed if he'd managed to place second in anything. August had never earned a trophy. Not one. Her trophies should have been on display, not hidden away. But now wasn't the time for that insight, so August kept it to himself.

Instead he leaned over and pulled a leaf from the helmet she was wearing. He hadn't meant to lean over, but the frown on her lips made his heart ache. His chest tightened as he looked at her and tossed the leaf to the side. There was no reason for him to have pulled a stray leaf from a helmet they were going to discard in a few minutes.

To cover the moment and try to take his mind off the fact that he wanted to kiss her, to touch her, to see her smile, he offered, "I've never earned a trophy. I would put any that I won on the mantel. First place, second or participation. Though I suppose we're passed the point where we get trophies."

He shrugged, placing his free hand on the pommel to keep it from reaching across to Kit. "Missed my opportunity, I guess."

"Trophies aren't all they're cracked up to be. At least that's what they tell me. But the experiences. Those are priceless." Her eyes met his, and August swallowed.

An invisible connection snapped between them. This wasn't anything he'd felt before. He never stayed in one place long enough to develop connections. His relationships were all short-term. Ending when he or the woman he was with moved on.

Lust and desire were emotions he'd felt before. But not this intensity. He'd never felt drawn to another. August let out a breath as he stared at her. She was gorgeous but it was her spirit calling to him. "Kit…"

Before he could ask whatever question his brain was trying to push forward, her horse whinnied.

"We should get them into the barn." She looked away and the spell broke. She nudged her horse forward and his followed.

Another missed opportunity.

And again he wished he'd acted.

"Whoa! Calm down. You're going to hurt yourself more!" The raised voice echoed from the barn as they got close.

Kit lifted off the horse with a grace that screamed equestrian, handed the reins to a waiting stable hand and disappeared into the barn. It took him a few seconds longer, and he suspected he was much less graceful dismounting.

"Patty, Patty. You're okay." Kit's voice was low and soothing as August stepped into the barn. "Shh. Shh." Her hands were up as the horse whinnied.

A large gash on the side of the mare's flank sent a flash of worry through August.

How had the mare done that?

Horses were intelligent creatures, but stubborn, and prone to spooking.

"Our med bag." Evie pushed it into August's hands,

her blue eyes dark with worry. "Do you think we need to sedate her?"

August looked to Kit. There was no way for him to answer that question now. Kit was calming the mare, but he laid the bag at his feet and started rummaging through it. Kit's calming method might work, but a horse, particularly an injured one, could do a lot of damage to itself, people and property. If Kit couldn't sooth the creature, he wanted to be prepared.

"Patty." Kit's singsong voice carried in the barn, and the horse snuffled and lowered its head. But the rigidness of its stance lessened, and its ears were no longer pinned back. Patty's tale still swished more than he'd like, but she was calming down.

"Grab a towel. Let's get the sweat off her." Kit kept her voice light, though everyone in the barn could hear the authority in it. "And, August, we'll need antibiotic, and cleaning solution."

He grabbed the supplies, and the syringe with the sedative. *Just in case.*

"What happened?" he asked as he stepped to Kit's side. She was standing on a small step stool, wiping sweat from the animal's neck.

Anya took a deep breath as she rubbed Patty's nose and offered the animal a treat. "Patty's eye sight's slipping." She hiccupped as she laid her head against the animal. "We've had a few incidents in the last month or so. Clumsy in her old age. She's nearly twenty-eight."

Horses lived longer than dogs and cats, averaging between twenty-five and thirty years. But owners could still expect to outlive their fur babies. And at twenty-eight, Patty was considered elderly.

"Something startled her as she was being led in, and she scraped her side against the post. Then that spooked her too. And…well here we are." Anya kissed the horse's nose. "My sweet girl."

"The cut doesn't look too deep." Kit glanced to August and held out a hand for the cleaning solution.

The horse stamped her feet as Kit flushed the wound. It was a normal reaction, not aggressive. Still, his heart raced as he watched Patty's stance, his eyes monitoring each movement. Each swish of the tail.

The horse was calmer now, but if she was losing her eyesight, Patty could overreact to any simple movement. A vet he'd served with in Maine had been kicked by a horse, breaking his leg in three places. And he'd been considered lucky.

Kit was sure of herself, confident next to the horse. But August was still nervous to see her so close to danger.

Breathe, he tried to remind himself. The horses knew Kit. He was the stranger. Passing items to Kit was the right place for him. No need to add additional stress to the situation with him trying to actively participate in the care. But that didn't stop the worries pulsing through him.

"Antibiotic."

He handed it to her, his body relaxing as the horse's stance loosened again.

"I just want to get every moment I can." Anya's voice was soft as she nuzzled the beast, continuing their unfinished conversation outside the barn. "Life is too short."

"Yes, it is," August agreed, keeping his eyes on Kit. Her gaze met his for just a moment before it dropped back to her patient.

Heat that had nothing to do with the warm evening spun through him. There was something between them. And the next time desire flared, maybe he'd finally give in to it.

Life was simply too short not to have an idea of how the woman before him kissed.

"Tonight was an experience." August reached for the air-conditioning and turned it down as they started driving down the dark path leading away from the ranch. The evening had cooled dramatically over the last few hours, but she was sure he was still warm from the activity in the barn.

Which meant he'd seen her shiver as the air-conditioning blasted. And he'd taken care of her. It was such a sweet gesture…one she could so easily get used to, if she were honest with herself.

But the chill was only part of the reason she'd shivered. The truth was it was August and the desire she couldn't bottle up when she was near him.

It wasn't his fault that she was hyperaware of how close his hands were. Wasn't his fault that she'd calculated the minuscule movements it would take for her hand to brush his across the console.

Would that be so bad?

She wanted to know how the man beside her kissed, wanted to explore the connection that bubbled between them. They were both single, and…

Desire raced across her skin. Of course she'd consider it tonight, when she was very aware that she had helmet hair. She'd been fine on her own for years—lonely, yes…but still fine. And now when she was finally interested in giving in to the feelings coursing through her, she had helmet hair.

In a lifetime of the universe being unfair, this shouldn't have surprised her. But still.

August had escaped the curse of helmet hair. Because of course he had. Somehow his soft short curls were only slightly mussed, giving him the kind of roguish unkempt look that graced magazine covers rather than the I've-been-out-on-a-horse-riding-trail-and-my-hair-is-plastered-to-my-head look.

He wasn't wrong though. Tonight had been an experience. Just not quite the one she fully wanted. When he'd leaned over and plucked a leaf from her helmet, she'd thought for sure that he was going to kiss her.

But then the moment passed. Or rather she'd pulled back after he'd hesitated. The walls she'd lost control of the moment August brought her a sandwich reassembling for just a moment before deserting her again. Why was whatever that was between them so hard to ignore?

Would it really be so bad to kiss him? And why would that thought not desert her head? Maybe then whatever was between them could vanish?

The connection, the electricity that she felt anytime he was around could evaporate. Like popping the seal on a jar. Once the pressure was gone…

"Tonight was definitely an experience." Kit let out a nervous laugh as she saw his fingers flex, closing the distance between their hands by millimeters. What was wrong with her that she noticed something so minor?

"I almost feel bad about inviting you."

"What?" Her voice was louder than she meant, and August's eyes met hers briefly as he pulled into her driveway.

He put the car in park, unbuckled his seat belt, then turned to look at her. "I'm glad you came, but I meant tonight to be a break from the clinic. A way to help us relax."

"Us? Or me?" Kit tapped his hand, needing the connection. But it did nothing to lessen the pressure dancing around them.

"Us. I needed a night out too." August raised his hand

and pushed a piece of hair behind her ear. "Balance is important, remember?"

She leaned into his palm. His thumb stroked her cheek. The motions were soft. *Gentle.* And her soul lightened at the simple touch.

"Though, I do worry about the amount of time you spend in the clinic. You deserve a break too." His thumb ran along her chin, and she saw him swallow. "But to be even more honest, I wanted to spend time with you."

"August." His name felt like a prayer on her lips as she leaned closer. Life was so short. Things could change without warning.

Tomorrow would come, with all its responsibilities, but she didn't want to go another day without knowing how he kissed. One kiss, to loosen the pressure building between them. And give her a memory to hold on to.

"Kiss me." Her fingers wrapped around his free hand as she watched him close the distance between them.

His lips were soft. Perfection as they connected with hers. *August.*

The kiss was light, not demanding, but the hand on her cheek felt like it was burning as it stroked her skin. She'd been wrong—one kiss with August was not enough.

When he pulled back, she wanted to scream. Or beg him to kiss her again.

"We should go inside." His voice was husky. Desire dancing across his eyes as he let his thumb trace along her jaw before dropping a feather kiss against her lips. So light. Airy…

Inside. Kit let out a breath. Dear God, what was she doing? She found August attractive. He was hot. And temporary. When his father was better, he'd be gone. Maybe that was why she should lean into this. Because she wanted more than to kiss him. Didn't she?

Yes. She hadn't dated much since Leo's passing. And no one had made her feel like this since Leo. August brought out the best in her, just like Leo had. He made her laugh and smile. Things she hadn't realized were so infrequent in life until August dropped in. But he wasn't Leo. Her brain spun in another direction. What was she doing?

She never rushed into things. But was this rushing, really? They'd spent every day, and most nights, together for the last week. More time than some families spent together.

The questions refused to leave her brain.

"Kit." August squeezed her hand. "We've had a long day. We should go inside, but that doesn't mean that this needs to go any further. You're in the driver's seat here."

She pursed her lips. Of course he'd be perfect about this too. "Sorry."

"No need to apologize." He squeezed her hand one more time and then opened the car door.

If she were daring, she'd open the car door, grab his hand and lead him to her bedroom. Or maybe suggest they shower together after a night on the trail. Options that any rom-com heroine might take.

But Kit wasn't the heroine in the made-for-television movies she loved to watch during the holidays. She wasn't the risk-taker, the fly-by-the-seat-of-your-pants-and-have-fun type. Though tonight she really wished she were.

Opening the front door, she stepped in and let August pass her. "Sleep well, August."

"Sleep well, Kit."

And then he headed up the stairs and disappeared from view.

Well, dang.

CHAPTER FIVE

KIT WATCHED AUGUST down another cup of coffee as she passed him in the back of the clinic. By her count, that was at least his fourth. Did the man not react to caffeine at all or was he as dead on his feet as she was?

She sent a quick look to her watch and barely kept the yawn from her lips. There were still at least another two hours left on their shift. Kit glanced at the tablet chart in her hands, then looked back at August.

The soft kiss they'd shared last night had done nothing to cool the desire building in her. Today she looked like how she felt.

Tired and unkempt. But not August. The man looked delectable, even with the small dark circles under his eyes. For the hundredth time, she wished last night she'd just taken a risk.

He looked up, and she looked away, certain he'd seen her staring but unable to meet his gaze. She'd spent most of the evening lying in bed, replaying their kiss. And her reactions to it.

All her reactions.

Particularly those related to Leo. Those were the ones that caught her off guard. She'd never felt like she was cheating on Leo before. Though she hadn't felt drawn to anyone this way since him. August made her feel alive.

But it wasn't guilt about finding another attractive. It was what August represented. *Freedom...*

August did what he wanted. What he wanted right now was to help her, but when this assignment ended, he'd go on to his next adventure. The next thing that caught his fancy.

And she wasn't free to do the same thing. Her brothers were here, her nephews, and Leo was here. They'd sworn they'd have a great clinic, and he'd hate how his parents had turned their dream into a corporate thing that cared more about profit margins than care. Her place was here, but part of her was jealous of the freedom August had created for himself.

Even if he was leaving, there were worse ways to pass time than a short fling with a hot man who cared for her.

God, I really have it bad for him.

And he'd be easy to fall for.

So easy.

That was what really scared her. She swallowed and refused to look over her shoulder to see if he'd already gone into another room. She'd lost the person she'd thought she'd spend the rest of her life with once. Kit knew that deep soul-crushing loss.

When August left Foxfield, he wouldn't return. Could she risk her heart on a short-term fling? She shook her head, forcing those questions to the back as she gripped the handle to the exam room.

"Hi, Kelsy," Kit hoped her voice sounded more upbeat than she felt as she stepped into the room. "My tech tells me you have a new family member."

"I do." Kelsy Richards smiled as she stroked a cat in a box that Kit couldn't see. "Amanda, the tech, scanned her, no microchip. Not that I expected one given the condition I found Pepper in."

"Pepper?" Stepping to the exam table, Kit did her best to keep her face clear. This was not the kitten she'd expected to find. The once black-and-white cat had a gray snout and cloudy eyes, missing half of one ear. Though that injury had healed some time ago. It was at least eight or nine years old, likely older.

"For the white-and-black and of course all the gray." Kelsy smiled as she stroked the cat's ears.

"I admit when Amanda told me that you were excited about your new kitty, I was expecting a younger cat." She'd have to have a quick chat with Amanda, their newest tech, about making sure she at least noted when a cat was a kitten, adult or elderly in the chart's notes.

Kelsy nodded as she looked at Pepper. "I called her a kitty, because she is. But I am also very aware that whatever time I have with her is going to be limited. Maybe very limited."

"Well, we need to get some blood drawn, check her teeth, ears and eyes." The cloudy eyes worried her most. Pepper had lived a hard life before Kelsy rescued her. If the eyes were cloudy from corneal ulcerations, keratitis drops could relieve the issue, but if it was cataracts or glaucoma, then all Kit could offer was palliative treatments.

And if it was feline AIDS, commonly called FIV, then Kelsy may only have months with her new baby. Better not to worry about that until she absolutely had to.

"My boyfriend thinks I'm crazy for adopting such an elderly cat. But she was laying by my car yesterday morning. When she looked at me, I swear she was asking, *Are you my mommy?* I know that sounds crazy, but she's mine. For however long I can claim her. That's enough."

Kelsy leaned over the box and gently lifted the cat out. Pepper nuzzled her head against Kelsy, and a soft purr echoed in the room. "That's right, girl, you're safe. But Dr. Bedrick is going to have to make you uncomfortable, so Mommy knows how you are."

Kit felt the tip of her lips lift. She loved hearing other pet parents talk to their animals like this. She talked to Bucky all the time, though the beast had taken to sitting next to August at dinner. At least the mutt still only cuddled with her.

"We'll do the blood draw last." Kit looked at Pepper's ears and was surprised by their good condition. But the cat's gums were inflamed, and Kit's heart sank as the likelihood of FIV rose. Unfortunately FIV was incredibly common in street cats, and untreatable.

She drew the blood from Pepper as quickly as she could and then rubbed the cat's ears. "Good girl."

Before Kit turned to leave, she looked from Pepper to Kelsy. "Kelsy, I want to be honest—"

"You think she has FIV." Kit's face must have registered surprise, because Kelsy quickly added, "I did that thing everyone tells you not to do. Went online and did a quick, well, actually, a not so quick search on what might be wrong with her. FIV and feline leukemia were the top results."

Kit nodded. She always recommended pet parents not search for information on the internet. It tended to skew toward the worst-case scenarios, but she was happy that at least it wasn't coming as a shock to Kelsy.

"Whatever comes, comes." Kelsy kissed Pepper's head and nuzzled against her. "You and me, girl, we got this."

"If it is positive, we'll do a retest in a few weeks just to be sure."

Kit closed the door and leaned against it. Kelsy's attitude toward Pepper was perfect. If more people looked at animals the same way, this world would be a better place.

But it was her reasoning that kept echoing in Kit's brain.

She's mine. For however long I can claim her. That's enough.

Except it wasn't the image of a cat in her brain.

"You okay?"

August materialized in front of her. Kit's heart picked up its beat, just like it had every time she'd seen him.

His eyes were soft as he looked at her. "You all right?"

His repeated question made her realize that she'd just been staring at him without answering. She barely kept her hand from slapping her forehead. "Yes, I just…" She gestured to the door. "A client adopted an elderly cat."

Kit held up the blood vial, "She's prepped for me to find FIV, but I still hate the idea of giving bad news. And I have two more clients to see and then it will be closing time." She was rambling, so she took a deep breath and met August's beautiful gaze. "Guess I am resigning myself to a late night in the clinic. Which after not sleeping much last night…"

She let that sentence run out and prayed he wouldn't ask why she'd failed to rest well. The last thing she wanted to do was find a plausible reason for her sleepiness when the real reason was standing before her looking far too handsome.

"Do you want me to look at the blood?" August held out his hand. "I'm done with clients for the day. Or I could look after one of your last appointments."

She pressed the vial into his hands, ignoring the pulse of energy flittering through her as her skin connected with his. Kit had to focus to calmly pull her hand back rather than react as though his touch burned her.

Which it did.

"I'll get the enzyme linked immunosorbent assay

ready." August nodded. "If it's positive, do you want me
to call the owner?"

"No, I'll handle notification. Though she is expecting
the results, I still want to be the one that relays the news
and discusses all her options."

"All right." August tapped her shoulder. The connection was brief, and platonic, and the opposite of everything Kit wanted in this moment.

He opened his mouth, then shut it. August hesitated
for a moment longer before offering her a grin and wandering off.

He'd meant to say something else, then thought better
of it. There was no way for her to ask what it was. But
she craved the knowledge.

And him.

August looked at the cup of coffee sitting next to the enzyme linked immunosorbent assay test and made himself look away. It was far too late in the day to add more
caffeine to his system. Besides, the coffee hadn't fixed
his sluggishness all day, and it wouldn't magically wipe
it away now.

He'd lain awake, thinking of Kit for hours after they'd
come home. Replaying the short gentle kiss they'd shared
in the car.

And the look of panic racing through her when he
suggested they head inside.

It wasn't personal. He knew that. And he'd meant what
he said. She was in control of where whatever was between them went. But that hadn't stopped the fantasies
from materializing last night.

One soft kiss, one perfect sliver of time. It should have
quelled his need for her, at least a bit. Instead it had ignited a fire he had no idea how to control. Particularly

when he worked with her each day, slept yards from her, shared coffee and walked with her dog.

He should find a way to put distance between them. But he didn't want to. He craved her.

Kit kept her eyes down as she walked past him into another room. Her last patient of the night. Outside of him asking her if she needed help, that had been her routine all day—never fully meeting his gaze.

He couldn't pretend that it didn't hurt. But he understood. Their relationship had shifted dramatically last night. They couldn't un-ring the bell.

August hadn't been able to keep his eyes from her today. She was gorgeous, but Kit looked tired too. A fact she'd confirmed.

The timer he'd set dinged, and he looked at the test. *Positive.*

He pulled at the back of his neck as he looked at the results. It wasn't a result that would surprise Kit. But it was still upsetting. Cats with FIV had shorter life spans and all a vet could offer was palliative care.

August loved caring for animals. Loved seeing them love on their owners. There was nothing he'd change about the career he'd chosen, but one never got used to delivering bad news.

Letting out a sigh, he went to grab the phone number for the owner. He knew Kit wanted to make the call, but he could have everything ready for her. He wrote out Kelsy Richard's number next to the test results and then left a short note.

He did a few more chores around the back of the clinic, making sure all she'd have to do when she was done was turn off the lights and come home. Then he grabbed his bags and headed for the small house they shared.

It wouldn't be fancy, but after a long day he could

make sure that there was dinner and a glass of wine ready when she made it home. August took a look at the clock and mentally added an alarm.

If Kit wasn't home in an hour, he'd come searching for her.

The front door opened, and August smiled as he looked at the clock. He'd fully expected to have to drag her from the clinic today. "In the kitchen!" he called as he put the meat for the burgers on the plate next to the buns.

"Burgers." Kit closed her eyes as she stepped into the kitchen and took a deep breath. She looked tired, but relaxed. "It smells delicious."

"It was quick and easy." August passed her a plate and nodded to the toppings he'd left out. "Ladies first."

She grabbed a patty and bun, piled it high with lettuce and tomato before moving to the kitchen table. "Thank you. You didn't have to do this."

"I had to eat too." August slid into the chair across from her and lifted the burger to his lips. He took a big bite and savored the taste. "We each had a long day yesterday and neither of us seemed to rest much last night…"

He bit the inside of his cheek.

Why had he said that?

"After we kissed you mean?" Kit rested her head on her hands and looked at him.

August's tongue was frozen in his mouth. She was right of course. But he would not have called it out so directly.

She was really something.

They sat for a few minutes finishing their dinner. Words hovering unsaid around them as they watched each other.

Finally August broached the topic she'd directly called

out. "Yes." He took a sip of wine as he looked at her. "I spent a long time last night thinking about kissing you." He watched her eyes widen and he rushed on, "But that doesn't matter if you don't want to kiss me…"

"What if I do?" Kit's cheeks reddened, and she stood and took her empty plate to the sink. She rinsed it off and then turned and gripped the edge of the counter. "I panicked last night. I haven't dated much since Leo passed. The clinic, my time…" She paused, and her eyes danced toward the Be the Best sign.

He didn't interrupt. This was something she needed to work out. And whatever she wanted…

"I know you aren't staying in Foxfield. I know this is temporary." She let go of the counter, and her gaze was steady as she looked at him. "But life is so short. And what if I wanted to reach for whatever is between us for however long it's there?"

A twinge of something tore through him at her words. At her acknowledgment that this was temporary. That she didn't expect forever with him.

She wasn't wrong, but that didn't stop the hint of pain that she was acknowledging it so openly. Or stop the wish deep in his heart that maybe, just maybe he could settle here. But Foxfield wasn't home.

Was it?

No, it wasn't. But that wasn't a thought he wanted to deal with right now.

Before he could waste any more time, August stood and moved to her side. He ran a hand across her cheek, marveling at her beauty and strength.

"I want to kiss you, August. Really kiss you." She let out a breath and reached up on tiptoes to brush her lips against his. "Then I think we should see where the night takes us."

"Kit." He bent his head and captured her lips. She tasted of hope. A word he'd never assigned to a kiss before, but as she deepened it, that was the only word that came to his mind.

Hope. His Kit, for however long she'd have him.

He ran his hands along her hips, then lifted her and sat her on the kitchen counter.

"We are a bit mismatched in height." Kit giggled as her hands stroked his chest.

Heat danced across his skin with each touch. He pulled her close, desperate to kiss her. Her mouth opened, meeting each of these demands.

She moaned as she gripped the edge of his shirt and ripped it over his shoulders. If her touch had tingled before, it burned now. She dipped her head and ran her tongue along the base of his neck. "God, you're beautiful. Or handsome, or… Man I'm out of practice at this."

August gripped the sides of her face and kissed the tip of her nose. There was no place for her questioning anything tonight. "There are no comparisons tonight. No need for perfection. Besides, I've never been called beautiful." Before she could say anything, he kissed her deeply. "I quite liked it."

"Take me upstairs." Kit's whispered words sent need wrapping through him.

He eased her from the counter and lifted her in his arms. Her body was distracting but he had all night to focus on her body. To claim every inch of her.

She could hear her heart pounding in her ears as August laid her on the bed. He backed away and reached for the light on the end table.

"I want to see everything," he murmured as he slid next to her on the bed.

Heat poured through her as August ran a hand along her side, his fingers grazing the edge of her breasts. She swallowed. She was really here, sitting on a bed with August Rhodes—desperate for him to touch her.

He was gorgeous. Tattoos covered one arm, and the stubble on his cheek made her mouth water. He looked like he'd stepped from the cover of a steamy romance novel. And he was here…with her.

She closed her eyes, letting the sensations wash through her.

"Are you okay, Kit?"

"Just a little overwhelmed."

"Look at me." His voice was soft but commanding.

She opened her eyes, still stunned by the hot man sitting beside her.

"This ends whenever you want it to." His thumb lingered beside her breasts, "No matter what. If you're overwhelmed—"

Kit let her hands wander along his thigh, edging close but not touching his erection. "Overwhelmed doesn't mean I want to stop." His eyes glittered as her fingers probed ever closer. "But you are an amazing specimen, August Rhodes. I think most people would be a little overwhelmed to be in your bed."

He grinned, then chuckled. "If you're trying to inflate my ego, sweetheart. It's working."

She let her fingers roam his chest, enjoying the catch in his breath as she touched him. Such power. She started to let her mouth follow her fingers when August gently lifted her face.

"Your touch is—" he kissed her as his fingers dove under her shirt "—breathtaking."

"But…" Kit raised an eyebrow as she let her fingers trace the edge of his hardness.

"But…" August lifted her shirt overhead and sighed. "So beautiful. I have plans for tonight, Kit. And kissing every inch of you is high among them."

His head dipped to her chest as his lips skimmed her breasts. He unclasped her bra and sat back, his eyes lit with fire as he stared at her. "So lovely."

August's lips captured one nipple, his tongue licking one raised bud as her need bloomed. His fingers wandered lower as his mouth suckled her.

He quickly slid her pants off, and she felt him smile as his hand slid into her panties. Electricity engulfed her as his fingers fondled her. His thumb putting pressure at just the right spot.

"August."

"There is no better sound than my name on your lips." He gently laid her back as his mouth wandered lower and he finished stripping the final clothes from her body.

She bucked as his tongue dipped lower and his thumb pressed against her mound. His kisses slowed as he moved even lower, closer to where she wanted him. Needed him.

Kit ran her hands through his hair. Gripping it, needing more. His lips caressed the inside of her thigh. It was nice, amazing, but not what she wanted. "August… please…"

"So demanding." His husky tone sent chills through her. "I love it."

His mouth replaced his thumb and Kit shattered into a million pieces.

"August." His mouth pressed against her, and he slid one finger and then another into her. Kit quivered as her body reacted to his deft explorations.

"I need you," Kit panted. "All of you, August. Please!"

His tongue flicked her bud and she let out a groan as

her body vibrated with ecstasy. It seemed to take forever for him to step out of his jeans and put on a condom.

When he finally hovered above her, Kit kissed his chest and wrapped her legs around him tightly as he finally joined them.

"Dear Lord, Kit." August captured her mouth as they moved together. Lost in the sensations of their bodies.

"Kit," August called as he reached his climax, and she smiled against his chest.

"That was amazing." Kit rubbed his back and then a yawn tore through her.

August kissed her cheek as he rolled over. "You're exhausted. Why don't I let Bucky out and you get comfy?"

"Here?" She swallowed as the question escaped her lips. "I…"

"Here works great." August winked as he stepped toward the bathroom.

She sighed as she lay against the pillow and waited for him to exit the bathroom. Her room was at the end of the hall. But she didn't want to sleep there tonight. No, tonight she just wanted to be next to August.

CHAPTER SIX

THE MORNING LIGHT was barely a hint in the window when August opened his eyes. His body was heavy but sated as he leaned up on his elbow. He felt rejuvenated after a night spent next to Kit.

Kit.

His hand ran along her side, so soft, and dropped a light kiss on her shoulder. He wanted nothing more than to wake her with kisses, lose himself in her body before the day started. But Kit needed her rest.

She sighed and rolled over. Her nipples rubbed his chest, and the loose hold he had on his control nearly snapped.

God, she was gorgeous.

He let his gaze roam her lithe body. Tiny freckles dotted her stomach, and his finger lightly traced the pattern they made. Kit…so perfect.

Her eyes fluttered open, and she smiled.

"I didn't mean to wake you." August dropped a chaste kiss to her nose.

Her hand ran along his cheek before she kissed him. "Somehow I doubt that." Kit's grin lit up his soul as she ran her hand along his thigh.

"But since I'm awake, I get to direct our early morn-

ing." She ran her fingers along his manhood before starting to kiss her way down his body.

Kit's lips and fingers roamed his bare skin, and August let go of everything, giving in to the overflow of
emotions as she touched him.

Her lips traveled across his body while her fingers
grazed over the tattoos on his arm and chest. When she
finally grabbed a condom from the bedside table and
joined their bodies, August was nearly ready to explode.

There truly was no better way to wake up than next
to her.

"I like your tattoos. Did you get the first one to make
your dad mad?" Kit passed him a coffee cup and kissed
his cheek before turning to make her own.

He blinked as the question rattled through his brain.
He was used to people asking about his ink. Used to them
asking where he got each idea, though being a vet, most
assumed the animals on his arm held little meaning. But
each one had been chosen with deliberate intent.

But no one had ever asked if the tattoos were rebellious. Of course no one he'd ever been with knew the
disapproving stare that he'd grown up under.

He'd visited his father in the rehab facility twice. And
looked at his watch more than he liked to admit during the tense visits where the questions revolved around
the clinic. Though to his credit, his father seemed genu-
inely concerned about Kit. He was a little jealous of that
given that their difficult relationship hovered unstated
in the room.

The turtle on his arm burned as he thought about stepping into the first tattoo shop. The rush he'd gotten as
he'd done something so permanent. A true and lasting

rebellious act. They'd become so much more since that initial visit, but it was rebellion that had lit the initial fuse.

"I wish I could say no." August took a deep drink and imagined the caffeine rolling through him. He'd slept well, but his body didn't seem to truly function before caffeine.

"Why?" Kit raised a brow as she drank her own coffee. "They're gorgeous."

"Thank you." August looked at the sleeve on his arm. "I love them. But. I wish I'd chosen to get the first one for me. Rather than because I knew it would upset my father."

A weird choice since he'd not expected to see him again after he'd failed to show up for his vet school graduation. Deep down he'd still hoped his father would see them, see him. But on his few visits his father hadn't acknowledged the visible ink on his left arm. Hadn't paid any attention to the rebellion.

Because it didn't involve the clinic.

He swallowed. August was not going to let the disappointment he'd buried so long ago surface. He was successful now, the man he wanted to be. That was all that mattered.

And he'd made the ink speak for him.

"I get one for each place I've been. The first was the box turtle." He pointed to his shoulder, though the turtle was covered by his T-shirt.

"What does it represent?" Her brows knitted together as she tried to piece together a puzzle that only August really understood.

His arm had animals, flowers and insects. All representative of the state or city where he'd resided. "The Eastern box turtle is the state reptile for Tennessee. It's where I started so everything else grows out from it."

And he'd never expected to return, so it was his memory piece. His goodbye to the place where he'd grown up, to the place that had made him who he was—even if he didn't want to admit it. But those were statements best left buried.

"I recognize the bluebonnet flower. I expect that's Texas. Where else have you been?"

He wrapped his arms around her waist and kissed the top of her head. "So many places. Being a relief vet has let me travel far and wide. I've been in Florida, Massachusetts, and Maine to name a few."

"The moose!" Kit exclaimed as she set her coffee down and stepped in front of him. "It's so big." She held his arm out and pointed to it.

He chuckled as she ran her fingers along the horned creature. "It is. But so are moose. I treated more than one pet that was unfortunate enough to come across a moose hanging out in its backyard. Maybe I should have chosen something else, but it's Maine. So…"

"And the crocodile is Florida! Even though I doubt you treated many crocs."

"Yes, the crocodile is Florida. And actually I treated quite a few." He smiled as the memories floated through him. The clinic he'd worked at had specialized in exotics and the local crocodile rescue had contracted with them to evaluate the crocs before being released back into the wild.

It was a bit of a weird experience treating patients with snouts that were duct-taped for the safety of everyone. But he'd loved every minute. Dogs and cats were lovely creatures, but treating reptiles always excited him.

A sense of ease and happiness swirled through him as her fingers followed the images up his arm. "The cranberries are Massachusetts; the goldfinch is Washington."

His voice sounded a little hoarse. No one had ever paid so much attention to the ink he'd put on himself.

The partners he'd had complimented the pieces, but any questions they had usually revolved around how much it hurt to sit in the chair. Not questions about the pieces, and what they meant to him.

He sighed as he watched her explore him. He could fall for her. Really fall for her. August waited for the panic that usually exploded when he thought of caring for someone long-term, of loving them.

His mother had loved his father, and in his own way, his dad loved her. But she'd always been second, until she put herself first. And it had broken their family. Love was risky… What if they didn't love you enough?

That had nearly destroyed his mother, but she'd loved being on the road. And so did he. Love was dangerous, but as he watched Kit study him, he felt a piece of fear fall away.

"What was your favorite place?" Her voice was soft, like she hadn't meant to ask the question.

Here. The word caught in his throat as he looked at her. It was the truth but saying it aloud felt like a step too far. So instead he settled on the statement he always used when he was asked this as a relief vet. "I've enjoyed them all. There was something to learn at each place."

Her eyes narrowed and her mouth opened, but before she could say anything, Bucky bumped into her leg and demanded pets. "Who is a good boy?" Kit kissed the top of his head and then looked to the clock.

The spell capturing them shattered, and he desperately wished there was a way to pull it back. To keep the world and its problems at bay forever.

"We probably need to head to the clinic." Kit patted Bucky again as she poured coffee into a to-go mug.

August looked at the clock but held his tongue. They still had time before their first patients showed up, but he knew she liked to arrive early. To make sure that everything was ready. She downed the rest of her first cup of coffee, tightened the lid on her to-go mug and then he saw her eyes stray to the sign on the wall. *Be the best.*

He looked at the words. What did they actually mean to Kit? He'd spent years letting his rebellion be the main part of his personality. He loved his tattoos, and what they represented, but the truth was that he'd done it as a rebellious act. But the follow-on ink, the designs he'd chosen had all been for him. To remind him of the memories and friends he'd made and said goodbye to.

Kit's mother and her in-laws had demanded more than they should have of the woman grabbing her backpack and hooking Bucky to his leash. But how much of her interactions now were because she wanted them? Life was too short to be chasing the reality that others wanted for you.

"Ready for the best day?"

"Best?" August grabbed his bag and held the front door open for her. "That's a high standard."

"True." Kit kissed his lips. "But it seems better to aim for the best day each morning than starting with the idea of settling."

"But it's okay if the day is just fine, right?" Best wasn't possible every day. It simply wasn't. They were vets. Some days were hard. Sometimes they had to recommend a pet parent say goodbye or treat an animal they weren't sure they could save. You could try your hardest, but not every day was going to be good. Sometimes bad days just happened, and it didn't mean you'd done anything wrong or failed. Besides, best was such a high standard.

"If fine is the best one can do, then of course it's okay."

Kit smiled but it was the determination hovering in her eyes that sent a bead of worry through him.

Kit couldn't keep the smile off her face as she moved from one patient to another. Who knew sleeping next to August Rhodes could make her feel more rested than she'd felt in forever?

And she felt more than just well rested.

Memories of last night and this morning floated through her mind. Such good memories. She placed the back of her hand against her cheek, grateful that it didn't feel too warm.

"You look happy." Amanda grinned as she handed Kit a tablet chart. "Like really happy."

Kit didn't try to keep the smile from her mouth as she met the vet tech's sparkling gaze. But she also didn't feel like getting into exactly what had resulted in her good mood. "I'm just really well rested."

"Dr. Rhodes looks well rested too." Amanda playfully raised her eyebrows as she looked at her. She winked at Kit before heading into another treatment room.

The two women were about the same age, but Amanda had three kids and a happy husband at home. She'd tried to set Kit up on more than a handful of dates. The dates had all been failures, though the men she'd set Kit up with had been nice enough.

But there'd been no sparks. She and Leo had had sparks. So many sparks. The kind of hot and heavy excitement that one really only feels in their early twenties when life is still fresh, before the real world gets a chance to truly touch you, if you are lucky...

Once you felt sparks, felt the connection that came with them, settling for less just didn't seem possible.

She'd accepted that that part of her life might be over when she lost Leo.

Then August arrived in her kitchen.

From nearly the moment her eyes landed on him her heart had raced, her cheeks had flamed, and her body had cried out with need. A feeling she thought might diminish after last night.

In fact she'd expected it to lessen. She'd figured that once the initial high of sleeping together was out of their systems, her fingers wouldn't itch to reach for him. Her lips wouldn't yearn for his caresses. But… She reached her fingers to her lips and let her eyes wander to the room where she knew he was seeing a patient.

Sparks…so many sparks still pulsed through her.

The emotions pulling through her were different than she'd had with Leo. Maybe because she'd accepted that whatever this was with August was temporary?

Or at least she was trying to accept it.

Still, when she'd asked him this morning where his favorite place was, she'd hoped he'd say here. After less than three weeks, in the city he'd run from. It was fanciful. A dream for a younger woman, but that hadn't stilled the hope in her heart.

Maybe she should have kept the question to herself. Particularly if she was going to let him get away with telling a half truth.

She'd nearly called him on it as his eyes darted away from the images on his arms. His voice had held an off tone when he'd answered. Forced, like he was trying to keep the words steady.

And she hadn't pressed. Hadn't said that of course one learned from everything, but he had to have a favorite place. Hadn't demanded to know if it was the heat of

Florida, the icy cool of Maine or somewhere else etched onto his arm.

She wanted to know. Wanted to know what had excited him so much. Wanted to know if he missed it.

How would he memorialize this stop in his life?

No. She was not going to travel that route. Not today.

Barks echoed in the front room as a small voice called out, "Hey! Biscuit, come back!"

"Biscuit!" the child's voice repeated.

Kit turned and saw August exit the exam room, closing the door behind him.

"Frank the German shepherd is going crazy with all the noise," August explained as he stepped to her side. "Figured if he bolted through the door, it was better to bolt back here instead of where all the drama is." He motioned to the waiting area.

German shepherds were stress balls at the best of times. The vet was a stressful place for most animals no matter how she'd tried to design the waiting room. The comfort was surface level and between confused pets and worried pet parents, the occasional drama happened while everyone was waiting to see the doctor.

She followed August through the door and was not surprised to find general mayhem.

"Biscuit!" The cry echoed in the room, dogs barked and a few cats were hissing from their carriers.

"Biscuit, please come here," her nephew, Wes, raced by a couple of chairs, tears streaming down his cheeks as he reached and failed to grab a small critter that Kit couldn't see.

"Wes?" The seven-year-old was too upset to notice his aunt Kit had stepped into the room.

"What is Biscuit?" August turned and asked her.

Kit shrugged and looked around the room for Stephen or his wife. They had a cat and dog, but neither were small enough to skitter through the room unseen.

"It's a bearded dragon," Stephen called as he peeked his head above the reception desk before darting back under and announcing, "He's not over here."

Bearded dragon?

Kit blinked. Stephen hadn't mentioned a new pet and their clinic rarely saw reptiles. Reptile bodies were completely different than the mammals most vets were trained to treat. Vets specializing in reptiles got additional certifications following their initial training.

She'd treated a handful of snakes and turtles through the years. However, her specialty, the clinic's specialty, was domesticated mammals and birds. But that was a problem for after they found the lizard.

"He's back here," August called from the corner of the waiting room where they kept the medicated pet food. "If you have a dog, could you please take them outside for about five minutes. Our receptionist will step outside and let you know when I've trapped this very scared and sick bearded lizard."

August straddled the cart, keeping the toes of his right foot wedged into the cart and placing his left foot along the other edge, limiting the lizard's options for escape.

After the room quieted, August lifted the top food bags from the cart. "Hi, Biscuit. You've caused quite a bit of a stir today. And I bet your jaw is sore."

"Wes brought him home from school today," Stephen explained. "A friend didn't want him anymore and was just going to release him on the playground. Wes, well, he didn't want that."

"Smart boy." Kit grinned at her nephew. "So you're here for a checkup?"

"Yes, but he has pus that has been oozing for days,

according to the friend." Stephen crossed his arms and shrugged. "Banking that our family vet knows what to do since it also smells terrible," Stephen added. "Alyssa is not thrilled but—"

"But I love him, Daddy." Her nephew bit his lip. "It's not his fault he smells, right, Aunt Kit?" Wes's eyes caught hers, desperate.

She looked at her brother before getting down to Wes's level. "It's not his fault. And it's good you brought him here."

Stephen sighed as he looked at his son. "I know, Wes. And Mommy knows too. It's just been a bit of a day." He patted his son's head before wrapping an arm around his shoulders. "It's why we're here. To make sure Biscuit is going to be okay."

"And lucky for us, Dr. Rhodes knows about lizards. Have you treated bearded dragons much, August?"

"Yep." August nodded to her brother and Wes. "But first we have to get him!"

August pulled more dog food from the cart, and Kit stepped to his side to take the bags he was pulling off. She could see the lizard. "You can't reach him?" Kit's arms might not be able to reach the lizard from the position she was in, but surely August could.

"Bearded dragons do best when picked up from the side. Grabbing them from above stresses them out, and this guy is already stressed enough." He reached through the cart and pulled the lizard out.

"Biscuit." Wes let out a sigh as August held the lizard. "That was a naughty boy to run away."

"It caused quite the commotion," August agreed as he bent and put himself at Wes's height. "But it isn't his fault. This is a very noisy and new place. Animals, and reptiles particularly, like to hide when they are stressed."

"So I should put him in a box." The boy hung his head. "Mom told me that, but I thought he'd do better if I held him. He liked me at home."

"I'm sure he did." August patted her nephew's shoulder.

Kit's heart melted as she watched the interaction. Not only was he great with pets, but he was also good with children. Was there anything August didn't excel at?

"Did you know that bearded dragons can wear leashes?" August stood, his gaze rotating between Wes and Stephen.

"Like a dog?" Wes's mouth fell open at the same time that Kit's did.

She knew a little about the lizards, but not much. And she wouldn't have thought to try to leash a reptile.

"They can." He made sure to make eye contact with Stephen before adding to his son, "It takes a lot of training, but it can be done. Maybe Aunt Kit and I can show you some training routines sometime."

"Well, I can tag along," Kit said. "But it will have to be August showing the tricks. He's the reptile specialist…or the closest we have."

Stephen looked at her and she felt her cheeks heat. Her brother smiled, then looked at his son, "I'd like that. You two could come to dinner sometime, maybe?" Her brother gave her a look that only older brothers gave, but August seemed oblivious to the subtle sibling communication happening. "Though today we should probably focus on the smell."

August looked at Kit and then gestured to room three. "I want to take a closer look, but I suspect it's infectious stomatitis, or mouth rot. It's a bacterial infection we can treat."

When he was gone, their receptionist placed her hands

on the reception desk and leaned forward. "That man may be perfect."

Kit nodded. "He certainly handled that crisis well." And her brother seemed to approve. She looked at room three and felt her lips tip up. August Rhodes was one of a kind.

The clinic is fine. Kit is handling things well. How is rehab?

August sighed as more questions regarding the clinic popped into his cell phone. This had become his father's nightly routine. Ask about the clinic but refuse to answer any questions regarding rehab.

The clinic was operating fine. Better than fine, according to more than a few clients. He'd not informed his father that several clients had mentioned that their animals preferred him. Or that the clinic seemed to run smoother with August and Kit at the helm rather than Dr. Jeff. Those were not words he shared with his father.

In fact, whenever he passed along information about how well things were going, his father's response was a flurry of texts with specific questions. Like he was looking for a reason to find fault.

Maybe he was.

August's stomach rolled as his phone dinged. No response on how physical therapy was going, but three questions about the supply of dog meds and a reminder that surgeries were always scheduled for Thursday unless it was an emergency. He'd been at the clinic for three weeks. He knew that procedures like spaying and neutering were done on Thursday.

"Your father freaking out because you run the clinic better than he does?" Kit kissed his cheek as she slid next to him on the couch.

His heart settled as she laid her head on his shoulder. It was such a small moment, but one that made his soul leap with happiness. He wrapped an arm around her and kissed the top of her head. August could get used to this.

"I doubt he thinks we're running it better than him. He doesn't think that highly of me. Today he made sure I knew when surgery schedules and med orders were." He kissed her head again.

"Or maybe he's trying to help you? Make sure you know everything." She kissed his cheek.

He'd never considered that. "More likely, it's just he believes the place will fall apart without Dr. Jeff."

"And it hasn't." Kit yawned. "That has to worry him." She held up her hands as he turned on the couch to look at her. "I'm not saying that is the right reaction. But the clinic is his life. If it doesn't need him…" She shrugged as she let the rest of the sentence die away.

His phone dinged with a few more questions, but now August looked at them with fresh eyes. His father was demanding. But what if he was trying to help? Worried that August didn't need him, and wanting to insert a piece of himself?

August still wasn't sure that was the case, but it was an interesting thought.

"So my nephew adopted a bearded dragon and let it loose in the clinic, and you knew exactly what to do." Kit tapped his shoulder.

She was trying to distract him. And he was more than happy to oblige.

"Wes is adorable and will be a great beardy parent. But, yes, since beardies are the most popular reptile pet, I saw a lot of them when I worked at the exotic vet clinic in Florida."

"An exotic vet clinic." Her eyes sparkled as she sat up.

Her hands rested on his thigh, but he missed having her right beside him. August grabbed her hand, letting his thumb roll over her palm. He doubted he'd ever get tired of touching her.

Which would be a problem since he'd be leaving at some point.

An internal shudder shook him. He didn't want to leave Kit. But her family was here. Leo's resting place was here. This was her home. He couldn't ask her to leave. And he couldn't stay... Could he?

"Well, come on." Kit kissed his cheek and squeezed his hand. She was nearly bouncing as she looked at him. "What was the most exciting animal you treated?"

August chuckled. "Mostly I saw beardies. The bearded dragon is the most popular reptile pet in the US. And ball pythons. It's amazing how many people get pythons not realizing that they can grow to five feet long and weigh thirty pounds. A small terrarium will not be enough!"

He leaned his head back and looked at the ceiling. Stepping onto his responsible reptile pet ownership soapbox was unnecessary. He cared when any pet was mistreated, and far too many were.

But reptiles were harder to rehome. Far too many owners got a reptile, realized it was too much for them and released it into the wild, like Wes's friend planned to do today.

"I remember when Florida instituted a ban on Burmese pythons." Kit's voice was quiet as her fingers stroked his.

"Yeah. Burmese pythons are invasive. Those snakes can grow to twenty feet and weigh over two hundred pounds. Makes the ball python look tiny in comparison. But it's not the snake's fault. It's bad owners."

"You like reptiles." Kit tilted her head as she looked

at him. "I don't mean in the we're-vets-so-we-love-all-animals way, though I admit that even though I understand their purpose in the ecosystem I am not a fan of spiders. I mean you love reptiles. They're your favorite. Aren't they?"

August nodded. He knew he was in the minority of vets. Those that loved the creatures usually ended up at zoos with reptile houses, severely limiting the number of vets that were qualified to look at cold-blooded pets.

Veterinarian school was shifting, more classes were being offered in exotics, but it was still a drop in the bucket compared to the classes on small and large mammals. Which he loved too.

But there was something about snakes, turtles and lizards that excited him. He mentally did a happy dance anytime one showed up at the clinic. During his year at the exotic vet, he'd learned so much. And loved every minute.

"They are my favorite." He laughed as Kit nodded in a told-you-so manner. "I mean, I love dogs, cats and horses. But when a lizard hides behind a food cart or a snake wanders in—I don't know how to explain it. Something inside me just goes gooey. I've actually looked at getting the additional certifications for reptiles and amphibians more than once."

And each time he'd pulled up the forms, looked at the additional jobs that would help him complete the last few months of his internship qualification, another new job popped up. Another new adventure.

It was a fun dream. But he was fine with who he was.

"The Zoo Knoxville's reptile house is pretty amazing. And they occasionally do internships for vets. That would let you qualify for the certification. You would be so good at it. I mean, we don't see a lot of reptiles…" Her cheeks colored as she looked at him.

"I…" Kit bit her lip. "I just mean there are opportunities that aren't far if you wanted to do that. Since you light up when you talk about the cold-blooded little guys."

"Something to think about." August offered her a smile.

"Don't do that." Kit blinked and shook her head. "If you aren't interested, say so. But don't give that flippant response."

He felt his mouth fall open as her bottom lip popped out. If her eyes weren't shooting daggers, the image might have been cute…or even sexy. But there was no mistaking the anger mixed with just a hint of disappointment.

How many times had his father's eyes looked at him in the same way?

Seeing it in Kit's gaze sent another shudder through him.

Her hand squeezed his and she dropped a light kiss to his cheek. "There's no judgment here, August. All I was saying was that if you love that field, there are options nearby. 'Cause I think I'd like it if you were nearby."

The air in the room felt heavy as he pulled it into his lungs. His body coursed with flames as he turned so he could fully look at her.

Her eyes were focused on her free hand, looking at a bit of chipped polish, but the brilliant color in her cheeks told him she probably hadn't meant to utter that last line.

"This is the first time I've been back to Tennessee. A short stop to help…" His throat tightened as he lifted her chin to meet his gaze. "But I'm in no hurry to leave."

He lost himself in Kit's eyes as that truth hung between them. Today had been hectic, hell the last three weeks had been one rush after another. But here, now, sitting on her couch, August wished he could push pause. Wished he could freeze this single moment. Hang it on a wall in his memory and just as it was now so he'd never forget any piece of it.

"So..." Kit grabbed the remote and laid her feet across his, settling in in a way that made his heart leap. "Want to watch the animal channel and see if we can guess the diagnosis before the TV doc?"

He couldn't help the chuckle that flew from his lips. "You want to race TV docs...knowing we don't get to see the test results they do? And knowing we're on a TV timer?"

"That's what makes it a fun game!"

"Then let's do it." He kissed her cheek and relaxed as she settled against him.

CHAPTER SEVEN

AUGUST YAWNED AS he locked the clinic's front door, then glanced at the silly wall calendar. Mentally he marked off another day in Tennessee.

Another successful day.

Time seemed to fly as the days turned to weeks. And August wished he felt that the rush was a good thing. That he could say the age old cliché that time flies when you're having fun.

Which was true. But that wasn't the primary feeling in his body. As much as he wanted it to be.

He should be having fun with Kit. And he was. He just wished he could enjoy it more rather than dealing with bone-deep exhaustion at the end of most days.

The exhaustion wasn't a surprise. He and Kit were covering the load of at least three vets and hadn't had a day off all month. Somehow he'd managed to be at the clinic every day. Even Sundays, though he'd made sure their Sunday time was only half days.

Only half days.

This wasn't going to work in the long term. He stretched his head, trying to work out the knots in the back of his neck. A nice long shower and night spent next to Kit were the first things his body needed. But the second was a day or two off.

And Kit needed time off too. Ideally he'd convince her to take a vacation, but he'd settle for two days off in a row. A real weekend together.

August pursed his lips and rolled his shoulders as he prepared himself to enter the office his father and Kit shared in the back. She needed a break.

We just need a relief vet for the weekend. A bit of a break for both of us. We can go hiking. Or horseback riding. Get some fresh air. Not interested in those options? How about a weekend of streaming movies and seeing how much popcorn we can consume? A weekend without stepping foot in here, just the two of us.

His mental speech sounded all right…but how would the woman he knew was bent over paperwork after a day serving more than three dozen patients feel? Kit prided herself on her long workdays. But burnout could happen to anyone. And he suspected she was teetering on it without realizing it.

How many vets had he subbed for that had worked themselves too hard for their clinics? One had nearly left veterinarian practice for good and August had never forgotten his colleagues' comments about how Dr. Burke had been so productive right before the burnout. Accomplishing more than any of them.

In an effort to stave off the rising cliff, to prove to himself that he was fine. Until he wasn't.

That was the thing about burnout. If you weren't actively giving yourself time to rejuvenate your body and spirit, they'd eventually demand it.

Her need for perfectionism, her constant concern for bettering herself and the clinic weren't sustainable. She didn't seem to understand that improvement wasn't a constant path of escalation. Eventually things had to level off or you went mad.

He took a deep breath. She was working herself constantly…taking pride in it and nothing else. It wasn't healthy.

"Kit?" He knocked when no one answered. Frowning, he looked at the door handle. The office was a shared space, but he hadn't claimed any of it. It was his father's and Kit's, and the door was closed.

Still, she always answered when he knocked. In fact most of the time the door wasn't even closed. Worry pierced his heart. It was an overreaction, he knew it. Maybe she had headphones in. Or was on the phone. He knocked one more time and when no answer came, he opened the door. If something was wrong, he needed to get to her.

His brain was screaming that he was overreacting, while also running through a list of worries. That she'd fallen or had a stress-induced health crisis. He'd seen that in Boston. They'd managed to revive Dr. Folles, but his doctors had put him on a strict regime to regain his strength and demanded he work no more than eight hours a day.

"Surprise!" Kit called as she held up a small trophy. Her body swayed as she beamed and held it out to him.

His heart rate settled as he looked at her. She was fine. His mind wrapped itself around that thought. She was fine.

And looked so happy. And clearly proud of the surprise she'd orchestrated.

August blinked as his eyes registered a copper turtle sitting on a base that he suspected was meant to look like seaweed, but it didn't quite look right. "What am I looking at Kit?"

"A trophy!" She beamed as she passed it to him. "Your trophy!"

He took the small trophy and felt his eyes mist as he looked at the inscription on its base: August Rhodes. Best Reptile Vet in Foxfield.

"They didn't have any lizards. Or snakes. Not sure why they had turtles, but you should have heard the awkward silence on the end of the line as I went through a list of reptiles, hoping they'd have one. Not one snake or crocodile!" Kit's cheeks were pink, and she crossed and then uncrossed her arms as she looked at him.

"It's just a silly trophy. The base is a little loose. The local trophy shop is mostly for sports teams, but..." She ran a hand through her hair. "I just... You said you'd never gotten a trophy and... I think you are the best reptile vet in the city."

"I'm not actually certified." His voice was thick as he ran his fingers over the nameplate. His body soaring as seeing the words in print sent a cascade of emotions floating through him.

"Pish." The noise left her mouth, and August felt a smile tip his lips.

"You have more qualifications than anyone else in the city. The vets at Love Pets Vet don't focus on reptiles and amphibians at all. Your father and I maintain a passing knowledge and the phone numbers for the specialists at the Zoo Knoxville if a complicated case or even an uncomplicated case comes in." She crossed her arms again as she looked at him.

"So in that way, it's very true. Besides—" she shrugged "—it's just a silly fun gesture. You know, since you mentioned never getting a trophy. If you don't like it..."

Maybe it was silly, and fun. But it wasn't just anything. At least not for him.

"I love it." August looked at her, his eyes stung, and he

couldn't believe that a hunk of iron covered in cheap copper could make him feel so many things. A deep-down wish that he'd finished his internship. That he could truly claim the words on the nameplate.

It was intoxicating. Maybe this was why people chased trophies and ribbons.

Kit danced to him and kissed his cheek. "I wanted you to have a trophy. You mentioned never getting one, and well, I know it's not technically from a competition, but that doesn't mean it's wrong either."

"Should I put it on our mantel or..." His tongue seized as he realized that he'd referred to her house as theirs. August blinked, trying to finish the sentence. Trying to find any words that might make sense.

"We could put it on our mantel..." Kit stepped into his arms.

Was it my imagination or did she emphasize our *in that sentence?*

His heart leaped at her inclusion of the word. He'd said it unintentionally, but Kit's words... He'd never tire of being part of an *our* that included Kit.

"Or," she continued, "you could put it in the waiting area with the other awards your father has out."

His stomach dropped at the idea. To put a trophy with his name on it with the ones his father had chosen to display. His body wanted to dash to the waiting room. Wanted to place this trophy with all the others, wanted his father to see it when he walked in.

Then reality took over. "Kit, I love this trophy. I love the idea behind it and all the meaning. It means more than I can possibly put into words." He ran his thumb over the turtle's shell, emotion clogging his throat as he reread the words she'd had engraved on it.

It meant so much, but it wasn't real. Not truly.

Even if he suddenly wished it were.

"It seems disingenuous to put it up there. I mean, I didn't really win anything, not in a real way."

"The only award that's real on that shelf, at least if you mean voted on by more than one person, is the Foxfield's Finest certificates from so long ago."

"What?" August felt his mouth fall open as he tried to register her words. That couldn't be right. Recognition was the only thing his father cared about as much as this clinic.

He still remembered his father putting up the floating shelf when he was a kid. Watching him buff the first awards he'd placed on it. His father had been so proud of it. And he'd wanted to include August.

After carefully laying out his awards, he'd told August that one day he'd put one of his on the shelf. That day had never come, though his father repeated the offer often. Then always added the statement, *If only you'd win one.*

His hands shook as he asked, "They aren't real?" It was such an important part of his father's mentality. How could they not be?

Kit shook her head. "Not really. He puts quotes from the reviews of the clinic on nameplates. He rotates them in and out. I think there are dozens in his house…or maybe he just tosses them when they get a little old. Though I guess my AVMA nomination certificate is framed up there too."

"You were nominated for an AVMA Award?" August stared at the woman before him. How had he not noticed that the night he'd arrived? He'd looked at that wall. Looked at the trophies and certificates. And felt inadequate. So he'd turned away before seeing her accomplishment. And he'd kept his eyes from drifting toward it anytime he'd been in the waiting room.

Kit nodded as though dropping that piece of information wasn't an incredible reveal. "I was nominated for the Animal Welfare Award several years ago."

"Are you serious?" The trophy in his hand was a lovely gesture, but that was one of the highest awards in veterinarian medicine. It was a true honor to just be nominated.

"Yeah, didn't win." Kit smiled, then shrugged. "Remember…always the runner-up."

She meant it as a joke, but the tone cut him to the core. Her mother had done that to her, just as his father had made him crave a place on his trophy shelf, and he'd spent so many years refusing to give in to that craving. Refusing to give his father the satisfaction.

But she should be proud of this accomplishment. Full stop.

"Kit." He set the trophy on the desk and pulled her hands into his. "That is amazing." Her eyes shifted and he wanted to scream at the woman who'd made her doubt herself.

He'd worked all over the place, with dozens of vets in his career, and he'd never met anyone that had been nominated for an AVMA Award.

It was an impressive accomplishment. If a relief vet had a nomination on their résumé, clinics would fight for the opportunity to hire them.

"I know it's great." She shrugged. "But that isn't the point tonight." She lifted on her toes and kissed his cheek again. "Tonight is all about your award."

She grabbed it from the desk and held it up. "Which was selected by a very prestigious panel, if I might be so bold." Her tone was playful, like she were a mock presenter. It was adorable.

I'm falling in love with her.

The thought flew through his brain as his heart raced.

The blood pounded in his ears as he stared at the woman before him. The truth rolled through him as he tried to find his footing in a world that had suddenly and irrevocably shifted.

Dear God, he'd fallen in love with her. It had happened so fast he'd barely noticed. But he loved her. What did one do with this information?

August had dated regularly. But he'd never had a long-term relationship. Never more than a few months of fun with a partner before going their separate ways.

He hadn't minded that pattern. In fact, before meeting Kit, he'd have said that was perfect. After all, he'd watched his parents' union. On their wedding day, they'd believed in forever. He could still remember the grainy home videos showing them happy. So happy.

That couple had vanished before his brain had been developed enough to form long-term memories.

He had no experience with love. Not really. But he was in love with Kit Bedrick. A woman who prided herself on working seven days a week. The irony was not lost on him.

Still, he loved her. Of that he was certain. And he had no idea what to do with the information.

"Where do you want to put it, Kit?" August took the trophy from her hands and pulled her close. This was a lovely gift. One that he'd had never thought to ask for. But seeing his name on a trophy, even a silly one with a turtle on messed up seaweed, was a gift he'd never expected.

The fact that it had come from the woman he loved only made it more precious. But it still didn't compare to the gift that was simply Kit. He kissed the top of her head, just reveling in this moment.

"I think it should go with the others out front." She

smiled, stepped out of his embrace and grabbed his hand, pulling him toward the quiet waiting room.

He stood in front of the award corner. The shelf was smaller than he remembered. Or maybe it was just that this area had held such a big part of his life for so long. Kit lifted the trophy from his hands, and he let her.

Kit put it in the center of the others, turned and smiled. "Ready to go home?"

Home. Such a simple phrase with so much meaning. August took a deep breath and let his eyes wander from the trophy Kit had ordered him to the framed certificate with her nomination.

"You are amazing." August kissed her, savoring the taste of her. The feel of her heat against him. The perfection of it all.

She hit his hip and let out a light chuckle. "I'm all right, I guess."

It was the *I guess* that ripped through him. Because she didn't believe that being nominated for such a prestigious award, even once in her career, was more than most vets ever got. Maybe Rhodes Animal Services hadn't gotten the Foxfield's Finest Award since she came to help his dad, but none of those things diminished her abilities.

And somehow he was going to find a way to make her realize that.

It was long past dinner, with Kit softly snoring beside him, when August realized he'd never brought up the idea of a day off. Of taking a break for their mental well-being.

Tomorrow, his exhausted brain called as he closed his eyes. *Tomorrow...*

Kit rolled over as carefully as she could in August's arms. He let out a soft sigh and her heart melted. Waking up next to someone you cared about was the best. It was the thing she'd missed most when she lost Leo.

There was something about sleeping next to someone. Feeling their movements, a heavy arm over your waist, a late-night snore. The heat of another body keeping you warm at night. Reminding you that you weren't alone. It was such a small thing…something most people hardly noticed.

Until it was ripped away.

August smiled in his sleep, and she wondered what he was dreaming about.

Selfishly she hoped it was her.

She was getting too comfortable with him. She'd slept better these last few weeks than she had in years. Like her body knew she was safe and cared for. It was invigorating.

And it was getting difficult to remind herself that it was also temporary. That when his father was done with rehab, August would start looking for a new place.

Even in the morning light when her heart wanted to lean into the belief that maybe…just maybe it could be more, her brain jumped in with the reminder.

August had only agreed to stay until his father finished rehab. That was the promise he'd given. But he'd agreed to it before they'd fallen into bed together. So much had changed in the last few weeks.

Hadn't it?

She kissed his jaw, enjoying how his lips tipped up even farther. But the enjoyment was tinged with a hint of sadness.

After Dr. Jeff was cleared to return to work, what would his son do?

It was a question that remained on the tip of her

tongue. A question she was desperate to know the answer to. And terrified to hear.

She wanted him to stay. She'd basically said as much the night they'd talked about him getting the certification for amphibians and reptiles. But basically saying it and flat-out saying it were two separate things.

How often had she counseled friends that if they wanted to know the answer to their relationship question, they should simply ask? Of course she'd been happily ensconced in a wonderful engagement and marriage then.

And now that she needed relationship help, her friends were happily married with young children. The get-togethers were few and far between with her work schedule and their busy lives. But they'd likely give her the same advice she'd given them.

Just ask.

It was solid advice. The right answer. But it was different on this side of the dating game.

August let out a gentle laugh and shifted on his side. She rolled with him, determined to enjoy these few minutes before the day started. A few minutes where she didn't have to share Dr. August Rhodes with anyone else.

She ran her hand along the turtle tattooed on his arm. It didn't look anything like the one on top of the silly trophy she'd given him. She still wasn't sure if the trophy was a good idea or ridiculous, but she wanted the words on it to be true.

Wanted him to at least consider her suggestion about finishing his certifications at the Zoo Knoxville.

The first reason was because it would make him happy. Watching him corner Wes's bearded dragon and then melt when he lifted Biscuit and stroked his back had been one of her happiest moments with August. He loved the creatures. Anytime a cold-blooded animal wandered through the door, he knew how to respond.

Unlike her and Dr. Jeff, August never had to search out the answer. Didn't have to call in help. He read the reptile and amphibian medical studies along with the studies on cats, dogs and other small animals. It brought him joy. So he should have the certification that gave him standing in the veterinarian world. And it would help with his relief vet assignments.

She'd looked at relief vets as soon as she heard about Dr. Jeff's accident. There was a larger pool of applicants than she'd expected but the vast majority were trained in small or large domestic breeds, like most vets. August was already cleared in both of those... If he added amphibians and reptiles, he could go anywhere.

Her heart broke anytime she thought about his next assignment. That was the second reason she'd mentioned the Zoo Knoxville. *The selfish reason.* Knoxville was only a few hours from Foxfield. An easy drive that meant they might still be able to see each other for a while.

She wasn't ready to say goodbye. Kit ran her hand on his side, across his stomach, just touching him. Memorizing him.

She'd never be ready.

She was only beginning to accept that. In the early morning light, Kit traced her fingers along his jaw, trying to memorize the subtle shift in his features. The small freckle on the edge of his jaw that was always covered in stubble in the morning. The light scar on his cheek from an injury so old he said he didn't remember it. The bump in the center of his nose from a baseball he'd caught with his face in elementary school.

All these and so many more things that made up her August.

"August." She whispered his name and dropped a light kiss on his lips.

She was falling in love with him. She kissed the tip of his nose and closed her eyes. No, she was in love with August Rhodes.

It wasn't something she'd planned. Wasn't what she was looking for. But she knew the feeling. She'd felt its absence for so many years and having it back sent a sense of fullness through her.

And dread too.

She'd never expected to lose Leo. Never expected to have to put herself back together after a tragedy. But she'd done it. Because she hadn't had another choice.

But when August left, he'd still be on this plane. Still alive but not with her. Unless she could find a way to convince him that staying in Foxfield with her was the best choice.

There had to be a way to convince him that staying, reclaiming his roots here, was a good option. To convince him that her clinic, *their* clinic, was where he belonged.

She feathered kisses along his neck, her tongue dipping into the space at the base of it that always made August sigh.

His hand cupped her breast, his thumb tracing along her already erect nipples. "Good morning, Kit."

She smiled and laid her head on his chest as his fingers wandered along her skin, sending rockets of desire through her with each stroke. "I didn't mean to wake you."

"Tsk." August dropped a kiss to her lips. "I don't think that is the truth."

She nipped his bottom lip as she moved her body over his. His eyes sparked as she rubbed against him. She loved turning him on. Loved watching the need pulse through him.

"Maybe it's a little bit of an understatement." She caught his mouth before he could say anything else. Deepening the kiss, she lost herself in his taste as his hands gripped her waist. The urge to strip and join their bodies was nearly overwhelming, but she wanted more.

Pulling back, she let her mouth start a slow descent while she continued to move her hips against his, relishing the groans pouring from August's lips.

"Kit." His voice was heady with need as she moved her mouth lower, his hands running through her short hair as she gradually made her way to where he needed her.

When she finally took him in her mouth, August's back arched. Kit let her nails scrape the insides of his thighs as she pleasured him.

"Kit... I..." August's breath caught. "Dear God, Kit. I need you." She heard him open the bedside drawer, then he sat up, pulling her with him.

Capturing her mouth, August sheathed himself, then let Kit join their bodies. He pressed his thumb between their bodies, kneading her pleasure point as heat, desire and love scorched her.

She shuddered as completion rocked through her. August gripped her hips, and she rode with his movements as he crested to oblivion too.

In the moments after laying on August's chest, completeness settled through her. It was intoxicating and she wanted to hold on to it for as long as possible.

August's fingers ran over her skin, the lightness of his touch bringing a smile to her lips. It was such a small moment, yet it meant more. "I love you."

His fingers paused and she lifted her head, heat pooling in her cheeks as she met his clear gaze. "I know it's cliché to say after we…" She dipped her head. God, she'd told him she loved him after making love to him.

But the words weren't a lie. And she was not going to diminish them by pretending they were.

"I could tell you it just slipped out, and in some ways it did, but it's true, August Rhodes. I love you. The world can be ripped away so quickly and those words matter." She smiled and kissed his lips. "You don't have to say anything. But I need you to know I love you."

He stared at her, and her heart pounded. She'd meant it when she said he didn't have to say anything, but the silence in the room was terribly loud.

"Kit." His mouth opened but no other words came out.

She swallowed as she kissed his lips. "I need to get ready for the day." She let her lips graze his once more, then slid from his chest. It was Sunday and there was work to be done in the clinic.

There's always work to be done.

"Want to go hiking with me?" August propped himself up on one hand, the sheet draped over his waist. He looked like he belonged in a rom-com movie rather than her bed. "Take the day off. Spend it with me. Please."

"Yes." She nodded. It wasn't a declaration of love, but there was a look in his eyes that sent a shiver through her. Besides, there was always work to be done at the clinic. And there always would be. But there were no guarantees with August, and she'd earned a day off.

Her stomach twisted at the idea of relaxation. She briefly wanted to list the mental reasons why she'd earned it…but that wasn't necessary. She was taking a day off with the man she loved. And she was going to enjoy it.

CHAPTER EIGHT

"IT'S BEAUTIFUL UP HERE." Kit stood still, looking at the scenery overlooking the Roan High Bluff.

It was beautiful. The Cloudland Trail in Roan Mountain State Park was one of the prettiest places in the world. Growing up, he'd spent as much time in the state park as he could manage.

He'd even hiked a portion of the Appalachian Trail senior year. The hardwood forests were his sanctuary, a place he'd missed more than he'd ever admitted—even to himself.

Coming back here, walking the paths soothed one of the aches in his heart. But today, it wasn't the trail or the mountain commanding his attention. The woman he loved was all he could see. And she loved him too.

The fact that he hadn't told her he loved her this morning burned his soul. He should have said them. The words were there. They just hadn't come forth.

She loved him. His heart soared with that knowledge. He wanted to tell her the truth, wanted to scream it into being. But he'd never spoken those words to another, because they meant things.

Love was a gift, but it meant changes. So many changes.

The last thing he wanted to do was hurt Kit. And leaving Foxfield would hurt her. Her brothers were here, Leo was buried here. It was her place. Besides, the clinic, her clinic for all purposes, was her life. She thrived as a veterinary practice owner. One who needed to learn to let herself relax.

Still, it was what she was meant to be. He couldn't ask her to leave it. He wouldn't.

So that meant he'd be the one changing. The one adjusting. The one shifting his path. The one to step into a new role.

When he'd stood waiting for his father to arrive at graduation, the minutes ticking by aimlessly, he'd promised himself he'd never work at his father's clinic. That he'd work anywhere, for anyone, but not for Dr. Jeff Rhodes. And not in Foxfield, Tennessee.

That promise had motivated him to find a job, and to keep finding them when his vet contracts ran out. But he'd never settled anywhere. He'd embraced the road in a way his mother hadn't been able to.

Seen so many of the places she never got to.

And he'd never planted roots.

He'd sworn it was because he didn't want to be like his dad. Didn't want to own a vet clinic. But what if it was because his home would always be here?

He stepped beside Kit as the wind rustled around them and his body settled. The wandering need that clawed through him for so long hadn't reared in his soul since he'd returned.

No, that wasn't true.

He'd planned to leave until he met Kit. She was home. The place where his roots felt like they belonged. So why hadn't the words slipped from his lips?

Fear.

Such a simple and complex answer. Was he ready to

commit to her? Ready to figure out what his new path was beside her? *Yes.*

August let out a soft breath and reached for Kit's hand. He couldn't pick a better setting. Or a better time. The wind heavy with the scent of the forest blew a piece of Kit's short hair across her eyes and August reached up to brush it away.

"Kit…" Her face turned and her lips parted. She was perfection.

He wanted to say the words, but his throat seized.

Before he could work through the emotions and fears clogging his mind, a yelp echoed not far down the trail. Kit turned on her heels, and August followed.

A dog's cry of pain was a sound no one liked hearing, but up here on the trail, almost a mile from the closest parking facility and nearly an hour from their clinic, the closest in the area, it sent a chill through him. There were many things that could go wrong when hiking with a dog. While August knew people loved bringing their pets with them, he only recommended hiking with an animal to avid hikers who knew the trailheads, and always kept their dog on a leash. Their clinic sold dog emergency kits and he'd added a hiking kit to the selection soon after arriving.

Now he wished he'd grabbed one today, but they'd left Bucky at home since he wasn't ready to walk on a trail yet. Though he was getting much better on his leash.

Another yelp lit up the trail, and Kit picked up her pace as she looked back at him briefly. "I hope it's not a snake bite. The antivenom I have at the clinic expired just after your dad had his accident. I put in a new order, but it hasn't arrived."

"The efficacy of expired antivenom is still better than no antivenom." August gulped air as he matched Kit's pace. Despite her shorter legs, and hiking up a mountain, she hadn't slowed at all. "Only the copperhead and timber rattlesnake are in this area. And those guys don't seek out active trailheads. So hopefully…"

The trail rounded and a young woman bent over a what looked like a Lab-mix came into view. Her shoulders were shaking as she looked through a bag and kept one hand on the dog, trying to calm her. "Hold still, Abby. You're going to be okay. You are. I promise. I'm so sorry, girl. I promised I'd take care of you, and I will. I promise."

She sniffled and looked up as Kit and August approached. She swiped her eyes with the back of her hand, and August's eyes shifted to the dog. None of the paws looked swollen and a poisonous bite would already be noticeable.

Kit bent and waited for the young woman to meet her gaze. "I'm Dr. Kit Bedrick and this is Dr. August Rhodes. We're both vets."

"You're kidding." A nervous laugh slipped from the woman's mouth, and she sat back on her heels. "Of course Mom would make sure that vets were on the trail when we came today."

August blinked at her words and looked around the trail. He didn't see anyone else. "Your mom's here?"

"Sort of." She pursed her lips and held up a small tin. Her eyes filled as she tapped the top of it and looked from August to Kit.

"I'm so sorry for your loss." Kit's words were soft, filled with sympathy for the grieving young woman.

"Thanks." She blew out a breath. "It feels weird to thank someone for saying they're sorry. Sorry, I'm rambling. I'm Layla and this is Abby. My mom's dog, and now mine."

"It's nice to meet you, Layla and Abby." Kit's sooth-ing voice carried over the situation and the Lab wagged her tail. Though not with the veracity that one typically saw with Labs.

The dogs were perpetually happy. Unless they were hurt or grieving. And this dog was both.

August bent so he was on the same level as Kit and Layla. Abby had her front raw paw lifted. He could see blood on her pad. "What happened to her pad?"

Layla rubbed Abby's back with one hand and wiped a tear away with her other. "She stepped on something and tore her pad. I think a rock, but I'm not sure. I bought a pet first-aid kit for hiking, but I can't find it." Layla sucked in a deep breath, "Mom asked that I scatter her ashes on Roan High Bluff. It was her favorite place.

"And Abby was her favorite child." Layla closed her eyes as she tilted her head to the sun.

"I'm sorry." August patted the young woman's shoul-der. "I understand how hard it is to come in second, or further back, with a parent."

"It sucks." Layla's eyes opened and grief mixed with anger as she looked from him to Kit, her cheeks coloring as she looked at the tin. "But it isn't Abby's fault. Still, I thought bringing her… Well, now here we are, and I'll have to come back another day."

She looked in her backpack and her shoulders re-laxed as she pulled out the travel-size dog first-aid kit. "I thought I'd forgotten to pack it. Guess I was panick-ing too much to see it."

"I've done that." Kit rubbed Abby's ears, then offered her hand. "Why don't you let me fix Abby. I can wait with here with her, and maybe…" She looked to August, and he nodded.

"I'd be happy to go up the trail with you. Unless you'd

rather be alone to say goodbye. Then I can carry Abby back down the trail for you."

"You sure you don't mind?" Layla held out the first-aid kit to Kit.

"Not at all. Taking care of animals is kinda my thing." She took the materials and rubbed Abby's belly. "We'll be okay. Take as long as you need."

Layla grabbed her mom's ashes and started up the path. She didn't ask August to come, but she didn't say anything when he stepped beside her. The climb to Roan Bluff took about fifteen minutes, and August didn't interrupt Layla's thoughts. If she wanted to talk, she would.

When they reached the peak, she opened the lid and grabbed a handful of ashes, releasing them into the wind. Tears raced down her cheeks, but she didn't say anything as she repeated the process again and again. Finally she closed the tin and accepted the water August offered to rinse her hands.

"Goodbye, Mom. I wish we'd found peace in this life, but I hope you find it in the next. And I want you to know that I'm charting my own path. The one I want, not to spite you but for me."

The words struck August like a hammer. That wasn't what he was doing. Except it was. Foxfield wasn't a trap…unless he made it one. His throat was thick as emotions tore through him.

The woman he loved, who loved him, was on this trail. She'd told him she loved him, and rather than open his heart and speak the truth to her, he'd hesitated. Because he was scared to consider staying in Foxfield.

Scared on some level that he was giving in to the thing he'd sworn he'd never give in to. It was ridiculous and shameful.

He and his father might never see eye to eye. But that

had nothing to do with Kit. He loved her. She was his home. The place where he felt safe and loved.

The urge to get to her was overwhelming. His heart pounded in his ears as he looked over the bluff, urging his feet to move. But he wasn't going to rush Layla.

She took a few deep breaths, then turned and offered August a watery smile. "Thank you for coming with me. This was important to Mom." She hesitated and wrapped her arms around herself. "And me. But now it's time to get back to Abby. Are you sure you don't mind carrying Abby down the path for me? I could probably get her, though it will take us longer. I don't want to hold up you and Dr. Bedrick anymore than I already am."

"We were headed down the trail anyway." It was admirable that Layla was taking over Abby's care. And clear that despite feeling like she came in a distant second to a dog, she wasn't punishing Abby for it. Far too many people dumped their loved ones' pets when they passed or went into senior care.

When Kit and Abby came back into view, August's heart leaped. Her gaze met his and he looked at her, hoping that the depth of his emotions was clear. As soon as he had her alone, he was going to tell her he loved her. Tell her she completed him. Tell her that his world had shifted irreparably since he'd found her.

Abby's tail thumped as Layla bent to pet her ears. "Ready to go, girl?"

Abby shifted and stood. She gingerly put weight on the foot Kit had bandaged. The dog took one step, sat, lifted her leg and let out a whine.

"Oh, no." Layla looked at Kit. "Do you think something else is wrong? I saw the cut on her paw...but what if..."

Kit held up her hand and shook her head. "I looked

over Abby while you were on the bluff with August. She is fine. That cut is little more than a paper cut. She's being a bit of a drama queen."

Layla let out a chuckle. "Well, she is a drama queen, so that is not new."

"She can walk on it." Kit sighed. "It's sore, but she's capable. However—" Kit looked to August "—we'll make better time if we carry her."

August bent and looked at Abby. "You ready to go, Abby?" The dog licked his nose and August took that as his cue to lift the dog and put her on his shoulders. Her tail thumped against his back as they started down the trail.

Abby was perfectly content to wag her tail at the people they passed on the trail who doted on the "injured" pup. Between the three of them, they made decent time to the parking lot. Abby licked the back of his hand as he slipped her into the car and buckled her in the pup seat belt Layla had for her.

"Thank you. Not sure what I would have done if you two hadn't popped by. Sorry I interrupted your date."

August laced his arm around Kit's waist, desperate to touch her. "I'm glad we could help. We run Rhodes Animal Services in Foxfield if you need a vet."

Layla smiled and nodded. "You'll be seeing us. But hopefully only for checkups."

"That's my hope too." Kit laid her head against August's shoulder.

They waved as Layla pulled her car out and drove away.

"We run Rhodes Animal Services?" Kit raised a brow as she looked at him. "We… I like the sound of that."

"I love you, Kit Bedrick. I should have said it this

morning. Should have told you when I realized it. I just…" August closed his eyes.

"You don't have to explain." Her lips grazed his cheek and his soul danced.

"I do." August kissed the top of her head. "I was scared to say them. Scared of the changes that saying those words out loud meant. But I refuse to deny the truth. I love you, Kit."

"I love you too." She placed both hands on either side of his cheeks and kissed him. The world disappeared as August lost himself in the moment with the woman he loved.

August loved her.

Her mind kept repeating that happy thought. His hand locked in hers. It was electrifying.

He loved her and she loved him. In this moment everything seemed possible. She knew there'd be challenges— all relationships had them. But she wanted to lock away this moment in her memories. Cling to these feelings as they settled in to figure out what life brought them now.

He'd spoken of the changes love brought, but had not named them specifically. Still, she was nearly certain he meant staying. Surely that was what he meant. He was staying.

With her.

Her body was relaxed, not a feeling she was accustomed to, but one she could get used to.

"You look relaxed." August squeezed her hand as they entered the outskirts of Foxfield.

A small giggle left her lips. "It's like you read my mind." She'd never believed the theories that people in love were in sync. But it was true that when you cared about someone, you noticed the little things about them.

It had been so long since she'd had that. She planned to savor it this time around. "I am relaxed. Amazing what a day off will do."

"Think about what a true vacation might do!" August winked.

A vacation? She hadn't taken one of those since she was a child. Even her honeymoon hadn't been a real vacation. She and Leo's focus then was on setting up Love Pets, strapped for cash and just excited to be wed. The idea of leaving for a week or even two was not something she'd considered.

"A vacation? That might be fun." She leaned her head against the back of the seat. Thoughts rolling around her head. She could take a vacation. Not anytime soon, maybe next year. Or after Dr. Jeff finally sold the place to her.

One day.

"Where would you go, if you could go anywhere?"

"Alaska." The word left her lips before she even considered other options.

"Alaska." August chuckled. "That was quick. So you'd prefer to bundle up and see the snow instead of stripping down and laying on a beach?"

"A beach would be fun too," she offered with a shrug. She knew her answer wasn't what most people might say for their first vacation in years, and the need to explain herself bubbled up.

"When I was in college, I saw an ad in the student union that said *Come Visit Alaska.* It had a snowy mountain and cabin on it. Not sure how it landed on the bulletin board, but…"

She squeezed his hand. "I have no idea why, but that poster burned its way into my brain. I've wanted to go ever since. Leo and I always talked about taking an Alaskan cruise. Seeing the Arctic and..." She paused. "Sorry."

"For what?" August pulled into the driveway of their cottage and put the car in Park.

Her throat was tight. She knew that Leo would want her to be happy. She didn't feel like she was being disloyal or cheating on him. It had been so long. But there was no rule book for dealing with the unfulfilled dreams his death left behind.

Should she let go of the dreams that he'd been part of? Even though she was the one who'd sought out Alaska? Was it better to make new dreams with August?

Those were questions that the books and resources on widowhood hadn't prepared her for. What dreams did she get to keep that were a blend of her and Leo?

Kit let go of his hand and he didn't reach for it again. But he didn't let her drop the question either. "Kit?"

"Leo..." Her voice tightened and this time August did reach for her hands.

"You still love him." Before she could answer, August traced his thumb down her chin and cupped her cheek. "And that's okay. Love shouldn't disappear because a person leaves this world. I would never ask you to give up your love of him for me. Promise. I figured your heart just expanded to include us both. And if you want to see Alaska, then we will find a way to make that happen. If you have something special of his, we could even take it with us, if you'd like?"

Of course he'd have the perfect answer. Her heart sighed as she looked at him. "I've always wanted to see Alaska. Did your travels ever take you there?"

"Yep!" August laughed. "I spent the winter in Blue Ash, Alaska. I even got to meet the television star Annie

Masters—well, she's Dr. Annie Bradstone now, but that's a story for another time."

"Maybe next summer we can—"

"Kit!" Her mother's screech carried through the closed windows and Kit shuddered. Her mother did not show up unannounced unless something was wrong.

Though her mother's definition of wrong and Kit's often differed. And usually had something to do with Kit's failings. But she couldn't think of any recent failure that would drive her mother to seek her out in person.

She gripped the door handle and took a deep breath. Hopefully this was quick. And not too embarrassing.

August exited the car too and leaned against the car as he looked at her mother. "You must be Kit's mother. I can see where she gets her good looks."

It was a sweet statement. One most women would like hearing. But Laurie Bedrick was not most mothers. She'd gotten none of the cliché motherly attributes that sitcom moms had. She wanted the best for her children, but she didn't use love and support. Rather it was cutting remarks and demands that pushed her kids.

And the effort had worked with her brothers. It was only Kit who hadn't met expectations. But Kit was working to fix that. Once she owned the clinic and made a few more changes…

Anxiety raced through her as her mother looked her up and down before turning her gaze to August. "She's prettier without the short hair." The complaint exited her mother's lips, and Kit heard August let out a low growl.

She turned and offered him a soft smile. One she hoped was comforting. It wasn't worth arguing with her mother. Besides, this was an old argument.

Kit had worn her hair in a short pixie cut since a stressed cat had latched onto her ponytail in vet school.

She'd done it on a whim and loved it. It was one thing she hadn't changed in her ever-present drive to find a way to please her mom.

"What can I do for you, Mom?" Kit shifted her shoulders, making sure she stood as straight as possible. It wouldn't make her close in height to her statuesque mother, but it was a habit she'd never managed to break.

"Where were you today?" Her mother huffed as she crossed her arms and tapped her foot. "You didn't answer any of my texts."

She didn't owe her an explanation. She was in her late thirties and a doctor of veterinarian medicine. But she still couldn't stop the need to please from welling up in her.

"August and I went for a hike in Roan State Park." Kit ached to lean against the car, to look relaxed. But her body refused to follow the command. "I didn't take my phone. Is something wrong?"

"You made me look like an idiot."

"That's not fair." August wandered to her side and put his arm around her waist.

It was nice to have his support, but she knew that her mother wouldn't appreciate the added commentary. Once Laurie Bedrick was upset, you took the heat and tended to the burns in your heart after.

"I'm not sure what is happening here," August continued, "but maybe we should go inside, have a cup of tea and talk this out—civilly."

"I am not going into my daughter's rented hut. Seriously, late thirties and still renting." She rolled her eyes, refusing to look at the cottage Kit loved.

Kit wanted to let out a moan. Wanted to explain that her rent was well under market value, letting her save to buy the clinic. Wanted to argue that there was nothing wrong with renting; many people did it their entire lives.

Besides, she hoped Dr. Jeff would let her buy the cottage too. Maybe it wasn't as fancy as the home she'd grown up in, or the one that Leo's parents had gifted him when they married, but she liked it.

Instead of listing those things, Kit squeezed August's waist. Her mother was in one of her moods, and it would be better to rip the Band-Aid off than try to hash this out in a civilized manner. "How did I embarrass you by not answering my phone?"

She saw August start to open his mouth, and she shook her head. His frown deepened but he didn't interrupt.

"David's new business partner, Trevor Crest, is in town." Her mother lifted her chin as she waited for a reaction.

It was not a name that Kit recognized but she heard August let out a soft noise. She looked up at him and raised an eyebrow.

"He's the founder of the Payme3."

"Payme3? The cash app?" Kit blinked. It was a payment app that nearly everyone used, but she had no idea why his presence in town would send her mother to her doorstep.

"Yes. The cash app. The man is ridiculously well off." She glanced at August and his arm around Kit's waist before adding, "And single."

"Well, that is nice information, but as you can see, *I'm* not single." She sighed as August kissed the top of her head. "This is not the way I would have liked to tell—"

"Not the point," her mother interrupted as she held up her phone with the image of a Persian cat. "He has a Siamese—"

"That's a Persian," August interjected. His voice was

smooth but she could hear the tint of annoyance. Her mother had cut off Kit, so August was interrupting her. It was sweet.

"The *point* is the cat goes with him everywhere. The creature got into something and got sick. *If* you had answered your phone, you could have taken care of him. David said your clinic was closed on Sunday, but I said you were always here and would be happy to help. I told him that."

"Well, David was right. The clinic is closed on Sunday." It was true she was here on Sundays. And true that she'd have opened up to help if she hadn't been on the trail. But it wasn't wrong to take a day off. It wasn't.

Even though her stomach twisted as her heart tried to reassure her brain.

Her mother continued like she hadn't even heard her. "He has a huge social media presence. Maybe you could have even gotten a blast on that. Did you think of that?"

How could I? I didn't even know about it.

Instead of saying that, Kit kept her voice level. "Is the cat okay?"

"Yes. They went to Love Pets Vet. Best clinic in town according to the Foxfield Finest. A lost opportunity because you went hiking. Shame." She reached into her purse and grabbed her car keys. "Here I am talking about how my daughter is a great vet. How she'd be happy to look after the poor thing. And then you didn't even answer your phone. Didn't even take my call."

"I'm sorry."

"You should be." Her mother pushed her long hair behind her ear and headed toward her car.

August started to move. But Kit squeezed him tightly, and he stilled. "It's okay."

"It most certainly is not!" August was shaking as he looked from her to her departing mother. "Are you okay?"

"Sure." She opened the car and grabbed her backpack. "It's not the first time I've let her down."

"Let her down? Jeez, Kit." August looked like he was vibrating. Like he wanted to ride into battle on her behalf. It was nice, but unnecessary.

"I'm fine, August. Promise." She kissed his nose. "Today was actually one of her smaller outbursts. She just wants the best for her kids."

August opened his mouth and shut it before whatever he planned to say popped out. He pulled her into his arms and just held her. "Whatever her intentions, you did not deserve that. Period."

She leaned into him, enjoying the heat and his support. "Thank you."

He kissed the top of her head and took the backpack from her. "Ready to go cuddle Bucky?"

"Yep." She nodded and followed him into the cottage. Before she closed the door, she looked toward the clinic. Her mother was wrong to yell at her, but that didn't mean she wasn't right about the missed opportunity.

If she'd answered her phone, Trevor Crest would have come here with his cat. Maybe he'd have promoted the clinic on his social media… Would that have helped the clinic? She didn't know, but it couldn't have hurt.

But there will be other opportunities? Won't there?

Her heart raced as her brain wrestled the worry back into its place. Today had been amazing. August loved her. He loved her. That was the feeling she needed to cling to.

CHAPTER NINE

THE CLINIC WAS quiet as August stepped inside. He took a deep breath and looked around. If he planned to stay, this was going to be his place. He waited for the anxiety he felt each time the clinic he'd been at asked him to stay. The need to separate himself from the situation to find a new place.

He let out a breath as those feelings refused to materialize. He loved Kit. Yesterday had been nearly perfect. Still, a kernel of fear had refused to dissipate. Fear that feeling of home he'd felt on the path with Kit would evaporate when he walked into the clinic today. Worried the fear that had dogged him for years would surface now.

He hated to admit it, even to himself, but that was why he'd suggested that he get everything ready this morning since Kit wanted to take Bucky for a walk. She'd said it would be good for the big guy so that he could join them on future hikes. A perfect little family.

It had made his heart melt, but the kernel in his brain popped with panic. This was something he needed to make sure of, without Kit. Heaven knew she'd had enough drama over the last twelve hours.

Now that his worry had evaporated, he needed to find a way to stop the flames of fury the memory of the encounter with Kit's mother induced. The woman had taken a great day, the day they'd told each other how they felt, and tarnished it.

Telling Kit she'd missed an opportunity. And Kit was worried about that. Worried she'd missed something important for the clinic. She hadn't said the words out loud, but he'd seen it in her eyes when she'd picked up her phone and flipped through the barrage of messages.

Life was full of missed opportunities. In fact each opportunity one took destroyed other possible paths. He'd never regret spending the day with Kit, telling her he loved her, starting their joined path. But what if she didn't feel the same?

What if her mother's voice—the one already imbedded so deeply in her brain—outshouted his love? How could he convince her that this was one missed thing? And honestly not that big of a thing. Their clinic was perfect.

Their clinic.

He smiled. That was a nice thought.

A grunt echoed from the first patient room, followed by a crash, and August took off.

He wasn't surprised to find his father in the room, though finding him on the floor wasn't ideal. "Dad. What are you doing here?" He slipped an arm under his father's shoulders and helped him get back to his feet. "And where is your cane?"

August looked around the area, noting the crushed glass and scattered dog treats from the cute treat container that Kit kept in each room. This room was now a hazard to animals and people until it was cleaned. They couldn't risk any furry friends getting a sliver of glass in their paw. And the clinic was set to open in thirty minutes.

"I'm here, because this is still my clinic, August. In case you forgot."

Heat crept up his neck. He was not going to admit it to his father, but that knowledge had slipped his mind.

It was something he and Kit both technically understood. But it had been so easy over the last few weeks to slip into the fantasy that this was truly their place. And he didn't appreciate his father popping the fantasy.

"And the cane?" August raised his brow and looked around the room, feeling his lips dip farther when he couldn't find it. Surely his father hadn't left it in the car...or at home?

"I'm not using a cane. I'm fine. I am. Besides, the clinic needs me." His father's words cut through the wanderings in his mind.

"Except it doesn't." The words flew from his lips, and he wished he could reel them back as he saw his father flinch. It was true that he and Kit were doing fine without him. But he hadn't meant to hurt his feelings.

Or maybe I did?

He didn't like that thought. Their relationship was complicated but hurting someone should never be a goal—even if they'd spent years hurting you.

Reaching for all his patience, August started over. "What I meant was that the clinic will be fine until you have completed rehab. And using a cane will help you reach that point first. Your health is important."

If his father came back, what was August going to do?

And how had he not considered that? He and Kit worked seamlessly, but he doubted that he and Dr. Jeff would have a similar relationship. Would his father even want him here?

If he were choosing today, August was fairly sure his father would say no, judging by the hurt look in his eyes. But August didn't look away. Dr. Jeff might not appre-

ciate being stood up to, but his health was more important than the clinic.

His father broke the eye contact first, and something
in him that August couldn't place shifted too.

He took a step toward his father, but his dad pulled
back. He tried not to let that hurt.

"I'm fine, but my cane is in the waiting room." The
frown cemented into his father's lips dipped even farther.
He let out a sigh and met August's gaze. "If you could
get it for me, I'd appreciate it."

August hustled for the cane but wasn't surprised to
see his father in the door of the room when he turned.
No one would ever say Dr. Jeff Rhodes wasn't stubborn.
But still, it would be nice if he'd waited for the cane before shuffling out.

"I noticed your trophy." His father's voice was soft as
he handed him the cane. He glared at it before leaning
on it to walk toward the corner displaying the awards.

"It's just something silly Kit had made up. I treated a
bearded dragon and mentioned I worked with quite a few
reptiles when I was in Florida. I love the cold-blooded
little guys."

"You certified for them?" His father looked at the trophy, his eyes holding an emotion August couldn't name.

"No." August shrugged. "But Kit says I'm the closest
thing between here and the Zoo Knoxville. I need one
more year of practice to meet the six-year requirement
for the American Board of Veterinary Practitioners. Kit
is trying to convince me to put in for an internship at
Zoo Knoxville."

"Of course she is. Kit would never settle for almost
done." His dad's chest puffed out a little, and his eyes
hovered on Kit's certificate. "One day that isn't going to
be a runner-up certificate. She's something else."

His father was proud of Kit. It was a look August had never seen directed at him. He hated the bite of jealousy spinning across his skin. He'd spent so long trying to achieve it.

And I should have it.

He swallowed the feeling crawling up his throat. It wasn't Kit's fault that his dad was proud of her. Conditional love and approval had been held from her too.

But knowing that, accepting it even, didn't steal away all the bitterness it brought.

Why can't he look at me that way? And why do I still care that he doesn't?

"She cares about this place as much as I do. It's her life." His father smiled and turned to survey the waiting area. "It'd be nice if it stayed in the family..."

August ignored the not-so-subtle jab about settling to focus on what his father said about the clinic. Even if he wanted it, which he didn't, he'd never take it from Kit. She needed it in a way he didn't.

"You know Kit cares about this place. How much it means to her, but you also want it to stay in the family? *And* you said you considered selling to her ex-in-laws. Not exactly the actions of a man who thought their colleague cared as much about the place as them."

Maybe it wasn't fair to bring up the hypocrisy. Maybe his father had had a change of heart, something he should celebrate. But August wanted his dad to know that he heard the duplicity.

"I was never actually going to sell to Karen and Robert. I can't stand them." He offered a small smile as August closed his hanging mouth.

"Then why is Kit not your partner?"

"Stubbornness and control on my part. I know my faults."

It's just taken you forever to work on them?

August kept that unpleasant thought to himself. Instead he crossed his arms and stared at his father.

His father shrugged, but he refused to meet August's gaze. "Kit's first husband was a good man. He's buried here, but I guess I still worried she'd leave. Start fresh somewhere else, particularly given Karen wanting to blame her. Then, well, time passes faster than you realize. Unless you're stuck in a hospital bed."

"Dr. Jeff?" Kit sounded surprised to see him as Bucky bounded toward him. "What are you doing here?"

"Just stopping by to see if you're still interested in purchasing the clinic." He shot August a look he couldn't quite decipher, before focusing on Kit. "I think maybe it's time I hung up my hat, though I'd love to stay on part-time, assuming I heal enough for it."

Bucky wagged his tail as his dad rubbed his ears. His father had many faults, but the man loved animals.

Kit beamed, and August wanted to be happy for her. She was getting what she wanted. What she longed for. But his father hadn't mentioned anything about selling it when he'd found him collapsed in the exam room. It almost felt like he was taunting his son.

God, August. Not everything is about you.

His brain hammered as his heart tried to process the onslaught of emotions invading it over the last fifteen minutes.

Their receptionist and the first clients would start arriving soon, and they still had an exam room covered in glass. That was why he started walking toward the back room to grab a broom.

"You'll make this place even better." His father's voice was raised. Making sure August caught it? Or maybe it was just because the clinic was quiet before their furry patients arrived.

"That's my plan. Foxfield's Finest."

She sounded so happy. It should be infectious. So why was it worry pulsing through his brain? He shook his head. It was fine.

Great in fact. And tonight they were going to celebrate Kit's success.

Kit felt like skipping. The nearly nine hours since Dr. Jeff asked if she was still interested in purchasing the clinic had done little to calm the excitement pulsating through her. It had taken all of herself control not to shout yes and ask if he wanted to go to the bank then and there before he could change his mind. Not that they'd actually be able to transfer anything to her today anyway, but she was so thrilled.

Her life was finally taking the path that she wanted. Over the last twenty-four hours, she felt like she'd gotten everything she wanted and more. August had headed home twenty minutes ago but she needed to get through a few more emails. Something that would be easier if she wasn't literally bouncing in her seat.

Focus!

She was excited, but she also wanted to get home. Wanted to have dinner with August and curl up on the couch to relax. Which couldn't happen until she finalized the last few items here. Putting things off always made her anxious, but it didn't even feel like an option anymore since the clinic was going to be hers soon.

She filtered through the emails that the office manager, Julia, had flagged for her review. The new hire was worth her weight in gold, and Kit was determined that one of the first changes occurring at the Rhodes Animal Services was the cessation of rotating office managers!

She clicked through the emails, answering only the

ones she needed to until her eyes caught one marked Zoo Knoxville Internship. Her heart leaped at the sender. Dr. Patrick Stepsard, the zoo's reptile house lead veterinarian.

Kit had reached out to him a few times when patients that were beyond her and Dr. Jeff's ability walked through the clinic door. He was always responsive, but her inquiry this time had been on August's behalf. To see what he'd have to do to complete his certification and if the zoo might have any positions besides the advertised internship that qualified.

Her hand shook a little as she hovered over the email. If Knoxville had an opening, she and August would be apart for a while. But he loved reptiles. He deserved to have the full recognition for his skillset.

They could handle a few months or even a year of long distance. Her heart quivered at the idea, but twelve months in the grand scheme of life were minor if it meant he got something he wanted. Something that made him happy.

She smiled as she read over the email. Dr. Stepsard said there were usually positions available that weren't publicly listed like the internship. He forwarded the link to the internal job listing board and offered to take a look at August's résumé whenever he wanted to send it. He also mentioned that the Reptile and Amphibian certification was one of the newest offered by the American Board of Veterinary Practitioners. Which meant August might be closer to qualifying than he thought if he'd worked with reptiles and exotics in Florida.

She let out a squeal as she pushed back from the desk. Literally everything really was falling into place. Today was one of the best days ever. She closed up quickly and rushed home.

She felt like she was floating when she swung open the door and heavenly scents struck her nose.

"You're home! I was about to come pick you up and carry you home," August joked as he dropped a light kiss along her lips.

"Really pick me up?" She giggled as she stepped into his arms. "Not sure that is much of a threat, August."

She looked up and sighed as his lips captured hers. His tongue teased hers and she melted into him. This was the perfect way to come home.

"Our dinner is getting cold." August frowned as he pulled away and looked toward the kitchen. "I already put everything out. What do you think the odds are of Bucky ignoring it if I carried you upstairs?"

"Less than zero." She grinned and her belly rumbled.

August dropped his gaze to her stomach and laid a hand against it. "Even if he would let it go, you're starving."

"Not starving, but close. The day got away from me and I forgot about lunch. Did you cook?" She reached for his hand as they walked toward the kitchen.

Where had he found the time?

"I'd love to take all the credit for the delectableness awaiting us—"

"Delectableness?" She leaned her head against his shoulder. "Such a fancy word."

"Well, we are celebrating. Dad finally offered you the clinic. That is a feat worthy of a special dinner. Which I ordered from a burrito joint in town. We'll have to go out somewhere nice another night."

She gasped as they walked into the kitchen. The table was set with her wedding china. The champagne flutes she'd toasted on her wedding sitting next to the bubbly.

"I know the food doesn't really match the fanciness.

But I figured it was a nice way to include Leo. 'Cause I'm sure he'd enjoy your success too."

Tears clogged her eyes as she looked at the sweet display. It was the perfect way to include her past while celebrating her future. "I love it. And you."

"Then let's dig in." August pulled out her chair before making his way to the other side of the table. He lifted up the champagne bottle and popped it open.

He caught most of the bubbly with her glass before filling his own. "To Kit Bedrick, soon-to-be owner of Rhodes Animal Services."

She clinked the glasses, and her heart swooned as the bubbles touched her nose.

"I am very impressed." Kit set the glass down and opened the foil wrapper on her burrito. "I'm even more impressed that you thought there was any hope that my dog might leave this alone. We got lucky he didn't investigate in the two minutes you were meeting me at the door."

August laughed before he took a big bite of his burrito. "He's a cutie, but his manners still need a bit of work. Still, maybe he understands tonight is a big night for you."

"For us!" Kit lifted the champagne glass, tilting it toward him. She'd meant to mention Dr. Stepsard's email as soon as she got home, but she'd gotten understandably distracted by August's treat. "I had an email that I think will make you quite happy."

"An email?"

August blinked, and her belly tilted for just a moment. *Did I overstep?*

She swallowed the bit of worry and let him know what was in Dr. Stepsard's email. Then she waited.

And waited.

"August. Did you hear me? You might be closer to the

certification than you realize. With just a little work, it could be yours!"

He nodded before lifting his burrito and taking another bite. He chewed it. *Achingly slow.*

"I heard you, Kit." He let out a sigh. "I appreciate you asking."

She opened her mouth to say that this didn't feel much like appreciation but shut it. Overreacting was her mother's specialty, not hers. "It feels like there's a but there?"

Her heart sank when he didn't immediately contradict her. She'd expected a celebration. Another toast. But his eyes were guarded. A wall she hadn't expected rising around him. This wasn't how tonight was supposed to go.

"I wanted to help." She hated the tinge of a whine she heard in her voice.

"Tonight's about you." He grinned, but it didn't quite reach his eyes.

She should appreciate him shifting the conversation to her success. How often did people, particularly men, try to take the spotlight from women? August was willingly giving it to her. All of it.

But she wanted to share.

Swallowing the tension crawling up her throat, Kit leaned on her hands and offered what she hoped was a convincing smile. "So what are the plans after dinner?"

"What if I carry you upstairs and see where the night takes us?" He leaned over her small table and kissed her nose.

The tension evaporated with his silly smile.

"I think that sounds like a plan!" Desire pulsed between them as his eyes burned into her. But there was an uneasiness that wouldn't quit her.

Something in his posture, the uneasiness hovering in his eyes unsettled her. Was he not as happy about her getting the clinic? Was he really mad that she'd asked about the qualifications? She just wanted what was best for him.

He knew that didn't he?

"I love you, August." Kit reached for his hand.

He squeezed it and winked. "I know."

Her heart relaxed at the playfulness. He knew she loved him. Everything was fine.

CHAPTER TEN

You going to complete your reptile qualifications?

IT WAS THE third time his father had texted the question in the last week. Though at least this time he was being direct. The loosely worded questions had nearly driven him mad.

Do you have plans for early next year? Should Kit plan for a relief vet for a few months?

Questions hovering on the border of today's directness but still designed to ferret out what his father wanted to know. He slid his phone back into his pocket and shook his head. It was too early for this!

August barely caught the groan in his throat as he stepped behind the reception desk and flipped on the clinic lights. Why wouldn't his father drop this? It was like he was dangling his acceptance on August completing the certification. But he was enough already.

If only Kit hadn't reached out to Dr. Stepsard.

August pushed a hand through his hair. That wasn't fair, and Kit had apologized, repeatedly. It had come as a shock to her that Dr. Stepsard and his father were such close colleagues too. She'd never expected him to reach out to his dad directly.

That wasn't the worst part though. She was still annoyed August was holding out on it too. Not that she'd said it directly. She didn't need to. He could see it in her eyes, hear it in the planning she was doing for when she took full ownership of the clinic.

He didn't need the qualification. Why didn't they understand that? The clinic only saw reptiles a few times a month. The knowledge base he had, and the fact that he read any veterinarian journal articles produced on reptiles and amphibians was enough. If they needed more support, they could ask Dr. Stepsard.

Assuming she wanted him to stay if he didn't get the certification.

He shook away that thought.

I'm already enough.

He repeated the mantra he'd learned in therapy years ago, but it didn't bring the usual calmness to his brain.

Enough had never been his father's goal. And it certainly wasn't Kit's. Still, she loved him for who he was. Getting the certification wasn't a condition of her love. He was letting past worries taint present happiness.

Wasn't he?

No.

His stomach ached as he sent the response back to his father. A certification wasn't needed. He was enough just as he was. Kit had even thought so when she'd gifted him that silly trophy.

August's eyes darted to the trophy display and his heart crashed. *No.* He stepped closer, though his brain already knew what his heart was praying his eyes got wrong. The turtle trophy was gone.

It had stood out on the small shelf. The one mis-

matched, unprofessional trophy in the lot. Kit had removed the review ones the day she'd signed the initial
paperwork to transfer the clinic into her name. The only
ones left had been her certificate, an award his father had
won, the old Foxfield Finest trophy and his. The others
all remained, but his...his was gone.

She'd joked that she had to make room for all the Foxfield Finest trophies they'd be getting. Except he didn't
really think it was a joke. But she'd left his trophy.

Hadn't she?

When was the last time I saw it?

August wasn't sure. And that killed him. Surely she
hadn't taken it down.

It wasn't accurate either.

It was just as misleading as the review ones. But Kit
had put it there, said it should be there. August swallowed
as he looked at the now-empty space.

There was an easy way to find the answer. If he asked,
she'd tell him where she put it. But what if she said she'd
give it back when he got the certification?

She wouldn't. Would she?

He hated that he wasn't sure of the answer. Hated the
uncertainty pooling in him since she'd found out his father was selling the clinic to her. It had been one week,
and she'd been here late each night. They'd canceled dinner with her brother twice this week.

But it was only one week.

August bit his lip. Kit loved the clinic. She'd apologized when he'd had to come beg her to at least join him
for dinner Sunday night. She was just so excited to have
everything in her name that she'd lost track of time while
making notes.

It was a silly trophy. It wasn't that important. That

was a lie, and he knew it. It mattered to him. Mattered that it had disappeared.

They were planning a life together. Visiting Alaska. In fact he'd started making nice progress on that trip. He thought visiting next spring was the right time. The clinic would be fine without them for two weeks by then.

He already had some feelers out for a few of his relief vets who'd be perfect subs for them. August smiled as the thought of two weeks alone with Kit materialized in his mind. Alaska might be the perfect place to propose too.

That was a life step he'd never really considered until meeting Kit. He'd moved so often that long-term relationships weren't possible. Or at least he'd never sought them out. But with Kit… He felt his lips tip up even farther.

With Kit, the idea of getting on one knee and asking her to spend her life with him made him weak. She was his person. His eyes moved to the trophy shelf and immediately shifted away.

She was his person, trophy or not.

"If your smile gets any bigger, it might walk all the way off your face." Kit beamed as she stepped to his side. "Do I get to know what's made you so happy this morning?"

"Just life." August sighed as he slung an arm around her waist. "Just life with you."

"I love the sound of that." She stood on her tiptoes and brushed her lips against his.

Her phone buzzed and she looked at it. "Stephen is wondering if we are free this weekend."

"We certainly can be!" August kissed the top of her head. He loved the feel of her in his arms.

"I was thinking of painting the office this weekend. It hasn't been painted in years." Kit pulled her bottom lip between her teeth.

August shook his head. Painting the office? That could wait. Family was more important than the clinic. She knew that…right? "We've worked almost every day this month. And canceled on Stephen and Wes twice…"

"I know." Kit nodded. She opened her mouth but before she could say anything, the clinic door buzzed and they broke apart.

"Are we expecting an early patient?" August asked as they walked to the front door.

"No." Kit's brows knotted. "Emergency?"

"Maybe. But Love Pets is open twenty-four hours." It was the wrong line. August knew it as soon as it left his lips. Her shoulders straightened and her chin lifted as she marched toward the front door.

"We can handle anything they can."

That wasn't necessarily true. But August wasn't going to argue in front of a patient.

A man holding, or rather doing his best to hold, his golden retriever stood at the front door, tears running down his face.

"Matt? What's wrong with Ginger?"

That was something Love Pets didn't have. Something they'd never have with the rotating vets. Kit knew her clients. Knew her patients. Had treated many of them since they were tiny puppies and kittens.

August reached for Ginger and the dog flopped in his arms. Not a good sign. Goldens wanted to please people and often put up with more than most breeds. But even older goldens, and Ginger didn't look to be more than about five, were bundles of energy.

"Room One," August stated and started there without waiting. He laid her on the exam table and his stomach flipped when she didn't react. Animals did their best to hide the pain. By the time they were demonstrating weakness, it was often late in a diagnosis.

"Tell me what happened, Matt." Kit stepped beside Ginger and ran her hand over her ear, her eyes on Ginger's unmoving tail. Goldens were happiness machines… Something was very wrong.

"We need the ultrasound machine." August interrupted and looked at Kit, then deliberately looked at the dog's lower region, where a mass was visible beneath the dog's fur.

Kit blinked and he saw the same thoughts roaming through her brain. *Cancer.* Goldens were prone to the disease. There was debate in the veterinarian and breeder community over why the incidents of cancer in the breed had steadily risen over the last two decades, but none of that mattered at the moment.

He stepped out and grabbed the ultrasound. Maybe it was just a fatty tumor. August wanted to hope for the best. But based on the dog's demeanor, he doubted they were going to get good news.

Still, Ginger was relatively young. With treatment, she might still have several years ahead of her.

Fingers crossed.

Matt was whispering to Ginger when August rolled the ultrasound machine in. Kit had already started shaving the dog.

"It's going to be okay, Ginger. Promise." Matt kissed his dog's head and looked at August for reassurance. He wanted to give it to him. He really did. But it would be unprofessional to offer hope before they had the full story.

August turned on the machine and handed the wand to Kit. He saw her take a deep breath before moving the wand across Ginger's belly. She kept her face still, but August could read the ultrasound. A mass in the lower abdomen.

It looked to be encased. With any luck it hadn't spread yet. This was the hardest part of veterinarian practice. Though he suspected a medical professional treating humans felt the same way about delivering bad news.

Matt's breath hitched and August turned to him. He might not be a vet, but it would be obvious to most that there was something abnormal about the mass.

"Matt." Kit's voice was soft.

Tear slipped down his face. "She's only three, Dr. Bedrick. Three. I know goldens get cancer. The breeder even warned me, but three. It's not fair."

"It's not," Kit agreed as August passed Matt a box of tissues. "The mass does look like it's encased in her lower abdomen. Hopefully that means it hasn't spread."

"There's a full-time oncologist at the Love Pets clinic. It probably would be a good idea to see them," August stated. He saw Kit's arms fold in his peripheral vision. They could operate, but if there was a vet better suited to giving Ginger the best shot, that needed to be the focus.

Kit took a deep breath and nodded. "August is right. I'll call and see if they can fit you in today."

"Thank you." Matt kissed Ginger's head. "She's…" His voice broke as he looked at the dog. "She's my best girl. I don't want to lose her."

August patted Ginger's head. "Pets are family."

"I'll be back as soon as I talk to the other clinic." Kit's shoulders were tight, not matching the false smile she'd plastered on her face.

August followed her to the back. "Want me to make the call? I know you don't like calling them."

"No, I want to talk to the oncologist myself. Get a read on them."

That made sense, but there was an undercurrent in her voice that August didn't like. She was upset. A difficult case could do that. Having to call the clinic owned by her ex-in-laws first thing in the morning also wasn't the best way to start the day. But they didn't work in the clinic, just ran it.

And called Kit to gloat when their clinic won the Foxfield's Finest.

He watched her step into the small office and close the door. And just like that, the walls rising between them seemed obvious. There was no need for her to close the door. No need to shut him out...but she was.

And August didn't know how to bridge the gap he felt opening between them.

By getting the reptile and amphibian certification?

The insidious thought chased him as he headed to the waiting room to speak to their receptionist about Ginger and the next steps.

Kit put down the phone and hung her head in her hands. The other clinic could see Ginger later this afternoon. And Dr. Mia Wambler had sounded delightful on the phone. Eager, even. She'd mentioned being a little bored at Love Pets, then caught herself.

No one wanted animals to get cancer, but she'd trained in the specialty to help. Kit had asked if she wanted to split her time between the two clinics. The question had just popped out, but it made sense. If Love Pets was lucky enough not to have enough patients for their oncologist, then splitting time with Rhodes Animal Services made sense.

But she hadn't talked to August about it. She swallowed. Technically his father had offered the clinic to her. And August hadn't seemed interested in being part of that sale. Still, they were partners in other areas.

She looked at the closed office door and cringed. She shouldn't have closed it. It was such a tiny thing, and maybe August wouldn't even notice. But she'd been frustrated that he'd immediately said they should call Love Pets. He was right—she knew that. It was just frustration that they weren't the best place for Ginger. But that wasn't August's fault...

She was just stressed and moving fast. A closed door didn't have to mean anything. They were in love. She didn't doubt her feelings for August. But things had shifted since she'd reached out to Dr. Stepsard.

Since she'd agreed to buy the clinic.

Last weekend had been tough. She'd spent all her free time here, even though she'd wanted to go hiking with him and Bucky. There was just so much to do. And she knew he was frustrated that they'd canceled on Stephen twice when things had come up here.

August had said he understood, but the doubt hovering in his eyes was still with her. It was almost like he was waiting for her to choose the clinic over him. But it wasn't either-or.

She'd asked if he wanted to stay with her on Sunday. Hang out while she reorganized the office...her office. Though she'd had to keep the filing cabinet in place since you could tell how much the paint had faded around it. Thus painting this weekend.

But he'd visibly shuddered as he said six days at the clinic was more than enough. She doubted he'd want to spend the weekend painting.

He was right—time away from the clinic was important. But sometimes one had to shift for a few weeks or months, and she was determined that her takeover be as seamless as possible. Determined to institute the changes that would make their clinic the best in the area.

Leo had supported her in that effort. August seemed more concerned with days off and vacations. Kit shook her head as she stood. That wasn't fair.

August was looking out for her.

Like she'd tried to do with the certification.

She hated the bitterness coating her tongue as she moved toward the door.

He patently refused to consider getting the certification for reptiles and amphibians. Despite the fact that he'd read three separate medical articles on the creatures this week. When he'd told her of the findings regarding a treatment for anemia in bearded dragons over dinner last week, he'd radiated happiness. He enjoyed it. It was his passion.

Rather than grow that passion, he was actively pushing it away. Sure, their clinic hardly saw amphibians and only maintained a small list of reptile patients, but if August was certified, more might come.

Surely there were clients driving to Knoxville to visit an exotic vet. But even if the clinic never gained another client, he enjoyed it. Bettering yourself for something you liked was the best kind of growth. But she had no idea how to make him see that.

A knock at the door brought her attention back to the day ahead as she reached for the handle.

"That was a quick answer." August winked as he leaned against the doorjamb, but his eyes were hooded as he looked at her. Her funny, sweet August was putting walls between them, and she didn't know how to tear them down. "Figured you'd just call me in rather than swing the door open."

"I was just heading out." She lifted on her toes and kissed his cheek.

"You okay?"

"Of course." The lie slipped between them, and he raised a brow but didn't call her on it.

She was mostly okay. And mostly okay *was* okay. She was tired, worried about Ginger, concerned about offering Dr. Wambler a part-time position without talking to August and worried about the distance she felt growing between them. Worries were normal though.

Besides, she was so close to her all her dreams. If she could just fake being okay for a little while longer, she'd hit her best. Then she'd find time to relax.

"Dr. Wambler can see Ginger this afternoon." She paused before exam room one and looked at August. "And she said there isn't enough work at Love Pets."

"I know that's a good thing, but as far as keeping a talented vet in the area, not the best either."

It was like he was reading her mind again. She took a deep breath. "I offered her a part-time position here. Between the two clinics…"

August's eyes widened and his mouth opened. "You just offered it to her? On a consult call?"

He wasn't wrong. It was unusual. And she should have checked. Heat flooded her body as she tried to explain. "It will be good for the clinic. Nice to have at least one specialist here rather than on call." She couldn't have chosen worse words.

He looked away and she felt the gulf between them widen. "August…" She hadn't meant the words as a dig toward him. She truly hadn't, but he didn't meet her gaze and her heart clenched.

"I should have talked to you about it," Kit offered.

"Why?" August sighed, "Rhodes Animal Services is

yours, Kit. If you think having her on staff is the right move, then I'm sure it is." He looked at his watch and then at her.

"I have a patient in room three. Why don't you go let Matt know what's going on? I'm sure he's beside himself with worry. We don't have answers yet, but at least there is a plan now."

"Right." Kit nodded.

"Right." He turned on his heel and disappeared into room three.

Kit's eyes hovered on the closed door. She should be glad that he'd said it was her clinic. Glad that she could offer positions to whomever she thought best. Happy that no one was going to take this from her. It was what she'd worked so hard for.

She looked at the back room of the clinic. At the operating table, the entrance to the four exam rooms, the scale... All of this was hers. Truly hers.

So why did it feel hollow?

But there wasn't time to examine that feeling. And even if there were, Kit didn't want to. She and August were a new couple. Not every day or week could be champagne and roses.

CHAPTER ELEVEN

"He just stopped eating." Gwendolyn Jones bit her lip as she looked at her box turtle. "And now he has this gunk in his eyes." She ran a finger along the turtle's shell in the small box she'd brought it in.

"Our usual vet is in Knoxville, and they're closed this week. Vacation. I called here and the receptionist said you might be able to help." She sniffled a little as she looked at August.

He tried not to let the idea that other vets were taking vacations when Kit had shifted the discussion back to the clinic's needs the last time he'd brought up a trip to Alaska.

"I know a turtle is not a cuddly pet like a dog or cat, but Fergus has been with me for almost ten years. He's moved with me three times, hung with me when my fiancée decided we made better friends than lovers, then ran away with my little sister last month."

She cleared her throat. "Sorry. I get talkative when I'm nervous. I just, I can't lose Fergus."

August lifted the box turtle from the container and rubbed the top of his head. The little guy looked under the weather, but he was nearly certain it was a vitamin A deficiency. But that usually happened when someone hadn't had a box turtle very long.

"You've had Fergus for ten years, and this is the first time you've had issues like this?"

"Yes," Gwendolyn confirmed.

"What are you feeding him?"

"Just crickets." She sniffled. "I used to feed him crickets, fruit and dandelion flowers, but my friend saw it and was horrified. She sent me an article about how crickets are best for box turtles. I hadn't meant to feed him poorly. I'd just always done what the pet store told me."

He didn't let out a groan, but he wanted to. Online misinformation was a problem for veterinarians, and medical professionals alike. But he also knew Gwendolyn had just wanted what was best for her turtle.

"Box turtles are omnivores. So while crickets are a good source of protein for them, they need more than just crickets. The diet you had for him before was perfect."

Her mouth fell open, then she nodded. "So if I go back to that, he'll get better?"

"Yes, but he also needs vitamin A now. The symptoms you are seeing are from a deficiency there. And it needs to be carefully administered. Because you can overdose on it.

"I'm going to take Fergus in the back, get him his first dose, then I'll make sure you go home with the right amount and instructions to follow."

"But he's going to be okay?"

August nodded. "Fergus is going to be fine." He lifted the cute little guy up and smiled at him. "Let's get you feeling better." Then he stepped out of the room.

"Is that a turtle?"

Kit sounded shocked, and he couldn't blame her. Box turtles were common enough pets, but usually had to be seen by exotic vets.

"Yep. Fergus, meet Kit. Kit, Fergus." He beamed as he

held the turtle up. "Fergus is feeling under the weather. Vitamin A deficiency."

"How do you know that?"

"Crusty eyes, lethargic, refusing to eat are the primary symptoms. And the owner confirmed that they recently shifted to an all-cricket diet, which will not provide the correct nutrients." August made soft noises to Fergus as he grabbed a vial of vitamin A from the shelf.

"It's probably not a bad idea for us to invest in the equipment to run blood work for reptiles. Then we can diagnose more things if the little guys come in."

Kit blinked as he looked at her. "Why don't we discuss that at home tonight?"

What is there to discuss?

August kept that question to himself. This was Kit's clinic. If she wasn't interested, then he didn't have a say. Except he wanted a say.

He swallowed. Where had that come from? His mother had hated this place. No, she'd hated that it came first, that his father chose it over her all the time. That when she'd tried to show interest and help, he'd ignored her aid and opinions. But Kit wasn't saying no—she wanted to talk about it.

He was just looking for things to worry over after a long few days. He needed a break. They needed a break. Exhaustion and overwork were a recipe for a disaster. "This is my last patient. You done for the day?"

"With patients, yes." Kit kissed his cheek, then patted Fergus. "But I need to see to some emails and paperwork before I head home. I won't be too long."

"Promise? We haven't had dinner together in two weeks."

"Yep." Kit nodded. "I'll see you shortly. Promise." She made a silly crossing her heart sign and winked at him.

August smiled, then turned back to Fergus. "Let's get you feeling better, buddy."

August rubbed Bucky's head as the clock struck eight o'clock. The plans he'd worked out for their trip to Alaska sitting next to her uneaten dinner mocked him from the kitchen table. Two hours since he'd left the clinic and Kit still wasn't home. How often had he watched his mother sit at their kitchen table, waiting, hoping that his father would show up?

He looked at the whiteboard by the pantry and bit his lip. *Be the best.* The words had worried him the first time he saw them, but now they tormented him. That mantra would continue to push Kit. It would drive her to reach for more. But would she ever be satisfied? Was one Foxfield's Finest award going to be enough?

He doubted it. Could he live with that? Live his life waiting for her?

No.

Tears coated his eyes. It was just two weeks, but weeks would turn into a month and then into years. He loved her, but he wouldn't sit around hoping to come first in her life. Hoping that she'd see their relationship as the best thing in her life.

His mother had never stopped loving his dad. She'd seen some of her favorite places in the two years she'd lived apart from him. But she'd always hoped he'd call and ask her to come home. Tell her she was first in his life.

But his dad hadn't been able to love that way. Maybe it wasn't fair of his mom to ask for what his dad wouldn't give. Maybe it wasn't fair of him to ask it of Kit. But that didn't stop the ache in his heart.

His mother had stayed for almost fifteen years. Begged

his father to choose her for fifteen years. And Rhodes
Animal Services had always come first. August wasn't
going to wait that long. Wasn't going to spend years of
his life hoping to be more important than a practice. He
couldn't.

He looked at his phone, then picked it up and sent a
text.

Can I stay with you tonight?

August patted Bucky's head while he waited for his
dad to answer. He should probably go to a hotel. But if
he was broken, then he wanted to be at home. As close to
his mom's memory as possible. He'd find another place
tomorrow.

Of course.

The quick answer surprised him. He'd expected his
father to say no. If he had, he'd have likely stayed tonight
with Kit. And then rationalized another night. Then another.

No, a quick break was best.

Kit yawned, then looked to the clock. Nearly ten o'clock...
Where had the time gone? And why hadn't August come
to get her? He'd come to get her each night this week.

Her stomach grumbled and heat flooded her face.
She'd missed dinner. *Again*.

It hadn't been intentional. She'd meant to head home
after checking her email. But time had slipped away as
she added a few more things to her to-do list. There was
always more to be done.

Her email dinged and she bit her lip. It was already late, so what was one more email?

Her heart leaped as she stared at the subject line from Dr. Stepsard.

Opening for weekend vet in reptile house.

She quickly read the email and couldn't stop the smile on her lips. If August spent the weekends in Knoxville for six months, he could complete his certification. And if he was here during the week…

She stood up and turned the computer off. If he could just see how he looked when he held a crusty-eyed turtle, he'd understand why she wanted this for him. One weekend in the reptile house would likely give him a week's worth of stories to tell her.

And she'd hang on each word. She just needed a weekend relief vet; luckily August had already contacted a few to help out if they took vacations.

Vacations.

She looked at the computer and then the calendar. August had talked about Alaska on a few occasions and she'd pushed it off each time. They'd get there eventually.

Just like they'd get to dinner with her brother and nephew.

There would be time for those things soon. But this job opening was perfect for him. She just had to make him see it.

Opening the door to the cottage, she slipped her shoes off and walked to the kitchen. The table was still set and her dinner sat on the plate, covered with plastic wrap. A travel guide to Alaska was sitting next to it.

The image tugged at her heart. August had eaten by himself again and their trip to Alaska was going to have to wait at least a few years. But they'd get there. They would.

"You're home." August leaned against the door leading to the living room. His face was devoid of the anger she expected. But the softness in his eyes and the way he was holding himself sent a shiver down her back.

"I lost track of time." She crossed her arms and looked at the dinner. "Sorry."

Kit took a deep breath and smiled. "But I have good news! I heard from Dr. Stepsard. He says that there is a part-time seasonal position in the reptile house open."

"Kit…" August's voice was soft.

She hurried on. He'd understand once she explained everything. "It means you can work with me during the week and there on the weekends and in six months you'll be certified."

"So, if I work seven days a week for the next six months, I'll get the certification and the clinic will have two specialists." His eyes held a look she couldn't quite understand as he continued, "Will that make you happy?"

"Yes." She blinked. "Of course it would."

He let out a sigh as he shook his head, "So working myself to the bone for something I've told you I'm not interested in. Kit, is that really what you want? What about what I think? And why can't you leave it be? I'm fine."

He had an opportunity to do something that made him truly happy. If she could have snapped a picture of him making silly faces at the box turtle, maybe he'd understand what she saw. He loved reptiles. Why was this so hard for August to do? "I just want what's best for you."

"Wanting what's best for me? How about just loving me for me? God, Kit, not everything is about being the best. Or earning the best."

"That's not fair!" Those were her words, but they were twisted. "I do love you. I love that you love cold-blooded creatures. That they make you go gushy like a giant dog

does for me. But right now, you aren't certified in them.
I know you can treat them, that according to state boards
giving the minimal care we do in the clinic is fine. But
with that certification, we could do so much more. We
could have the full treatment suite with the fancy blood-
work panels you mentioned today. People in the local
area would come to see us. Like Fergus."

"So it is about the clinic." August sighed.

"No, but…" Her words died away as he raised a brow.
She wrapped her arms around herself. They were at a
crossroads. One she was terrified was splitting them in
different directions. "But it is good for the clinic."

Couldn't he see that it could be both?

"And working all week, and on the weekends. That's
good too, right? Provided it's good for the clinic. When
are we going to Alaska, Kit? Or even just taking a few
days off?"

"I mean…" She shrugged as her eyes flitted to the
brochure he had put next to her uneaten meal. How was
she supposed to answer that question? The date had to
be fluid. "When the clinic is the best."

"What does that mean?" August looked at her board.
"What does *the best* mean to you, Kit? Is one Foxfield's
Finest Award enough? Or will you feel honor bound to
win it each year? What happens after you have ten? Is
that enough? Because best is a moving target."

She opened her mouth, but no words came out.

"Or does best mean when your mom accepts you?
What if she never does?"

"Now who's being unfair?" Her voice shook and tears
clouded her vision.

"Maybe I am. But I won't come in second to the clinic
again, Kit. I won't eat dinner alone and hope that I can
convince you to clear a few hours out of your weekend

schedule for me. I spent my entire childhood being second to it."

"I love you." Kit barely kept the sob from her lips.

"I love you too." August closed his eyes. "But I need to know if you're okay with me never earning my reptile certification, if we never win the Foxfield's Finest Award, never get the external recognition but know we love each other and have a balanced life between work and fun."

She wanted to say yes. In the movies that was how this played out. The heroine realized that the hero was enough. That she didn't need the other things. But this wasn't the movies. Could she really throw the other dreams away for him? Was it even fair for him to ask it?

Her eyes shifted to the whiteboard. The bright letters she'd written out so long ago. Her tongue felt thick as she replied, "Why does it have to be either-or?"

"Because I'm not willing to give everything to the clinic. I'll give it to you—"

"It's the same thing!"

August's lips dipped as he stared at her. "No, it's not, Kit."

He picked up his duffel bag and her mouth fell open. "So you'd already decided to leave? No matter what I said." Tears slipped down her face as anger pooled in her.

"I knew the answer two weeks ago when I saw the trophy you gave me was gone from the shelf. I just wasn't willing to admit it until tonight."

Trophy?

Her mind spun as he stepped past her.

"Goodbye, Kit. I'll stay on at the clinic until you find my replacement."

She waited until the front door closed to let the sobs come.

CHAPTER TWELVE

AUGUST STARED AT the screen, scrolling past relief jobs that held no excitement for him. He used to love this part. Picking out a new place. Heck, he'd even thrown a dart on the map a few times, then seen how close he could get to the location.

This was supposed to be the fun part. But his heart refused to even consider leaving Foxfield, no matter how often he tried to remind it that staying wasn't an option. Seeing Kit every day. Losing himself in work in the hope that they could carve a few hours of time out. He couldn't do that.

He rubbed his eyes, rolled his neck, and tried again to focus. After a few minutes, he lifted his phone and pulled up Kit's number. His finger hovered over it for just a second before he put it away. It had been less than twenty-four hours but what was there to say?

They loved each other but wanted different things. There was nothing wrong with wanting different things. Needing different things.

Was this how Mom felt?

He leaned his head against his palm and started scrolling again. The road had soothed her soul… Maybe in time it would do the same for him. A job caught his eye. Relief vet needed at Miami Exotics. He clicked on it. The clinic looked after all types of reptiles. It promised excitement at every turn.

Vet qualified in reptile care highly desired.

He was qualified, but there was no way to truly demonstrate that without the certification. His heart thumped at the idea of seeing his name framed in recognition—seeing his name on the website. It was an exciting thought. But unnecessary.

Except…

What if I want it?

August pushed back from the computer in his dad's home office. His mother's picture sat on the corner of the desk, and August wished there were a way to ask her thoughts. Ask if she thought he'd acted too hastily. Or if she thought he was right to leave before he got too hurt.

He picked up the small frame and ran his thumb along the frame. His mom had been gone decades now. In a few years he'd be older than she'd ever been. And his dad still had her picture on his desk.

He'd loved her. Still loved her, but the clinic had come first. He wanted to hate his father for that. But it was pity filling his soul as he looked at his mom's picture.

"What would have happened if you'd stayed?" His mouth was dry, but his eyes watered again. "Would you have been happy enough being second but getting to be with Dad?"

Happy enough?

That shouldn't be an option. Love took compromise, but surely he didn't have to compromise that. He opened the top drawer of his dad's desk and his mouth dropped open. The trophy, *his* trophy, separated into two pieces, sat on top of a bunch of pictures.

Pictures of him graduating from vet school.

"What?" His brain spun as he pulled the pictures out of the drawer and set them beside the pieces of his trophy.

He ran a finger along the silly turtle that looked more ridiculous separated from its base. His throat tightened as he tried to make sense of it. His dad had the trophy he'd assumed Kit had taken down. The trophy that had started so many of his doubts. The one he'd accused her of removing last night.

His body felt thick with too many emotions darting through it. His heart ached and his brain didn't understand. Looking away from the trophy, he picked up the pictures, trying to make sense of the images. They didn't look like the professional photographs the school had sold.

These were far from the stage. Zoomed in as much as possible. August was fuzzy, but it was him.

Gripping the stack of photos and the trophy, he headed to the kitchen. He'd avoided his father since he'd used his old key to enter the house late last night.

His father had left a stack of fresh sheets beside his door but hadn't asked any questions. Welcoming was not an adjective that one would attach to his father, but he'd let August be as he worked through his feelings today.

The kitchen was still the bright green his mother had painted it right before they left. The small flowers she'd painted by the light switch still intact. His fingers itched to run over them, to feel close to her, but he was terrified he might rub them away.

Besides, it was his dad he was here to see.

He laid the trophy pieces on the table, and the pictures. "Explain." The word was harsh. He crossed his arms but that didn't stop his body from shaking.

His dad looked at the items, then looked at him. "Which do I explain first?"

August shrugged. He was getting answers. He didn't really care about the order.

His dad looked at the pictures, his hand pushing through them. "I came to your graduation. But…" His dad held up one of the photos, set it down, then grabbed another. "I will never be the warm fuzzy man your mom wanted me to be. But that doesn't mean that I don't love you. That I didn't love her. But working, providing, pushing you to be your best…all the things that drove her away…are the only ways I know to show how I care."

His dad looked around the kitchen, and he smiled. "Maybe she deserved more than I could give her, but it hurt more than I dreamed possible when she asked me to choose between the practice I'd built and her."

"If you'd hired a few more vets, or taken time off, she'd have stayed." August's chest tightened as he stated the truth. A truth he'd have accepted last night if Kit had offered the same.

But his dad hadn't been willing to make that compromise…and neither had Kit.

His dad looked at him, "You ever been on the receiving end of an ultimatum?"

August shook his head. "No." But he'd given one… less than twenty-four hours ago. He suspected his father knew it had been August delivering one. His bag had even been packed.

Because he'd never expected Kit to change for him.

And he hadn't been willing to meet her halfway.

"Funny thing about ultimatums. They make you want to say no. Your defenses rise and you pick the opposing side, to prove you're right. I'm not proud that I let your mother walk out. That I didn't chase her. If I'd known…

"I always thought we'd find a way…" His father choked up and looked at the ceiling. "If I'd known her time was so limited, I want to believe that I would have chosen a different path. But life doesn't give do-overs."

He held up the picture of August walking across the stage. "Another moment I'd redo. My flight was late, and I drove directly from the airport. I should have come in the day before, should have let you know I was coming. But I didn't. And the one time I called, you didn't answer, which I understand.

"Then you went on the road. So much like your mother. I knew if I asked you to come home, to work with me... Well, I suspect you'd have told me where I could stick the job offer. So I buried that desire and became even more grouchy, though I doubt anyone noticed."

"You wanted me to work with you?" August felt his mouth fall open. "We never got along."

"I can see how your memories would look that way." His dad shrugged. "I won't pretend that I knew how to raise a teenage boy who'd just lost his mom, while I was also dealing with the grief, but I've only ever wanted what was best for you. For you to be your best you."

"And the trophy? Why is it here...and in pieces?"

"Because the universe seems determined to let me make an ass of myself." His dad pulled his hand across his face. "I picked it up when I was visiting one day, and the base came off. Figured I could just paste it back together, but—" his dad glared at the turtle "—it refuses to stick. And I have no idea where Kit found it! She must have searched the entire state for the thing. I was planning to bring it back tomorrow with an apology."

"I thought Kit removed it because it wasn't true." August's voice was tight as he looked at the pieces. "That she was trying to push me. To better me. Like you did and I..." His eyes misted as the words stuck in the back of his throat.

His father handed the pieces to him. "There is nothing wrong with aiming for the best you. And the best August is qualified in the practice you like most. If you don't want that, fine. But then this trophy and where it sits shouldn't matter."

August opened his mouth, but his dad held up a hand.

"I'm done pushing you, August. You get to decide what you want, but make sure it's not a decision from pride. That you aren't saying no because Kit thinks it's a good idea or because I put too many standards on you as a teenager. You're a grown man. Choose the path *you* want."

His father stood, grabbed his cane and headed toward the door. "And if I can give you one more piece of advice." His dad didn't wait for an answer, "Life isn't fair. It takes more than it gives. If you love Kit, truly love her, don't walk away without trying to find the middle ground."

Then his father was gone. August fell into the chair, the pictures still scattered around the table. His father had come to his graduation. Come and watched him. A small part of his soul knitted together with that knowledge.

Looking back at his childhood, he reevaluated the arguments they'd had. What if instead of being disappointed in his failures, his dad was trying to push him? To make him be his best?

What if Kit really wanted him to get certified because she could see how much it meant to him? Had he really let the first two weeks of her owning the clinic drive his fear that he'd end up like his mom?

The thing she wanted most was finally hers, and he'd asked her to shift her focus.

August laid his head in his hands. Had he really let a

childhood wound destroy the love of his life? He grabbed his phone, then set it back down.

He wanted to come to her whole. And the best way to do that was to show her that he believed her. His résumé needed a bit of updating, but he was reaching out to Dr. Stepsard today. And talking to Kit tomorrow.

Tomorrow...

So close and so far away. But he needed everything perfect for her.

Kit's coffee had cooled, and the day was moving but she didn't have the energy to move from the chair. Bucky laid his head in her lap, and she scratched his ears as her to-do list mocked her. She should have completed at least three things on it by ten o'clock.

Why do I have to do anything? It's Sunday. No clients are coming in. I don't have to do anything.

She tried to shake the intrusive thoughts from her mind. She was supposed to be productive...supposed to always be moving toward her goals.

But those goals had cost so much.

She stared at the *be the best* writing and wanted to scream. That phrase, that mantra had been drilled into her since she was a child. And having an off day wasn't a good reason to not accomplish something.

Her phone dinged and she grabbed for it, hoping it was August. Instead an image of Wes and Biscuit crossed her home screen.

Miss you, Aunt Kit! Biscuit says come visit soon.

Bitterness swelled in her as she looked at the image and then the be the best sign. She should just be able to sit here or take a few hours to visit her brother and nephew.

Those were things that were fine, maybe not *productive*, but important.

Get up... Move past it.

The very idea of doing nothing made her internal voice scream.

"Knock-knock, anyone home?" Her brother's voice echoed from the front door, and she hated how much she wished it were August. But he'd delivered an ultimatum, and she'd let him walk.

"In here." The words weren't very loud, but the cottage wasn't big. And if he hadn't heard her, it wouldn't take him long to find her.

"Ahh, great. I stopped by the clinic, but you weren't there. Taking a Sunday off." David smiled as he slid into the chair across from her.

"Just haven't made it there yet." Kit sighed. "Did Stephen send you to check on me? I keep canceling on dinner plans with him."

"No. Should he have?" David looked at her, his eyes wandering over her features.

Kit wasn't sure she believed him, but she didn't have the energy to argue.

"Mom's favorite having a bad day?" His eyebrow raised as he set his hands in his lap and smiled.

"Mom's favorite. That's hilarious." Kit stirred her coffee, even though she had no plans to drink it.

"I mean, she tells me you're her favorite. I think she tells Stephen that I'm her favorite, so you hear that he's her favorite, right?"

"No, I hear about you. Well, sometimes it's Stephen." Kit blinked, trying to understand the words coming from her brother. "But it's never me." No matter how often she tried to please her mother, nothing ever worked. She was a disappointment.

Always second.

"No one is her favorite. I thought you knew that. Well, she loves herself." David gripped Kit's hand. "But I didn't come over to talk about our mother and her unrealistic demands."

She blinked as her brain tried to process those words. It took a minute for her to realize David had kept talking. "Sorry, what?"

"I need to know if you'd be able to look after a cranky Persian beauty next month."

"You're getting a cat?"

"No, well, sort of. It's Trevor's cat. But we're going on vacation and Polly is his baby. He doesn't want to board her."

"Wait." She looked at her brother. The man who'd never taken a vacation. Who'd worked nonstop to build a tech empire. "You're taking a vacation…with your new business partner?"

"New business partner?" David raised a brow, "Trevor and I have a business relationship, but he's much more than that."

"Mom said he was in town for business and that he was single." She looked at David, really looked at him. The tension around his eyes was gone. He was smiling. He looked relaxed.

Was that how I looked with August?

"I mean, does it surprise you that our business relationship and the tech glory it could bring would be her focus? And he is very much not single." David winked and then laughed. "And I plan to keep it that way."

Kit let out a laugh, "Actually, she was mad that I was hiking and unable to look at his cat. Said it could have been all over his social media, and I lost an opportunity." She laughed again. "Gosh, it sounds so ridiculous!"

She squeezed her brother's hand. He was happy. That was all that mattered. "Congratulations, David. I'm thrilled for you. Guess I'm a little stunned you found someone who makes you want to take a vacation." Kit had wanted to take a vacation with August. Visit Alaska. Then the clinic had become hers. And she'd stopped even thinking it was possible.

But of course it was. People took vacations all the time without the world falling apart.

"What's the point of work if you can't have fun too?" David grinned. "So you'll watch Polly."

"I'd be happy to. Assuming you're willing to do the same for me when I go to Alaska." The words slipped out, but her soul felt lighter the moment she uttered the words.

With or without August, she was going. The clinic was important. It always would be. But it wasn't everything.

August was right. She'd been so focused on being the best that she hadn't even considered what that meant to her. She'd measured it by the unrealistic expectations of her mother.

But her mother didn't see her children as people with their own paths, their own dreams. Instead they were extensions of her, and if they didn't meet every goal she wanted, then they failed.

It was an impossible measuring stick.

So what did she want?

A full life. A rich life. The life she'd had with August. Where work was important because it was her passion, but family came first.

Where were these realizations last night?

"Alaska! Of course we'll watch Bucky." David paused and looked at her. "Are you okay?"

"No," Kit answered honestly. "But I will be."

And the first step was wiping that mantra off the board in the kitchen. She was already her best.

CHAPTER THIRTEEN

AUGUST WIPED HIS hands on his scrubs before he stepped out of his truck. Rhodes Animal Services looked the same as it had the day he'd arrived, but he was a different man. And he was tired of rebelling.

He looked at the résumé in his hand and the email he'd printed out behind him. Kit was right—he wanted to be a reptile vet. Wanted to look after turtles, snakes and lizards.

And he wanted it with her. *Here.*

He sucked in a deep breath. The morning air was crisp, and the lights were already on in the clinic.

One foot in front of the other, August.

He opened the clinic door and sighed as the feeling of rightness came over him. This was where he belonged. Now he just needed to find the woman who completed him.

A crash echoed in the clinic, and August rushed inside. "Kit?"

She was in the corner, picking up the pieces of the glass shelf previously holding her trophies. "Kit. Let me get a broom."

"August?" She turned. "It's not quite six, what are you doing here?"

"I could ask you the same." He grabbed the trash can

and handed it to her. She dumped the glass in, and he inspected her hands. "It's early."

"I couldn't sleep." She shrugged.

"So you figured you'd do some redecorating?" August crossed his arms to keep himself from reaching for her. There were so many things to discuss. None of which involved the trophy shelf. But now that he was here, fear crawled through him. What if she didn't accept his apology?

Kit looked at the broken glass, then at him. "You ever have a realization and you just had to act on it?" She gestured to the floor.

"Yes." August held up the papers in his hand. "I couldn't sleep either."

"August, I'm so sorry."

"Kit, I'm sorry."

They both laughed as their apologies echoed together in the empty clinic.

"I sent an email to Dr. Stepsard last night." He gestured to the papers in his hand. "You're right. It's what I want. I just…"

He pushed a hand through his hair, "I let my past, my parents' relationship and my fear of getting overlooked like my mother get in the way of what we have. I was so worried that you were trying to improve me. To make me worthy of you."

"August…"

His name on her lips sent his heart racing.

"I want you to have that certification, August. But only if you want it. It's not for me or the clinic. I promise." Her bottom lip shook.

"I know. I was just too pigheaded to see it. Particularly once my dad broke my trophy. I thought you were sending me a message. It was ridiculous, and rather than asking you about it, I let my fear fester."

"Your dad? Broke? What?"

August nodded. He quickly recapped what he'd learned yesterday, watching her eyes get wider with each piece of news.

"That's a lot." Kit wrapped her arms around herself. "But I get it. I learned yesterday that my mother tells David that I'm her favorite."

"Really?" August hated the surprise in his voice. Parents shouldn't have favorites, but if the reaction he'd seen Kit's mother have was what she did to her favorite…what was it like for the others?

"It's what she says. But the reality is that she doesn't have a favorite. We're all disappointments."

August took a step toward her then. But she held up a hand. "It's okay."

"Kit—"

"It really is. I was chasing something that I'm never going to get. No matter what I do, what awards I win, there will always be more that could fill this shelf. As you pointed out the other day."

"I was angry, Kit. I shouldn't have…"

"Maybe not. But that doesn't mean you weren't right. I get to define what best looks like." She smiled, and gestured to the clinic. "And this is it.

"I love this place, and I love you. And I don't care if I win any awards. Thus the damage I've inflicted here this morning. Plus, we are going to Alaska. I contacted one of the travel companies you had on the list…"

Her voice died away as she looked at him. "Assuming you still want to go with me. If not, then you'll have to look after this place with a relief vet, because I'm going to see them northern lights."

August let out a whoop and rushed toward her. Dropping his head, he held her gaze. "Just try to keep me away."

She captured his lips then. The kiss was deep and long and everything that he'd craved for so long. August Rhodes had found his roots, and he was never leaving again.

EPILOGUE

"HERE, GECKO... COME HERE..."

August laughed as Kit tried to coax one of the six baby crested geckos that Killian Polts had accidentally unleashed in the waiting room from under the bookshelf.

"Do lizards respond to their names?" His dad raised a brow as he covered his lips, trying to hide his smile.

August shook his head, enjoying a moment with his father he'd never expected to come along as he scooped up the lizard at his foot.

"Sweetheart, most lizards don't respond to their names." He pursed his lips and his pregnant wife looked up and glared at him.

"Well, last time I checked, we weren't even supposed to be here today." Kit wagged a finger and pointed to her watch. "Dr. Jeff and the relief vets are on duty while we, the owners of this fine establishment, get a much-needed break."

She was right. Their car was packed for a week in the state park. A babymoon before their son was born in four months. But his father had called to ask if he could take a quick look at the baby crested geckos.

He'd agreed. And by the time they'd walked down from the cottage, the box of lizards had gotten loose in an episode the teenager still hadn't been able to explain. They'd now caught all but the last one.

"You're right." August walked over to the bookcase, where this year's Foxfield Finest Award sat, and got down on his wife's level. The gecko was hovering along the back wall.

"So what does the lizard expert recommend?" Kit sat on her heels, her hands over her belly.

"Not picking up the phone when we're headed on vacation?" August winked.

Kit kissed his cheek. "Obviously. But I was speaking more in the immediate sense of getting the lizard out from under the bookcase."

"We could leave it. Have a clinic lizard? Think Bucky might like a friend?" August laughed as Kit put her hands on her hips. "All right, no office lizard. But honestly, I'm not sure."

"And you call yourself the best reptile vet in Foxfield."

She grinned at him, and his heart lit up. He'd never tire of working with his wife.

"Actually, you call me that." He bent and wedged his hand under the bookcase, palm up. It took a few minutes, but the lizard finally crawled in, and he closed his hand and pulled him out.

"Because it's true." Kit eyed the lizard tail in his palm. "Now go check these nuisances out so we can get on the road."

"I love you, Dr. Rhodes." He grinned as he walked toward the exam room.

"I love you too, Dr. Rhodes. But I will leave for my vacation without you if you don't hustle."

* * * * *

COMING SOON!

We really hope you enjoyed reading this book. If you're looking for more romance, be sure to head to the shops when new books are available on

Thursday 23rd June

To see which titles are coming soon, please visit

millsandboon.co.uk/nextmonth

MILLS & BOON®

Coming next month

THE NIGHT THEY NEVER FORGOT
Scarlet Wilson

She met his gaze. There was so much there. Twelve lost years between them. She lifted a muffin from the plate and walked around her desk, gesturing to the seat at the other side as she moved to flick some switches on her coffee machine.

He could sense she was trying to decide how to play this. He'd turned up unexpectedly. They'd had literally no contact since that last awkward morning after graduation. He'd replayed that day over and over in his head so many times. It had seemed clear that Caitlin had thought they'd made a mistake; she'd made a quick comment—'at least we got that out of our system'—and that they could get back to being rivals again. He hadn't said a word. Hadn't told her how much that cheapened what had happened between them and how, after one taste of Caitlin, she would never be out of his system. He'd let the hurt feelings go; he'd wanted to respect her wishes. The embarrassing retreat and hasty exit he'd had to make had been imprinted in his soul. He'd lost the person he'd been closest to for six years. It shouldn't have been worth it. Not for one night.

But, strangely, that night had meant everything. And he was still glad they had gone there. Even if the next morning had been a disaster.

He couldn't help it. His eyes went to her left hand. No ring. The sense of relief was unexpectedly overwhelming.

Ridiculous. And he knew that. He also knew he couldn't take a lack of ring to mean anything at all. Caitlin might well be married and just not want to wear a ring—she was a surgeon after all. She could also be in a long-term relationship. But he couldn't help but hope not...no matter how shallow that might make him.

He swept his arm around the room. 'Corner office? They must like you.'

'Of course they do. I'm their shining star.'

It was the way she said those words. The confidence in herself that had brought him here.

He glanced out at the dark view of the beautiful city of Barcelona, with all the familiar structures easy to pick out.

'You've done really well for yourself.' He said the words with a hint of pride. When any other physician mentioned Caitlin he always said that they'd trained together, and that she was a fine surgeon.

'I like to think so.' Her gaze narrowed slightly. She was getting suspicious of the small talk.

'We should catch up?'

Her eyebrows raised.

'I mean, twelve years is a long time. You could be married, divorced, a mother of ten.'

Her eyes widened.

Continue reading
THE NIGHT THEY NEVER FORGOT
Scarlet Wilson

Available next month
www.millsandboon.co.uk

MILLS & BOON

THE HEART OF ROMANCE

A ROMANCE FOR EVERY READER

ODERN

Prepare to be swept off your feet by sophisticated, sexy and seductive heroes, in some of the world's most glamourous and romantic locations, where power and passion collide.

STORICAL

Escape with historical heroes from time gone by. Whether your passion is for wicked Regency Rakes, muscled Vikings or rugged Highlanders, awaken the romance of the past.

EDICAL

Set your pulse racing with dedicated, delectable doctors in the high-pressure world of medicine, where emotions run high and passion, comfort and love are the best medicine.

ue Love

Celebrate true love with tender stories of heartfelt romance, from the rush of falling in love to the joy a new baby can bring, and a focus on the emotional heart of a relationship.

Desire

Indulge in secrets and scandal, intense drama and plenty of sizzling hot action with powerful and passionate heroes who have it all: wealth, status, good looks…everything but the right woman.

EROES

Experience all the excitement of a gripping thriller, with an intense romance at its heart. Resourceful, true-to-life women and strong, fearless men face danger and desire - a killer combination!

To see which titles are coming soon, please visit

millsandboon.co.uk/nextmonth